MW00355624

On a Dark Deadly Highway

A Black Horse Campground Mystery

by

Amy M. Bennett

Aakenbaaken & Kent

On a Dark Deadly Highway

A Black Horse Campground Mystery

Copyright 2021, all rights reserved.
No part of this book may be used or reproduced in any manner whatsoever without written permission except in the case of brief quotations for use in articles and reviews.

Aakenbaakeneditor@gmail.com

This is a work of fiction. Names, characters, places and incidents are either the product of the author's imagination or are used fictitiously. Any resemblance of the fictional characters to actual persons living or dead is entirely coincidental.

ISBN: 978-1-938436-87-1

Prologue

Somewhere on the outskirts of Bonney, New Mexico, early-November

J.D. Wilder jogged along the shoulder of U.S. Highway 70, trying to clear his head and wondering just what was wrong with him.

It was almost two in the morning, not the hour most people would choose to exercise. An hour that most people were sleeping peacefully. He envied them.

He followed a familiar path, two and a half miles from the Black Horse Campground and two and a half miles back. It was one he'd often taken during brighter hours of the day. Now the beam of his flashlight bobbed in front of him as it illuminated the asphalt shoulder dotted with rocks, weeds, and other potential stumbling hazards. Not that he was really seeing what was in his path. He had too much on his mind to notice.

The late fall weather in south central New Mexico had surprised J.D. It was unseasonably warm, prompting concern among the locals that the nearby ski resort in Ruidoso, Ski Apache, would not be able to open on Thanksgiving weekend as usual. While this would normally affect the local economy in a negative way, it had proved to be a financial boon to the campground which was enjoying an unusual influx of visitors who were determined to enjoy the Indian summer for as long as it lasted. Corrie Black, the campground's owner, made no secret that she needed the business; the last few weeks, to say nothing of the last few months, had been rough on her and her campground. Her livelihood. Her home.

If J.D. had a choice, right now he would be sound asleep in his cozy cabin at the Black Horse, instead of running in forty-five degree weather in the middle of the night. However, a solid night of sleep had eluded him for a long time. It had been almost two months since the San Ignacio fall fiesta had taken place at the campground, in the midst of yet another murder in the quiet mountain community, sending ripples of change through all their lives, particularly Corrie's. Two months since Corrie's best friend, Shelli Davenport had reunited with her ex-husband and moved her family, which now included three orphaned children, to a different part of the state to start their lives afresh. Two months since RaeLynn Shaffer had disappeared, after NOT stealing the fiesta receipts to bail her father out of jail, though it meant defying her violent, criminal family and placing herself in danger.

Two months since J.D. and Corrie had had a real conversation.

He had shed the jacket he had been wearing, but he now felt a chill travel down his back. No one J.D. had ever met in his life could be more understanding or forgiving than Corrie Black. She had proven it, time and again, and he had seen her reach out with open arms and genuine warmth in her dark brown eyes to anyone and everyone who had ever hurt her – even Sheriff Rick Sutton who had broken her heart years earlier, was still welcome for a cup of coffee every morning at the campground store. And while everyone, friends and family, had cautioned Corrie that she needed to be careful about trusting RaeLynn too much, she seemed to have taken J.D.'s warnings as personal insults. He had been so sure – almost smugly too sure – that RaeLynn had finally broken Corrie's trust when it appeared that she had run off with nearly seven thousand dollars that had been raised by the fiesta. Then RaeLynn had proved them all wrong and vindicated Corrie's belief in her, which had only served to harden Corrie's heart against J.D. All his apologies, though cordially accepted, seemed to count for nothing. Whatever had been building between them had come to a complete standstill, had turned into a wall, not a bridge. And J.D. had no idea what he could do to make things right again.

So when his mind refused to let him sleep, when he couldn't take the restless thoughts any longer, he went for a run, hoping to tire out his mind and body enough that he could finally rest.

The rumble of tires on asphalt broke into his thoughts. He had already reached the two-and-a-half mile mark on his run and was returning to the campground. His runs used to be along the hiking trail between the campground and the village limits, but he'd been unable to bring himself to use the trail after he had discovered three cold-case victims' bodies along that path a few months earlier. Since the highway ran past the campground, he'd switched his daily run to that path, figuring there was a far slimmer chance of him running—pardon the pun—into any more hidden surprises. He always took his run on the side of the highway which had a shoulder that stretched to the base of the tall hillside that bordered the village of Bonney on one side of the highway. The opposite side of the highway was defined by a guardrail that was frequently damaged while keeping motorists who took the winding road at too high a speed from ending up in the irrigation canals that ran alongside the highway. It was easily a ten-foot drop from the asphalt down to the ditch that separated the road from the Hondo Valley and J.D. didn't want to take a chance of being caught on the narrow strip of shoulder between the guardrail and the highway by a careless driver.

The growl of the approaching vehicle told him it was an 18-wheeler whose driver was judiciously keeping the rig's speed to barely below the posted speed limit. J.D. slowed his pace and stepped as far off the paved shoulder as he could, blending into the darkness of the shrubs and tall grasses growing among the rock-strewn base of the hillside. He kept his flashlight aimed downward, in order not to distract the driver. The truck's air horn blasted twice as the behemoth roared by and J.D. grimaced, turning his face away from the dust storm stirred up by the big rig. Most truckers announced their approach to the turnoff toward the Black Horse Campground, which sat in a hollow off the main highway, but the sound as it was carried on the wind toward the campground was soothing and muffled. This close, it reminded J.D. that one of the worse parts of police work was having to deal with the aftermath of close encounters between vehicles and human beings... especially when the vehicle topped out at 40 tons.

Once the truck's taillights disappeared around the next bend, J.D. began to pick his way out of the brush and back onto the pavement. Weariness began to seep into his muscles and brain, but he knew that it would still take him a long time to fall asleep once he returned to his cabin. He shivered and shook his head. Just when he thought he'd found a safe haven, a place to call home, and someone he could share it with, it all came undone. And he had no idea how he could put it back together again.

Before he reached the shoulder, he heard another vehicle approaching. This one was obviously not an 18-wheeler; the sound was more of a high-pitched whine and, unlike the trucker, this driver was in a much bigger hurry to get someplace. J.D. wondered whether he'd even be able to identify the vehicle, much less catch a glimpse of the license plate, then laughed at himself. What was he going to do, try to ticket a speeder without even being able to catch him? He shook his head, sighed, and stepped back into the brush.

The car—that much was all he was able to identify—sped by, sending gravel and small stones flying in all directions. J.D. shook his head. The driver was taking some stupid chances on the sharp curves of the winding highway, not to mention that he was fast approaching the village limit. While he might have been lucky in avoiding the county LEOs who were spread out covering a larger area, there was sure to be at least one police officer on night patrol near the edge of the village who might succeed in convincing him to slow down.

Before J.D. could return to the pavement and his run, he heard the sudden screech of brakes ahead of him, around the curve where the driver had disappeared. He tensed, listening for the crunch of metal and glass that signaled a collision and mentally prepared himself for the worst as he broke into a run, pulling his cell phone out of his pocket and praying he wasn't in a dead zone.

To his surprise, silence followed. He picked up his pace until he rounded the curve. The car was stopped nearly a quarter mile ahead. Its lights were off, but the sound of the engine running reached J.D.'s ears over the pounding of his heart. He could only make out the shadowy shape of the vehicle in the dim moonlight. Both driver's and passenger's doors were wide open and he faintly heard the "whump" of the trunk being shut. His flashlight's beam didn't reach far enough for him to see anything clearly, but the bobbing light caught the attention of the two people who were standing on either side of the vehicle. They froze.

"Hey!" J.D. shouted as he moved toward them. "Are you guys okay? Do you need help?"

Their response was to bolt for the doors of the car and dive inside. Doors slammed and the driver floored the gas pedal, peeling out and leaving behind the faint smell of burnt rubber. For a moment, J.D. was too dumbstruck to move, then his flashlight beam illuminated a shapeless form on the pavement where the vehicle had been. He jogged closer, wondering if the driver had hit a deer—but no, unless it was a very small deer... perhaps a dog? He grimaced at the thought of having to move the carcass, but he also couldn't just leave it in the middle of the road to be run over repeatedly. No other drivers should have to deal with....

He stopped short when his light was strong enough to reveal that the figure on the road was covered with clothing, not fur.

His stomach lurched and he sprinted for the figure, only taking his eyes off it long enough to check his cell phone's screen. No signal. He muttered something between a curse and a prayer as he got closer, and his mind raced. Was this a hit and run accident? But who would be out on the highway at this hour—besides himself? A hitchhiker? But where did he or she come from? He hadn't seen anyone walking along the highway earlier, and not once in all the times he'd gone running in the middle of the night. If only he'd been able to see the license plate....

He reached the huddled form on the ground. Ratty, shoulder-length blond hair and a slim, slight figure indicated that it was a woman. J.D.'s heart began to pound; there was something familiar about the person on the ground. He reached for the throat to check for a pulse and his flashlight beam fell across the pale, bruised face of RaeLynn Shaffer.

He drew back and blinked, not sure if his eyes and the darkness were playing tricks on him. He felt a weak pulse and a slight gurgle escaped the young woman's throat. Questions spun in his mind. Where had she come from? What had happened to her? It was impossible to see the extent of her injuries and he knew that moving her could be dangerously risky—paralyzing or even killing her—but he couldn't call for help and leaving her on the road was....

The blare of another 18-wheeler's air horn, coming from behind them, sent a chill down his spine and made up his mind. There was no way the trucker would see them before he rounded the curve and by then it would be too late for him to stop....

In a flash, he scooped RaeLynn up in his arms and dashed for the opposite side of the highway. She seemed no heavier than an armful of feathers, as fragile as delicate crystal or fine china. He grimaced as the truck blasted by behind him, the horn sounding frantic to his ears and he was sure that the sight of him running across the rig's path with the unconscious woman in his arms had taken several years off the trucker's life. He gritted his teeth and kept running.

He didn't stop till he reached the Black Horse Campground's door.

Chapter 1

The glare of the fluorescent lights in the waiting room of the Bonney County Medical Center emergency room made it hard to tell how much time had passed. Corrie stared bleakly at the bland face of the clock on the wall near the registration desk, willing the hands to move faster.

It was nearly four in the morning, almost two hours since J.D.'s shouts and insistent pounding on the front door of the campground store roused her from sleep. She had leaped from her bed in the apartment over her business, tripping over her dog and cat, Renfro and Oliver, as she stumbled to the window. She was greeted by the nightmarish sight of J.D. standing below with the seemingly lifeless form of RaeLynn in his arms. He shouted at her to let him in and call for help and she flew down the stairs with the cordless phone in her hands as she punched in the speed dial number for Rick.

Everything that happened since she let J.D. in was a blur now. She couldn't remember getting dressed or how she got to the hospital. Flashes of memory showed Rick arriving at the campground with the ambulance right behind him; then Jerry and Jackie Page, her long-time friends and employees, arriving with wide, frightened eyes at the commotion; her frantic, shrill voice calling out RaeLynn's name and demanding answers from J.D.

Once RaeLynn had been taken into the emergency ward, there had been nothing for Corrie—and everyone else—to do but wait. None of them, not even Rick or J.D. as law enforcement officers, had been able to gain entrance into the back where RaeLynn was being examined. Corrie shuddered and closed her eyes, trying to drive out the image of RaeLynn's face, bruised and hollow-cheeked.

She jumped as Rick's strong hands gripped her shoulders and began to knead the muscles in her neck. It had been years since he had touched her that intimately and, instead of relaxing, she stiffened. "Easy," he said, his voice soothing and soft. "She's going to be okay."

She shrugged his hands off and stood up, wrapping her arms around herself. She wasn't sure if the chill she felt had to do with her emotions or with the temperature in the waiting room. In her haste to join Rick and J.D. as they followed the ambulance carrying RaeLynn to the hospital, she had forgotten to grab a jacket. She had yanked on a pair of jeans and her sneakers and hadn't bothered to change out of her usual sleeping attire: a University of New Mexico jersey that was emblazoned with Rick's number. Though it had been over a decade since he graduated from the university, over fifteen years since they had broken up, she had never worn anything else to bed. She fought back a rush of heat to her face, even though Rick didn't seem to notice what she was wearing, and glanced away from the concern in his deep blue eyes. She ended up staring directly into J.D.'s silver-gray eyes. He had retreated to a corner in the waiting room where he leaned back against the wall in a wooden chair, just like he always did. He was still wearing his jogging clothes and, despite the chilly night, his t-shirt was stained with sweat and his hoodie was tied around his waist. Fleetingly, she wondered why he had chosen that time of the night to go for a run, but it didn't seem to be the right time to ask. Now he watched her, his own eyes filled with sympathy and worry. She knew she looked like she was on the verge of hysteria—her hair in a disheveled braid, her eyes swimming with tears. Only the thought that RaeLynn had no one else she could call a friend kept Corrie from completely falling apart. RaeLynn needed her.

The sliding glass doors that led to the parking lot opened, letting in a cold blast of early morning air. Deputy Dudley Evans strode in and made a beeline for Rick. He removed his hat and nodded to Corrie before turning his attention to his boss. "Anything?" Rick asked tersely.

Dudley shook his head. "No, sir, Sheriff," he said, his normally soft voice even quieter than usual. "No answer at the door, or on the phone. No lights or sound in the trailer. That's not to say they aren't there and just refusing to acknowledge us. We checked with the folks who lived on either side of them. Even the neighbors said that they hadn't seen Mrs. Shaffer or anyone else around for a while." The expression of exasperation on his usually placid face, coupled with Rick's snort of disbelief, indicated that neither man believed that the neighbors were being truthful. "We checked a few other places where the Shaffers were known to go, but no one's claimed to have seen any of them." Rick nodded and Corrie felt her heart twist.

"So none of RaeLynn's family is around to come see her, be with her?" she said, her voice cracking despite her best efforts. Deputy Evans glanced at Rick then back at Corrie and shook his head. Rick cleared his throat.

"That's nothing new, Corrie," he said. She blinked back tears and tossed her braid over her shoulder as she sank back into the chair she had abandoned. She looked at J.D.

"Tell me again what happened, where you found her," she said, her voice calm. Rick had already taken his statement—the place where RaeLynn had been found had been in the county's jurisdiction—and he hadn't bothered to talk to J.D. privately, knowing that Corrie wasn't about to leave them to talk without her present. But she wanted to hear it again, for herself, not an official police report. J.D. let the front legs of the chair down, without the customary bang that normally punctuated the action. He leaned forward, his elbows on his knees and cleared his throat.

"I was coming back from my run, heading back to the campground," he began. He didn't take his eyes off Corrie's face as he told her, step by step, what had occurred out on the highway. She shuddered when he got to the part about hearing the 18-wheeler coming up behind him and he paused, but she motioned for him to continue. "And I brought her straight to the campground store," he concluded. She nodded and took a deep breath, straightening up in her chair. She looked at Rick then back at J.D.

"You don't think that car hit her, do you?" she asked them. They hesitated and she shook her head impatiently. "I'm not asking for an 'official' theory or statement!" she snapped. "I know we have to wait for the doctor to examine her and see what her injuries are like! I just want to know, here, among the three of us—four of us," she amended with a nod to Deputy Evans, "what you think happened, how she ended up in the middle of the highway, in the middle of the night."

Rick looked at J.D. and gave the slightest nod. J.D. stood up and folded his arms across his chest. "Whoever was driving that car left her there," he said, his voice and demeanor leaving no doubt that he didn't only think that was what happened. He knew. He ran a hand over his hair and tugged at his disheveled ponytail. "As fast as they were going... there's no way they could have hit her and not—" He stopped when he looked at Corrie. She had felt the color drain from her face and she was sure he thought she was going to faint. He sighed and cleared his throat again. "They must have had her in the vehicle. I heard the trunk slam shut. That's probably where they had her. They took her out and left her there."

"Why?" Corrie said. "Of all places along the highway, why right there? Did they expect someone to find her and help her?" J.D. was shaking his head before she finished speaking.

"They didn't expect her to get help," J.D. said, and Corrie's blood ran cold. She had tried not to think too much about the reason why RaeLynn had been left in that particular place on the highway but the way J.D. was looking at her told her that her suspicions had been correct. Rick shifted his weight and J.D. went on, "That spot was on a blind curve. Anyone coming around that curve, even if they were going the speed limit, by the time they saw her," he paused as Corrie put her hands up to her mouth. "It would have been too late to stop," he finished.

"They left her there for another driver to kill?" Corrie shook her head and tears spilled over her fingers. "How could anyone do that? And why?"

J.D. shrugged and glanced at Rick, who was jotting down notes in his ever-present pocket notepad. Though he wasn't in uniform, he looked just as official and imposing despite his faded jeans and plain gray sweatshirt. And unnaturally distant. He looked up, his brows knitting together. Instead of his customary Stetson, he was wearing a dark blue ball cap which he hadn't bothered to remove. It shaded his eyes from the waiting room lights and kept Corrie from reading the expression in them.

"There are a number of blind curves on that particular stretch of US 70," he said in a clipped voice. "There was one just about a half mile before the spot where she was left and a couple more up to three miles away. They left her on the outskirts of the village, where she was likely to be found more quickly." He sighed and pushed his ball cap back, his blue eyes ringed with exhaustion and some other emotion Corrie couldn't place. He cleared his throat. "They left her right near the Black Horse. If they had wanted help for her, they could have taken her to the campground, gone into the village, even taken a detour to the church before they got to the campground, if they didn't want to answer any questions by bringing her to the hospital. They had a reason for leaving her where they did." He looked directly at her. "They wanted her dead and I think she was supposed to be a warning to you."

Corrie sucked in a breath so deep it hurt her chest. She looked at J.D. and saw that he agreed with Rick's suspicions. She glanced toward Deputy Evans but he had turned away and was talking softly into his cell phone, no doubt calling his wife of two weeks, Myra, to let her know what was going on. Corrie found herself feeling sorry that the first call he got on his first day back from his honeymoon was to have to track down the Shaffer family. She swallowed hard. "What was I supposed to be warned about?"

"RaeLynn obviously didn't give her family the money to bail her father out of jail," Rick said, his face growing dark. "And they're all aware that you're not only her employer, you're probably her only friend. I think they blame you for turning RaeLynn against them."

"I didn't turn her against them," Corrie retorted. "All I did was what any good friend would do... I tried to help her!"

"Help her get a job, help her get out from under their control, help her turn her life around. Help her stand up for herself. All things that made you the enemy in the Shaffers' eyes," Rick responded, his face like granite. "You're not their most favorite person in the world right now."

"Oh, give me a minute to get over the tragedy!" she snapped, jumping to her feet and planting her fists on her hips. Her face was still streaked with tears but anger burned her cheeks. J.D. raised a brow but said nothing. "Do you really think I care about that?"

"No, but you need to realize that what happened to RaeLynn could easily have happened to you," Rick said in a deadly calm voice. A chill shot down Corrie's back.

"So you're sure it was her family that did this to her?" Corrie asked. She found herself wrapping her arms around herself and fighting back the shivers. Rick shifted as if he wanted to step toward her and take her into his arms, but he kept a distance between them.

"So sure that we could arrest them and charge them, no," he admitted. "And as much as I'd like to do that, I'm not willing to take a chance of letting them walk because we don't have any hard evidence. Wilder didn't get a good look at the car, much less the license plate...."

"Sorry, Sheriff, I was a little distracted," J.D. said coldly. His gray eyes were icy as he glared at Rick. Before Rick could respond, Corrie spoke up.

"You did more than enough by saving her life," she said, stepping closer to J.D. and placing a hand on his arm. She caught a glimpse of his surprised face before tears clouded her vision. She blinked. "If you hadn't been out there on the highway...." She stopped and swallowed hard.

Before anyone spoke again, the double doors to the emergency ward swung open. Instead of the doctor on duty, Noreen Adler, the head nurse who was also the longtime girlfriend and now fiancée of Corrie's maintenance man, Buster, emerged. Her face was drawn and tired-looking and Corrie's heart began pounding with dread. Noreen beckoned them to follow her. "Let's go to the conference room." She didn't specify who was included in the invitation. She turned and headed down the hallway. Corrie, Rick, and J.D. followed her.

J.D. shut the door behind him as he joined Corrie, the sheriff, and Noreen. He had glanced back, but Deputy Evans had gestured for him to go on as he continued his conversation with his wife and moved to a position where he could watch the doors that opened out to the parking lot. It occurred to J.D. that there was a likely chance that whoever had left RaeLynn Shaffer—most likely her own family, if the sheriff's suspicions were correct—might have returned to the portion of the highway where she had been left and, not finding her there nor any evidence of her having been there, decided to see if she had been taken to the hospital.

Not that any true concern or care about her was what would prompt them to make the visit. J.D. was sure that their motives would be simply to finish what they had hoped would be accomplished on the highway by an unsuspecting motorist.

Noreen leaned back against the conference table, folding her arms across her chest. She didn't offer them any seats nor wait for anyone to ask any questions.

"I have to make this fast but I'll do my best to tell you everything I know. First off, I'm not even supposed to be talking to any of you, except maybe Rick, in his official capacity as sheriff, because none of you are RaeLynn's family. At least, not legally nor biologically," she added quickly, even though no one had appeared ready to argue. "The new resident intern here is very much a 'by-the-book' man, but he just left for a break and said he didn't want to know what went on while he was gone. So here we are," she said, spreading out her hands. "And here's what's going on. First, RaeLynn is still unconscious. Her heartbeat is very erratic and she's having trouble breathing. She's had a couple of seizures—minor ones—since she was admitted. We're running tests, scans, x-rays, blood work, everything, to find out just what happened to her and what we can do to help her. So far, not all the test results are in yet, but here's what we know for certain. She was NOT a victim of a hit-and-run, though she has multiple bruises on her body and a fractured jaw. No broken bones, no cuts or lacerations that indicate that she was in a car accident. The bruises," she went on, looking at each of them in turn, "seem to indicate that she was being restrained. There are bruises around her throat, her upper arms, her forearms," she indicated the locations on herself as she spoke, "and there are needle tracks in her arms. And, yes, we found drugs in her system—meth, heroin, cocaine. It was a hellish cocktail that was administered to her in the last twelve hours. It's probably the cause of the seizures and it's a miracle it hasn't killed her yet." She paused for breath and the sheriff spoke up.

"What do you mean, 'administered to her'? Aren't you saying she overdosed?" There was a hint of skepticism in the sheriff's tone and manner. J.D. almost asked the same question and he was glad he hadn't when Corrie shot a glare at Sutton. Noreen held up a hand.

"Yes, but I—and the doctor—don't believe she took it herself," she said firmly. "Of course, until and unless RaeLynn can tell us herself what happened, there's no way to prove it. The bruises I mentioned earlier are fresh enough to have been administered earlier today, or rather yesterday," she amended, glancing at the clock on the wall. "And the position of the bruises indicates someone holding her down, or at least holding her arm steady. There are no other scars or needle tracks to indicate she'd been shooting anything else into her veins anytime in the last few months." She paused and when no one spoke, she continued, "However, it's not my place to speculate about what happened. I leave that to the professionals." She nodded at J.D. and the sheriff, then took a deep breath. "There is one other thing that I think I should mention." She looked around the room and saw that every eye was on her. "She was pregnant. Hard to tell how far along, but probably not more than a few weeks. She started miscarrying while she was being examined. Probably as a result of all the drugs in her system. The baby never had a chance."

The silence was unbroken for several seconds except for the ticking of the clock on the wall. Corrie finally spoke up. "Is she going to make it?" Her voice, hushed though it was, echoed in the room. Noreen gave a helpless shrug then reached out to Corrie and the two women hugged.

"We're gonna do our best to give her a chance," Noreen whispered. She stepped back but she held onto Corrie's hands. "She needs medical attention, lots of rest, and probably an intensive detox, not to mention emotional support. Once she wakes up, we'll have a better idea of what her recovery will entail." She grimaced slightly as she released Corrie's hands. "I'm not sure we can give her all that she needs here. There are facilities that are better suited to treat her in Albuquerque or Santa Fe. However, if she doesn't have insurance...."

"Is that all you can think of that you need to tell us, Noreen?" the sheriff said. There was a strange, emotionless tone to his normal voice. It sounded like it came from far away. J.D. saw that he had shoved his hands in his pockets, his note-taking forgotten. Noreen nodded. He went on, "We may have some more questions for you later on. I know you're not supposed to be discussing RaeLynn's medical information, but would you be willing to talk to us? I know it will get you into trouble...." Noreen was shaking her head before he finished speaking.

"Rick, I'm willing to risk that in order to help RaeLynn," she said. "That poor girl has no one, except the people in this room and the folks at the Black Horse, who care about her. I doubt she'll have any member of her family who would be willing to make medical decisions on her behalf... and I doubt she'd want them to," she finished dryly.

"Can we see her?" Corrie asked, clasping her hands together. It was a plea more than a request. Noreen sighed and shook her head.

"Not at the moment, Corrie. She's still undergoing tests and her condition isn't very stable. I'm not sure if...."

"I don't want her to feel that she's alone," Corrie interrupted. "I want her to know that we're here. If I can't see her now, I'll wait till I can, but I won't leave the hospital until I do." J.D. knew by the set of her jaw and the way her fists dug into her hips that she meant every word. Noreen flashed a sideways glance at him, her eyelids flickering. Apparently, she could tell she wasn't going to convince Corrie otherwise.

"All right," Noreen said.

Chapter 2

J.D. managed to convince Corrie to go back to the campground only after promising that he would personally take her back to the hospital in time for the eight a.m. visiting hours, as long as the doctors in the ICU allowed it. The brief visit that he, Corrie, and the sheriff had been allowed with RaeLynn before she was moved to a room hadn't held out much hope for that happening, but he knew that wouldn't stop Corrie from wanting to be there in the event that RaeLynn woke up. In the stark light of the emergency ward, her injuries were more obvious and underscored just how serious her condition was. Noreen had confided that the doctor had hoped that the battered young woman would show some signs of consciousness returning, but she still had an erratic heartbeat and her breathing was still shallow. Her body was fighting hard against the effects of the drugs in her system, effects that were magnified after months of being clean, but the battle was taking a toll on her. The fact that she had also suffered a miscarriage in the process only made her weaker and pathetically frail. The bruises on her face, throat, and arms—the only parts of her body not covered by a blanket—stood out garishly against her sickly pale skin. The sooner she was transported to a facility that was equipped to deal with detox and her emotional turmoil, the better off she would be.

If she lived long enough to get there.

While Corrie was allowed five minutes alone with RaeLynn, Sutton pulled J.D. aside. "Are you working today?"

"I'm supposed to be off, but you know how that goes," J.D. responded. He was still acting chief of police though the actual chief, Eldon LaRue, had recently returned from an extended bereavement leave of absence in the wake of the death of his dispatcher/fiancée earlier in the year. If LaRue had minded that J.D. continued to hold the reins of the Bonney P.D. since his return, he didn't show it. "There's nothing pressing at the moment... except this," he added, jerking his head back toward the emergency ward.

"Can you stay with Corrie at the campground?" J.D. raised a brow as the sheriff's face reddened slightly. "I wouldn't ask if it wasn't important. I'm just...."

"Worried that the Shaffers—assuming that's who left RaeLynn on the road this morning—will come by to make good on the warning they meant to send Corrie?" Sutton nodded and

19

J.D. went on, "Sure, I'll stay with her, but I'm surprised you haven't volunteered yourself to do that."

"There's a good chance RaeLynn will be transferred to another hospital later on today," he said. "I've got Mike Ramirez coming to relieve Dudley here at the hospital at seven a.m. I've got deputies looking for the Shaffers, any of the Shaffers, including RaeLynn's mother. She might very well be in danger as well. I'm also keeping it quiet about RaeLynn being transferred, because I don't want to take any chances of her being followed, so I haven't even said a word to Corrie."

"You think that's wise?" J.D. said. "You know you can trust her not to breathe a word...."

"It's for her own protection that I'm keeping it quiet," Sutton interrupted. "Once RaeLynn is moved, I'm going to make arrangements for her safety, even if it means hiring security. The place where she's going protects their patients very well, but I don't want to take any chances." J.D. was about to ask when he had made all these arrangements when a voice interrupted them.

"Sheriff."

They spun toward the door where Deputy Evans was standing. He beckoned to them urgently and they hurried toward him, their hands instinctively moving toward their weapons. Before they could ask what was going on, they saw a slight, gray-haired woman, whose lined face made her look twenty years older than her actual age, standing just outside the emergency room doors. She was wearing a faded t-shirt and jeans with a threadbare sweater draped over her stooped shoulders. J.D. blinked, feeling a shock of recognition and disbelief, then the sheriff spoke. "Mrs. Shaffer, we've been looking for you."

"Yes, Sheriff, I know." The woman's voice was a raspy whisper and her eyes, a darker shade of amber than her daughter's, swam with tears. She reminded J.D. of the day, months earlier, when he had seen RaeLynn for the first time at the Black Horse Campground. Mrs. Shaffer cleared her throat and licked her lips. "Took me a while to find someone to bring me. Jake wouldn't let me answer the door or the phone and he wasn't gonna let the deputy or any other official person give me a ride. Finally told him I was comin' if I had to walk, I had to come see my girl. He got mad but I didn't care. I went to a neighbor—I ain't saying who, they don't want Jake finding out they helped me—and he gave me a ride." She took a deep shaky breath. "I wanna see her."

"Of course," the sheriff said quietly. He started to turn toward the emergency room desk, but the woman caught his arm.

"How bad, Sheriff? How bad is she? She gonna make it?" She pressed her lips together as her tears slipped down her cheeks. "I gotta prepare myself before I go in, or else I'm gonna lose it. I have to be strong for her." Sutton took her hand.

"Mrs. Shaffer, she's in bad shape," he said, keeping his voice low. The woman's face paled and the sheriff's grip on her hand tightened. "She's hanging on. She's fighting. But it's going to be a battle. Do you know what happened to her?" She was shaking her head before the sheriff finished asking.

"I don't know nothin' about any of that, just that she's here and she's in a bad way. That's all I know." She pressed her lips together again, letting both J.D. and the sheriff know that she wasn't going to say anything else.

Sutton nodded and spoke to the nurse behind the desk. She quickly buzzed them in.

J.D. didn't wait for an invitation. He fell into step behind the sheriff and Mrs. Shaffer. She seemed to shrink even smaller as they walked down the hall, their footsteps echoing in the near-empty ward. J.D. wondered if she was going to make it to RaeLynn's bedside. She kept glancing over her shoulder as if she were considering turning back and running. Presently, they arrived at the door where Noreen Adler was waiting for them. Corrie stepped out into the hallway, her own eyes glazed with tears. Her mouth dropped open at the sight of RaeLynn's mother.

The woman hesitated when she saw Corrie, but she moved forward, reaching for Corrie's hands. "Shoulda known you'd be here with her," she said when Corrie pulled her in for a hug.

"I'll always be here for her," Corrie said, her voice cracking. She glanced at the sheriff and J.D. and shook her head. "She's still unconscious, but...."

"I just need to see her," Mrs. Shaffer said, straightening her shoulders. Corrie glanced at Noreen who looked uncertain. "Just for a minute. Might be the last time I see her," the woman added, her voice fading to a sob. She cleared her throat. "Can I see her? My neighbor's gonna wonder what's keeping me and I don't want to make trouble for him."

"Come this way," Noreen said, extending a hand to the frail woman and ushering her toward RaeLynn's bedside. She managed to convey to everyone else that only Mrs. Shaffer was included in the invitation. Corrie reluctantly stepped back between the sheriff and J.D., glancing up at each of them with questions in her eyes. Before any of them could say anything, a loud half-sob, half-moan came from the room and RaeLynn's mother came staggering out of the room with her hands covering her mouth, Noreen right behind her. Corrie rushed up to her, as if to catch her if she should fall, but the woman straightened up, waving away all offers of help and practically ran down the hallway toward the doors.

"Mrs. Shaffer, wait!" Corrie cried as J.D. and the sheriff ran after her, with Corrie right behind them. The double-doors to the waiting room slowed the frantic woman as she blindly fumbled with the latch, not realizing that the button on the wall would open the doors. She spun and faced them, her breathing ragged and her face pale and contorted with tears. She was shaking her head even more violently than her body was shaking. The sheriff caught her by the shoulders, keeping his voice low as he tried to soothe her.

"Mrs. Shaffer, I know it's hard to see her like that, but she's going to be all right. She's going to make it...." The woman moaned and covered her face with her hands, shaking her head even harder. The sheriff pressed on, "Yes, she is, Mrs. Shaffer, RaeLynn is strong, she'll be fine...."

To their surprise, the woman showed impressive strength by wrenching away from the sheriff's grasp and slapping the button to open the doors. Before they opened fully, she slipped through them and ran for the exit. The last thing they heard her say was, "She should have died! It woulda been better for her...."

Corrie stared bleakly out the window of the police cruiser that J.D. had borrowed to take her back to the campground. In the early morning darkness, the quiet village seemed deserted, matching the desolate feeling in her heart. She had been aghast at the way RaeLynn's mother had reacted on seeing her only daughter in such a sad state. Corrie had hoped that RaeLynn would have awakened at sensing her mother's presence, as well as Corrie's presence, that she would have sensed the love and support around her. Now, Corrie thought with a wince, she was glad that RaeLynn had been unaware of her mother's visit.

"You holding up okay?" J.D.'s voice dragged her back from her dark thoughts. She turned to him, feeling a pang at the sight of the care and concern in his silver eyes. She knew she hadn't been very friendly to him since RaeLynn had vanished and she marveled that her coldness hadn't made him turn away from her for good. She straightened up in her seat and couldn't refrain from wiping her eyes, hoping J.D. would think it was tiredness, not tears, she was trying to erase.

"All things considered," she said. She'd never been able to hide her true feelings from J.D., just like Rick had always been able to read her. She took a deep breath. "I just realized that I never thanked you," she said.

One of his dark brows rose as he took his eyes from the road to look at her. "For?"

"For finding her. For rescuing her. For bringing her home."

He shook his head. "I didn't do much more than what any decent human being would do," he protested. She let out a flat laugh.

"There aren't many decent human beings out there, if RaeLynn's condition is any indication," she said. "It was providential that you were there when they—whoever those people were—left her on the road to be killed. You could've just called for help, an ambulance...."

"There wasn't time," J.D. said bluntly. "What was providential was that whoever dropped her there chose that spot. It was close to the Black Horse so I didn't have to take her too far. It was providential that she wasn't injured by me moving her. I just... I just happened to be there."

"You cared."

He shot her a look she couldn't decipher then turned his attention back to the road. His brow furrowed with thought then he cleared his throat. "You're glad she's back."

"Of course I am," she said, blinking with surprise. "In spite of her condition... I mean, it's going to take a while for her to recover, to heal, but now she's back and she's safe...."

"I'm not so sure she's safe, Corrie," he interrupted. "Whoever left her on the highway intended for her to die. She didn't. If they don't know it by now, they will soon, and they might be back to finish the job." He looked at her squarely. "You have to realize that they left her where they did for a reason."

She had been trying to push those suspicions that both Rick and J.D. had voiced earlier out of her mind. Her concern for RaeLynn had helped her keep those thoughts at bay, but now she had no choice but to face her growing fear. "That's what you and Rick think."

"You don't?" he asked. She shrugged, shaking off a chill.

"I guess I don't have a choice. But why am I a threat? You heard Mrs. Shaffer; her husband is home. It doesn't matter that

RaeLynn didn't take the fiesta money. Obviously they found some way to bail him out. So why the warning? I mean, I get that they're angry and maybe vindictive enough to want to take it out on me as well as RaeLynn, but don't you think that this is a little over-the-top?" She was trying to convince herself as much as she was trying to convince J.D. It wasn't working on either one of them.

"I haven't had the pleasure of meeting any of the Shaffers other than RaeLynn," he said dryly. "But I've heard stories. Even though it's well-known that they engage in a lot of illegal activities, including dealing drugs, they've managed to keep out of the law's reach, mainly through intimidation and threats to anyone who would be willing to press charges or testify against them. I've also heard that Jake Shaffer himself has done a bit of time behind bars for aggravated assault, including on a police officer. So, to answer your question, no, I don't think this is over-the-top behavior for them."

Corrie wrapped her arms around herself, even though the car's heater was on full blast. She was grateful for the warmth but neither the heater nor J.D.'s hoodie, which was draped over her shoulders, could touch the coldness deep inside her. "They know now that she survived," she said. J.D. responded with a grunt. "So you think they're going to try to finish the job... if it was the Shaffers that did that to her."

"I'm sure they're afraid if she recovers, that she'll be able to identify her attackers and probably testify to their identity in court," he said. Corrie drew in a sharp breath.

"Then that's probably what her mother meant when she said it would have been better if RaeLynn had died!" She choked back a sob and didn't try to stop the tears that blurred her vision. RaeLynn had defied her family by refusing to steal the money for them. They believed she would defy them again. When J.D. reached over and covered her hands with his, she gripped them as if he were throwing her a lifeline.

"We're going to do all we can to keep her safe... and you." His fingers tightened around hers. "She's got enough to worry about with recovering. We'll make sure no one will hurt her again."

"How can you be so sure?" Her voice came out as a strangled whisper. She couldn't stop thinking about all the times RaeLynn had <u>not</u> been protected by the police... and what happened to the Law Enforcement Officer that had tried to help her. The thought of something like that happening to J.D. or Rick made her sick to her stomach.

"Hey," J.D. said, giving her clasped hands a little shake before disengaging his own to make the turn toward the Black Horse. "It's our job, Corrie. We'll do what we have to do. And that includes keeping you safe as well."

It hadn't occurred to her that she could be in as much danger. Somehow, that didn't frighten her near as much as the thought of the danger that Rick and J.D. would be in for trying to protect her and RaeLynn. "I don't understand why I have to be protected. Why would they want to hurt me? Just because I'm RaeLynn's friend."

"And because some of your best friends are cops. You're their enemy," J.D. said ominously as they pulled off the highway and down the ramp to the campground office. "You turned her against them. At least, that's the way they look at it," he added when she started to protest. "You're going to pay for meddling in their business. That will also serve as a warning to anyone else who dares to interfere in the future."

Corrie said nothing as they parked in front of the building. The campground wasn't filled to capacity and a glance at the dashboard clock told her it was barely five in the morning. It would be a while before any of her guests were up and about. She reached for the door handle but J.D. stopped her with a hand on her shoulder.

"Wait," he said. He took the car's radio and softly spoke. "Detective Wilder checking in."

She stared at him, then came the response, "One-fourteen responding. All clear."

"Ten-four," J.D. said. He returned the radio to the rack then nodded. "Let me come open your door for you."

"Who was that? What's going on?" Corrie asked. She waited until J.D. had walked around the cruiser and opened her door. "Was this your or Rick's idea?" she asked as she realized that her campground had been under guard since they had left for the hospital earlier.

"Does it matter?" J.D. raised a brow. "Both my officers and the sheriff's deputies have been keeping an eye on the campground for the last few hours. Jerry and Jackie know what's going on. In fact, they're the ones who let Officer Camacho into the store. He's been watching for us."

Corrie didn't know whether to be relieved or annoyed. She saw the ramrod-straight figure of Aaron Camacho standing in the doorway, his piercing dark eyes searching the area even as she and J.D. stepped inside, and felt safer, in spite of herself. "Good morning, Officer Camacho."

"Miss Black, how are you holding up?" he asked, his eyes flicking toward her for a split second before resuming his scrutiny of the dark campground. She smiled at his concern.

"I'm fine, thank you." She made her way through the store, turning lights on as she went. She glanced in the direction of the door that opened into the laundry room and was reassured by the sight of the lock securely fastened. She wasn't surprised to see that there was a half pot of coffee on the courtesy table. "I see that Jackie made sure you had something to help you get through the morning."

"Yes, ma'am," Officer Camacho said, still keeping his position by the door, even though J.D. joined Corrie inside the store. "I told her she didn't need to do that, but she insisted. I'm sure there's plenty for you and Detective Wilder."

"I'll brew some piñon coffee for us, if you don't mind," she said, smiling at J.D. "It's going to take more than regular coffee to get rid of the taste of whatever that stuff was that we had at the hospital." J.D. returned the grin. Before she could respond, he spun toward the front door of the campground store as Officer Camacho stiffened and reached for his weapon. Corrie froze and nearly dropped the coffee pot. Then she heard a faint, gruff voice from outside.

"Don't shoot, Officer, it's just me and the missus!" Corrie sagged in relief as J.D. went to the door and let Jerry and Jackie Page in. The older couple were fully dressed and had obviously been watching for Corrie to return. Jackie rushed to Corrie, her long silver hair loose from its customary ponytail and flowing behind her, and enveloped her in a fierce hug.

"I'm fine, Jackie," Corrie said, correctly interpreting Jackie's maternal reaction. "Really, I'm okay. It's RaeLynn that needs our concern."

"And she has it," Jackie said, releasing Corrie and taking the coffee pot from her. "I'll do this. You and J.D. sit down and tell us how that poor child is doing." She bustled into the small kitchen that opened off of the campground store and returned with a loaf of banana bread that she had set out to thaw earlier in the morning. While she made a pot of piñon coffee, J.D. and Corrie filled her in on RaeLynn's condition, with Jerry interjecting an occasional question. Officer Camacho remained by the door, still vigilant.

The fact that J.D. was confident in the young officer's abilities was evident by the way he was able to focus on the conversation with Corrie and the Pages with undivided attention.

"So Rick's going to make sure she's got round-the-clock guards at the hospital?" Jerry asked. His walrus mustache bristled and he ran a hand over his bald head. He shrugged. "I guess he's aware that it is RaeLynn's family he's dealing with? Eventually, she'll be released and then what? He can't assign her a personal bodyguard for the rest of her life."

"I'm sure Rick's planning to have whoever did this to RaeLynn in custody before she's released from the hospital," Corrie said. She looked at J.D. for confirmation and was surprised to catch a fleeting look of apprehension on his face. It was gone before she could blink and she wondered if she had imagined it. He appeared to be as casually confident as he always was, the grim set of his jaw a common expression when he was determined to solve a case. "You probably already know what Rick's plans are, don't you?" Corrie asked him, then immediately added, "No, I know, you can't tell me. 'Official police business can't be discussed with us lowly civilians, right?" She winked at him to take the sting out of her words. His smile seemed strained, but perhaps it was just tiredness.

"A lot depends on what her doctors say and how her recovery goes," he said, accepting a cup of coffee and a plate with two slices of banana bread from Jackie.

"This ought to take the edge off," Jackie said, as she prepared the same thing for Corrie. "I'll fix you a real breakfast. You must be starving."

"This looks like a feast to me right now," J.D. said, taking a generous bite of his bread. While Jackie took a plate to a grateful Officer Camacho, Corrie eyed J.D. over her coffee cup. Something was off; she couldn't say exactly what it was, but she could sense a tension in J.D. that was different from what she had been seeing in previous weeks. Almost as if he were keeping something from her. He must have felt her gaze. He looked at her and wariness clouded his steel-gray eyes for a split-second. He stood up, his manner becoming brisk. "Camacho, when you're done with your coffee, you can go back to your regular duties. I'll take over here."

Officer Camacho looked dubious. "You sure, Detective? I mean, you're supposed to be off today and I don't mind...."

"It's fine, Camacho," J.D. said, his tone a little sharper than anyone expected, if the startled looks he got from everyone in the room meant anything. Now Corrie knew she wasn't imagining things. He immediately softened his tone. "You've pulled a couple of double shifts this week and hanging around with Corrie isn't exactly what I'd call work. I'm sure I'll manage just fine." He gave Corrie a wink that would have set her suspicions at rest if it weren't for the fact that she knew J.D. too well to dismiss her earlier feelings.

Chapter 3

Despite J.D.'s insistence that she get some rest, Corrie found the only way to deal with her nerves and exhaustion was to shower and dress and begin the day like a regular work day. Visiting hours at the hospital started at eight, which meant she would be able to get the campground store opened up and then leave it in Jerry's and Jackie's capable hands. Red and Dana Myers, the other couple who stayed at the campground and helped her out, had left the day before to take a couple of weeks off to visit family for the upcoming Thanksgiving holiday. Corrie knew that she could call Myra Evans, formerly Myra Kaydahzinne, to help out but she had promised her newly-wed employee a hiatus through the holidays to help get her grandmother situated in the new home she and Deputy Evans had built on the old woman's former home site. She didn't have any new guests arriving, only two checkouts, and there was no reason why Buster, her maintenance man, couldn't get all of his tasks done within a reasonable amount of time. She finally admitted that it was her concern and anxiety over RaeLynn that had her worrying about things and decided that it wouldn't hurt to head over to the hospital a little early.

She hurried down the stairs from her apartment, followed by her ancient black Labrador, Renfro, and her black and gray tabby cat, Oliver. Once she reached the campground store, the two animals scooted around her and headed for the door for their morning trip outside. Corrie quickened her steps, knowing that her dog, especially, needed to get to the dog yard as soon as possible. She cast a quick glance around the store, surprised that J.D. wasn't in sight. She pulled the door open, only to have it yanked out of her grasp and nearly slammed shut on Oliver's tail as he managed to slip through the gap. Renfro wasn't as fast and his yelp matched Corrie's as the door almost caught his snout. She blinked and, after a stunned moment, she reached for the door just as J.D. pushed it open and she jumped back to avoid getting hit in the nose.

"J.D., what are you doing?" Corrie sputtered. J.D. stumbled as Renfro pushed past him, the old dog grumbling in his throat while J.D. muttered under his breath. He shoved his cell phone back into its holster, his brow furrowed with concern. "Is everything all right?" she asked, wondering if he'd gotten a call about RaeLynn and her heart started pounding with dread.

"You shouldn't be going outside without checking to see if it's safe!" J.D. snapped in response. Corrie's mouth dropped open and he went on, "You know there's a chance that the Shaffers might try to take it out on you for turning RaeLynn against them!"

She ignored the chill that his words sent down her spine and bit back her natural impulse to argue with him. "Was that Rick? Or the hospital? Is RaeLynn all right?" she asked, restraining the urge to clutch at his arm.

Several emotions flickered in his eyes though his expression became wooden. She didn't know what to think; she only knew that his reaction was making her expect the worst. "J.D., talk to me!" she cried.

"RaeLynn is all right," he said, his voice as expressionless as his face. He caught her incredulous look and shook his head. "I mean, as well as can be expected, under the circumstances." He glanced around the campground store, but Corrie got the distinct impression he was avoiding her gaze rather than checking to see if all was well. "Yeah, that was the sheriff. He said everything is under control."

"What's under control? What does that even mean?" She planted her fists on her hips as J.D. slipped inside and shut the door behind him and locked it. "You know, my campground is open for business. I can't very well lock my guests out!" He unlocked the door without a word and then motioned for her to move toward the front counter. She did, her heart hammering wildly. "Come on, J.D., just talk to me! Tell me what's going on!"

He sighed and ran his hand over his hair, giving his ponytail a tug. "You know that everything the sheriff and I do is for your own good and safety," he began. Corrie fought back her initial urge to tell him that she was perfectly capable of taking care of herself. She didn't want to get him sidetracked. She folded her arms across her chest to keep herself from tapping her fingers on the counter, but she kept her eyes fixed on his face. He straightened up and mirrored her stance. "All right, here's what's going on," he said and he rolled his eyes heavenward. "Sutton's going to kill me, but he, of all people, should know that there's no way to keep anything from you, so there's no point in even trying."

"I'm flattered, truly," Corrie said dryly. "But if everything is 'all right' and 'under control'," she asked, hooking her fingers into air quotes, "why are you worried about Rick killing you?"

"I'm not. In fact, it would save me from *you* killing me." He muttered. He took a deep breath. "Okay, the plan is to have RaeLynn transported to a rehabilitation facility."

"Rehabilitation? You mean she's regained consciousness and...." Corrie's excitement was cut short by J.D. holding up a hand.

"No, she's still unconscious, but stable. Somewhat. Normally, the doctors wouldn't give the green light to have her moved, but the sheriff explained the situation to them and that keeping her here is more dangerous to her health and safety than moving her."

Corrie nodded soberly, aware of how serious the threat to both RaeLynn and herself was. She knew J.D. and Rick were not the type to overreact, no matter how concerned they were. Their protectiveness irritated her at times, but she knew it was because they cared about her more than she was willing to admit... or hope for. "Okay, well, I'm sure Rick knows what's best and that the doctors know what they're doing. So how soon is she being moved? I was going to see about going to the hospital a little earlier than the regular visiting hours...."

"They left about thirty minutes ago."

Corrie stared at J.D., not sure if she had heard him correctly or if her stress and tiredness had caught up with her and she had imagined the words coming from his mouth. She waited for him to speak again, but he kept silent. "What?" she stammered. She shook her head. "But... we were just at the hospital a... a couple of hours ago. How...?"

"He didn't want to wait too long, in case word got out about her condition and the plans for her treatment. He wanted it to be kept quiet. He and Noreen got with the doctor and made the arrangements as fast as they could." He paused and Corrie shook her head again.

"Why didn't he tell me?" she asked, her voice strained. J.D. sighed.

"I told him he should," he said, rubbing the back of his neck. "I told him you had a right to know what was going on. But he... well, you know how the sheriff gets. I don't blame him, because I know why he did this and I kind of agree with him. Until he gets Miss Shaffer someplace he feels she's safe and taken care of, he can't focus on you." His eyes met hers and she could see the concern in his gray eyes. "Not that he doesn't trust me to look after your safety, but he's got a case to solve and he needs to give that all his attention."

"Where...? I mean, can you tell me where she's going? I can go see her, can't I?" J.D. straightened up and shook his head.

"Those are questions you'll have to ask Sutton when he gets back," he said firmly. "I'm not sure how much he'll tell us or anyone else who asks. He needs to protect her privacy. By law, her medical condition and information are all supposed to be kept private, anyway. But I'm sure as soon as she's in a condition to have visitors, you'll be the first to know." She gave a short laugh.

"After Rick. And probably you, as well," she said dryly. She sighed and flopped onto the stool behind the counter. "Anything else I should know?"

J.D. shook his head and leaned his hip against the counter. "Nothing you haven't already heard. The only thing you need to worry about is keeping an eye out for the Shaffers. We don't know what they might do when they find out that RaeLynn is alive and gone from Bonney."

"You're pretty sure that RaeLynn's family had something to do with what happened to her," Corrie remarked, swallowing a yawn as she rested her chin on her hand. She didn't want to admit that she was tired; she knew J.D. had to be tired as well. She was afraid he'd start worrying about her, order her to get some rest, and then keep any new developments from her. One of his brows rose as he stared at her and she wondered if he would attribute her glassy eyes to exhaustion or concern. She fought the urge to reach for a tissue to wipe away the moisture.

"So far as we know," J.D. said, handing her his handkerchief, "they're the only ones who have any kind of axe to grind. You should get some more sleep," he added.

Corrie snatched the handkerchief and dabbed at her eyes, cursing herself for being so transparent. "I'm fine and, like you said, that's only as far as we know. We don't know where she was or who she was with after she left here the night of the fiesta." She thrust the handkerchief back at him and he stuffed it back in his pocket.

"True," J.D. acknowledged with a nod. "But you would think that, if she had been attacked by someone else, her family would be cooperating in helping us find whoever that might be."

"You don't know the Shaffers," Corrie said with a snort. "If there's any police involvement, they're not going to volunteer any information or even express any interest. They're too afraid that the cops will find something on them that isn't even related to the case and they're not willing to take that chance. Not even for one of their own."

"I had hopes that RaeLynn's mother would offer some help. But she's apparently too scared...." He broke off, frowning. "But scared of whom?" he went on, almost to himself.

"That's what I'm wondering," Corrie said, sitting up straight. "I get that she didn't want to answer the door this morning when a deputy showed up... but was that because she knew it was about RaeLynn or because she *didn't* know?" J.D.'s eyes widened slightly.

"She did say that her husband didn't want her answering the door when Deputy Evans showed up," he said. "I wonder how she found out about RaeLynn then?"

"I can venture a guess," Corrie said. "One of the other tenants in the trailer park where the Shaffers live spends almost all his time listening to a police scanner. His name's Benny Gonzalez. Rick will tell you that Benny applied to both the sheriff's department and the village police several times over the years. But he had numerous health issues that prevented him from passing the physical and he's a self-avowed couch potato since he retired from working at the hospital. So he's been living out his dream of being in law enforcement by listening to a police scanner almost constantly...."

"He worked at the hospital?" J.D. interrupted, raising a brow. Corrie nodded.

"He was an orderly in his younger days, then he volunteered at the information desk when a heart attack put him on disability. He keeps his finger on the pulse of the community—almost literally—by maintaining his friendships with his old co-workers. No doubt he heard the call come in about RaeLynn and then called someone at the hospital to get what information he could. I'd be willing to bet that he's the one who told Mrs. Shaffer about RaeLynn and I can almost guarantee that he's the neighbor who gave Mrs. Shaffer a ride to the hospital."

J.D. grunted. "I wonder if he was also one of the neighbors who told Deputy Evans that he didn't know where the Shaffers might be."

"Oh, he wouldn't have admitted to seeing them around. If the police are asking about the Shaffers, Benny will immediately say he hasn't seen or heard anything. One time, several years ago, he did tell the police about having seen one of the Shaffer boys hanging around a house that was vandalized. The very next day, his car's tires were slashed. All four of them. He got the message and didn't report it. He lives on a fixed income and really didn't need the expense of replacing his tires, but he figured it was a small price to pay for learning his lesson." Corrie shrugged. "I'm sure he was concerned when he heard the news over the scanner and he just went to see Mrs. Shaffer and promised to be discreet about taking her to the hospital. He's probably a bundle of nerves, hoping that the police don't question him or do anything that makes Jake Shaffer think that Benny ratted him out to the cops."

"Well, there's no way we can look the other way regarding the Shaffers, even if Mr. Gonzalez is afraid he'll be in their cross-hairs," J.D. said dryly. "At this point, we're just looking to notify them about a family member. We're not looking to arrest them. Yet."

"You don't have anything to charge them with, do you?" Corrie asked, her brow furrowing.

J.D. sighed and ran a hand over his head. "If I could have identified the car or the people I saw last night who left her in the middle of the highway... but I can't even venture a guess." He blew his breath out in frustration and Corrie knew that it was anger at himself for not having gotten a closer look—no matter how impossible it might have been. "It was just a shadow. All I know is, it was a car, nothing sporty, definitely not a truck or SUV. I couldn't make out any details—no make, no model, certainly not any color at that hour of the morning. At most, we could question the Shaffers about RaeLynn's whereabouts for the last few weeks and who they think might have attacked her. But they could just say that she's an adult and they're not responsible for her and she doesn't have to tell them anything about where she goes, who she sees, and what she does. All of which is true," he said with a shrug.

Corrie chewed on her lower lip, then stopped, realizing that she was adopting Rick's signature nervous tic. "So how are you going to find out who hurt RaeLynn and left her out there?" she said, indicating the highway outside the campground with a tip of her head. "If the Shaffers won't talk to you...."

"They're going to <u>have</u> to talk to us," J.D. said, his face darkening. "If they want to know what happened to RaeLynn, they're going to have to help us find some answers."

Corrie was quiet for a long time and she stared down at the floor. She noticed that the baseboard needed dusting. When RaeLynn had come to work for her, Corrie had found her one day on her hands and knees, scrubbing the baseboard all around the perimeter of the campground store. She did it about three times a week and Corrie had told her that, while she had appreciated RaeLynn's work, she didn't need to be THAT meticulous. RaeLynn had blushed and told her that she felt better knowing that all her jobs were done more thoroughly than they needed to be done—that she wanted to be sure she was making herself as useful as possible because she really needed her job. RaeLynn had been so diligent in keeping up her work that Corrie had discovered that she never had to check up on her to make sure things were being done. In fact, she'd gotten so used to it that she hadn't checked in weeks, since RaeLynn had disappeared. With a jolt, she realized that she had come to take RaeLynn and her work for granted. Had she ever let RaeLynn know how much she was appreciated? Did RaeLynn realize how much Corrie cared about her friend and wanted to help her have a good, happy life? She could feel J.D.'s gaze fastened on her and she jerked her head up to look at him, his face hazy through the glaze of tears in her eyes.

"They won't care, J.D.," she said softly. She sniffed and groped blindly for the tissue box on the counter. She snagged one and wiped her eyes, but the tears came faster than she could stop them. "They won't care," she repeated with a sob. "They've never cared about her, only what they could get from her. She wasn't important to them. Even if her mom did care about her, she kept it under wraps because she knew her husband didn't want her to waste any time or energy on her daughter. Only he and his sons mattered. When she didn't deliver on the fiesta money to bail him out, despite his threats, he probably washed his hands of her. She was useless to him and his family. So I doubt he cares what happened to her. He's probably wishing she'd never turned up again."

J.D. frowned. She could almost see the wheels spinning in his head and she kept silent. At last, he shook his head and sighed. "Then maybe we're overreacting about protecting you. Unless you approach the Shaffers yourself or directly defy them, you shouldn't be on their radar. It's just—" He broke off and stared down at the floor, lost in thought. The jingling of the bell over the front door made him look up with a jerk and a shift toward the weapon at his hip. His reaction made Corrie jump, but then she and J.D. both relaxed when Buster ambled in, making a beeline for the courtesy table.

Chapter 4

"Mornin'!" Buster called out with a cheery wave. "How's it going today?"

"Fine," Corrie and J.D. responded in flat tones. Buster didn't seem to notice as he poured himself a cup of coffee and doctored it with several packets of sugar and a hefty dose of pumpkin spice creamer. He hummed happily as he proceeded to slather two slices of banana bread with butter and took a healthy bite before turning toward his employer. He stopped in mid-chew when he noticed their somber faces.

"Whah?" he asked through a mouthful of banana bread, spewing crumbs all over his dark beard. "Fumthin whong?" He swallowed and took a huge swig of his coffee, grimacing as the hot liquid burned down his throat. He shook his head and looked at the clock. "I'm not late, am I?"

"No," Corrie said. She looked at the clock as well and blinked in disbelief. "As a matter of fact, you're early." It was only by five minutes, but since Buster's usual arrival time was at least fifteen minutes past his scheduled time, Corrie felt properly shocked.

"I am?" Buster looked almost as shocked as Corrie felt. He nearly dropped his coffee. "Wow, and here I was, thinkin' that Noreen was hollering 'cause she was mad at me because I overslept or something. I didn't even look at the clock, just jumped out of bed, got dressed, and jumped in my car." He patted his pockets, dropping banana bread fragments all over the floor. "Man, I even dropped my cell phone... oh, man, I dropped the phone while Noreen was talking to me! She probably thought I hung up on her! Oh, she's really gonna be mad at me now!"

"Buster," Corrie interrupted him as his voice rose hysterically, "I doubt Noreen called to wake you for work. Did you even hear what she called you about?" She took his coffee cup out of his hand before he dropped it and added to the growing mess on the floor, wondering if she was going to have to clean it up or if he was going to pull himself together in time to do his job.

"Um, I dunno," Buster admitted. His brow wrinkled. "She was at work last night.... I thought she was supposed to get off work around eight. I wonder why she was calling me so early?"

"So you didn't hear what she called about," J.D. said. Buster cringed and glanced at J.D. his wide face reddening with embarrassment. He shuffled his feet, his huge work boots in danger of pulverizing the crumbs on the floor, and Corrie quickly grabbed the broom and dustpan before her employee made an even bigger mess.

"Um, no, Detective Wilder, I guess not," he mumbled. In spite of herself, Corrie bit back a grin. She doubted that Buster would ever get over his nervousness around J.D. or any law enforcement officer, even Rick whom he'd known since kindergarten. "I mean, I was sound asleep when she called and it kinda shocked me...."

"It's okay, Buster," Corrie said soothingly, as she shot a glare at J.D. who had put on his "stern cop face", probably just to rattle Buster. He gave her a wink that Buster didn't notice. "It's just that it was a busy night at the ER. Maybe she wanted to let you know she wouldn't be by to see you this morning."

"Yeah, maybe," Buster said, uncertainty tainting his words. He frowned. "How'd you know it was busy at the ER last night? Did you talk to Noreen this morning?"

Corrie grimaced. She hadn't planned on telling everyone she saw about RaeLynn's mishap and she wasn't even sure she should talk about it. J.D. read her face correctly and gave a shrug, leaving it up to her how much to tell Buster. "Yeah, we talked to Noreen... Rick and J.D. and I," she clarified when Buster seemed perplexed. She chose her words carefully, hoping the story wouldn't spread too far out of control. "RaeLynn had an, uh, accident last night. Just down the road from here."

Buster's brows shot up into his hairline. "Oh, wow, RaeLynn's back? And she was in an accident? Is she okay?"

"It's pretty serious," Corrie admitted, though she didn't attempt to correct any misconceptions. She couldn't really say how RaeLynn was faring or what had actually happened, so she just hoped that her vague explanation would suffice. "She was taken to the ER early this morning. That's probably why Noreen called you. Just to let you know."

Buster nodded, his eyes wide with concern. "I better call her back. You know, just to make sure she knows I didn't mean to hang up on her and all. I really wasn't awake when she called." He patted his pockets again and grimaced. "Uh, can I use the phone? My cell phone is...."

"Go ahead," Corrie said, gesturing to the phone on the counter. She made her way around the counter and she and J.D. headed back toward the laundry room door to give Buster some privacy, stopping for cups of piñon coffee on the way. As she filled her cup, she glanced at J.D. and noticed he looked preoccupied. Of course, it was probably due to the events of the last few hours. She decided to try to distract him. "It looks like it's going to be a beautiful day," she said.

"Mm, hm," J.D. responded as he sipped his coffee.

Corrie tried again. "You think I might get more guests if the weather holds?"

"Uh, huh." His eyes were fixed on his coffee cup, he was frowning, and it was apparent his mind was a million miles away.

She wondered if he'd even heard her. "Maybe I'll end up hosting Thanksgiving dinner here for about a hundred guests," she said cheerily. "You can help Jackie cook the turkey and maybe contribute a pie or two!"

He only nodded.

"J.D.!"

His head snapped up, his eyes coming into focus. "What?"

She sighed. "Detective Wilder, you just allowed yourself to be volunteered to cook Thanksgiving dinner this year."

"What?"

She waved a hand and shook her head. "I'm kidding, J.D. But it's obvious you have something on your mind. Care to share with me?"

He gave her a rueful smile and tilted his head back toward the counter where Buster was engaged in conversation—heavily sprinkled with apologies—with Noreen. "Not much to share," he said. "I'm just wondering why Noreen felt she had to call Buster this morning."

"You think there's something strange about that?" Corrie asked, her brow furrowing.

"She knew he was coming to work and he'd be bound to hear about it from you or me or even Jackie and Jerry," he said. "And it's not like Buster and RaeLynn were such good friends that he would be one of the first people notified about what happened to her." He looked back at Buster at the exact same time Buster glanced over at him. Buster blanched and quickly spun back around, lowering his voice as he continued his conversation. J.D. and Corrie exchanged a look and moved toward Buster just as he hurriedly ended his call.

"What's up?" Corrie asked, not bothering to try to sound nonchalant. Besides, J.D. was watching Buster with narrowed eyes.

Buster's face paled and he gulped. "Uh, nothing. Nothing at all. I gotta get to work," he stammered and edged toward the door.

He stopped when both Corrie and J.D. stepped toward him and he swallowed hard. He managed a sickly smile. "Uh, something wrong, guys?"

"You tell us," Corrie retorted. Buster's grin faded. "What was Noreen telling you? Why did she call you about what happened to RaeLynn so early this morning?"

"Um," Buster began and his face flushed bright red. "Well, she wanted me to know what happened because... 'cause she knew that... I'd probably get a call from Benny. Benny Gonzalez," he explained. "You know, he lives near the Shaffers...."

"Yes, we know who Benny is," Corrie interjected. "What about him?"

"Well, I sometimes go by and visit him. And he sometimes calls and asks me to do stuff for him around his trailer. His uncle and my dad were friends, so I help him out when I can. I feel sorry for him, you know, 'cause he can't do so much and he gets lonely. Anyway," he went on hurriedly when he saw the impatience growing on Corrie's and J.D.'s faces, "Benny probably heard about RaeLynn's accident on his scanner and he knows me and Noreen are dating, and she wanted to make sure I didn't tell him anything about her. About RaeLynn. I mean, not that I've heard anything except what you guys have told me 'cause I haven't really talked to Noreen...."

"You mean, Noreen is afraid that Benny might try to pump you for information about RaeLynn's condition and what her treatment plans are," J.D. clarified. "And she's worried he might say something to the Shaffers?"

"Yeah," Buster admitted. "She was warning me not to say anything and that she wasn't gonna tell me anything, either. Not because she didn't trust me to keep it secret," he added quickly, "but because that way, I could honestly tell Benny I didn't know anything." He shrugged. "She asked if Benny had called me yet and I told her that, if he did, I didn't know because I left my phone at home after I dropped it. She said that was probably a good thing... and that she wasn't mad at me. Never was!" His face brightened, then clouded as he took in Corrie's and J.D.'s somber faces. "Hey, uh, RaeLynn... she's gonna be okay, right? I mean...."

"We hope so, Buster," Corrie said quietly, touched by the concern in the big man's face. Buster could look threatening and act less than brilliant, but he was really all heart. He was biting his lip and his look of concern deepened.

"Wow, I didn't know she was that bad. Noreen wouldn't say what happened to her. She said she'd tell me what she could later when we had some privacy." He shook his head. "That's so sad. I hope she gets better soon. She's nice."

J.D. made a sound deep in his throat. Corrie shot him a glare, positive that he was trying to hold in a sarcastic comment, but his face appeared to be carved from stone. His eyes met hers and the emotion she saw swimming in their silver depths wasn't scorn or disbelief. She blinked in surprise and J.D. glanced away before she could study the look further.

Buster spoke up, "Well, I guess I better get to work. Noreen said she'd stop by later, when she's on her way home from work. That's okay, isn't it?"

"Of course," Corrie started to say, but then J.D. straightened up with a look of concern.

"Buster, have Noreen call to let us know when she's leaving the hospital." Buster's face mirrored the surprise Corrie felt. Before she could ask what J.D. meant, he went on. "I need to talk to her and I want to make sure I catch her before she goes home to get some rest. I don't want to bother her," he added. He avoided Corrie's eyes.

Buster nodded. "Oh, yeah, sure, J.D. I mean, Detective," he corrected himself, blushing. He pointed to the phone and raised a brow at Corrie. "Can I use the phone again?"

"Sure. Just tell Noreen to call the campground and ask for me or J.D. I'll let you know when she calls." Buster nodded happily and turned toward the phone as Corrie and J.D. moved back toward the laundry room door. "What's that all about?" she asked him, keeping her voice low.

"I'm going to guess that Noreen warned Buster about Benny Gonzalez because she's worried that he's already gotten some information about RaeLynn already. Benny knows that Buster and the head ER nurse are a couple and I don't want to take a chance on Noreen's safety in case someone wants to get information on RaeLynn's condition."

Corrie drew in a sharp breath. "You think someone might follow her from the hospital?"

"Maybe, maybe not," J.D. admitted. "I'm not planning on a police escort because that would only draw too much attention to Noreen, but I can arrange to have an officer follow her and keep an eye on her home discreetly. I just don't want to take any chances." Corrie nodded mutely.

Buster turned from the phone. "Hey, J.D.... I mean, Detective Wilder," he stammered, "um, I just talked to the receptionist. Noreen left right after I talked to her."

Chapter 5

J.D.'s temples were throbbing as he pushed the police cruiser past the posted speed limit. Normally, he would have taken his Harley, but leaving Corrie behind without a LEO to guard her and the campground was out of the question, and her father's old truck wasn't in any condition to make the trip to the hospital at the speed J.D. was driving. Corrie's face was grim and pale and she asked no questions, just kept her eyes focused on the road. He knew she was looking for Noreen's dark-green Subaru SUV or her Harley as diligently as he was.

About two miles from the medical center, they spotted the SUV pulled over on the opposite side of the road with the flashers blinking and J.D. let out a stifled oath. Corrie gasped and J.D. hoped he hadn't made a mistake in bringing her along. Behind the dark-green hatchback was a black sedan with rust spots and dents in the body. He didn't see Noreen or anyone else around the vehicles and J.D. flipped on the siren and lights as he cut across the oncoming traffic lanes and stopped in front of Noreen's Outback. "Stay here," he ordered Corrie as he checked his weapon and opened the car door. She nodded without a word, crouching down slightly in her seat, her eyes wide with fear—for herself, for him, or for Noreen, he wasn't sure. Probably all three.

He slipped out and, using the Subaru for cover, swept the area around the two vehicles. It didn't take long; they were out in the open except for a few scrubby bushes that lined the road. There was a ditch that dropped off next to the shoulder where the vehicles were parked and, near the bottom, he saw Noreen in her pale green scrubs, her face grim, talking to two rough-looking men who were gesturing wildly. J.D. decided not to take any chances. He stepped out from his cover, his gun aimed. "Police department! What's the trouble over here?"

The two men looked up, startled, and instinctively put their hands in the air, their faces registering more fear than any other emotion. Noreen turned, frowning at the unexpected intrusion. Her eyes widened in surprise, then her brow cleared when she saw J.D. "It's okay, Detective, everything is all right," she said as she waved.

"I'll be the judge of that," J.D. responded. He moved closer, his gun still covering the two men. "What happened?" His gaze was trained on the two men who looked both nervous and guilty. "Who are these guys?"

"They're maintenance workers at the hospital," Noreen said. "Joe Trejo and Alan Rivers." The two men nodded respectfully at J.D., keeping their eyes on his weapon. "They've been working there for about ten years now," Noreen went on. "They were heading home from their night shifts and blew a tire. While they were changing it, they lost the wheel cover that was holding the lug nuts. They accidentally kicked it down the ditch," she said, pointing into the tall grass. "I stopped to help them look, but we've only managed to find one and I doubt we'll find any others. We were just discussing what to do next when you showed up." Now she raised one brow quizzically. "Is there something going on that I should know about?"

"I'll tell you in a minute," J.D. said, lowering his weapon. "I'll call a mechanic to come meet them with some spare lug nuts to get them on their way."

"I was going to give them two of mine, to get them back into town to get their tire replaced," Noreen began, but J.D. shook his head.

"No, let's get you home and let a mechanic take care of these gentlemen. I'll make sure they get home safe, too," he assured Noreen. Her look of surprise was tempered with suspicion, but she nodded. She said good-bye to her co-workers, who thanked her, and got into her SUV. J.D. went back to the police cruiser where Corrie waited with barely-concealed impatience. Before she could ask him anything, he held up a hand and called dispatch, explained the situation, and requested assistance for the two men.

Corrie watched him silently until he was done and put the patrol car in gear. "I take it Noreen is safe and all is well?" she asked quietly.

He was glad she hadn't pointed out that his actions had verged on over-reacting. He couldn't help but feel slightly foolish for assuming the worst, but he told himself that it was better to be safe than sorry. "All is well. I'll brief her at the campground, make sure she keeps an eye out for anyone who might take an unnatural interest in RaeLynn's case...."

Corrie held up a hand. "J.D., right now, RaeLynn is safe. She's on her way to wherever Rick and you have decided to send her to recover. I doubt Noreen even knows where that is. So unless the Shaffers have been advised of where RaeLynn is going, there is no danger. Whoever left RaeLynn in the road is not going to risk showing themselves. They know the police are deeply involved now. If it is her family, then for sure they aren't going to make

44

waves. They might be criminals, but they haven't resorted to murder...."

"Yet," J.D. interjected.

"Yet," Corrie agreed. "But I don't think they're going to start now, especially since RaeLynn is being watched very closely by the police."

"And if—when—RaeLynn recovers," J.D. said correcting himself hurriedly, "and there's a chance she'll testify against her family, do you think they won't panic and try to silence her... and anyone else they feel is a threat to them?"

Corrie said nothing for a long while. They followed Noreen's SUV as it drove into the Black Horse parking lot. J.D. quickly got out of the patrol car and gave the area a quick but thorough glance before gesturing for Corrie and Noreen to get into the campground store. Corrie stopped in the doorway and turned to look at J.D. He could see shadows moving in her eyes and the gravity in her expression made him pause. She shook her head, and her own gaze traveled around the campground. Her home.

"I don't think it's RaeLynn or the police the Shaffers are afraid of," Corrie said, her voice low. "I don't think they're the ones who hurt her. I don't know who did," she went on quickly. She shrugged and sighed. "But whoever it is, I think they are a bigger threat to the Shaffers than they are to anyone else. You have to find out who it is that the Shaffers—particularly Jake Shaffer—is so afraid of."

Corrie watched the clock, her frustration mounting as the hours crept by. Rick had left nearly ten hours earlier to accompany RaeLynn to wherever he had found a facility to take her and help her recover. She hadn't heard a word from him since she had left the hospital. She debated asking J.D. if he had heard anything, but knew that he would have told her if he had. Assuming, of course, that Rick hadn't sworn him to secrecy as well.

J.D. had stayed in the campground store all day, after giving Noreen and Buster stern warnings not to give anyone any information about RaeLynn's condition or possible whereabouts. The seriousness of his demeanor had impressed Buster to the point that he promised to avoid any contact with Benny Gonzalez—a promise made easier by the fact that his cell phone was at home—including his usual weekly stop to see if his friend needed anything from the store or any help around his house. Noreen had confirmed that she didn't know much about whatever arrangements Rick might have made and that, in any event, she was bound by patient's privacy not to talk to anyone—Buster included—about what she might know about RaeLynn's condition and treatment at the medical center. She promised to keep an eye out for anyone who might be following her in hopes of gaining information, but Corrie noted a note of humor in the nurse's voice and when she caught Corrie's eye, her slight headshake indicated that she believed that J.D. was overreacting.

J.D.'s feverish concern for her safety and his suspicion over any vehicle that drove into the parking lot had slowly dwindled as the hours went by and nothing remotely resembling a threat occurred. Corrie did her best to keep her "I told you so" expression off her face, but J.D. refused to give her the satisfaction of admitting it out loud.

The sun had set long before the closing time of the campground store. As usual, despite the smaller number of campers than usual during her peak season, it seemed everyone converged on the store at the last minute to make purchases. She spent the last forty-five minutes of the day steadily ringing up sales, grateful that both Jerry and Jackie, along with J.D., were helping the customers find what they needed so she could stay on the register. With a sigh of relief, she saw the last customer out of the store and flipped the "Closed" sign around only one minute past the posted time on the door.

"Not a bad day," Jerry commented. He glanced at his watch, as if to make sure that the clock on the wall was correct, then said, "I take it that Rick hasn't called?"

"If he had, I would have known," Corrie said, indicating that both the campground phone and her cell phone were on the counter next to the register. While she hadn't been nervous about any possible danger, she had been impatient to hear what Rick had arranged and where RaeLynn might be and how she was doing. She glanced at J.D., who was checking his own phone. He looked up at her and shook his head.

"Not a word. But that's not surprising," he added, as he went around the room, checking the doors to make sure they were all locked for the night. "He wanted to make sure that Miss Shaffer was safely transported and admitted to whatever facility she'll be in for a while. And no, he didn't make it clear where, exactly, she was going. And I imagine that the sheriff, being as thorough as he is, won't leave until he makes sure that everything is arranged to provide the best care and protection for her." He stopped in front of the counter and folded his arms across his chest, as he looked at each of them in turn. "I know it's not easy for you all to accept the fact that the sheriff is keeping you all in the dark. You've known him for years, he's a close friend. Yeah, I understand that. But in this case, he has to be a cop first. And, as a cop, his priority is Miss Shaffer's safety and to find the people who did this to her. In that order," he added. "So it's best that everyone keep that in mind and not take his silence as something personal. It's got nothing to do with whether or not he trusts you all. You know he does." His gray eyes fastened on Corrie's face and she felt a slight prickle of warmth. She was glad he looked away before her entire face burst into flames. "Sutton will tell us what he can, when he can. And it's safe to say that everyone here will be the first ones to hear about it. So let's call it a night and say a prayer that everything went well and Miss Shaffer is on the way to recovery."

If anyone was surprised at J.D. mentioning prayer, they kept it under wraps. Jerry and Jackie nodded soberly. Corrie raised a brow but said nothing. She knew if there was anything Rick had told J.D. in confidence, no one would ever hear it. What surprised her was that it seemed that J.D. was just as much in the dark as she was.

Jerry and Jackie left for a late dinner at home, after receiving assurances from both Corrie and J.D. that they would be notified if they were needed for anything. J.D. went around the store once more with Corrie, checking to make sure everything was locked up and turned off for the night. "I'll lock the side door behind me when I leave," J.D. said as he waited at the bottom of the stairs that led up to Corrie's apartment.

"No need," Corrie said as she went to the storage closet under the stairs and retrieved her denim jacket. She slipped it on as she made her way to the side door, pulling her truck keys out of her pocket as she went.

J.D. stared at her. "Where are you going?"

She raised an eyebrow at him. "I'm going to go wait for Rick to get back." J.D. blinked, and Corrie went on before he could say anything, "I know he can't tell me a lot. Maybe he can't tell me anything, really," she said, hurrying to speak before he found his voice. "But all I want to know is that RaeLynn is really safe. That she's going to be okay."

J.D. shook his head. "Corrie, you can get that information from him just by calling him."

"I know that," she said. "But I'll find out more if I see him when I ask him."

"What?"

"Never mind," she sighed. "The thing is, he's not answering his phone. So the only thing that's left for me to do is to go and...."

"Why don't you let him call you or come over once he's back?" J.D. suggested, moving toward the door. She raised her brows and he leaned against the door jamb. "You don't know when he'll be back and it's already late."

"So I'll wait for him. You know as well as I do that if he does get back late, he won't call or come over because he won't want to wake me up or bother me," she said. She cocked her head and folded her arms across her chest. "Are you trying to stop me from leaving?"

"Yes," he deadpanned, and he straightened up. "I thought we established that you might be in danger from whoever attacked Miss Shaffer."

"We established that you and Rick think that whoever attacked RaeLynn might have a bone to pick with me because I'm a friend of hers. Given that the entire day has passed and no one has so much as left a threatening note on my door or called with a warning, I think what we've established is that there is nothing to worry about as far as my safety is concerned."

"You think I'm overreacting," J.D. said stiffly.

Corrie gave him a smile, hoping to take the sting out of her words. "I know you care about me and you're worried. I know it's your job and I appreciate it...."

"I'm not doing this because it's my job," he growled, his brows knitting and his bronzed face growing darker.

She held up her hands. "All right," she said quietly. "I understand your concern. But the fact is, you can't stop me from going to wait for Rick to get back and ask him for information."

There was silence for a long time. His gray eyes were fixed on her face and she looked back at him just as steadily. She lost count of how many ticks of the clock went by before he let out a long sigh and raked his fingers through his hair. To her surprise, he stepped away from the door without saying a word.

For a moment, she stayed where she was, not sure how to react. J.D.'s face was set like stone, his lips in a grim line. He gave her a nod. She went to the door and he opened it for her and followed her out.

She hesitated as they stood on the wooden porch, listening to the late evening sounds of the campground settling down for the night. The scent of campfires, tinged with various cooking aromas, including the faint sweetness of marshmallows and chocolate, sent a pang through her heart and she wasn't even sure why. J.D. remained silent and she wondered what was going through his mind. Part of her wanted to reach out and touch his arm, thank him, though she wasn't sure if there was a need to; another part of her wanted to put her arms around him, reassure him, explain her actions and feelings, but she wasn't sure if she needed to do that, either. For once on this emotionally exhausting day, his eyes weren't busy scanning the area, keeping an eye out for danger. They were trained on her, studying her every move, trying to read her every thought. She was torn between wanting to explain and wanting to keep to herself. In the end, she forced a small smile. "I'll let you know when I'm home," she said.

He raised a brow. "I'll know," he said as he turned and headed toward his cabin.

Chapter 6

Rick Sutton pulled into the parking lot of the apartment complex he called home and, as his Silverado's headlights illuminated the battered Ford pickup parked in one of the two spots reserved for him, he shook his head. He should have known she'd be here.

He slid into his spot, dimming his lights in order not to blind Corrie who was sitting on the steps leading up to his apartment. Though it was mid-November, the night was mild and she only wore jeans and a gray flannel shirt. Her knees were drawn up with her arms folded across them and she had been resting her chin on her forearms. She sat straighter as he cut the lights and shut off the engine, and stood up as he got out of the truck.

"You should be in bed. You had a long day," he said, keeping his voice down as he slung his sport jacket over his shoulder and approached her. She didn't respond, waiting until he got close enough for her not to have to raise her voice. He stopped a step or two below where she was standing and looked up at her, trying to read her expression by the dull glow of the complex's safety lighting.

"How is she?" Her voice appeared to be controlled. He sighed and removed his Stetson.

"Want to come in?" He gestured toward the door of his apartment. To his surprise, she shook her head.

"Just talk to me, Rick. Please. I need to know what's going on."

He stood for a few seconds and chewed his lip, noting with a hint of amusement that she was doing the same. He nodded and motioned for her to sit down again. She did and he climbed up and sat beside her, replacing his Stetson on his head. "Cold?" he asked, offering her his jacket.

She shook her head again. "My jacket's in the truck. I'm fine," she added and waited again, her dark eyes fixed on his face.

He had changed out of his uniform to something less official, yet still professional, to take RaeLynn to the facility that had been arranged for her. Her scrutiny made the night air seem warmer and he loosened his tie. "You could have called me," he said, hoping he wasn't going to antagonize her.

It seemed that she was willing to let him take the roundabout route, now that he was sitting beside her. "If you were busy or driving, you wouldn't have answered. I called once and it went straight to voice mail. I figured you'd be too busy to get back to me so I didn't bother to leave a message." She stopped and bit her lip again. "I know you probably planned to call me in the morning or come by the campground, since you got back so late. I appreciate your consideration, Rick, but I don't want to wait to get some answers about RaeLynn. I need to know how she is and what's going to happen to her."

He nodded and gave her a half-smile. "I figured," he said. He leaned back and rested his elbows on the step behind him, wishing he could erase the lines of worry and fatigue he saw etched on her face. "Okay, here's all I can tell you, Corrie, and I'm not going to sugar-coat any of this." She nodded impatiently and he went on, "She's stabilized, although she still hasn't regained consciousness. That's not unexpected, considering the condition she was in when she arrived at the hospital, but it's also not good." He sat up and reached into the pocket of his jacket and retrieved a sheet of paper. "The plan is to keep her under observation and, if necessary, under sedation for the next forty-eight hours. She hasn't had a seizure since she was checked in, but they want to make sure she doesn't hurt herself if she does. She's going to have a nurse in attendance with her around the clock. And a twenty-four hour security guard outside her room."

"Is that really necessary?" Corrie interrupted, her voice strained. Her brow was furrowed and the dim lighting reflected off the gleam of tears in her eyes. Rick had handed her the paper, but she ignored it. Against his better judgment, he reached for her hand and squeezed it.

"Maybe, maybe not," he said with a shrug. "I'm not taking any chances with her safety."

"I should have told you what was going on with her… during the fiesta and everything," Corrie blurted, her voice breaking. She pulled her hand from his grasp and fumbled in her pocket blindly. He reached into his hip pocket and wordlessly handed her his handkerchief. She mumbled a barely-coherent "thank you" and he waited while she wiped her eyes and pulled herself together.

"What happened to her is not your fault," he said when she had cleared her throat and taken a few deep breaths. She shook her head and he turned to her, capturing her chin with his fingers and forcing her to meet his gaze. His heart twisted at the sight of the anguish in her coffee-brown eyes. Even in the darkness he could see it. She tried to turn away, knowing that he could read her thoughts as if they were written on paper. It had always been that way between them. Even after everything that had happened.

"Stop blaming yourself. What happened to RaeLynn was probably inevitable. I'm not saying she got what she deserved; no one deserves what happened to her. But she knew what her family was like and still refused to cut ties with them and she ended up being used as a scapegoat. She's too loyal for her own good." He stopped before he could go on and say that Corrie was the same way. However, he could never imagine Corrie's father having treated her the way Jake Shaffer treated RaeLynn.

She shook her head free of his grasp and he tried not to take it personally. He'd done enough damage to their relationship over the years. She was a generously forgiving person and he harbored a crazy hope in his heart that someday she'd be willing to give him another chance... but he also knew she believed him to be validly married to his ex-wife and, so far, his appeals to the marriage tribunal hadn't produced a verdict that was contrary to that. He had kept Corrie in the dark regarding his petition for annulment and the fact that he had already filed two appeals. He didn't want to raise false hopes in either of them, but he was determined to stay positive despite the tribunal's previous two judgments. He might have made a huge mistake in marrying Meghan but he had vowed to make sure that his bad decisions didn't ruin Corrie's life.

"She deserved my loyalty and trust," Corrie said, unaware of Rick's inner turmoil. "All she ever asked of me was a chance to earn an honest living and give her an opportunity to live a normal, boring life," she added, choking on the words. He drew his hand back and waited for her to continue. "I knew what her life was like at home and she never complained about it, she tried so hard to make her dream a reality, but I should have done more to help her. It was just easier to pretend, like she did, that it would all be okay if we just didn't dwell on it. If only I had...."

"If *we* had," he corrected her. "If we – me and the local law enforcement – had done more, had done something different, then maybe this wouldn't have happened, either. Or maybe, if Jake Shaffer had been a different man, a better man, a better husband and father, then none of this would have happened and maybe RaeLynn would have had a happy and normal life without any of our help. But that's not the way things worked out and we can sit here all night and play the blame game, whether we deserve it or not. In the end, no one wins anyway." She stared at him, her tears locked away for the moment. He took a deep breath, removed his Stetson, and ran a hand over his head. "Look, I know you can't help feeling like you should have done more. No one knows that feeling more than I do, believe me. But we can't change what we did or didn't do, so now all we can do is focus our energy and efforts into her recovery. And believe me, Corrie, RaeLynn's going to need all the help she can get."

"Is her condition that serious?" Her voice was strained.

"We won't know until she regains consciousness," Rick said, doing his best to keep his own fear and uncertainty under wraps. However, Corrie knew him well enough to sense the feelings that mirrored her own. Her eyes widened and Rick went on hurriedly, "We have to hope for the best and know that she's getting the best care possible and that we're doing everything in our power to keep her safe while she gets better."

"Can I go see her?" The question came out in a ghostly whisper. At first Rick wasn't even sure he'd understood her question correctly. The way Corrie's face had gone white made him think she might faint, though she'd never been the type to flinch at bad or hard news.

He cleared his throat. "Not for a while," he said. "Not until the doctors have evaluated her and she's had time to heal. It's not just her body that's been damaged, Corrie. Mentally and emotionally, she's probably worse off than she is physically. She's also lost a child; whether she was aware she was pregnant or not, we don't know. There's no way of telling how she'll react when she regains consciousness and gets that news."

"Shouldn't she have someone there to be with her when she does get the news?" Corrie persisted and Rick realized that telling her the truth wasn't going to scare her away. It was only going to make her more determined not to abandon her friend.

"Corrie," he began and then hesitated. He couldn't look at her; he understood what she wanted to do and why, and part of him, the part that loved and admired her generous spirit and loving heart, wanted to allow her to do what she felt was the right thing to do. He knew she would sit at RaeLynn's bedside and walk every inch of the road to recovery along with her, encouraging and supporting her.

But another side of him that also loved and admired her was also the law enforcement officer side of him. That side saw the danger in allowing her to get too close – physically and emotionally – to RaeLynn. Keeping her away from RaeLynn kept her off the radar of anyone who might be looking for revenge. Revenge for what still wasn't clear. But Rick had been a cop too long to let his guard down. He tried to tell himself that it wasn't just because it was Corrie who was involved, but he knew that if it were anyone else, he'd have been satisfied with simply giving them a stern warning to be on his or her guard and perhaps had a deputy keep an eye on him or her for a few days. He might have even kept a close watch on the Shaffers, in case they did have something to do with RaeLynn's "accident".

But it *was* Corrie. So....

"I promise you," he said, not allowing himself to think too much about what he was saying, "I promise that as soon as it's safe, you'll be allowed to see RaeLynn, you'll be able to spend time with her, and she'll come home and finish her recovery surrounded by the people who love her. But right now.... right now, it has to be this way. You have to trust me." And he winced as his own words reached his ears and he braced himself for her reaction.

She sighed and shook her head, turning away from him, but said nothing. Maybe she was trying to get her emotions under control. Or maybe she was just tired of arguing. Heaven knew he was, but it seemed like every time they talked, it turned into an argument – one that neither of them could win. He waited; there was nothing else he could say that would change anything. The night breeze stirred the trees and the only other sounds were from cars passing on the street and the occasional sound of an owl hooting in the nearby trees or a dog barking in the neighborhood.

Finally she turned back to face him. "I guess I have no choice but to trust you," she said. Her voice was flat, emotionless. She stood up. "I'd better go. I know you must be tired and you've got a busy day tomorrow. Thanks for talking to me, Rick. Good night."

"Hey," he said. He stood up as well, reaching for her arm as she started down the stairs. Her bland reaction bothered him far more than if she'd gotten angry at him. At that moment, he wished she would lash out at him, call him names, even slap his face. He would have settled for her treating him coldly. She turned to him, her face blank. She didn't even try to shake off his hand, but he let go anyway. "You okay?" he asked. She simply nodded. "I can drive you home," he went on before she could turn around again. "I can drop your truck off tomorrow...."

"It's all right, Rick," she said, a thin shimmer of anger or hurt threading through her words. "I'll be fine. Good night." She turned and went to her truck, not looking back. He wanted so badly to hurry after her, to stop her from leaving, to say something that would fix everything. He watched her get into her truck and start the engine and just barely stopped himself from raising a hand to wave goodbye.

He stood still until her tail lights faded down the road then he turned toward the corner of the building. "Does she know you were here, too?" he asked.

J.D. Wilder stepped out of the shadows and moved toward him, shrugging his shoulders. "I wouldn't be surprised if she did, but right now, she's not letting anyone know what's going through her mind." He climbed the steps until he was level with Rick. "You didn't keep anything back from her?"

"Just the actual location where RaeLynn is staying," Rick answered. There was a long silence. Wilder's quicksilver gaze burned into his, but Rick wasn't about to share that information with anyone. Especially not out in the open where hidden ears might hear.

Finally, Wilder nodded. "All right," he said, a curious tone in his voice, but then it became brisk and professional. "If you haven't already checked in with your deputies, there isn't much to report. No one has come and gone at the Shaffers', no suspicious vehicles or individuals around the campground, nothing out of the ordinary has surfaced."

Rick raised a brow. "And you're okay with letting her go back to the Black Horse alone tonight?" He hadn't meant to sound so sharp but Wilder cracked a grin and shook his head.

"Easy, Sheriff. Officer Camacho was just leaving as Deputy Mike Ramirez was pulling in for his turn at watch. And Deputy Evans will follow her home from here. She might get irritated enough to accuse us of police harassment. But at least she's safe." His smile vanished and his eyes narrowed. "She's beginning to convince me that maybe we're overreacting. Nothing indicates that she's in the same danger as Miss Shaffer."

"I still find it suspicious that RaeLynn's own family won't come forward to talk to me or even the doctors regarding what happened to her. They refuse to give us a chance to question them and maybe find some clues as to what happened to her. That can only mean that they're behind what happened to her...."

"Or they're afraid of whoever attacked her." Wilder said. "At least, that's Corrie's take on the matter. I'm beginning to think she might be right."

"Then that's an unknown person or persons we should be concerned about," Rick said, frowning. "And what's more, we have no clue who it might be. Since the Shaffers won't talk to us and RaeLynn can't just yet, we're completely in the dark as to who and why someone wanted to kill her and might be targeting Corrie next."

Wilder nodded. "I let Corrie think we were backing off, especially since it did seem like I overreacted a time or two. But I don't plan on relaxing my watch. I know you can't spare your deputies for too long...."

"I can be there when you can't," Rick snapped, and instantly regretted it. He hadn't meant to sound so defensive, so threatened. Wilder cocked an eyebrow at the outburst but said nothing. Rick cleared his throat. "If she's going to be irritated at anyone, let it be you or me, not one of our officers or deputies. They don't need to be in the middle of it."

"Right," Wilder said. "Just you and me, Sheriff."

He stood silently, scanning the parking area of the apartment complex, and Rick did the same, his mind racing. It wasn't hard to figure that they both had the same thoughts going through their minds. Whoever attacked RaeLynn had to know by now that she had survived; would they make another attempt on her life? Or would they focus their attempts on Corrie? Rick wished that RaeLynn had awakened before he had left her earlier today, and not only so that she could have given him some clue as to what had happened to her and why. Like Corrie, he wanted her to know that it was her friends who rescued her, not just a passing stranger. Awakening in a strange place, surrounded by strangers, all alone, would be alarming and stressful for her. He had taken every precaution, making sure that there were at least two armed security officers outside her room and one female officer – armed as well – in her room, ready to hear anything and everything that RaeLynn might say, if she were to regain consciousness, that could lead them to whoever was behind her attack. It might be hours or it might be weeks before that happened. It didn't matter. She was safe and that's all he could do for her now.

But for Corrie, he knew that wouldn't be enough. Corrie wanted to go to RaeLynn and just be with her, as well as do everything she could to find whoever did this to her. And she wouldn't care if Rick or Wilder told her to stay away from the investigation. Nothing would stand in the way of her helping RaeLynn. And Rick knew, all too well, that he was going to have his hands full trying to protect Corrie as well.

That's why he had no choice but to accept Wilder's help.

He cleared his throat, not sure how long it had been since either of them had spoken. "I hope to get a report from the doctors tomorrow. They're supposed to call me if there are any changes, but they didn't seem to expect anything to happen overnight."

"Are you planning to let anyone else know where she is?" Wilder asked. He turned toward Rick with his eyes narrowed and his voice barely above a whisper.

Rick hesitated. He could cite HIPAA rules and regulations, he could flat-out refuse on the basis of lack of "need to know", he could argue a half-dozen reasons that made some sense or no sense at all for not telling Wilder where RaeLynn was. But it all boiled down to just one reason.

It was the only way he could be sure that Corrie would be safe.

He trusted Wilder, probably more than any other person he'd ever known. But he also knew that any information he gave anyone put that person – and Corrie as well – at risk of being tracked by whoever attacked RaeLynn. And might lead the attacker straight to her.

Wilder watched Rick without blinking and the tension between them grew. Rick knew that Wilder would think he was keeping the information from him just so he could be the one to tell Corrie, or that he wanted to keep Wilder out of the loop out of jealousy. And maybe, to a small extent, that was partially true. But no matter what his personal or professional feelings were toward this man who he had come to regard as both an ally and a rival, no matter how much he needed his help, he couldn't take any chances. He took a deep breath and met Wilder's gaze directly.

"No, Wilder. Not yet."

Seconds ticked by. Neither man moved, nor broke eye contact with each other. Rick doubted that either of them breathed. Finally, Wilder nodded slowly. "Okay," he said, and Rick silently drew air into his lungs. Wilder stepped back. "Then I guess you'll keep Corrie posted about Miss Shaffer's condition."

"I'll keep everyone posted with whatever information I can share," Rick said firmly. Wilder said nothing just nodded. "I'll stop by the campground in the morning."

"I'll be there," Wilder said and he turned and vanished into the shadows.

Rick stood still until he heard Wilder's Harley start up then roar off into the night. He shook his head, wondering what the next day would bring.

Chapter 7

Corrie was up before her alarm went off, which would have been more impressive had she been able to sleep for longer than fifteen or twenty minutes at a time all night. She threw the covers off her bed, only realizing too late that she might have startled her pets awake with the action. Renfro and Oliver, however, had given up on a solid night's sleep in their owner's bed a few hours earlier. Renfro had curled up in front of her father's old recliner and regarded her with heavy eyes and a half-hearted "woof". Oliver had curled up into a tight, striped ball on the old Lab's back and opened his jade-green eyes a mere slit and allowed a begrudging "meow" before settling himself with his back to Corrie.

"I guess I can't blame you guys," she said with a rueful smile as she slid out of bed. She gave each one a quick head rub in apology. Renfro accepted it with a few thumps of his tail while Oliver let a purr slip out before resuming his sulk. Corrie chuckled as she headed for the bathroom and a shower, grateful for little things that helped alleviate the heaviness in her heart.

She headed downstairs and took a quick tour of the campground store, flicking lights on as she went, including the floor lamp next to her Barcalounger in the TV room where she planned to sit and watch the morning news. The dog and cat went straight to the side door and waited none too patiently for her to let them out. Despite the fact that nothing remotely threatening had happened in the last twenty-four hours, Corrie figured that it wouldn't hurt to be cautious and she peered out the window of the side door as her pets vocalized their displeasure at her delay. Seeing nothing out of the ordinary, she flipped on the porch light.

To her combined amusement and annoyance, the porch light of the cabin across the way – J.D.'s cabin – went on a split second later. He was approaching the campground store with long strides before she could unlock the door and let Renfro and Oliver out. The dog and cat didn't even glance at him as he stepped up onto the porch. "Did you get any sleep at all last night?" Corrie asked him with a wry grin.

"Good morning to you, too," he responded, then yawned. "Got the coffee ready?"

"Almost done brewing." She studied his face, her amusement and annoyance quickly replaced by concern. She had been joking about him being awake all night but it was all too evident that he probably had NOT slept at all. His eyelids were heavy and his silver eyes were dull as lead from tiredness. Her heart twisted. She quickly took his arm and tugged him toward the TV room. "Come in and sit down," she said. He didn't resist, just cast a quick glance over his shoulder at the door. "I locked it," Corrie assured him as she led him to the Barcalounger. He flopped down in it, trying and failing to suppress another enormous yawn. "I think you need sleep more than you need coffee," she said, shaking her head.

"You're right, but I'll take the coffee," he said, flashing a quick smile that chased away the haggard lines of his face for a fleeting moment before they returned.

She hurried to the courtesy table and quickly poured two cups of coffee, debating briefly with herself about whether she should grab some banana bread from the refrigerator. She gave a quick shake of her head, deciding that J.D. deserved a real breakfast and he could enjoy a cup of coffee while she fixed it, and she returned to the TV room.

She was greeted by the sight of J.D. sleeping soundly in the Barcalounger. He hadn't even bothered to recline the chair. Tears stung her eyes. As exasperating as it was to deal with his and Rick's overprotective attitudes, she couldn't deny that everything they did for her was out of a deep sense of friendship... and maybe something more. She set her own cup down on the long table where guests played games and worked puzzles, then quietly stepped toward him and the chair. Before she set his coffee cup down on the end table, she reached across him for the switch on the floor lamp.

He bolted upright and grabbed her left wrist, yanking it downward. She gasped as his other hand shot up toward her face and she instinctively threw her right hand – the one holding his coffee cup – forward to block his fist. Hot coffee showered them as the cup flew from her grasp and shattered on the floor and she shrieked as she tumbled, off balance, onto J.D.'s lap. He uttered a barely-stifled oath as the Barcalounger rocked backward, miraculously not tipping over completely, and he propelled himself to his feet. Corrie shrieked again as she rolled off his lap and landed on her back in a puddle of coffee on the floor. J.D. stumbled and fell, stopping himself with his forearms before he landed on top of her, his nose a mere inch from hers.

"J.D.!" "Corrie!"

They stared at each other for a long moment, their breathing ragged, and Corrie wondered if her eyes looked as wide and shocked as J.D.'s did. In the next instant, she became acutely aware of how close they were and what position they were in and she stifled a gulp. J.D. shook his head to clear it and sprang up and away from her. She continued to lay immobile on the floor until he cleared his throat and offered her his hand. "Are you all right?" he asked hoarsely.

"Just dandy," she managed to say as she took his hand and sat up. She grimaced, feeling the dampness of the coffee seeping through her shirt. "It's not my scheduled day to mop, but I don't think I have a choice now," she remarked, tugging on her braid. Drops of coffee hit the floor and she silently acknowledged that she'd be taking another shower as well.

J.D. rubbed his hand over his face. "You scared the daylights out of me," he said, the testiness in his voice as easily attributed to his exhaustion as to his fright.

"Sorry, I was going to shut the light off and let you get some rest. I didn't mean to startle you. I thought you were sound asleep." She took a deep breath and willed herself not to snap at him, but her previously tender feelings toward him had hardened with his reaction... and the sensation of the coffee soaking her clothes.

"You shouldn't have let me fall asleep," he muttered. He slumped against the folding table, crossed his arms and gave her a stern look that was foiled by a yawn. He shook his head irritably and grabbed the coffee cup – her coffee cup – that was sitting on the table and took a huge gulp. He grimaced. "I'm supposed to be keeping an eye on you, making sure nothing happens to you."

"Well, so far, your reaction to me shutting off the light has been the most dangerous thing that's happened to me in a long time," she said, trying to control her temper. She shook her head. "I guess I should be thankful you didn't clock me when I startled you."

That seemed to pierce his annoyance and his eyes widened. "I didn't hurt you, did I?" he said, straightening up, his tiredness vanishing in an instant. He took a step toward her and she held up a hand, stopping him.

"No, you didn't. I'm fine," she assured him. She wasn't in the mood to have him fuss over her. He hesitated and looked her over critically.

"You're sopping wet."

"Spilled coffee does that to you. Look, J.D.," she said, raising her eyes to heaven, "I'm sorry I startled you. It never occurred to me that you were that strung up about protecting me. But it's crazy for you to lose sleep over it. You haven't slept in over 24 hours and that's not helping anyone, least of all yourself."

"I'm fine," he argued, barely stopping himself from yawning again, though his eyes turned glassy. Corrie pretended not to notice.

"All right, then," she said, resigned. He wasn't going to back off. And she didn't have the energy or interest to argue with him. She glanced at the clock. "The store opens in an hour. Let me just clean up the floor and grab another shower and I'll fix us some breakfast."

He looked at her through narrowed eyes. He didn't seem to believe that she was willing to back down. He shook his head. "I'll clean up the mess while you go shower. And maybe I should fix you breakfast."

"You don't have to do either one. You should get some sleep. But do what you want," she added abruptly, putting her hands up. "I'll be back down shortly." She headed out of the TV room and J.D. caught her arm as she passed by him.

"Hey," he said when she stopped. She looked up at him, cocking one eyebrow. He let go of her and shoved his hands into his pocket. "Uh, you sure you're okay?"

She hesitated for a fraction of a second before she decided to answer the question as if he were referring to her spill and not her frame of mind. "I'm fine, J.D. Just fine." Try as she might, she couldn't muster up a smile for him before she turned away and went up to her apartment.

J.D. had cleaned up the coffee spill in the TV room and brewed a fresh pot of coffee before he heard Corrie's steps on the stairs. He had considered starting breakfast in the small kitchen of the campground store, but decided that his cooking skills – limited even when he was at his best – weren't going to be as impressive in his half-asleep state. He downed the last of his third cup of coffee and poured her one before refilling his own.

"Thanks," she said, and took a sip. She turned towards the side door of the store.

"Hey, where are you going?" J.D. came fully awake and went after her. She stopped and threw him a glance over her shoulder, not bothering to hide her impatience.

"I'm letting Renfro and Oliver back in. Remember? They went out earlier when you came over. I figured you'd forgotten about them."

He grimaced. "Sorry. You're right, I did. But let me get them," he said, moving past her toward the door. She sighed and rolled her eyes.

"J.D., would you stop already? You're driving me nuts! Nothing has happened and nothing is going to happen!"

"You don't know that!" he countered.

"You don't know that anything *is* going to happen!"

"Which is why we're trying to be careful!"

"'We're trying to be careful'? We, who? You mean, you and Rick? Yes, I know you followed me out to his place last night and had Deputy Evans follow me home. And I think you're well aware that I've been extremely patient up till now. But you guys are really starting to get on my nerves!"

"Your memory can't be that short, Corrie," J.D. snapped back. "Have you forgotten what's happened to you in the last few months? And you weren't directly threatened any of those times. This time...."

"This time, you and Rick *think* I'm being threatened. You both think that whoever left RaeLynn on the highway meant to send a message to me. Well, so far, nothing's happened and I think you guys are worrying about something that only exists in your imaginations. There is no threat to me. What happened to RaeLynn has nothing to do with me. You should be focusing on *her*, not me! She might still be in danger, wherever she is!"

J.D. bit his tongue hard before he responded in a way that would be sure to ruin any chances he and Corrie might have of rebuilding what they once had... or might have had. He took a deep breath. "Corrie, listen to me. I know the sheriff and I are getting on your nerves. What else is new? You should be used to it by now." She didn't smile, but she snorted. J.D. went on, "We are doing everything that we can for RaeLynn. She is getting the best medical care available and the sheriff has taken every precaution to make sure she is safe. So you don't need to worry about her. And I know you don't feel that we need to worry about you, but just humor us. There is always a chance, however slim, that the sheriff and I might be right." He stopped and watched as she blew her breath out and glanced away from him. He took a chance to go on. "Until we find out exactly what happened to her and why it happened, we can't risk leaving any possibility that her attackers might take advantage of your friendship with her to try to get to her. Whether you're the target or not doesn't matter; if they can't hurt RaeLynn directly, they might try to hurt her through the people she cares about the most."

That got Corrie's attention. Her head snapped back and her eyes grew wider. "So you're saying that, even if something were to happen to me, RaeLynn is still in danger."

"Uh, essentially," J.D. answered warily. He wasn't sure what she was getting at, but he knew from past experience that it was probably something that was going to create more headaches for him and the sheriff. Before either of them said another word, there was a sharp rapping from the front door that made them both jump and J.D. reach for his weapon.

Corrie didn't argue when he led the way to the front counter and they peered out the window. He had been prepared to concede that he had overreacted if he had seen one of the Pages at the front door, but framed in the window opening was a slight, stooped figure of a man with a thin face and brown eyes that were magnified by the thick glasses he wore. J.D. slipped the safety off his weapon and prepared to call out to the man but Corrie let out an exasperated sigh behind him.

"It's Benny Gonzalez," she said, moving past J.D. He caught her arm and stopped her.

"And?" he said.

"And, what?" Corrie snapped. "It's Benny, probably one of the most harmless people in the village."

"And he's here, knocking at your door at—" J.D. glanced at the wall clock over the counter, "—at five minutes after seven in the morning. You're not the least bit concerned?"

"Yeah, I'm concerned," she said, shaking his hand off her arm. "It's five minutes past my usual time to open and I don't have the courtesy table set up or my register, either. It's Jerry and Jackie's day to come in late and I'm falling down on the job. Put the gun away before you give Benny a heart attack." She turned and unlocked the door, hitting the light switch as she did. "Hi, Benny, good morning. How's it going?" she said as she swung the door open.

"Oh, good morning, Corrie! I'm fine and how are you?" The older man looked past her and his already-huge eyes seemed to bulge like a pug dog's when he saw J.D. and he stopped before he stepped over the threshold. "Oh, good morning, Officer... I, I mean, Detective Wilder." He made a motion as if to tip his hat, except he wasn't wearing one. He transferred the cane he was leaning on to his other hand and straightened his heavy denim jacket. Though he wasn't much past sixty years of age, his thinning dark hair was shot through with yellowish-white strands. His pinched face was blotched with age spots and he had a grayish pallor. His bent frame probably topped out at five feet, ten inches, if he were to stand upright, but he limped through the door as Corrie stepped back and ushered him in. "I'm sorry to bother you so early, Miss Corrie, but I thought you opened at seven?"

"I do, normally," Corrie said, her eyes shooting daggers at J.D. "It's been a busy morning and far from normal. What can I do for you, Benny?"

J.D. moved his gun behind his thigh, not quite willing to concede that he had, once again, overreacted. He stepped back beside the counter, nodding a greeting to the early morning visitor and waited to hear why he felt the need to visit the Black Horse before the sun was up. Benny leaned his cane against the counter and blew through his gloveless hands. Corrie quickly remembered her manners and moved over to the courtesy counter to fill a cup with piñon coffee which was all she had made. Benny nodded gratefully and thanked her. "That's sure good coffee, Miss Corrie," Benny said, as he took a sip. He looked around the campground store. "Actually, I came by to see if Buster might be around."

"You're looking for Buster?" Corrie shot a look at J.D. and he did his best to keep his expression blank. Benny nodded, his thin face pinched with concern.

"Yes, he usually stops by to see me once or twice a week but I haven't seen him since last Thursday and I wanted to see if he could help me out by fixing a leak in my roof. I noticed it a while back and I told him I'd let him know when I had a little money to make the repairs. I'm sure he's forgotten about it, but I wanted to see if he could get to it this weekend before the weather gets much colder and we start getting rain or snow." He took another sip of coffee. "I tried to call him yesterday but he didn't answer. Tried all day. Then I thought he might be at work and couldn't answer his phone so I waited till yesterday evening to try again." He shook his head. "Still no answer and I was getting worried. So I thought I'd stop in and see if he was here so I could talk to him and make sure he was okay."

"Well, I can tell you he didn't have his cell phone all day here at work yesterday, Benny," Corrie said. J.D. knew she was wondering, just as he was, if concern over Buster's welfare was the only reason Benny was trying to locate him. "He left it at home when he came in, on accident, and the battery probably went dead. That's probably why you couldn't reach him," she added. J.D. bit back a smile at Corrie's attempt to keep Benny from being annoyed with Buster. He could imagine Buster cringing as his phone rang all evening long, afraid to answer Benny's calls after the warnings he'd been given.

Benny seemed to relax. "So he's okay, then? That's good to know. He's a young man, but you never know, he could've had an accident or something, like... uh, well, probably ain't my business," he added hurriedly, his face reddening. "Anyway, I'm sure that young lady of his who's a nurse is taking good care of him. Well, that's a relief." He cleared his throat and took a long pull on his coffee cup. "Is he going to be here soon, Miss Corrie? I could wait for him a little bit, if you don't mind me talking to him. I won't keep him too long...."

"Actually, Benny, I'm afraid you're out of luck," Corrie said with a grimace. "Buster's off today so he won't be by here at all." Benny's face fell.

"Oh... oh, that's too bad. Oh, man, I guess I never thought of that," he said. His brow furrowed and he shook his head. "See, I thought... I caught a ride over here from a neighbor. I don't drive much anymore," he said, apologetically. "And I don't have so much gas in my car and I don't want to drive it too much until I get some money to buy gas. So I got a ride from a neighbor who works in town. I thought that maybe you wouldn't mind if Buster gave me a ride home after I got done talking to him...." He let his voice trail away. J.D. wondered if he was hoping that Corrie would offer him a ride home.

Corrie, however, wasn't in her usual generous mood. She shot a glance at J.D. that he was able to read loud and clear. "I'm sorry, Benny, I wish we could help you. But I can't leave the campground store, since I'm the only one here now and Detective Wilder is on duty. But let me call the local cab service...."

"Oh, no, Miss Corrie, I can't afford that!" Benny stammered, shaking his head. "I'll just walk home, it ain't that far...."

"No, Benny, I insist and the ride is on me," she said firmly, reaching for the phone on the wall behind the counter. Benny stood by silently, looking embarrassed and refusing to make eye contact with J.D. while she made the call. She reached the driver, who happened to be less than five minutes from the campground, then poured Benny a second cup of coffee which he hadn't finished before the driver arrived. She escorted Benny to the cab while J.D. waited, trying not to fidget. She came back in to the store, looking relieved.

"Everything okay?" J.D. asked. She gave him a half-hearted smile.

"Oh, yeah. I kind of feel bad... I know Benny is lonely, but if I hadn't gotten him a cab ride home, he would have spent the day here, talking to anyone and everyone he could get hold of... and fishing for gossip."

J.D. raised a brow. "You mean, he's more concerned about pumping Buster for information about RaeLynn than he is about Buster's well-being?"

"You didn't get that impression?"

"Yeah, I did," J.D. admitted. "He was being very careful not to mention anything about RaeLynn, even though it's probably already common knowledge in the village. To be honest, I thought it was just me being overly suspicious." Corrie laughed.

"No, you hit the nail on the head. Everyone knows that Benny is just plain nosy. It's probably because he is alone and he lives vicariously through his neighbors and friends, but he's one of those people you can't help but feel sorry for... poor health, missed career opportunities, hard luck. So everyone tries to be nice to him and he's so eager to have company and a connection to the community that he sometimes takes advantage of people's kindness."

"Or uses a portion of his meager gasoline reserves to drive Mrs. Shaffer to the hospital?"

"He's known the Shaffers for years," Corrie explained. "In fact, according to legend, he and Jake Shaffer used to be friends and worked together at the race track in Ruidoso Downs. Yes, I know it's hard to believe, but Jake Shaffer actually did have a real job at one time, although he didn't keep it for long. He got fired and rumor has it that it was because of Benny. Supposedly, Benny caught Jake stealing and turned him in. I don't know all the details – I don't know if anyone really does, except Benny and Jake – but that was the end of their friendship and the start of Jake's so-called 'reign of terror'. He let it be known that no one crosses Jake Shaffer and doesn't pay for it."

J.D.'s brows rose. "And how did Benny pay for it?"

Corrie gave a shrug. "He won't say. As far as I know, he's never told anyone what Jake did to him, won't even elaborate on what actually led to Jake getting fired, but he steers clear of all the Shaffers...."

"He gave Mrs. Shaffer a ride to the hospital," J.D. pointed out.

"And she made it clear that she didn't want Jake to know about it," Corrie said. "Like I said, people feel sorry for Benny. Whatever happened, it was when he started his downhill slide. It's why he's never been able to afford to move out of the same trailer park the Shaffers live in." She cleared her throat. "That being said, while people feel sorry for him, they also tend to avoid him. I don't know if it's because of his tendency to pry gossip out of people or if they're afraid of Jake and think that their association with Benny will put them in the crosshairs."

"Jake seems to have really taken his anger over Benny's betrayal, if you want to call it that, to an extreme. How long has this been going on?"

"Since the dinosaurs roamed the earth," Corrie said. "I think Clifford may have been about five or six years old when this got started. He grew up believing that his family was above the law. He was the epitome of the school bully and RaeLynn and Teddy got the worst of it. There's another brother, Johnny, who's a year younger than Cliff, and generally kept his hands clean for the most part. But he's always been more of a con man rather than a bully. And he got away with just about everything, too, either because of his smooth talk or his brother's fists."

"What's he do for a living?" J.D. asked, as he refilled their coffee cups.

"I have no idea," Corrie said. "But he's got expensive taste in clothes, drives an expensive sports car, always seems to have money to blow at the casinos and racetrack. Rumor has it he has a second home in Vegas. I couldn't tell you where his first home is, but I don't think it's in Bonney. Maybe Ruidoso or Alto. He only comes around here once in a while, mainly to show off how much better off he is than the rest of his family, but he never stays long. He's only ever seen around town with Clifford."

"So he doesn't help out at home with whatever money he's got?" J.D. asked.

Corrie shook her head. "If, and that's a big 'if', he helps out his family, gives them money or whatever, they spend it on booze, drugs, or expensive toys – cars, electronics, stuff like that. The place is practically falling apart. And it's not because the Shaffers are impoverished. They've got money coming from somewhere, although I think RaeLynn is the only one with a legitimate job. You'll see an assortment of cars and trucks – expensive ones –

coming and going at their place at all hours of the day or night. The drivers make sure no one sees them and the police suspect there are drug deals involved, but they don't have any evidence and no one is talking. They could afford a much nicer home, even without any help from Johnny, but they'd rather spend their money on other things."

"Mrs. Shaffer doesn't get a say in how it's spent, I take it," J.D. said, sourly. "Or much of a say in anything at all. Neither did RaeLynn."

"What I pay her is probably what buys groceries and keeps the rent and utilities paid."

Before J.D. could respond, his cell phone buzzed. Welcoming the distraction, he didn't look at the screen as he unclipped it from his belt. "Detective Wilder."

"Get over to the Shaffers' place right away," the sheriff growled. "I'm on my way."

"Copy," J.D. responded, wishing he had checked his screen before answering. He would have stepped out of the room so that Corrie wouldn't have overheard the conversation. He snapped his phone back in place. "I'll have one of my officers come right over. I've got to go."

"So I heard," Corrie answered dryly. She cocked her head on one side and raised a brow at him. "You know where the Shaffers live?"

He had started to turn toward the door but her question stopped him in his tracks. He drew a deep breath but didn't turn around. "No, but I'm sure I'll...."

"Find it? With my help? In no time at all," she said cheerfully as she grabbed her jacket from the coat rack and yanked it on. "Let me call Jerry and Jackie and we'll be on our way!"

Chapter 8

J.D.'s stomach tightened into knots as he and Corrie approached the Riverside Trailer Park. He hadn't been out to the place in all the time he had lived in Bonney and he wasn't sure what to expect. Despite the fact that the majority of the residents were on low, fixed incomes, many of the trailers were well-kept up, with only a few showing signs of neglect. He drove slowly down the lane that Corrie indicated and he noticed a moderately dilapidated trailer in the middle of the lane that had a dim light showing through the window. The blinds parted furtively, then immediately snapped shut at the sight of the police cruiser and the light went out. "That's where Benny Gonzalez lives," Corrie told J.D., breaking the silence that had filled the vehicle since they left the Black Horse. "The cab must have just dropped him off a few minutes ago. The Shaffers' place is at the end of the lane on the left."

He would have been able to identify the Shaffers' trailer from what Corrie had told him about the family, even if the sheriff's Tahoe hadn't been parked across the lane from it. Though the yard was choked with weeds and the paint was peeling, a large TV satellite dish was attached to the roof along with a cell phone signal booster. Two off-road vehicles and a dirt bike were parked in the empty lot next to the trailer under a large metal carport alongside a black four-by-four Dodge pickup truck. All the vehicles were in far better condition than the trailer. J.D. pulled in behind the Tahoe. "Wait here," he told Corrie. She nodded silently and he couldn't read the expression on her face.

He approached the Tahoe and Sutton stepped out. "You brought Corrie?" J.D. couldn't tell if the sheriff was annoyed or incredulous.

"Long story," J.D. answered shortly. "What's the plan?"

"We got a tip that the Shaffers are home. All of them. And it seems like they're planning to skip town. Clifford Shaffer was in town yesterday, trying to rent a large moving truck and car hauler. He was told nothing was available immediately, he'd have to wait a few days, and he lost his temper and stormed out. He and his brother, Teddy, visited a few of their friends in town, guys who have large trucks and trailers. Not sure if they succeeded in making any arrangements, but they were out all night and got back home a short while ago." Sutton tipped his chin toward the truck under the carport. "That's Clifford's truck. Teddy and Jake moved their respective vehicles around back about twenty minutes ago."

"Did they see you out here?" J.D. asked. Sutton nodded.

"Teddy looked scared to death, like he was ready to make a run for it, but Jake gave me a not-so-friendly wave and shoved Teddy toward his truck. They both have pickups, but not as new as Clifford's so they park them in front of the place without cover."

"You sure they haven't left while you've been watching the front?"

"Mike Ramirez is watching the back of the place. I dropped him off before I pulled in."

"I thought there was another Shaffer brother. Johnny?"

"I see Corrie's filled in the Shaffer family tree for you. Johnny hasn't been around in several months. Not unusual." The sheriff straightened up. "I let the Shaffers think I came alone for a friendly chat but they probably know you're here by now."

"So you ready to go 'chat' with them?" J.D. asked. The sheriff nodded and they crossed the lane to the Shaffers' front gate. J.D. was surprised a stiff gust of wind hadn't already knocked down the rickety wooden fence. A faded "Beware of the Dog" sign was loosely wired to the gate, but there was no evidence of a dog anywhere. They went up the gravel walkway toward the front steps, carefully scrutinizing the area. A long-discarded box from a 60-inch screen TV lay flattened in the dirt next to the trailer's front steps along with a few plastic trash bags that looked like they had been out in the elements for weeks. The steps were only wide enough for one person to stand on them at a time. The sheriff motioned J.D. to wait on the ground while he climbed the steps. J.D. nodded, noting that the sheriff's weapon was still in its holster, but he decided not to take chances. He slipped his own weapon out and held it close against his thigh. Sutton nodded approval and then pulled open the screen door and knocked.

Several seconds passed and the trailer seemed to be unnaturally silent. He pounded on the door a little harder. "Mr. Shaffer? Mrs. Shaffer? Sheriff Sutton here. Can we talk for a minute?"

A creaking noise came from the back of the trailer. J.D. started to move, but Sutton held up a hand and shook his head as the lock rattled and the front door opened a crack. "What is it, Sheriff? What do you want?"

J.D. recognized the voice of Mrs. Shaffer, though it was a shaky whisper. The sheriff rested his hand on the door to prevent the woman from slamming it shut in his face.

"Just wanted to talk to you and your husband about your daughter," Sutton said. "I thought you might want some updates on her condition."

"I'll call the hospital," she said and tried to push the door shut. In vain. The sheriff didn't budge.

"Where's your husband, Mrs. Shaffer? There are a few questions I'd like to ask him."

"I don't know. He was here earlier, but he left. He don't want to talk to you. He don't know nothing."

"About what?" Sutton asked.

The woman hesitated. She had stopped trying to push the door shut and her voice sounded weary. "He don't know what happened to RaeLynn. It ain't his business. He ain't seen her since she left and that's fine with him. So there's no reason for you to talk to him, Sheriff."

"What about Clifford? Is it possible he might know what happened to her?"

"Leave Clifford outta this!"

J.D. raised his weapon and the sheriff turned around as Deputy Mike Ramirez appeared around the corner of the trailer with Jake Shaffer in his grasp. The man's scruffy appearance made him look far older than his sixty-odd years, but the much-younger deputy was still having trouble keeping a tight hold on him.

"He tried to sneak out the back door. Told him to stop and he ran for his truck and told me to do something really rude to myself. Thought he'd be able to get away 'cause I didn't take the keys... but I did disconnect the battery, so...."

"That's vandalism!" Jake Shaffer cried. "You heard him! He damaged my vehicle!"

"No, he didn't, Jake, but you ignored a direct order from a law enforcement office to stop and he hasn't arrested you. Yet," the sheriff added. "We just want to talk to you."

"I'll call an attorney! I don't have to talk to you! I know my rights!"

"Fine. Call your attorney. But you're coming down to my office to talk to us. You can come peacefully, or we can arrest you and haul you down in handcuffs. Your choice." Sutton paused. "Or maybe we'll talk to Cliff and Teddy first, see if they know why you tried to run when we came by to talk to you." Jake stopped struggling and glared at the sheriff. "Clifford's a tough nut to crack, so questioning him might get us nowhere, but Teddy...."

"All right!" Jake snapped. He threw his head back and glared at the deputy. "We'll go talk, but you ain't got nothin' on me or my boys! You leave 'em out of this!"

"Leave them out of what?" J.D. asked raising a brow. Jake Shaffer narrowed his gaze and shot a baleful look at J.D.

"Nothin'," Jake said sullenly. "Let's go."

Because J.D. had Corrie in his patrol car, the sheriff and Deputy Ramirez had the honor of escorting Jake Shaffer back to the village. J.D. braced himself as he made the detour to drop Corrie off at the Black Horse."

To his relief, she didn't argue. The campground store was busy and it was apparent that Jerry and Jackie could use her help. She quickly jumped out of the cruiser as J.D. slid to a stop near the door. "Officer Camacho is here. You don't have to worry. Go do the cop thing and I'll see you later," she said. She turned and hurried into the store before J.D. could say anything.

He pushed the cruiser just above the speed limit and arrived at the sheriff's department not long after the sheriff and Deputy Ramirez had arrived. He started past the front desk toward the interrogation rooms. The dispatcher, Laura Mays, who was on the phone when he walked in, waved him down and covered the mouthpiece with her hand. She pointed to the sheriff's office. "They got Mr. Shaffer in there," she mouthed to him, then went back to her phone call.

He managed to mask his surprise, then wheeled around and headed toward the sheriff's office. Sutton was out in the hallway, on his way back from the break room with two Styrofoam cups of coffee. He handed one to J.D. and paused outside his office door to take a sip. "Did you offer Mr. Shaffer any?" J.D. said, tilting his head toward the office. Through the glass upper half of the door, he could see RaeLynn's father hunched in one of the two chairs in front of the sheriff's desk. His head was down and his right knee was bouncing – from nervousness or impatience, J.D. couldn't tell. The sheriff shook his head.

"He's jumpy enough without caffeine. And this isn't a social visit." Sutton took another sip and watched the man fidgeting in his chair. He looked at J.D.. "You ready?"

J.D. hadn't expected to participate in the interrogation. He shrugged. "Sure. Can't wait to hear what he's got to say. How do you want to play this?"

"You'll know," the sheriff said as he grabbed the knob and went in.

Chapter 9

Jake Shaffer jumped and glared at them over his shoulder, his eyes shifty as they slid from the sheriff to J.D. and back. He glanced around the room, as if expecting someone else to join them. The sheriff went around his desk and sat down without a word. He took a sip of his coffee but didn't look at Mr. Shaffer. J.D. leaned against the wall next to the door, hooking a thumb in the front pocket of his jeans. Jake Shaffer eyed him warily as J.D. raised his cup to take a sip and watched him over the rim. His gaze locked with Jake's and he reached up behind him and pulled down the shade over the door's window.

Jake's eyes widened and then narrowed and he spun back to face Sutton. "So, what's going on, Sheriff? You gonna arrest me?"

The sheriff didn't look up. "For what, Jake?" Sutton asked, as he perused a file on his desk. J.D. doubted it had anything to do with the Shaffers or RaeLynn. The sheriff was keeping Shaffer on edge. Jake snorted.

"I'm sure you'll find something. You think you got something on me or I wouldn't be here. I ain't talking without an attorney."

"Fine." Sutton pushed a phone across the desk, still not looking at Jake. "Call him."

Jake's lip curled. He looked back over his shoulder and J.D. saluted him with grin and a raised Styrofoam cup. The man shook his head. "Just tell me what you wanna know so I can tell you that I don't know nothing and I can go!" he spat.

The sheriff leaned back in his chair and tossed his pen on his desk, fixing a stony gaze on the older man. "You're pretty sure you don't know why I want to talk to you?"

"Yeah, I know," Jake muttered. "You wanna know what I know about the girl and what happened to her. Well, I don't know nothin', Sheriff. Nothin' at all. Don't know where she went, don't know who she was with, don't know what happened to her!"

"Did you know she was asked to get the money to post your bail a few weeks ago?"

"I never asked her to do anything!" Jake snarled, half-rising from his chair. J.D. shifted his position just enough to make Jake Shaffer settle back in his chair. "I posted my own bail," he added, glancing at J.D. over his shoulder. "I never got a dime from her." J.D. took a noisy sip from his cup and Jake shook his head irritably. "Look, does he gotta be standing there?" His voice teetered on a whine.

"No, he doesn't 'gotta be standing there'," Sutton answered deadpan. "Detective Wilder stands wherever he wants to."

Jake threw another wary glance at J.D. before shaking himself and turning back to the sheriff. "Anyway, that's all I can tell you. Can I go now?"

"No," Sutton replied. "I have some more questions."

"Well, ask 'em so we can get this over with and I can go!" snapped Jake. "I got things to do, people to see, places to…." He stopped and his lips snapped shut as a flush crept up his face.

Sutton leaned back in his chair and fixed his gaze on Jake's face. "Going somewhere, Jake? Is that the reason Cliff and Teddy were trying to rent a truck and trailer? You must be planning to make a major move if you need more than your own vehicles to go someplace."

"You got no reason to be checking on my boys!" Jake blazed, lunging forward and pointing a finger at the sheriff. Sutton didn't move nor change expression, but J.D. moved silently up behind Jake. He reined in the impulse to grab the man's shoulders and pull him back but he was ready if Jake made any other threatening moves.

Something, perhaps the silence, made Jake realize he might be creating problems for himself. He eased back into his seat and jumped as J.D. dropped into the chair next to him. J.D. gave him a smile but said nothing. Jake drew away from him and glanced at the sheriff. "Leave Cliff and Teddy out of this, Sheriff! They got nothing to do with what happened to that girl!"

"Clifford tried to get RaeLynn to steal the fiesta money to bail you out." The sheriff's voice had a slight edge of steel though his expression didn't change. "Not sure how you expect me to keep him out of it. Especially if, as you say, *you* didn't ask RaeLynn to do anything."

"She's lying!" Jake rasped, shaking his head. "Clifford didn't ask her to do nothin', not for me, not for him! She tried to steal that money for herself! She was gonna steal it and take off on her own! So it's got nothing to do with me or my boys!"

"If RaeLynn wanted the money for herself, why didn't she just take it without telling anyone that she'd been asked to steal it? Why did she bother to make up a story that would implicate you and Clifford? And why would she raise suspicions that there was a possibility that the money might get stolen?"

"Ask *her*," Jake snapped stubbornly. "It was her idea! She probably wanted to make it out like Cliff asked her in case she got caught so she could blame it on him!"

"So then what do you think happened to her?" Sutton asked. He put his hands up behind his head and rocked back in his chair. "She didn't steal the money, but she disappeared for several weeks. Then she shows up, half-dead, on the highway. Your wife tell you about her condition, Jake? RaeLynn's fighting for her life. What do you suppose happened to her?"

"Don't know, don't care," said Jake. He shrugged and leaned back in his own chair and smirked. "If she don't make it, that's too bad, but it's got nothing to do with me. She's been nothing but trouble all her life and I say good riddance. She got what she deserved and...."

The crash of J.D.'s chair overturning stopped Jake in mid-sentence and he jumped. He turned and his mouth dropped open at the sight of J.D. standing over him with his gun drawn and aimed directly at Jake's head. "Keep talking, Shaffer, till you say something that gives me a reason," J.D. said quietly, his voice and temper under tight control.

"What?" Jake spluttered. He glanced from J.D. to the sheriff. Sutton hadn't made a move, hadn't even looked at J.D. He appeared to be unaware of what was happening. Jake's wary expression relaxed and he sneered. "Oh, I get it. Time to play 'good cop/bad cop', huh? Don't you get tired of being typecast, Sheriff? Doesn't that white hat get boring?"

"Now, Jake," Sutton said, allowing a half-smile, "if I were the good cop, I'd stop Detective Wilder from shooting you." Jake's leer vanished and he shot a nervous look at J.D. The gun still loomed steadily.

"You wouldn't," Jake said, his voice betraying a slight tremor. "Why would you? You got nothing on me. I didn't touch that girl, I don't know anything about what happened...."

"But Cliff might," the sheriff said. Jake wheeled around.

"You're trying to pin something on Cliff! You got something against him! Why? Leave him alone! He ain't done nothin', he don't know nothin'!"

"He allegedly tried to bully his sister into stealing for him. Threatened her if she didn't do it. That makes him a suspect in her assault. I'd like to hear his side of the story."

Jake was shaking his head before the sheriff finished. "Oh, no, you don't. You're trying to pin this on Cliff. You got something against him and I ain't about to hand him over just because that worthless mess of a girl said…."

J.D. cleared his throat sharply, stopping Jake's tirade. Sutton glanced at him. "Easy, Detective, I just had the carpets in here cleaned."

"I'll gladly replace them," J.D. hardly recognized his own voice and red rage flooded his field of vision. He'd heard enough stories about Clifford Shaffer and his criminal activities as well as his responses to anyone who dared to defy him. The man would just as easily beat anyone who cut him off in traffic or at the grocery store half to death as key their car, slash their tires, or throw a brick through their window. Clifford sneered at police authority, and "bullying" was too soft a word to describe what he did to those who crossed him… even his own family. For a moment, it occurred to J.D. that perhaps even Jake was afraid of his own son. But listening to RaeLynn's father defend his monstrous son against his timid, hard-working daughter sparked an anger in him he hadn't been aware he was capable of. If Clifford was responsible for RaeLynn's condition, and his father was covering for him, that made Jake just as culpable as far as J.D. was concerned.

Jake's mouth dropped open. "Listen, Sheriff," he stammered, his eyes flitting from J.D.'s eyes to the gun in his hand, "I ain't touched the girl, I ain't even seen her in weeks, and I don't know nothin' about any of this! Just leave Clifford out of this, please, for God's sake, Sheriff, you know you don't want to make him mad."

"Clifford doesn't scare me or Detective Wilder near as much as he seems to scare you, Jake," Sutton said, his half-smile still in place. "Of course, Detective Wilder and I have nothing to hide. Anything you'd like to share with us, we can offer you protection…."

Jake let out a barking laugh. "Are you crazy? I don't need your protection and it's worthless anyway! I'll look after myself by keeping my mouth shut, thank you very much, but you and the detective better watch yourselves, Sheriff. And anyone you care about, as well."

Sutton's brows rose and then his eyes narrowed. "That sounds like a threat, Jake. Care to elaborate?" The half-smile was gone and the steel edge in his voice had become razor sharp.

Jake's face darkened. "You know good 'n' well what I'm talking about, Sheriff." He shook his head. "Clifford don't like to be crossed. He does what he wants and nobody better get in his way. Not his friends, his family, definitely not anyone in authority. Hell, even I don't mess with him, unless he's going too far, and then he don't always listen to me. But anyone who gets in his way or makes him mad... they're gonna pay the price." He lowered his voice and leaned toward the sheriff. "That girl knows now... she learned the hard way. And your own little girlfriend's gonna find out it's best to leave well enough alone. She shoulda never turned RaeLynn against her own kin. It'll be her fault if RaeLynn don't make it. That'll teach her not to stick her nose where it don't belong and if you all don't back off on me and my boys...."

"This is really sounding a lot like a threat, Jake." Sutton had leaned forward across the desk, his hands linked in front of him. Jake drew back slightly and Sutton went on, "You're as good as admitting that Clifford attacked his own sister and is responsible for her current condition. And I'm also hearing that your son is intending to do the same thing to someone else. Someone who absolutely has no dog in this fight...."

"Consider it a warning, Sheriff," Jake snapped. "She's a real pretty girl, a lot prettier than RaeLynn. Any damage done to your little girlfriend would be a shame, a real shame. Whoever beat up RaeLynn – and I ain't saying it was Clifford, mind you – probably done her a huge favor, messin' up her face...."

"Sheriff...." J.D.'s voice was a shaky growl though he managed to keep the gun steady. "You got a color in mind for this new carpet?"

Sutton never took his gaze off Jake Shaffer's face. "Maybe maroon, Wilder. The stains won't be as noticeable."

"You got it." J.D.'s grip tightened, though it took every shred of self-control to keep his finger off the trigger. Jake let a strangled squawk. "I think it would be in your best interest, Mr. Shaffer, if you gave the sheriff some solid information about your son's whereabouts and what your involvement is in your daughter's assault before you end up begging us to throw you in jail where you'll be a lot safer than where you are right now!"

"You wouldn't...."

"You sure?"

Jake's mouth worked and his eyes ping-ponged between the gun in J.D.'s hands and the sheriff's narrowed eyes. His chest heaved and he shot a glance toward the door. Any hope that a passerby might look in and rescue him was dashed by the blinds that J.D. had closed earlier. His hands shook and he tugged at his collar. "All right," he said hoarsely. "I'll tell you what I know, but then you gotta keep me locked up until Cliff calms down...."

"You think he's telling the truth?"

J.D. had managed to rein in his temper and return his weapon to his holster after he and the sheriff spent forty-five minutes listening to Jake Shaffer tell all he knew about his son's involvement in RaeLynn's assault... which wasn't much. Jake admitted to knowing that Clifford had approached RaeLynn about the ten thousand dollars to bail Jake and that he had threatened her if she didn't get the money, even if it meant stealing the fiesta funds. He also admitted that his bail for that particular arrest was nowhere near the amount Clifford had demanded and, in fact, Jake had not even asked Clifford to bail him out.

But he claimed he didn't know why Clifford had demanded that amount and that he didn't know whether or not Clifford had anything to do with the attack on RaeLynn.

Sutton shrugged. "Actually, I do, but that's not exactly a testament to Jake's honesty. I think he's either only told us what he knows, which, as you can see, isn't much, or he's only told us enough to keep his own hide safe. What I'm not sure is whether he's trying to keep it safe from Clifford... or someone else."

J.D. nodded silently. The sheriff had whisked him out of his office as soon as they got Jake's statement, leaving Jake to be escorted to a cell by Deputy Gabe Apachito. Sutton led J.D. to the empty break room and poured him a strong cup of coffee, no doubt intending to give him time to recover. J.D. didn't protest, hoping he would stop shaking and gather his wits so he could discuss things with the sheriff in a calmer, more rational manner than he exhibited in the office earlier. He took a sip and was surprised to see that it was piñon coffee. He shot Sutton a glance, but the sheriff poured himself a cup from a different pot on the dual burner.

He caught J.D.'s look and shrugged. "No one drinks decaf and it's cheaper than buying flavored creamer." He put his cup down and folded his arms as he leaned against the counter. "You okay?"

"Yeah, I'm fine," J.D. responded, grimacing as he chugged down the coffee. He tossed the empty cup into the trash and mirrored the sheriff's posture, leaning against the wall. He blew out his breath and forced himself to meet Sutton's gaze. Part of him was ashamed at the way he had allowed Jake Shaffer's behavior to push him to the edge of losing control. He wondered if the sheriff really thought he'd been acting the part of the "bad cop" or if he was aware of how close J.D. had come to crossing an unspeakable line. Another part of him was still reeling in shock at how strongly he had reacted.

In the course of his career as a law enforcement officer, especially the years he spent undercover investigating drug dealers, he had encountered every imaginable type of low-life, scum-of-the-earth, poor-excuse-for-humanity criminal. He had hauled in men who had beaten their wives, girlfriends, even their own children and mothers, as well as innocent bystanders who had been in the wrong place at the wrong time. At one time, he had been confident that the system would mete out justice for the victims and make the guilty pay. Over time, he'd become jaded and at times had, half-jokingly, wished for a return to frontier justice where the criminals had less chance of escaping the consequences of their actions. However, the urge to take matters into his own hands had never hit him as hard as it had today. And he still wasn't sure just why. Was it because Jake had threatened Corrie as well? Or was it because he, J.D., had felt guilty over his own previous judgmental attitude toward RaeLynn?

One thing was certain: Jake Shaffer was a bully and had gotten his way in life by bullying everyone around him, including his own wife and daughter. Now, however, J.D. wasn't completely convinced Jake was the hardened criminal that common opinion had led him to believe. Jake had built up an intimidating reputation that gave the impression that he was a tough, callous criminal lord, but it seemed that Jake's reputation was built on the strength of his son's actions... and J.D. was beginning to wonder if the orders came from Jake or from Clifford.

He dragged himself back from his thoughts when the sheriff spoke up. "You're beginning to wonder if Jake is the mastermind of this whole thing or if he's taking orders from someone else," Sutton said. "I am, too."

"The thought never occurred to you in the past?" J.D. asked.

The sheriff shook his head slowly. "Jake has never given any indication that he might be operating under someone else, much less his own son. He's been like this for as long as I can remember. Clifford is a few years older than I am, Johnny is about my age, Teddy is a couple years younger. We were warned away from the Shaffer place from the time we started school – not that we needed much convincing. Jake was much scarier back then and

Clifford was learning the ropes of being a world-class bully. If you were smart, you steered clear of the Shaffers."

"Was there a specific reason Jake was throwing his weight around, beating up people, or whatever, even before losing his job at the racetrack?"

Sutton was shaking his head before J.D. finished asking his question. "I'm sure you've heard a few stories. Jake's always had a short fuse. He didn't need a reason to go off on anyone. If he felt you were looking at him wrong, that was reason enough for him to let loose with his temper, either just verbally or physically. I remember once that he took his truck to get an oil change and one of the locals happened to get there a few seconds ahead of Jake. No big deal, there were two mechanics on duty and Jake had to wait maybe two minutes before he was attended. You'd think the guy had side-swiped Jake on a freeway. Jake started shouting and threatening to make the guy pay for jumping ahead of him. It was ridiculous, and the other man laughed it off... until he woke up the next morning and found all four of his tires flat and his gas tank filled with water. He filed a complaint at the police department and he was advised by the chief of police at the time that without any evidence or witnesses, it would be impossible to prosecute the Shaffers. It was always like that; he knew how to cover his tracks so that even if everyone knew Jake had done something, there was never any way to prove it."

J.D. felt his stomach churn. "What about people he assaulted? Surely they knew who had attacked them...."

"Yeah, the same person who left them with a warning that their next beating would be even worse." Sutton sighed and pushed his Stetson back. "Then they wouldn't even bother to file a report. And as you know, if no one presses charges, much less files a report, there isn't a whole lot we can do. And Jake was always careful to make sure he was never seen except by his victims." He chewed his lip, frowning. "There was never any reason for anyone to believe that Jake was working for anyone else. Whatever he stole, or sold, or did was always on his own, for his own benefit. He never worried or cared about anyone but himself."

J.D. immediately picked up on where the sheriff was going. "And now, all of a sudden he's worrying about keeping the spotlight off his son. How often has Clifford shown up on your radar? I've heard he's a chip off the old block."

"Clifford learned well. And he's always given the impression that he's operating under his old man's orders. Jake's never disputed that. He's always seemed proud of the fact that Clifford took after him so well. Teddy's always been a disappointment to him... like RaeLynn, Teddy has found safety in keeping his head down and staying out of his father's and brother's way, although when Jake or Clifford go on a rampage, no one and no place is safe."

"What about his other son, Johnny?"

"Johnny is a wild card. Half the time, most people even forget that there is another Shaffer son besides Teddy and Cliff. You never know if he's going to join forces with his family or back off and pretend he's got nothing to do with them. That's why it's no surprise he hasn't been around in several months. As for RaeLynn, Johnny pretends she doesn't even exist."

J.D. felt the rage that had begun to fade away suddenly roil deep in his gut again. He took a deep breath, hoping the sheriff wouldn't notice. "How long are you planning to hold Mr. Shaffer?" he asked.

Sutton had raised a brow but his voice remained neutral. "It depends. Might let him go in an hour, might keep him overnight. If I get some answers, real answers...."

"From Clifford?"

"From anyone. Mainly I want to know who Jake is afraid of and whether or not that person or persons is responsible for RaeLynn's condition. And what, exactly, their point was in leaving RaeLynn by the Black Horse Campground. I can't help but think that Corrie is still in someone's crosshairs."

J.D. let out a short laugh. "Try telling that to Corrie. She thinks we're both overreacting. And we're getting on her nerves."

"Nothing new there," the sheriff said, rolling his eyes. "How did you end up bringing her along to the Shaffers?"

"She was more reliable than my GPS," J.D. said dryly. "And she happened to be standing right in front of me when you called. Hard to keep anything from her."

Sutton nodded. "It's one of the reasons I've been staying away from the Black Horse."

J.D. had moved toward the coffee maker for another cup of coffee but the sheriff's words made him turn around. "What's that supposed to mean?"

The sheriff sighed and shook his head. "Just what you said. Corrie's too easy to talk to. I'd have to keep my guard up around her constantly regarding RaeLynn's whereabouts. I know if I'm not careful, I'll not only end up telling her exactly where RaeLynn is, I'll probably end up taking her there."

"Is that really a bad thing?" J.D. asked. He remembered the mishap in the TV room at the campground earlier in the day and fought back a rush of heat to his face. Not only was the incident embarrassing, it highlighted just how tightly wound he was. The tiredness of two sleepless nights in a row was starting to catch up to him and he knew that he wasn't going to be able to keep that up much longer. And while the sheriff seemed much his usual self, J.D. noticed the lines of tiredness despite Sutton's determination to stay alert and on the job. "Corrie really thinks we're overreacting. Seriously, Sutton, how much danger is she in? And RaeLynn? You've got Jake Shaffer locked up and you now know that it's really Clifford you need to keep an eye on. Clifford may be a threat, but you really think he's stupid enough to try something with both the police and sheriff's department watching him?"

"I'm hoping not," Sutton said. "But if we're wrong...."

"We'll never know, not as long as we're keeping our guard up and he knows it. Maybe Jake didn't care about flaunting his power to terrorize people, but I get the feeling Clifford is a little more prudent. He's letting everyone think his dad is still the kingpin and the only reason we know he isn't is because Clifford might be crossing a line that's making Jake nervous."

"Jake is afraid of his son. That's what you're saying."

"That's what it looks like. Maybe Jake decided to let Clifford off the leash and see how he did on his own and now he's wondering what kind of monster he created."

"One he's having a hard time controlling," Sutton said, nodding. His eyes looked far away and he shook his head. "And now he's afraid that Clifford will turn on him if he doesn't take the heat for whatever Clifford does."

"Including assault?"

"Jake's never shied away from beating up someone. Not even his own family, including his wife and daughter. But what happened to RaeLynn goes far beyond anything Jake ever did. It's not that I'm excusing his behavior, but whenever Jake took out his anger on someone with his fists, it was always in the heat of the moment. Never cold-blooded, never premeditated. Oh, he might wait a few days to slash tires or throw a brick through a window, but if he was mad enough to beat up someone, he wouldn't wait a few days to jump them. That's why I'm not convinced that Jake had anything to do with RaeLynn's assault. What he was saying in there," he added, jerking his head back toward his office, "sounded more like a warning than a threat."

"For Corrie?" J.D. felt his stomach twist.

"Corrie, us, anyone who tries to get justice for what happened."

"What about protecting RaeLynn? Is that a punishable offense, according to the Shaffers?"

"It could be," Sutton said quietly. A barely perceptible buzz came from the sheriff's cell phone on his belt. He removed his Stetson and rubbed the back of his neck as he read the message. He sighed, replaced his hat, and straightened up. "You got anything planned for the rest of the day?" he asked unexpectedly as he snapped the phone back into its holster.

J.D. bit back his initial response that maybe sleep would be a good idea. "Nothing I can't put off till later."

The sheriff gave him a slight grin as if he read J.D.'s mind. "You can sleep on the way. That was a text from RaeLynn's doctor. She's showing signs of regaining consciousness. Believe it or not, we can still get there by one o'clock if we leave right now."

J.D. doubted he'd be able to sleep at all. "What about Corrie?"

"With any luck, we'll come back with good news and she'll be able to see RaeLynn in the next few days."

Chapter 10

Corrie was both annoyed and glad that the campground store was busy on this particular day.

She took several reservations for the coming weekend, noting that it was still nearly two weeks till Thanksgiving and there was a good chance she would have a "full house" for the holiday. She was also busy helping guests find items in the store while Jackie kept running the register and Jerry assisted campers with their sites and information about local attractions and services. Buster surprised them all by showing up on a scheduled day off, claiming he could use the additional hours with the holidays approaching, though Corrie suspected he was also trying to avoid Benny Gonzalez. She decided not to mention that Benny had stopped by that morning to look for him. He had also worked steadily with only one coffee break and a half hour lunch break and it was unusual for Corrie not to have to be constantly checking on him to make sure everything was getting done on time. Even with Buster there, having an extra employee would have given them all a breather, but it also would have given Corrie time to wonder what Rick and J.D. were up to and what information Jake Shaffer had given them.

She was walking around the store with a notepad, making a list of items that needed restocking and reordering. She glanced out the side window of the campground store that was also used to display locally handmade stained-glass ornaments and she saw that Rick had made arrangements to have someone on the premises to keep an eye on her.

Deputy Gabe Apachito had been assigned to maintain a low-key watch on the campground. He wasn't in uniform and he had elected to take a leaf blower as a means of patrolling the campground in an unobtrusive manner. Buster had been happy to have help – he hadn't asked the real reason why a deputy was hanging around the campground store and didn't care, as long as it meant that he didn't have to do all his work on his own – and Deputy Apachito seemed equally enthused to help out.

His enthusiasm and eagerness had faded as the realization hit him that Corrie didn't have anyone else scheduled to work for the day… in particular Dee Dee Simpson. His not-so-subtle questions about her part-time employee's schedule made Corrie smile, though she kept it hidden from the young deputy. She knew Apachito was a huge movie fan and he'd been star-struck by Dee

Dee who had, once upon a long time ago, gotten a tiny bit part in a straight-to-video cheesy western that somehow managed to include ninjas and vampires in a nearly incomprehensible storyline. Dee Dee's role was that of a beautiful girl in a skimpy outfit whose only line of dialogue was a giggle and a scream before she was dispatched by the villain in the first ten minutes of the film. That was enough to make her a serious Academy Award contender in the deputy's mind and to call him a "fan" of Dee Dee's was an understatement. Ever since then, he immediately volunteered for any duty that required him to be at the Black Horse Campground. His only disappointment was that Dee Dee was a part-time employee and he never knew when he would actually get to see her.

He had, so far, not advanced to the point of actually speaking to her, when he did have the opportunity. Any time he laid eyes on her, he was not only star struck, he was dumb struck.

For a moment, Corrie was tempted to call Dee Dee just to see if she was available to work, but she immediately vetoed her own idea. Calling Dee Dee in on a weekday almost guaranteed that she would expect to have a weekend shift cancelled and Corrie couldn't afford to be short-handed on a weekend.

Corrie started to turn away from the window when she noticed the deputy reach for the cell phone at his side. She paused when she saw him stiffen and shoot a furtive glance toward the campground store. Instinctively, she stepped aside, hoping he didn't see her through the colorful merchandise hanging in the window. She watched him turn his back toward the store and nod several times before he ended the call and returned the phone to his side. This time, when he glanced toward the store, she noticed his expression was bordering on nervous. She wondered why and wished she could find out....

She spun and headed toward the front counter. She grabbed the phone and Jackie raised a brow at her. "I think I'll see if Dee Dee wants to pick up a few extra hours and it'll give us a chance to catch up on a few things," Corrie said, hoping she sounded casual and non-committal.

Jackie nodded slowly, one brow raised, and Corrie knew there was no keeping any secrets from her old friend.

Dee Dee arrived less than twenty minutes later and appeared eager to get to work.

"You have NO idea how much I appreciate this, Corrie!" she bubbled as she shrugged out of her embroidered suede jacket. It appeared to be brand new and expensive. She gave it a gentle caress as she hung it carefully in the coat closet before turning to Corrie. "With the holidays coming up, I could use some extra money and I'm already tapped out on the number of hours I can get at the salon and the sheriff's office!"

"I thought you had an acting job coming up," Corrie said. "Weren't you doing a holiday commercial for tourism in the state?"

Dee Dee pushed her lips – a deep bronze shade today – into a pout that managed to look both provocative and hurt at the same time. "They started to run behind on production and, even though I spent two hours getting my makeup and hair done, they decided they didn't need me after all! They decided to cut the three segments I was supposed to be in, so I only got paid a cancellation fee, which is hardly nothing, compared to what the other actors and actresses got. They said I didn't have 'the look' they wanted… whatever that was. Not that the pay was great, but the exposure would have helped and it would have looked good in my portfolio." She shook her hair back from her face, and twisted it into a messy bun that made her look casually glamorous. Today, Dee Dee's hair was the shade of autumn leaves and her eyes were a mysterious hazel color. She wore jeans and a flannel shirt but somehow managed to look like she was ready for the runway rather than the campground. Corrie suspected that the producers of the commercial were looking for actors that looked like "real" tourists rather than fashion models but she said nothing, just gave her employee a sympathetic look. "Anyway," Dee Dee said, reverting back to a dazzling smile and sunny disposition, "I need the money and you need the help, so what can I do? You want me to work the register?" She glanced toward the front of the store where Jackie was ringing up a purchase.

Corrie mentally crossed her fingers and hoped her proposal wouldn't make Dee Dee decide she suddenly didn't need the money as badly as she thought. "Actually, I had something else in mind for you to do," she said. She drew Dee Dee toward the kitchen just off the main store and Dee Dee's eyes widened in alarm. "It's nothing to do with cooking or food prep," Corrie quickly assured her. "But I think you could be a big help to me with customer relations."

"How? What customer relations?" Dee Dee asked as Corrie dove into the refrigerator and began rummaging through it. In a matter of minutes, Corrie had assembled a platter of sliced cheese, crackers, and other snack items. In addition, she put together a plate that included a hearty ham sandwich with a generous helping of Jackie's potato salad on the side. She picked up the platters and nodded toward Dee Dee's jacket.

"You're going to need that. I want you to take this around the campground and offer samples to the guests. Tell them we're giving them a 'taste of the region' with cheeses from Noisy Water and a couple of other gourmet goodies to encourage them to patronize the local businesses here in Bonney and even Ruidoso." Corrie hoped that Dee Dee would pick up on her feigned enthusiasm and work whatever acting skills she claimed to pull this off.

"Uh, okay, but what's with this sandwich plate? I mean, how am I supposed to sample this out to a bunch of people?" Dee Dee asked.

"Oh, this," Corrie said with a laugh. "This is for Deputy Apachito. You saw him out there when you came in, didn't you?"

"Oh, yeah, he was out there doing something," Dee Dee said and she frowned. "What's he doing here? He doesn't work for you. Is there a reason why Rick's got a deputy here at the campground? Did something happen again?"

Corrie tried not to bristle at the word "again". She took a silent breath and prayed she didn't scare off her employee. "Well, you heard about what happened to RaeLynn, right?" Dee Dee nodded, her hazel eyes widening. "You know how Rick and J.D. are… they're being a little overprotective. So they just want to make sure that everything is fine and everyone is safe. That's why they have Deputy Apachito here for the day, just to keep an eye on things."

"Oh," Dee Dee said. She looked uncertain. "I'm just wondering why Rick or J.D. aren't here. I mean, if it's not something serious, it seems weird that they would have a deputy here."

Corrie decided to take a chance. "Dee Dee, I have a favor to ask you and I need you to be completely discreet. If you could maybe ask Deputy Apachito to help you take the samples around, after you give him this for his lunch, and maybe talk to him a little…."

Two hours later, Corrie was getting antsy. Surely it wouldn't take Dee Dee and Gabe Apachito this long to take samples around the campground? They weren't completely full. She was busy enough with phone calls from prospective guests inquiring about campground availability for Thanksgiving weekend as well as placing orders for supplies, that she didn't have time to stroll by the windows to see if her employee and the deputy were in sight.

Jackie, as usual, seemed able to read her mind. "They're sitting on the patio in the back and they're engaged in very animated conversation," she murmured, as she slipped behind the counter on the pretense of looking for something. She looked directly at Corrie, who was losing patience with the contemporary Christmas music she was being forced to listen to while on hold with one of her suppliers. "The samples are all gone and so is Deputy Apachito's lunch and I hope you're not expecting a great deal of information to be gained by whatever they're talking about. They're enjoying themselves far too much."

Corrie felt her cheeks redden. "I don't know what you're... yes, I'm still holding," she interrupted herself to speak to the person on the phone. Jackie moved away with a smug grin and Corrie had invested too much time waiting for service to abandon the call in order to defend herself. Besides, there was no sense in trying to argue with Jackie.

She ended the call just as Dee Dee strolled in, both platters empty but with a glow on her face that had nothing to do with the crisp fall weather. "How did it go?" Corrie asked, trying to mask her impatience.

If she failed, she couldn't tell by Dee Dee's expression. "Oh, it went great, Corrie! That was a lot of fun. Thanks for letting me do that today." She sighed and her hazel eyes looked dreamy. Corrie had worried that perhaps her idea had meant that Deputy Apachito would end up with a bruised ego or broken heart, but she had a feeling that something else may have come up.

"Uh, sure. You want to tell me what you found out?" Corrie tapped her pen on the counter, thankful that the store was empty for once. Jackie had retreated to the kitchen to rinse out the coffee pots and make fresh coffee for the afternoon wave of customers and Jerry had gone back to their trailer for five minutes of peace and quiet. She didn't want to take a chance of Deputy Apachito wandering in and finding out that Dee Dee had been on a mission from Corrie.

Dee Dee sighed and her eyes brightened. "Gabe is a HUGE fan of mine and my work! Did you know that?" She shook her head and there was wonder and awe in her voice. "Can you imagine that? I have a fan! See, I know I'll make it big someday, Corrie! He's so excited to be able to say that he knows a movie star! Did you hear that? He called me a movie STAR!"

"That's great, Dee Dee," Corrie said, hoping to drag her employee's attention back to the information that Corrie had sent her to get. "I'm glad Deputy Apachito has noticed your work and all, but did he...."

"You know what's really sweet?" Dee Dee was off again. She had deposited the two platters on the counter and now she plunked her elbows on either side of them and rested her chin in her hands. Her eyes were still faraway and Corrie wondered what it would take to get her back to focusing on what Corrie had asked her to go do in the first place. "He asked if I would consider going out to dinner with him. He said we'd go someplace really nice and it was no pressure, he wasn't, you know, looking for anything else except a chance to get to know me better. Isn't that sweet? You know, a lot of guys have hit on me, but they were after only one thing. With Gabe... it was like I was doing him, you know, like an honor to go to dinner with him. It made me feel really special, you know?"

"That's terrific, Dee Dee. I've always thought Deputy Apachito was a real gentleman," Corrie said, trying not to make her answer short. She could hear Jackie finishing up in the kitchen and she wanted Dee Dee to hurry up and get to the information she wanted. "What else did you two talk about?" Dee Dee's eyes came back into focus for a second and she stared blankly at Corrie. "Like, did you find out what I asked you to find out for me?" Corrie hinted.

Dee Dee blinked. "Oh, yeah. Well, everyone liked the samples and all. They said they'd be sure to check out Noisy Water and the other places in town that you recommended. Gabe helped a lot with that. His mom likes to entertain so she goes to a lot of those places to get stuff for parties. And he really enjoyed the sandwich you made him. He thought I made it," she said, dropping her voice to a whisper. She blushed. "I toyed with the idea of telling him that I did, but then I remembered what you wanted me to ask him, so I told him you made it."

Alarm bells went off in Corrie's head. "You didn't tell him I made it just so he would tell you what I asked, did you?" Corrie wasn't sure that subtlety was one of Dee Dee's strong points.

Dee Dee giggled. "No, of course not, but it gave me that opportunity to bring your name up without making it sound forced."

"Why did you need to bring my name up?" Corrie felt a sense of doom. All she could think was that Dee Dee had blurted out that Corrie had wanted her to ask the deputy something specific about Rick and there was no way that Gabe Apachito wouldn't have been suspicious.

Dee Dee seemed unaware of Corrie's inner turmoil. "Well, I told him how nice and considerate you are, you know, how you're always thinking of other people. And then I mentioned how nice you've been to RaeLynn Shaffer, giving her a job when most people might not have given her the time of day, considering who her family is," she said. If she felt a twinge of guilt because she, at one time, had been "most people", she didn't show it. She went on, "And we talked about what happened to her and how awful, that no one deserved that kind of treatment and how bad she was hurt. And I said I wondered if it would be okay to send her flowers or something at the hospital. I didn't let on that I knew she wasn't here in Bonney anymore," she added quickly. "And he told me that Rick and the doctors had moved her to another hospital. So I kind of played dumb and said I couldn't understand why this hospital wasn't good enough and how mean it was for them to move her away from friends and family. And I guess he really, really admires Rick because he stood up for him right away, said that he knew what he was doing and that it was the best for RaeLynn's health and safety. That it was nothing against the medical center here 'cause even the doctors here agreed. Anyway, I said it was a shame that her friends couldn't go see her and he told me she wasn't in great shape but that he'd heard that she might be waking up and that was why Rick and J.D. had to go to see her...."

Corrie had been leaning forward on her stool behind the counter so as not to miss a word Dee Dee said, but at the mention that Rick and J.D. had gone to see RaeLynn, she slipped off the stool, nearly smacking her chin on the edge of the counter. She straightened up like a jack-in-the-box and stared at Dee Dee. They went to see RaeLynn? And didn't tell her?

Dee Dee hadn't noticed Corrie's near mishap. She went on, "…because they had to see if they could find out more about what happened to her, you know, maybe she could tell them who attacked her and all that. Personally, I'm surprised she regained consciousness that quickly, from what Gabe told me about how injured she was. But anyhow, I told him I thought it would be nice if a group of us friends of RaeLynn's could go see her and he was, like, no, that's not going to be possible anytime soon and she was too far away, people would have to take time off from work and stuff to go see her and it would be too hard to organize. Which, he's got a point, I've got three jobs and it would be almost impossible for me to get a whole day off from all three of them on such short notice. So I said maybe we could all send her cards and flowers, try to arrange it all so it all gets there on the same day, you know what I mean? I think that would be fun for her. I was really talking it up, getting excited about it, and I think he was really getting into it, too. So I asked him if he could get us an address to send it to."

Corrie forgot her hurt for a split-second and held her breath, waiting for Dee Dee's next words. "Well? What did he say?" she asked, when Dee Dee hesitated.

Dee Dee crinkled her nose and twisted her lips. "Well… he didn't say. Not exactly where she is," she added quickly. "He said he didn't know the address. I… I said we could look it up but he said he didn't know the name of the place. Just that it was in Santa Fe…."

Santa Fe. Corrie's disappointment was tempered by the information. At least she now knew where to look, although she was still stinging over the fact that both Rick and J.D. had left town without even bothering to tell her they were going. She almost didn't hear what else Dee Dee had to say.

"And that he wasn't sure if he should be telling me that much, because it kind of sounded to him that Rick didn't really want anyone to know where they were going. He, uh, he asked me not to say anything so…."

"I won't tell anyone what you told me," Corrie assured her. Of course, that meant she would be unable to take action on the information she had received. The last thing she wanted was for Deputy Apachito to get into any trouble. Santa Fe might not be a huge city and it was bound to have several hospitals or clinics where a person with RaeLynn's injuries would go to recover, but just knowing that RaeLynn was in Santa Fe gave Corrie a measure – however small – of satisfaction.

She started when Dee Dee greeted Jackie coming out of the kitchen. "Did Deputy Apachito enjoy his lunch?" Jackie inquired pleasantly.

"Oh, yes, he loved it!" Dee Dee said with enthusiasm. She glanced at the wall clock behind Corrie. "Hey, Corrie, I know you said you needed help this afternoon, but it's already almost two o'clock and Gabe said he went off duty at six and if I'm going to dinner with him, I'm going to need some time to get ready, so...."

Corrie doubted that Dee Dee would be able to improve her appearance anymore than it already was, but she was glad that Deputy Apachito's daydream of going on a date with Dee Dee was coming to fruition. She smiled at her employee, marveling at how excited she was over the prospect of a date with the young deputy. "You're fine, Dee Dee, I just needed a little help for a couple of hours. You can go, and have fun tonight."

Dee Dee squealed with delight, clapped her hands, and scurried out the door before Corrie had a chance to change her mind. Jackie had been refilling the coffee maker and now she approached the counter. "So did you find out what you wanted?" she asked, not bothering to hide her disapproval.

Corrie felt her face heat up under Jackie's gaze and she shrugged. No sense in denying what she had done. "Not everything," she admitted. "In fact, Dee Dee and Deputy Apachito seem to have made out better than I did."

"So it seems," Jackie said. She raised a brow and shook her head, sending her long, silver ponytail swinging. "Has it occurred to you that Rick, especially, and J.D. would have taken you directly to RaeLynn's side if they felt that was an option? Don't you realize that they are simply doing what's best... for RaeLynn?"

Corrie's face felt like it had burst into flames. She had been too busy feeling hurt, as if she were being left out of the loop because she wasn't trusted. Perhaps Jackie was right.

Corrie sighed. "All right, let's forget any of this happened... except for the part where Deputy Apachito finally asked Dee Dee out on a date!"

Chapter 11

J.D. was glad that the sheriff wasn't expecting him to be chatty company on the drive to Santa Fe. Exhausted from lack of sleep and too many unanswered questions, he had dozed off less than ten minutes after leaving Bonney.

The drive took nearly four hours, with only one pit stop in a place called Clines Corners, which didn't seem to be much more than an over-sized truck stop at the junction of Interstate 40 and U.S. 285. J.D. was shocked that he had slept the entire time; he always had a fear of sleeping on a road trip because he worried that the driver would doze off as well, but his tiredness was stronger than his anxiety. He shook his head as he stepped out of the truck and stretched. A cold, sharp wind was blowing and he was amazed at how much clearer his mind felt after getting some rest. The sheriff said nothing and J.D. followed him into the convenience store/gift emporium, sensing that Sutton wanted to get back on the road as quickly as possible.

J.D. was back at the truck before the sheriff returned and they quickly climbed in to get out of the chilly weather. A glance at the dashboard clock told him that they still had an hour to go on the trip and would be in Santa Fe at nearly one in the afternoon. As if reading his mind, Sutton broke the silence.

"We'll go see RaeLynn first. I want to know exactly what her condition is and whether or not she can talk to us. The doctor wasn't inclined to give me a lot of information over the phone… probably because he didn't want to take a chance on anyone overhearing the call."

"Is she still being guarded? You said you were going to make sure she had security around the clock." J.D. knew that the sheriff wasn't taking chances that someone might follow them. They had stopped at the sheriff's apartment long enough for Sutton to change into faded blue jeans and a flannel shirt and he had traded his Silverado's keys for Deputy Mike Ramirez's GMC Sierra pickup truck. One thing he didn't stop for was breakfast and J.D. wished he'd thought to mention it. All he had in his stomach was the cup of coffee – well, three cups – that he'd managed to chug down at the campground, followed by two cups at the sheriff's office. In his hurry to get back to the truck and back on the road, he hadn't even thought to stop in the convenience store to grab something to eat. He hoped his stomach rumbling wasn't going to get too loud but the sheriff apparently wasn't one to blast the truck's radio.

As usual, very little got past the sheriff and he handed J.D. a king-sized candy bar from the paper bag he pulled out of his jacket pocket. "This will have to hold you, but I'll make it up to you later. I know a good place in Santa Fe for a late lunch. There are a couple of water bottles under the seat."

"Thanks," J.D. said, trying to control his eagerness as he tore open the candy bar. He noted with some amusement that the sheriff was pulling out a similar sized one for himself. "Glad you're not the type to think that a granola bar was going to cut it."

"I'm not a cruel man, no matter what the prevailing opinion may be," Sutton replied with a grim smile. They busied themselves with settling the hunger pangs in their stomach for a few minutes before the sheriff spoke again. "I got a call from the clinic while you were asleep. RaeLynn's doctor wants to meet with us before we see her. He wants to prepare us for seeing her again and let us know what we can expect from her, considering what she's been through and how her treatment has progressed."

"How much can that be in... what? Twenty-four, thirty hours since she was found?" J.D. shook his head in disbelief. It seemed to him that it had been a week since he'd discovered her on the highway and taken her to the Black Horse.

Sutton shrugged. "It's a miracle she's progressed this much, that's for sure. And she has a long way to go yet. But he knows it's a long drive from Bonney and he wouldn't have asked me to come if he didn't think she was ready to talk."

"Ready to talk," J.D. said pensively. "Do you mean physically, or mentally as well?"

Sutton shrugged again and shook his head. "I'm not sure. The doctor didn't give me a lot of detail, said that it could wait until we met." He paused and glanced at J.D. "He did tell me that the first thing she did when she awakened was ask if her baby was all right...."

"Oh, God," J.D. blurted out. His hand went to his stomach, as if he'd been physically punched in the gut. He wished he hadn't scarfed down his candy bar; the chocolate and caramel sat like a heavy lead ball. Sutton nodded and focused on the highway ahead of them.

"She took it well, all things considered," he said, his voice tight. "That's all the doctor told me. They gave her a sedative and she fell asleep again...."

"When was that?" J.D. asked, his thoughts swirling, wondering how on earth RaeLynn could possibly be all right after a shock like that.

"Sometime during the night. Or rather, early this morning. He said she'd been showing signs of regaining consciousness so they were monitoring her pretty closely. Like I said, he didn't give me all the details. But that answers the question of whether or not she knew she was pregnant before she was found."

They rode in silence for several miles until they reached the outskirts of Santa Fe and U.S. 285 met with Interstate 25. J.D. took notice of the difference between northern and south-central New Mexico – mainly the drop in temperature. Here, he saw a light dusting of snow on the tops of the mountains. He was glad he had dressed in layers since the jacket he wore wasn't much more than a windbreaker. He had thrown a hoodie on over his long sleeve t-shirt before he'd gone over to see Corrie in the morning, but hadn't bothered to grab his winter jacket.

Again, Sutton pulled his mind-reading act. "Mike keeps an extra jacket behind the seat, in case he needs it while he's hunting. We won't be outdoors too much but if you need it...."

"I think I'll be fine," J.D. said, aware that the sheriff was wearing a fleece-lined denim jacket over his flannel shirt. The truck's heater was keeping them both warm and J.D. tried to recall the last time he'd ever really experienced snow. It wasn't a common weather event in Houston. "What made you decide to have her brought to Santa Fe?"

"There's a clinic here that specializes in rehabilitation, long term and short term, for patients who have a history of drug or alcohol abuse," the sheriff said. "I explained that RaeLynn had been clean for a while but there was some concern that, if she survived, the drugs that were introduced into her system might make her a candidate for a serious relapse. Naturally, it wouldn't do her much good to simply treat her physical injuries without making sure she had the appropriate support to fight off addiction." Sutton became quiet as he exited off Interstate 25 and turned onto Old Pecos Trail. They drove through an area that was part residential, part offices of doctors, lawyers, and realtors. Every building seemed to be made of adobe and J.D. wondered if it was real or merely cosmetic.

He was surprised when the sheriff pulled up to a driveway that appeared to belong to a large weathered adobe house. An eight foot high adobe wall surrounded the property, which seemed to take up the entire block, and a gate that appeared to be made of solid wood barred the entrance. Sutton pulled alongside an adobe pillar and lowered his window. J.D. saw a speaker with a keypad and a screen that lit up when the sheriff pressed a button. A pleasant woman's voice asked him to identify himself and enter a code on the keypad. The sheriff did, as J.D. looked on with interest. The woman's voice thanked them and the gate – which was actually metal that looked like wood – swung open. Sutton turned to him and explained, "The doctor gave me a visitor's code when I first brought RaeLynn here. It's an extra security measure, after I explained the situation and told him I'd be coming back."

J.D. nodded, his eyes widening at the sight of the clinic. It was set down in a hollow and, from the road, it wasn't readily obvious that it was a three-story building. There were no signs or anything to identify the purpose of the building and he understood why the sheriff had chosen this place for keeping RaeLynn safe. It was discreet and well-protected. Security cameras were strategically placed around the building and grounds, so skillfully hidden that the average person would probably have never seen them.

The sheriff drove around the side of the building to where there was a parking area designated for visitors. The front door was solid wood, heavy and weathered, with narrow stained glass windows on either side. J.D. wondered if it had once been a private home. A bronze plaque on the wall beside the door was engraved with the image of a man and a woman and the names Ramon and Regina Echeverria, but he didn't have time to examine it closely before Sutton stepped up to the door and pulled it open.

The lobby resembled that of a luxury hotel. The heavily textured walls were painted a soothing, neutral shade of cream which set off the expensive artwork that adorned them. J.D. recognized paintings by R.C. Gorman and he knew they had to be originals. Several comfortable chairs and sofas formed a seating area to the right of the entrance, complete with end tables and several potted plants, but the area was empty. To the left was a plain wooden desk with a computer, a phone, and not much else on it. A woman with a no-nonsense demeanor despite her pleasant smile, nodded as they approached and she stood up. "Sheriff Sutton? Detective Wilder? May I please see your identification?" she asked. After examining their badges and licenses, she nodded again. "Dr. Pruett is expecting you. Security will escort you to his office."

A uniformed guard was standing by a single door that was painted the same color as the walls. He unlocked the door, ushering them into a corridor that finally looked like something one would see in a regular hospital or clinic. A door on the left had the name "Pruett" on a plaque. The guard tapped on the door and opened it, stepping aside to let J.D. and the sheriff enter.

"Come in," said the man in the white rumpled lab coat who was rising from behind the desk and extending his hand. Unlike the lobby area, the office was crowded with filing cabinets, shelves of books, and several hard plastic chairs placed along the wall. "Sheriff Sutton and Detective Wilder? Grab yourselves a couple of chairs and have a seat."

"Thank you, Doctor," Sutton said. He had removed his Stetson upon entering the lobby but he replaced it as they sat down. He immediately got to the point. "You said you'd fill us in on Miss Shaffer's condition once we were able to meet face to face."

"Yes," the doctor said, rubbing a hand over his face. He was gray at the temples and there were deep lines in his face, but he didn't appear to be much older than fifty. He studied the sheriff and J.D. closely. He cleared his throat. "Refresh my memory, uh, Sheriff...."

"Sutton. Rick Sutton. Bonney County sheriff's department. This is Detective J.D. Wilder of the Bonney police department." J.D. nodded, receiving a brief nod back from the doctor. "You want to know what our interest is in Miss Shaffer's situation," the sheriff said.

"Well, yes," Dr. Pruett replied. He picked up a pair of glasses and put them on as he flipped open a manila folder. "According to the personal information in her file, neither of you are listed as her family, nor are you listed as contact persons. Before I give you any information, I'd like to know exactly how and why law enforcement officers are involved in her case."

"Of course," Sutton said, nodding. "Obviously, it wasn't possible for Miss Shaffer to list her contact information when she was admitted." He paused when it seemed that the doctor was about to interrupt, but then he motioned for the sheriff to continue. "She isn't a criminal, if that's what your concern is. She was found in the middle of the highway on the outskirts of the village in the middle of the night. She was transported to the emergency room in Bonney where doctors determined that her condition warranted care that was beyond what they could provide. Since her condition was partly caused by drugs, it only made sense to have her taken to a facility that specialized in both physical rehabilitation as well as drug detox and rehab."

Pruett cleared his throat again. "We aren't the only facility that provides that kind of care...," he began.

"But you are the best," Sutton interjected.

Pruett didn't argue. "Sheriff Sutton, forgive me if I sound elitist or arrogant. This young woman was found on a rural highway with severe injuries that have not been explained. I have a bare bones file on her as far as her personal information goes. You claim she's not a criminal, but is she indigent? Perhaps you're not aware that this clinic does not accept...."

"Her bills will be covered in their entirety, if that's your concern," Sutton said, his tone as icy as his dark blue eyes. J.D. had felt his own ire rise at the realization that the doctor seemed to be more concerned with getting paid than taking care of RaeLynn. Pruett's eyebrows rose and he glanced from the sheriff's face to J.D. as he cleared his throat.

"I didn't mean...."

"You did, and your concern has been addressed, and now we can move on to discussing Miss Shaffer's condition and treatment plan," Sutton said, his voice not thawing one degree. The doctor glanced in J.D.'s direction and blanched. He dropped his gaze to the file in front of him and cleared his throat again.

"Very well, uh, Sheriff Sutton, here is what we found." He glanced over the sheets of paper in the file. "No fractures in her back, arms, legs, or extremities. She does have a minor jaw fracture and a few of her teeth were wired back into place. Bruising indicates that she acquired these injuries in a physical altercation. They were not injuries sustained in an accident involving a motor vehicle."

Sutton's eyes had grown colder and his jaw clenched, but J.D. was positive it wasn't directed at the doctor's concern for his payment this time. "You're sure?" the sheriff asked, his voice tight. Pruett nodded.

"Oh, yes. We've treated many victims of domestic violence. Her injuries are classic examples. As far as her drug screen... well, suffice it to say that it was a wonder she didn't die immediately. I'm actually surprised that she regained consciousness this soon."

"So she is conscious?" J.D. surprised himself by speaking up. He had made up his mind to let the sheriff do all the talking. The doctor frowned and glanced at Sutton as if asking permission to answer J.D.'s question. The sheriff gave a slight nod.

"She's drifting in and out," the doctor said. "Her condition is stable, though still serious. We are trying to ease her out of the coma and keep her heartbeat steady. We honestly don't know, at this point, just how much damage her internal organs, not to mention her brain, have sustained from her ordeal. She did suffer a miscarriage as well, though it doesn't seem like she was more than a few weeks pregnant. I want you to understand that just because she is able to talk, I have no idea how much sense her words will make nor can I guarantee that whatever she tells you is the truth or a hallucination." He paused and took a deep breath. "Also, and I'm sure you already have a very good idea about this, she looks... terrible. That's the only way I can describe her. Her face is badly bruised and swollen, her arms are like matchsticks. I can only surmise that she has been malnourished for some time. That may or may not have contributed to the miscarriage, but the drugs in her system would certainly have been enough." He paused again, his eyes searching both their faces. J.D. wondered if Sutton felt as numb as J.D. did. The sheriff's face was frozen in an expression that appeared to be horror, anger, and compassion. It wasn't an attractive combination. The doctor got to his feet. "Do you still wish to see her?"

"Yes," Sutton answered as he and J.D. stood up immediately. The doctor nodded.

"I will have a nurse escort you. I have another family to talk to in twenty minutes and I need to prepare for that meeting. I just want to ask you both," he said, his eyes darting between the two of them, "is Miss Shaffer really just an unknown stranger to whom you've rendered aid in the line of duty?"

Sutton glanced at J.D. and shook his head. "No, Doctor Pruett, she is not. She is actually a friend of ours. Her family has not shown any interest in learning about her condition, nor are they willing to take any responsibility for her treatment. You are certainly welcome to ask Miss Shaffer, herself, if she wants us to take on the role of responsible parties when she is able to make that decision for herself. In the meantime, her bills will be paid and her treatment will entail the very best you and this facility can give her. I will be your contact person."

Pruett nodded and then gave a self-conscious cough. "That's fine, Sheriff. And the, er, security measures...?"

"Will remain in place," Sutton said, his voice razor sharp. "I know that's not commonly a part of a patient's stay, but in this case it's warranted, for Miss Shaffer's safety."

The doctor sucked in a breath. "If she's not a criminal, then what is she? A witness to a crime? Is she in some kind of a protection program?"

"Not officially," Sutton said. "However, we have not been able to track down the person or persons who left her in the middle of the highway and who, presumably, were responsible for the condition in which she was found. Until suspects are in custody, we feel it best to make sure that her whereabouts are kept quiet and that her visitors are kept to a minimum and carefully screened." He paused for a moment and when the doctor seemed about to speak, he added, "As you are probably aware, an outside security firm has been retained and the clinic is not responsible for that. Those are the arrangements I made with the director, Hector Echeverria."

"Yes, Mr. Echeverria did mention that to me." Dr. Pruett nodded. "All right, Sheriff Sutton, I'll let the nurse escort you to Miss Shaffer's room. Please let me know if I can be of further assistance or provide any more information to you."

"Thank you," Sutton said, his tone indicating that he didn't think that he would be needing anything else from the doctor. J.D. was itching to get going; the doctor's report on RaeLynn's condition only made him more impatient to see exactly whether the doctor had exaggerated. He couldn't imagine her looking worse than she had the last time he'd seen her in the Bonney Medical Center.

They were met outside the doctor's office by a slender woman with frosted blond hair neatly coiled at the nape of her neck. She didn't appear to be much older than he or the sheriff and she was attractive in a serious, professional way. Her welcoming smile suddenly froze when she saw the sheriff and she blinked her dark eyes several times. It seemed to take her a long time to find her voice and when she did, it shook slightly. "Hi, I'm Eleanor Price, the ward nurse where Miss Shaffer is. You can call me Ellie." J.D. extended his hand, noting that the sheriff's own expression had become wooden and his manner stiff. He added it to the list of things he was going to ask the sheriff about later. He decided to take charge of the situation himself.

"I'm Detective J.D. Wilder of the Bonney Police Department. This is Sheriff Rick Sutton, Bonney County Sheriff's

Department." Sutton touched the brim of his Stetson and nodded, his only greeting. Ellie's face bloomed crimson and her fingertips barely brushed the sheriff's. J.D. cleared his throat, wondering what was going on but deciding that they had more important matters at hand. "We'd like to see Miss Shaffer now, if you don't mind."

"Sure," Ellie said, turning away quickly. She cleared her throat. "Come this way. You'll be able to talk to the nurse who's been in charge of Miss Shaffer's care since she arrived."

J.D. was finding that he couldn't respond while he and the sheriff were picking up their pace to keep up with the young woman. They arrived at the nurse's station and Ellie slipped behind the desk. "Miss Shaffer's visitors are here, Rosa," she said to the older woman behind the desk who was busily entering information into the computer on the desk.

She looked up from the screen and pushed her glasses up onto the top of her head. Her dark hair was liberally streaked with gray and pulled back severely into a tight bun. "Hello, gentlemen," she said, as she stood up, looking formidable in her pale blue scrubs. "You're in luck, Miss Shaffer is semi-conscious right now. She was in a deep sleep earlier, but I think she'll very likely wake up and be able to talk to you."

"Thank you," Sutton said, and while the nurse seemed to be nothing short of professionally courteous, J.D. could sense tension emanating from the sheriff. Ellie had excused herself and became busy perusing the charts on the desk. Rosa had not, as yet, introduced herself formally but she motioned for them to follow her down the hall. She arrived at a door at the end of the corridor that was flanked by two men in security guard uniforms. They seemed to recognize Sutton and nodded to him without saying a word then scrutinized J.D. carefully. Without prompting, he whipped out his badge and identification. That seemed to make the two men relax slightly. Rosa waited until they had moved aside and allowed her to reach the door. She tapped lightly, then leaned in and whispered something to the person that had opened it. She stepped back as a slight woman with her long dark hair in a ponytail and wearing casual clothes came out of the room. Her eyes were bright and her face, though set in a professional expression, exhibited good humor and spunk.

"Hi!" she said, her voice low but friendly. "I'm Officer Debbie Yellowcloud. I believe we've met, Sheriff Sutton?"

The sheriff had relaxed, although only J.D. would probably be able to tell. "Yes, Officer Yellowcloud, just yesterday. This is Detective J.D. Wilder."

"Hi," she said, extending her hand to J.D. He was impressed by her firm grip. "Just call me Debbie. Nice to meet you, Detective."

"Likewise," J.D. said. "How's Miss Shaffer doing?" he asked, forgetting again that he was going to let Sutton do the talking.

"Not bad," Debbie said with a shrug. "She's awake now but not in a mood to talk. I haven't told her you were coming and I don't think the nursing staff has either?"

It was a question directed at Rosa, who shook her head. "No, Dr. Pruett didn't want to get her upset or overly excited. I'll be waiting out here while you go in to talk with her," she said, turning to the sheriff and J.D., "just in case I'm needed."

"Thanks," Sutton said. Debbie nodded and held up a finger.

"Give me a second to prepare her for a visitor. You're the first she's had, not counting doctors and nurses." She slipped into the room for a moment and J.D. heard a low murmur of the officer's voice, then she opened the door. "Come on in."

J.D. was surprised when the sheriff motioned for him to go in first. He stepped into the room and was even more surprised to find himself in what looked like a luxury hotel suite. He had expected sterile walls, but the room was warmly furnished in Southwestern décor with earth tones and a comfortable seating area. The hospital bed was the only discordant note in the room, despite the bedding also having a subtle Navajo tribal pattern woven into the blankets and sheets.

RaeLynn half rose from her semi-reclining position in the hospital bed. Pale didn't begin to describe her complexion. The only color in her face and arms came from the bruises and other marks of her injuries. Her tawny eyes seemed to have faded from their usual vibrant tiger-eye color to a dull brown. Only the merest spark of recognition gave her face any semblance of life. She shook her head slowly. "Rick. Detective Wilder." Her voice was raspy and faint as a breeze blowing through dead leaves. She coughed and Officer Yellowcloud stepped to the bedside table and picked up a plastic cup with a straw in it. She gave RaeLynn a sip of water. RaeLynn nodded and cleared her throat and the young officer stepped back. "What are you doing here?" she asked weakly, allowing her head to fall back on her pillow.

The sheriff had removed his Stetson and gave her a gentle smile as he moved toward the side of the bed and took her hand. "Just checking to see how you're doing, RaeLynn. You gave us a scare for a while there."

"Oh," she said, looking confused. Her brow furrowed, and she looked around the room. "Where am I? This isn't the hospital, is it?" She shook her head slightly. "At least, I don't recognize any of the doctors and nurses here. Where am I?"

Sutton's smile faded and his face looked grim. He cleared his throat. "Well, you're in a hospital, RaeLynn. But it's not in Bonney. You were very badly injured. You were in a coma for a few days." He hesitated and J.D. knew he was debating with himself about whether or not he should mention her miscarriage. She nodded, her eyes fixed on the sheriff. The expression on her face seemed more weariness and resignation than anything else, as if discovering where she was and what had happened to her didn't matter very much. Sutton went on, "I don't know how much the doctors have told you about your condition." She made a movement halfway between a shrug and a shake of her head, but still said nothing. "RaeLynn, I want to know what happened to you. You disappeared from Bonney the night of the church fiesta. I think I know who took you that night and who is responsible for what happened to you. You were assaulted. I need to know who did this to you. Do you remember what happened? Can you tell me who hurt you?"

She seemed to retreat into herself. Her brow wrinkled as if in thought, but then it seemed as if the effort were too much. She took a shaky breath. "I'm not sure what happened," she murmured, closing her eyes. J.D. blinked in surprise and he looked at the sheriff. Sutton's jaw was clenched and his eyes narrowed.

"Are you sure, RaeLynn?" The sheriff's voice was soft but J.D. could feel the tension behind the words. "Surely you remember some of what happened? You were gone for several weeks, I'm sure a lot happened in that time...." He let his words trail away.

RaeLynn's face grew even paler; she looked as if she were on the verge of fainting. Her eyes seemed to be looking into the distant past and her breathing became shallow. She shook her head again. J.D. felt his blood run cold as he took in the sight of the dark circles around her eyes, the sunken cheeks, the angry purple bruises and bright red welts on her face and arms. Her blonde hair hung in straggly wisps around her face and the acne scars in her face from her earlier years of substance abuse appeared to have been carved into her pale skin with a knife. She looked far worse than J.D. could have imagined. The only thing that would make sense of her inability – or rather, unwillingness – to give them any information was that she was afraid.

Deathly afraid.

She cleared her throat and gave a quick shake of her head. "I don't know. I don't remember. I'm sorry, Rick. I'm... I'm just sorry. I think I need to rest now...." She turned away, swallowed hard, and then dropped her gaze to the floor.

Rosa, the nurse, slipped into the room, her face grim. She stepped around J.D. and the sheriff and checked RaeLynn's vitals. "Her blood pressure is up and so is her heart rate. I think it's best if you gentlemen leave now." She didn't look at the two men, but it was easy to see that there was no arguing with her. Sutton stood up, jerked his head toward the door. J.D. followed him, casting a backward glance at RaeLynn.

She looked up and her eyes met his for a brief moment while the nurse was occupied in adjusting the IV. He wasn't sure if he was imagining things, but it seemed to him that there was an appeal in her gaze, as if she wanted to say a lot more but her fear was greater than her faith in their ability to protect her.

But who was she afraid of?

Officer Yellowcloud was waiting for them and she stepped out into the hall with them, keeping the door ajar and one eye on RaeLynn and the nurse. The two security guards moved away slightly, giving them some privacy. Apparently that was the arrangement they had with the sheriff and neither Sutton nor Officer Yellowcloud paid any attention to them. "Did you find out anything from her?" the young officer asked, keeping her voice low.

"No," Sutton said, his tone clipped. "Has she said anything while she was semi-conscious? Anything at all about what happened?"

"No," Officer Yellowcloud said, shaking her head so that her ponytail swayed. "She mumbles a lot when she's asleep, but I haven't been able to make out any clear words." She sucked in one corner of her cheek and glanced back into the room. She leaned closer to J.D. and the sheriff and lowered her voice. "I understand she lost a baby?"

Sutton nodded. "How did you find out? Did she tell you?"

"No," Officer Yellowcloud said. "At least, she didn't say so explicitly. The doctor briefed me, of course, when I took up my post. He said there was a good chance she might have an emotional breakdown and he told me to be on the watch for any signs that she might become seriously depressed or have a meltdown. She hasn't really been awake for long periods of time. Once or twice, she seemed alert enough to actually talk and I kind of chatted with her, you know, 'How are you feeling', that kind of stuff." She paused and glanced back in the room. J.D.'s eyes followed her gaze and he saw the nurse pulling up the covers to RaeLynn's shoulders. RaeLynn's eyes were closed and her lips were trembling. The woman murmured something he couldn't hear. She turned and made her way toward the door, joining them in the hallway.

"She'll probably sleep for a little while. She seems agitated. I hope you gentlemen aren't going to be upsetting her every time she sees you." She raised her brows as she looked from J.D. to the sheriff and her voice was tart.

"It's not our intention," Sutton said, his own voice deceptively neutral. "But we are here to find out what happened to her. That means having to ask her questions that may upset her."

"Hmm," Rosa said, her expression showing that she didn't approve. She looked at Officer Yellowcloud. "Let me know if I have to give Miss Shaffer any more sedatives. I only gave her a small dose, just enough to relax her, and I doubt she'll fall asleep. But just in case she doesn't calm down...." She let her words trail away and she threw a glance at J.D. and the sheriff.

"Yes, ma'am," Officer Yellowcloud said, her face solemn. Rosa gave them a single nod and went back to her desk. After she was out of earshot, the young officer turned to them. "So she's the victim of a crime? What, exactly, is your relationship with her? If you don't mind my saying so, you seem awfully concerned for her to be a stranger to you. Or else you guys take your jobs more seriously than most other cops."

"She is a friend. I've known her since we were kids." Sutton stopped and the young woman nodded, waiting for him to go on. He didn't. "You were telling us about how you tried to talk to her, Officer Yellowcloud?" he prodded.

"Call me Debbie. My official title is a mouthful and we're all cops here." If she expected them to offer their first names, she was disappointed. "I was feeling sorry for her, being so far from home and no one coming to see her but doctors and nurses. I thought maybe she was an indigent case except...." She pursed her lips and motioned around them, indicating the clinic. "Well, I've seen the inside of county hospitals and clinics. Nothing like this place, that's for sure. She seemed so lost. But she didn't say much. She did ask me who I was and why I was here."

"Did you tell her?" the sheriff asked.

"I told her my name and that I was providing security. She didn't seem surprised to hear that, which seemed odd. But then she didn't seem too terribly shocked to see you two, either." Debbie raised an eyebrow and glanced at the two men in turn.

The sheriff was being even more cagey than usual. "Told you we were friends," he said. "So did she ever say anything about what happened? Anything coherent?"

Debbie seemed to realize that the sheriff wasn't going to give her any more information until she gave him some information. "Not really. Mostly she mumbled but when I asked her if she said anything, she'd stop. When she was awake, she looked at me kind of the way you two are looking at me... like she wasn't sure if she could trust me." She gave them a lop-sided grin.

Sutton nodded and his manner became brisk. "All right, Officer. Debbie," he added, pointedly, when it seemed that she was going to correct him. "We're going to go catch a bite to eat then come back and see if she's willing to talk to us. I know she was probably more surprised to see us than she let on, and I don't want her to feel pressured. It's important that she understands that we're here to help her and we want to get her home as soon as it's possible."

Debbie nodded. "Anything you want me to tell her... or DON'T want me to tell her?"

Sutton glanced at J.D. "Not really. Just pay close attention to anything she does say. And if she asks if we're coming back, tell her the truth. She would expect that of us."

Debbie seemed impressed by his words. She shook their hands, told them to enjoy their lunch, then she went back into RaeLynn's room. J.D. and the sheriff waited until the door clicked shut behind her before they turned and headed down the hallway. J.D. was itching to ask the sheriff several questions but he knew better than to ask before they had left the building.

They made a brief stop at Rosa's desk, where Sutton informed the nurse that they would be back in an hour or so and made sure that they had both his and J.D.'s cell phone numbers in the event that they were needed. Ellie, the younger nurse, was behind the desk as well and she stared at the sheriff while he spoke to her superior, studiously ignoring her scrutiny. In silence, they made their way down the hall, past Dr. Pruett's closed door, to where the security guard let them out into the lobby. The low murmur of voices in the waiting area told them another family was waiting to visit someone. The receptionist at the front desk nodded when Sutton told her that they would be returning later on.

When they stepped outside, J.D. felt as if he'd been holding his breath for hours. He sucked in a lungful of cold, clear air and his mind immediately felt less foggy.

Sutton nodded. "Let's go get lunch. And talk."

J.D. wondered which of the two they needed more.

Chapter 12

Two-thirty in the afternoon in the middle of the week was a perfect time to find a place to eat lunch that wasn't too crowded. Although Sutton informed J.D. that The Pantry normally had a line out the door with a waiting time of up to an hour on the weekends, they were able to secure a table in the back corner of the restaurant with no other diners in close proximity to them.

J.D. was relieved to see that the restaurant served a Reuben sandwich that did not seem to include the ubiquitous green chile he'd noticed on just about every menu he had encountered since he arrived in New Mexico. The sheriff ordered the carne adovada stuffed sopaipilla without even looking at the menu, and J.D. realized he was quite familiar with the restaurant's offerings.

"Can I get you gentlemen something to drink other than water?" the server asked. J.D. hesitated; in the last twenty-four hours, especially the last hour, he'd learned a lot of things he hadn't expected and found more questions than he ever thought possible. Though he was not officially "on the clock", he doubted that requesting a beer – however badly he felt he could use one – would be all right with the sheriff. Sutton, however, could read him like a book.

"I'm driving and it'll be a few hours before we get on the road again," Sutton said, nodding slightly with a glint in his eye. "You look like you could use something stronger than iced tea. Which is what I'll have," he added, addressing the server.

J.D.'s eyes narrowed. He wasn't sure if this was a test, but he decided to let the chips fall where they may. "What do you recommend?" he asked the server.

The young woman had bright purple hair, several facial piercings, and a tattoo of a compass on her right wrist, and yet J.D. felt he'd seen her somewhere before. She grinned. "How 'bout a Modelo? Something a little more exotic than your sandwich?" J.D. raised a brow at her.

"I'd think a Reuben would be more exotic in New Mexico than anything else on the menu," he said. The server laughed.

"You got that right. I grew up in Hoboken, New Jersey, and spent weekends in New York, visiting my grandparents. We always had Reubens for at least one meal each time we visited. They make good ones here. The locals like to add green chile...."

"Don't ruin it for me," J.D. interrupted, handing her the menu. "Reuben and Modelo, no chile, please."

"You got it. I'll bring your beer and tea and your meals won't be long." She moved away and J.D. looked at Sutton.

"Sure you don't mind?"

The sheriff shook his head. "Nope. Like I said, you look like you could use it."

"Yeah, well, I've got a lot of questions and I almost feel like I've already gotten the answers to questions I don't even know I have to ask." He paused as the server deposited their drinks on the table. They thanked her and she was professional enough to sense they wanted to talk privately and she moved away. J.D. waited a second or two before picking up his beer bottle. "Sure you won't join me? I can help with the driving."

Sutton shook his head. "Thanks, Wilder, but I don't drink." He leaned back and pulled his notepad out of his shirt pocket, leaving J.D. staring at him. "Let's start with a few questions we both have," Sutton went on, apparently unaware of J.D.'s confusion.

J.D. set down his beer before taking a sip. He wondered if he should ask what the sheriff meant by that comment, but decided that he was too focused on the case and wouldn't want to discuss it at the moment. "Okay, here's one. Is it really possible she doesn't know or remember what happened to her?"

Sutton shook his head. "I think we both know that she's hiding something. She doesn't seem to be suffering from amnesia, not that I'm a doctor." He paused. "She's afraid."

"Next question: Just WHO or WHAT is she afraid of?" J.D. asked. "Any ideas?"

Sutton frowned and shrugged. "It would be easy to say that she's afraid of her attacker and, considering what we know about what she was afraid of before she disappeared, that means she's afraid of her brother or father... but after our little chat with Jake Shaffer, I'm beginning to think there's someone else that she – and he – are afraid of."

"Her brother, Clifford?"

"Maybe, but...." Sutton stopped as the server approached the table with their food.

"Everything look okay?" she asked as she set the respective meals down. "Need anything else? Another beer?" she asked, although J.D. hadn't taken one sip yet.

"No, thanks, we're good. And we'll flag you down if we need anything," Sutton added.

114

The server nodded with understanding and pulled a brown leatherette folder from her apron pocket. "I'll leave the check now, but don't worry and don't feel in a rush. If you need anything else, just let me know. My name's Mandie." She flashed a smile and left.

For a few moments, J.D. and the sheriff focused on assuaging their hunger pangs before they continued their discussion. J.D. was pleasantly surprised at how good his Reuben tasted and took a long pull on his beer to wash it down. Sutton gave him a half-grin. "I take it you're enjoying your meal?"

"Sheriff, I was starving and it's been a while since I had a Reuben." He raised his bottle. "If we were back in Bonney and I was tucked in my cabin for the night, I'd have another, but this one's taken the edge off and that's all I need."

The sheriff shrugged. "You'd hardly be impaired by another one, if you want one. I'm picking up the tab...."

"No chance. I got the tab and I'll arm wrestle you for it if I have to. And one beer's enough. I hate to drink alone, and no, iced tea doesn't count." He pushed the bottle to one side. "Mind if I ask a personal question?"

Sutton took his time cutting a piece of his stuffed sopaipilla before conveying it to his mouth. He chewed slowly, avoiding J.D.'s eyes. J.D. knew the sheriff wouldn't speak until he was ready. Finally, after taking a drink of iced tea, Sutton quietly said, "I guess I don't."

J.D. waited a few seconds, trying to figure out exactly what it was he wanted to ask. Sutton didn't seem like he was going to rush him, and J.D. felt that the sheriff knew exactly what it was J.D. wanted to ask him. Finally Sutton spoke up, "You want to know how RaeLynn ended up at this particular facility."

It wasn't really a question but J.D. nodded. "I doubt this was a place you chose by opening a phone book to a random page and flipping a coin."

Sutton managed to maintain a completely neutral expression. "My main goal was to get RaeLynn someplace where she was going to be safe... where whoever hurt her couldn't get at her again. That's why I had her come so far from Bonney. My secondary goal was to make sure that she received the best medical care possible. And along with that, the best therapy to help her fight any relapse that overdose might have pushed her to. I know this place is the best...."

"And you know that, how?"

The sheriff ducked his head and pushed the last few bites of his lunch around on the dark red sauce on his plate. It seemed like his appetite was gone. Again, J.D. waited until his patience was rewarded. Somewhat. The sheriff cleared his throat. "Let's talk about RaeLynn and her case now and then we'll talk about other things on the way home. We should head back soon...." His cell phone buzzed just then and he unholstered it and glanced at the screen before he answered. "Sheriff Sutton." He listened for a few seconds, caught J.D.'s eye and nodded. "Sure, that's fine, we'll still be in town. Four-thirty, then. Thanks." He ended the call and gave J.D. a look of satisfaction. "I think we'll be getting some answers from RaeLynn soon."

"Really?" J.D. said, unable to hide his surprise. "Who was that?"

"Rosa, the nurse. She said RaeLynn asked her if we were still in town. When she was told we were planning to stop back by, she asked if she could be assisted in taking a shower and washing her hair." Sutton leaned back in his chair and allowed a slight grin. "That tells me she wasn't completely comfortable when we stopped in earlier. Sure, the caregivers cleaned her up after she was picked up and brought to the hospital, but you could tell she was stressed while we were there. Even the nurse mentioned it." He paused and noticed J.D.'s look of confusion. "She hated that we saw her looking, to put it mildly, not her best. Since she's been back in Bonney and working for Corrie, she's tried her best to always look neat, clean, well-groomed... anything but a washed-up ex-junkie. She might buy her clothes at a thrift shop, but you can bet it's the best she can find. And then she wakes up after a horrific trauma, sees us, is mortified, and the first thing she thinks of is her appearance. She was trying to get rid of us so she would have time to clean herself up and look 'presentable'."

J.D. stared at the sheriff, not sure if the man was pulling his leg or not. He shook his head. "You're telling me she'll talk to us once she looks, uh, 'presentable'?"

Sutton nodded. "She doesn't want to look like a victim. She doesn't want us to feel sorry for her. You can thank Corrie for giving her a little shot of pride. The fact that RaeLynn cares enough to worry about her appearance before we come talk to her tells me she's willing to fight to get better and put a stop to whatever it is that put her in someone's crosshairs."

J.D. raised a brow. "And that means she's still in danger."

The sheriff nodded, glanced at his watch. "Rosa asked us to give her another hour or so to help her shower and change her bedding and clothes. I think we can...."

He stopped when Mandie approached them, her face showing signs of agitation though her manner was just as friendly as it had been when they first sat down, even if it seemed slightly forced. "Everything okay?" she asked. So far, neither J.D. nor the sheriff had even reached for the check, but she grabbed the folder and stuffed it into her pocket.

"Everything's fine, but we haven't...," the sheriff started but she interrupted.

"I'll bring your change in just a minute," she said and hurried away.

J.D. glanced at Sutton. "What was that all about?" he said. Sutton shook his head in a daze, then Mandie returned with the folder.

"Oh, sorry, I thought you were ready! Here's your check," she said, her voice slightly louder than was necessary. She widened her eyes at them and then cleared her throat as she set the folder on the table and tapped on it with her fingers. "You can take care of this at the register up front, okay?" Again, she moved away before they had a chance to say anything.

Sutton frowned and took the folder. He flipped it open and froze. He cleared his throat, as Mandie had, and said to J.D., "Is this what you ordered?" as he pushed the folder toward him.

J.D. raised a brow then he saw the note, written in purple ink, tucked into the folder on top of the check. "YOU'RE BEING FOLLOWED. COME TO THE REGISTER UP FRONT TO PAY AND I'LL EXPLAIN."

It took all of J.D.'s willpower not to look around the room. "No," he said, raising his voice slightly, "this isn't what I ordered. I don't think this is our check."

They stood up and got their jackets off the backs of their chairs, being careful not to look like they were in a hurry, and fighting the urge to glance at the other diners. They made their way to the front of the restaurant where Mandie was waiting for them at the register. Sutton pushed his credit card across the counter toward her along with the folder. J.D. stood back, watching the back room where they had been sitting out of the corner of his eye while the sheriff asked Mandie, "What's this supposed to mean?"

Mandie glanced toward the back dining room. "I got a call from my sister. She works at a clinic here in town." The sheriff stiffened and Mandie went on hurriedly, "She wasn't sure you were here, but she said she had a pretty good idea you might be and she described you. She said a man came by after you left and asked about a patient you guys visited. And he asked if she'd had any other visitors. The receptionist up front didn't give them any information, not about a patient and not about you two, either. My sister...."

"Who's your sister?" Sutton interrupted, keeping his voice low.

"Eleanor Price. She's a nurse."

That explained why Mandie looked familiar. Ellie was an older version of the young server, minus the purple hair, piercings, and tattoo. Sutton glanced at J.D. and nodded. "Go on," he said. "Did she tell you what the man looked like?"

"Yeah, but it wasn't much to go on. Just a tall guy, with a black trench coat and knitted hat. She thinks he might have been wearing gray slacks and black boots. She didn't get a good look at his eyes 'cause he was wearing shades, but he did have beard stubble on his face."

"Great disguise," J.D. said dryly. "Anyone matching that description come in for lunch?"

"No," Mandie said, shaking her head for emphasis. "When she told me, I made it a point to check before I dropped off your bill."

"It's easy to lose a knitted hat, black trench coat, and shades," the sheriff said. "Was he alone?" Mandie nodded.

"Ellie – my sister – said she went to the lobby when the man headed for the door and she watched him leave. He was driving a white Honda Accord. She said no one else was in the car that she could see. But she didn't see the license plate number because...."

"...There was mud on it," both J.D. and the sheriff said at the same time. Mandie's eyes widened and she nodded again, apparently awed by their detecting skills. Sutton sighed. "Thanks for the information. I'm sure you know not to tell anyone who might ask that we were here?"

She shook her head. "Are you guys cops or something? Undercover or DEA or...?"

"The less you know, the better, Mandie," Sutton said, glancing at J.D. and nodding toward the door. J.D. understood; the sheriff wanted him to check the parking lot for any white Honda

Accords while he took care of the bill. He slipped out the door, wondering if he was going to run into the mysterious man who was looking for them.

It only took a moment to check the parking area. There were less than a dozen vehicles and none were white. The sheriff joined him and they headed for the pickup truck. "Really wish Mike wasn't so fond of red," J.D. muttered as he buckled his seatbelt. "This thing only needs white stripes on it to make it look more like a target."

"I didn't think our unknown friend had any idea what we're driving," the sheriff said, even as he continually scanned the road and checked his mirrors. "But he must and he's clever enough to not be sitting in the parking lot waiting for us. He probably expects us to know we're being followed. Who knows how many clinics he hit, hoping to find us." Sutton went on, "I'm not sure that we should head back to the clinic or not. If our friend is still cruising around and following us, there aren't too many places to lose him in the neighborhood. And the neighborhood alone might clue him in to where RaeLynn is and where we're going."

"You said Rosa told us to give RaeLynn some more time," J.D. said. "If we head back and get behind that wall, there's less of a chance that we'll be spotted. If we try to kill time cruising around town, we're likely to get noticed." Sutton nodded.

"Agreed. We'll head back and...." He stopped, his gaze riveted on his rearview mirror. J.D. checked his side mirror and immediately saw a white sedan about three cars behind them.

"It's a Honda," he confirmed.

"Probably one of several hundred in town," Sutton groused. "Let's see if he's following us." He quickly moved to the left lane and made a left turn at the next light. The white Honda stayed three car lengths behind them. "Can you make out the driver?"

"Not without turning around and I'm not letting him know we're on to him," J.D. said. "What's the plan, Sheriff?"

"As much as I'd like to get a look at him and see who he is, we need to ditch him and get back to the clinic," Sutton said tersely. He knew J.D. was watching the car behind them so he concentrated on finding a way to lose it. "I'm worried about RaeLynn's safety and we need to find out what she can tell us. She might know who this guy is."

"If he's looking for her. He might just be looking for us," J.D. put in.

"Hoping we'll lead him to her. That's why we need to lose him. We can't let that happen. But if he finds out that we know he's following us...."

J.D. nodded as they cruised along at a normal rate of speed. He cursed the lack of traffic that would make it easier for the sheriff to lose the white Honda. He could only hope that Sutton knew Santa Fe better than their mysterious tail did.

Though he wasn't familiar with the city, J.D. sensed that Sutton was leading their tail away from the area around the clinic. Soon they found themselves in the tourist district around the Plaza and the government buildings. Here, the streets were lined with vehicles parked along curbs on narrow streets which were, for the most part, one-way streets with limited parking times. Parking lots – some private, some public – were only partly full. They circled through the streets as the traffic remained steady. "Are you looking for something?" J.D. asked as they drove past the same building for the second time.

"A parking spot along the curb. I'm hoping someone will be pulling out soon...."

J.D. glanced in his side mirror and saw that the white Honda had gotten closer, with only one vehicle between it and their truck. It was clear that the driver thought they were looking for a parking spot because their destination was close by.

The sheriff slowed down and flipped on his right turn signal as a large SUV pulled out of its space along the curb. Quickly he parallel parked and it took only a second for the car behind them to speed up and pass them. "Make like you're getting out and don't look at the Honda," Sutton hissed as he made a show of removing his seatbelt. Peripheral vision gave J.D. a quick glimpse of a face that matched the description Mandie had given them, complete with sunglasses, a face twisted with chagrin and frustration as the line of cars behind his Honda honked their horns, urging him to keep moving. He accelerated and moved forward, signaling a right turn at the next street.

No sooner had the Honda disappeared around the corner, Sutton immediately gassed the truck and shot out into the lane and cut off another motorist whose annoyance turned into gratitude as he slid into the vacated space. Sutton slowed as he reached the street where the Honda had turned and J.D. saw that it was a one way street. No white cars were in sight and the traffic was growing. The sheriff gunned the truck and drove through the intersection, to the next street, and made a left, heading away from the downtown area.

Chapter 13

Corrie had stayed busy after Dee Dee left, though business had slowed down in the campground store as the guests began to settle in for the afternoon and evening. Now that it grew dark by five o'clock, there was little business at the end of the day. It gave Corrie and Jackie time to restock shelves, tidy up the store, and talk.

"You have no idea where in Santa Fe RaeLynn might be," Jackie was saying as she folded and organized a pile of t-shirts that had been disarranged by shoppers earlier in the day. "And even if you did, it wouldn't be a good idea to try to contact her. There's a reason why Rick hasn't given you any information. You could just be making his job harder... and putting RaeLynn in danger. And yourself," she added.

"I know," Corrie said as she restocked the jars of salsa and chile sauce that had sold like crazy after Dee Dee and Deputy Apachito had taken the samples around the campground. "I don't have any intention of asking around blindly, making any phone calls or sending emails or anything that would give a clue to where RaeLynn might be." She straightened the jars so all the labels faced forward and made a mental list of what needed to be reordered. "Besides, it would be a waste of time. They can't give out information on a patient anyway; it's against the law. But I feel better just knowing where she is."

"Hmmm," Jackie said, eyeing Corrie. She turned away, hoping Jackie didn't see the color rise in her face. It was true that she had no intention of calling clinics and hospitals in Santa Fe to find RaeLynn and it wasn't just because she knew she wouldn't get any information.

She already knew where RaeLynn was.

She went to the front counter to write down her order for the product she needed when the front door opened. To her surprise, Officer Charlie White walked in, his dark face pinched with a combination of anger and another emotion that she couldn't quite place. He glanced around, then addressed her without so much as a greeting. "Where are Wilder and the sheriff?"

"Hello, Cousin," she said dryly, hiding her shock at seeing her estranged family member. She had known for months that he was now with the Bonney police department, but he had made it a point to avoid seeing her. Not that she was surprised; her father's side of the family had never made any attempt at mending fences while he was alive. There was no reason to expect things to change now that he was gone. "Long time no see."

His face flushed and now he seemed torn between anger and embarrassment. He gave her a slight nod. "Yeah," he said. "How you doing, Cousin?"

"I'm all right. And you?" She wondered how long she would be able to keep this awkward conversation going. "I heard you had moved to Bonney."

"You heard wrong, Cousin," he muttered. "I just work in Bonney. I still live in Mescalero. With the rest of the family."

Corrie tried to ignore the stab of hurt his words sent through her. "That's quite a commute every day," she said, trying to sound neutral.

"It's not bad. I got friends in town here so I got a place to stay when I need to." Jackie had straightened up from her task and shot Charlie a narrow glare. He jumped slightly when he saw her and muttered a greeting in her direction. "Listen, I need to talk to Wilder. Where is he?" he asked, turning back to Corrie, his earlier urgency becoming more pronounced.

"Maybe you should check the police department," Corrie said. "He's your boss, isn't he? He's just one of my guests."

"Sure he is," Charlie said with a smirk. "Whatever you say, Cousin. But he's nowhere to be found, not at the department, not anywhere in town. Figured he's probably hanging around here, providing security at the sheriff's request."

"I have no idea where Detective Wilder is, nor the sheriff," Corrie said stiffly, folding her arms across her chest. "Whatever rumors you've heard, the fact is Detective Wilder is a friend of mine and a guest here at the campground and has no obligation to report in to me about his whereabouts. He's got a cell phone; why don't you have dispatch call him?"

"He's not answering his phone," Charlie said, his face reddening. "I figure if you call him, he'll be sure to answer."

"Maybe, maybe not," Corrie said, knowing it was the truth. "I don't know where he is or what he's doing. As far as I know, he was on duty today and I'm not going to call him at work just because you can't get hold of him." A sudden chill spiraled down her back. Why wasn't J.D. answering his phone? Especially if one of his officers was trying to get hold of him? Was it possible he was somewhere that had lousy cell phone reception? Surely there was a way to get hold of him in an emergency. "What's the big rush to get hold of him? Did something happen?"

Charlie started to shake his head, then his shoulders sagged. "I really need to talk to him... I'll talk to Rick if I have to...."

"I don't know where he is, either," Corrie interrupted, her heart beginning to pound. A closer look at Charlie told her that something was terribly wrong and he wasn't able to keep it under wraps any longer. "Charlie, what's going on? What's happened?"

"I can't...."

"Oh, for heaven's sake!" Corrie cried, slapping her hands on the counter. "I get enough of that 'I can't tell you because it's police information' baloney from Rick and J.D.! Can you forget you're a cop for five minutes and remember that we actually ARE family? Pretend we're at a feast and gossiping over a bowl of Grandmother's mutton stew and a pile of fry bread! Just talk to me, Charlie!"

He had jumped and stared at her. She knew she probably sounded hysterical. But judging from the look on her cousin's face, it was the best way to get him to talk. He swallowed hard.

"Okay," he said, gesturing with his hands to get her to calm down and lower her voice. "Okay, this is what's going on. Clifford Shaffer showed up at the department about an hour ago, raising hell about police harassment and who knows what all. It took us a minute or two to figure out that his dad was hauled down to the sheriff's department and questioned about RaeLynn's assault. We told him we didn't know anything about it and he threatened to sue all of us – village, county, even state – if we didn't leave him and his family alone. Then he stormed out. Not five minutes later, his brother, Teddy, showed up, looking scared to death and asking if we had arrested Clifford or his dad. Of course, we told him we didn't have anything to do with either of them. Then he said something that kind of seemed weird. He said we should've arrested them. All of 'em. Including him, Teddy. He didn't say why, but he said it would have been better for them all to be in jail." He paused, pulled off his department cap, and ran a hand over his head. "I didn't know what to say or do. I mean, Wilder's the acting chief and Chief LaRue... well, he shows up whenever he wants to anymore, just leaves Wilder to handle things. It's supposed to have been Wilder's day off but it's not like him to be unavailable all day."

"So who's in charge at the police department today?" Corrie asked.

"No one, really. I mean, Ernie Villegas has been there the longest, but he's usually on night patrol. Most everyone is new, except for Duane Jessup. And he's all talk, no idea what he needs to do. He told us to ignore the Shaffers, but he kind of looked shook up." Charlie took a deep breath. "I just know, and I'm sure Rick's told Wilder this, that when Cliff Shaffer goes on a rampage, someone's gonna get hurt. And we got no idea what's going on. Why'd the sheriff pick up Jake? Did he arrest him?"

"I wouldn't think so, unless he had a reason to," Corrie said carefully. The last thing she wanted was for her cousin to find out that she was actually along for the ride when Rick and J.D. picked up Jake Shaffer. "I know they're working on trying to find out what happened to RaeLynn and who was responsible. I'm sure they'll question the Shaffers...."

"If they got the Shaffers riled up, that's probably why they want you to have security around here," Charlie groused. "You're all BFF with RaeLynn, right? Gave her a job here and all, and now they're mad at you for turning her against them."

"Where'd you get that idea?" Corrie asked. She'd never talked to any of her family members about hiring RaeLynn. Of course, the Bonney grapevine was notorious about spreading news faster than a wildfire and everyone in town had connections everywhere. But that didn't explain why everyone would assume she had turned RaeLynn against her family.

Charlie shrugged and waved off her question. "It doesn't matter. Listen, I need to get ahold of Wilder and let him know what's going on and see what he wants to do about it."

"I think I already explained to you, Cousin, that I'm not J.D.'s or Rick's boss," Corrie said, her exasperation tempered with worry and anger. "I can't call them just because you need to get hold of them. And why are you so worried about the Shaffers? The sheriff's department hauled Jake in, not the village police. You told Clifford you had nothing to do about it, so you're off the hook. And anyway, why aren't you talking to Rick's deputies if you're so worried? Deputy Evans is the unofficial undersheriff and everyone knows it. Take your concerns to him and I assure you he'll get in touch with Rick if he feels it's necessary, and J.D. as well. You're wasting time coming here and asking me to do his job."

Charlie's bronzed face had paled and then grew dark. His eyes snapped sparks of fury. He pulled his shoulders back and huffed, "Well, I guess that only proves that you really don't care about your family. Just like your father never did. Grandmother was right."

"This has nothing to do with the family and you know it," Corrie said, her voice quiet and calm though she was trembling with fury. "You're only here because you want something from me and you thought you'd get it just because we share blood. Well, I'm sorry, Cousin, but even if I could tell you and wanted to share that information with you, the truth is I have no idea how to get hold of J.D. or Rick if they won't answer their own dispatchers. They are, first and foremost, law enforcement officers; they're on duty whether they're on the clock or not. You, as a law enforcement officer yourself, should understand that better than anyone in the family. And if they aren't answering their phones, it's because they have more pressing matters to attend to." Corrie had seen her father's attempts at reconnecting with his family met with cold shoulders so many times over the years that she wasn't easily swayed by family connections. She'd learned to make her own family from people that didn't share blood with her but who shared their hearts.

She was willing to do whatever she could to keep RaeLynn, along with J.D. and Rick, safe from the Shaffer family. Even if it meant harming whatever little was left of her relationship with her cousin. She took a deep breath. "I've always cared about my family, Charlie, even if none of you feel the same about me. If you want something from me, you can always ask. But don't use the word 'family' like a secret code to get something you want and then turn your back on me the rest of the time."

Charlie's face had undergone dramatic color changes, from white-hot fury to cherry-red embarrassment to purple rage. "I need to get back to work. I guess there's nothing else to say." He wheeled around and headed for the door.

"Yes, there is," Corrie said as she walked around the front of the counter. He stopped and turned, then eyed her warily. "Thanksgiving dinner is at two o'clock if you want to join us. And anyone else in the family as well. I know you all probably already have dinner plans, but there's always room at the table and plenty of food. Feel free to stop by."

He said nothing and Corrie looked at him steadily. He managed to keep eye contact with her for a full minute, then he shrugged and looked away. "Just be careful, Cousin," he said, his voice husky. "Sometimes the wrong people get hurt when certain people get angry." He left before Corrie could respond.

Jackie moved up toward the counter, worry puckering her forehead. "What do you suppose he meant by that?" she asked.

"I'm not sure," Corrie said, keeping her voice steady. "But maybe I will try to call both J.D. and Rick and let them know Charlie's trying to get hold of them."

"Even though, according to what you just told Officer White, they might not necessarily answer just because it's you?" Jackie raised a brow and Corrie gave her a grim smile.

"They just might if I keep blowing their phones up."

The trip back to the clinic proved uneventful, even as J.D. kept a sharp eye out for the white Honda. The streets around the clinic were busier than they had been earlier, but they were able to pull into the clinic parking area without any sign of being followed.

They entered the lobby and this time the receptionist stood up to meet them, visibly agitated. "Sheriff, Detective, I'm so glad you came back so soon," she began, apprehension clouding her features.

"Is there a problem, ma'am?" Sutton inquired and J.D. bit back a smile at the sheriff's innocent question. They had agreed not to say anything about knowing they were being followed, not only to keep certain people from getting into trouble but also to find out just how much information they would get.

The receptionist clasped her hands, her previous calm, professional demeanor nowhere in evidence. "Not long after you left, a man stopped by, asking if you'd been here and who you had come to see." She went on to tell them almost exactly word-for-word what Mandie had told them. Sutton exchanged a glance with J.D.

"And of course, you didn't tell him about our being here or who we came to see," he said.

"No, of course not, Sheriff!" she said, clearly shocked at the idea. "That's completely against our policy and against HIPAA regulations!" she added.

"Was anyone else here who might have overheard the conversation?" Sutton went on. Again she shook her head vehemently.

"No, no, there was no one here. There had been visitors here waiting to see a patient when you left, but they had already gone in to the back before this man showed up!"

"I mean," Sutton said. "Anyone who works here? Like...." He glanced in the direction of the security guard who still manned his post by the door leading into the clinic.

"Oh!" The receptionist frowned. "Well, no, I don't think... wait, besides Jimmy," she said, nodding toward the security guard, "one of the nurses was up here. Ellie. Eleanor Price. She had come up to see how many other visitors were scheduled to come in today."

"And she was here when the man asked about us? She heard that conversation?" J.D. broke in. He could sense the sheriff's tension, though it was unlikely that the receptionist could tell there was anything wrong. She was nodding.

"Yes, she had just come in, she hadn't even had time to ask me about visitors before the man came in." She stopped and pursed her lips. "She never said a word the whole time the man was here, but she did sort of gasp when she heard his question. I don't think he noticed. He kept asking if I was sure I couldn't give him information. I told him that I couldn't tell him anything and, since he didn't have an appointment, he had to leave or I would have security escort him out. Jimmy came over to the desk to see if I needed help but the man backed off and left."

"And the nurse? What did she do?" J.D. asked. The sheriff still said nothing, but his eyes were like ice. A chill seemed to have settled in the room.

"Well, after he went out the door, she went to the window in the waiting room," the receptionist said, pointing toward the area to the right of the door. "I imagine she looked to see if the man had really left, you know, wasn't hanging around outside to wait for anyone. Then she came back and asked about any further visitors. I told her that you and Sheriff Sutton were the only other ones scheduled to come back this afternoon, though I understand that Rosa had said it would be later than this...."

"You didn't discuss this man with the nurse... or the security guard?" J.D. asked, trying to keep his tone casual. He was itching to ask about Ellie's behavior after the man had left, but didn't want to create problems for the young nurse or alarm the woman in front of him. The receptionist shook her head.

"No, I didn't. He really didn't seem to be a threat, he didn't become belligerent or anything like that. He was quite pleasant, even if he did try to insist I give him information." Her face reddened slightly. "I have to be honest. Something about the man and his questions were unnerving. I don't understand why he would come here to ask about you or a specific patient...."

"How did he get past the gate?" the sheriff asked suddenly. The receptionist jumped. He moved forward, his gaze intense.

"We had to be buzzed in at the gate. I had to provide a security code. This isn't the kind of place where anyone can just walk in. There's no way to tell what this place is from the outside. How did he even get into the parking lot, let alone the building?"

The woman's mouth opened and closed but no sound came out. She blinked and then she blushed. "Honestly, Sheriff," she said. "I... it never occurred to me to ask that. I had just gotten off the phone with Rosa about your visit...." Her voice trailed away and she shook her head.

"Is it possible that they followed another visitor through the gate?" J.D. asked. He could have kicked himself for not realizing the incongruity of the man being able to get into the clinic. The receptionist shook her head.

"No, Detective, there were no other visitors I had buzzed in...."

"Could someone else in the clinic have buzzed him in?" Sutton's question was stone cold, like the expression on his face. "Would you have been aware of it, if they had?"

She started to shake her head, then her brow cleared. "The only other person who can buzz someone in is the doctor on duty...."

"Pruett?" Both J.D. and the sheriff said. The receptionist nodded, but she looked uneasy.

"I can't imagine why he wouldn't tell me though. He knows I have to check their identification and verify their appointment."

"I'd like to speak to Dr. Pruett, please," Sutton said, his voice deceptively calm. The receptionist nodded eagerly and waved them to the door as she picked up her phone to notify the doctor that he had visitors.

"Absolutely not, Sheriff! I did not authorize anyone to come through the gate today, nor did anyone else. I'm the only doctor on duty here today and the only one who...."

"I get that, Doctor," Rick said, not bothering to keep the steel thread of anger out of his voice. "But someone did and we need to know who it was."

Dr. Pruett had not appreciated their sudden appearance as he was wolfing down a late lunch. Jimmy, the security guard, had knocked once on the doctor's door, mumbled an apology to the doctor, and retreated quickly after letting Rick and Wilder into the clinic area. They hadn't bothered to knock on the doctor's partially opened door, just pushed it open all the way and walked into his office. Wilder made it a point to close it firmly behind them.

The doctor had shot a nervous glance at the door then at the two angry lawmen in front of him. "I don't understand what's going on. You're telling me someone got into the clinic as far as the reception desk without authorization? And they were looking for you and Detective Wilder?"

"And trying to find out who we were here to see," Rick added. He rested his palms on the desk and leaned toward the doctor who was still seated with his half-eaten ham sandwich in front of him. "Look, Dr. Pruett, I understand your consternation, but this indicates a breach in your clinic's security. The safety and well-being, not to mention the privacy, of your patients could be compromised. Detective Wilder and I need to know who might have had a reason to allow an unauthorized person into the building. I know we don't have jurisdiction here and I would rather not get local law enforcement involved, especially since there hasn't really been a crime committed and it will only serve to cause bad publicity and reflect unfavorably on you." He paused a moment to let his words sink in and Dr. Pruett blanched. "Just tell us how you would have buzzed in a visitor and how someone else might have done it."

Pruett rubbed a hand over his face and sighed. He spun his oversized desktop monitor around for them to see. Wilder left his post at the door and came over to look as well. Pruett pointed to a small window in the upper right hand corner of the screen. "That's the feed from the security cameras on the grounds," he said. "It changes according to movement detected in the area that's being filmed. If someone pulls up to the gate, it triggers the camera to zoom in on the driver." He pointed to the phone on his desk. "You have to punch in a code to get an outside line on this phone. The other buttons are intercoms for the gate, the front desk, and the nurses' station." He paused and Rick exchanged a glance with Wilder.

"And this is the only way someone back here could have buzzed in a visitor?" he asked.

"Yes," came the doctor's terse reply.

"No other screens or intercoms?"

"No."

After a few seconds, Wilder spoke up. "How long were you gone from your office, Doctor?"

The way the man's face went from sickly white to brick red in the blink of an eye almost made Rick call for medical assistance. The doctor choked out, "I left some files in my car, okay? I needed them for a meeting I had with the family of one of the patients. I told the nurses...."

"Which ones?" Rick snapped.

Pruett jerked his head in the direction of the nurses station. "Rosa and Ellie. The others were tending to patients. I just wanted someone to know where I was in case I was needed. I was coming right back to my office. I never left the grounds of the facility."

"You didn't tell the receptionist or any of the security guards?" Wilder asked.

"There was no need to," Pruett said curtly. "I was gone for only a few minutes, ten at the most. The staff parking is in the back of the building, away from the front gates."

"Could someone have looked out a window and seen you going to your car?" Rick asked.

Pruett's face had returned to some semblance of normalcy. He shrugged. "Maybe. Those are all patient rooms facing the staff parking lot. Sure, a patient may have looked out the window and saw me going to my car, but they wouldn't have known to come to my office to buzz someone in. And they don't have phones in their rooms, either," he added quickly. "Nor are they allowed personal cell phones for the duration of their stay."

"I'm aware of that, Doctor," Rick said before he could stop himself. He sensed, rather than saw, Wilder give him a sideways glance. He wasn't sure if he succeeded in fighting the rush of red to his face. "So if you didn't buzz in this particular guest, the only other possibility is someone on the staff who was aware of you being away from your office at that time."

"I don't want to accuse anyone...."

"You're not," Rick said brusquely. He knew that what they were about to do was going to stir up even more questions in Wilder's mind than there already were. He just hoped that he could put them off until they were headed home.

Good thing it was a four hour drive.

Chapter 14

"What's your plan?" J.D. asked as they left Dr. Pruett's office.

They were making their way down the hall to the nurse's station and he could see the sheriff chewing his lower lip furiously. J.D. felt as if he were stuck in the middle of a puzzle with no clues on how to proceed. The sheriff stopped abruptly and J.D. almost walked past him.

"I need you to question Nurse Price," he said. "I'll talk to Rosa, the other nurse. Maybe they weren't the ones who buzzed in our mysterious friend, but they might have seen someone near Pruett's office who might have."

J.D. nodded. Deep down, he doubted there was anyone else on the staff, like maintenance, who would know about the security set up in Pruett's office. However, he understood that Sutton didn't want to antagonize the nurses and create a hostile environment for RaeLynn. He was intrigued by all the hints that there was a lot more to Sutton's knowledge about this clinic that he wasn't divulging. There were cracks in the normally cool veneer that J.D. had come to accept as part of the sheriff's overall personality. While people who didn't know Rick Sutton personally might not be aware of it, the man was under a lot of stress and J.D. wasn't sure exactly what was causing it. He cleared his throat. "What about the security around RaeLynn's room? Surely they have to be familiar with the clinic's security measures?"

"I'll check into that, too. But I'd take it as a personal favor if you'd talk to Nurse Price yourself." Sutton surprised J.D. by keeping his eyes averted. Not once in all the months that J.D. had known and worked with the man had he not been able to keep eye contact with him.

"You planning on telling me just what's going on?" J.D. failed to keep the bafflement out of his voice. Sutton even flinched and then his dark gaze fastened on J.D.

"Yeah, but I can't right now. Just trust me on this. I need you to have my back."

"You know I do," J.D. said. He shook his head. "You sure I don't need to know anything before I talk to Nurse Price?"

The sheriff's response was to stand straighter and look directly into J.D.'s eyes. "Two things. I've never lied to you and there have only been two women in my life. And you know who they both are. Now let's get to work. We're burning daylight and it's a long drive home."

Their initial request to speak privately to the two nurses was met with immediate suspicion. Rosa's, however, was directed at Nurse Price. She shot the younger woman a sharp glance as she reluctantly left her station to talk to the sheriff.

Eleanor Price had been unable to hide the "deer in the headlights" look that immediately came to her face when the sheriff made his request. Her apprehension diminished slightly when she saw that it was J.D. who would be speaking to her, but her face still burned a bright red. "What can I help you with, Detective?" she mumbled, glancing back to where Rosa and Sutton were standing in a remote section of the corridor, speaking in quiet tones.

J.D. caught the eye of one of the two security guards on either side of RaeLynn's door and motioned for him to approach. The man did, raising an eyebrow. J.D. flashed his badge at the man and then pointed into an empty conference room with a window in the door. "I need to speak to the nurse privately, but I want to make sure I have a witness that there isn't any impropriety. You can still watch the patient's door from here." The man nodded and J.D. opened the door, gesturing for Ellie to go in first. She glanced back to where Rosa and Sutton were talking, with Rosa's dramatic gesturing taking the place of raising her voice, and went in.

Her unease seemed to increase again as she went into the room. She stepped around the table, keeping it between her and J.D. "Yes, Detective?" she asked, a slight tremor in her voice.

He said nothing for several seconds, studying her closely and weighing how to ask his questions. She was doing her best not to fidget, trying to maintain a professional demeanor, though her hands were thrust into the pockets of her scrubs and she shifted her weight from one foot to the other. He decided to give her no chance to try to lie and he had to make it seem like he was her ally. "What made you call your sister about that man who stopped by?"

Her eyes grew round. She swallowed hard but before she could say anything, J.D. spoke up. "She told us you called her, to warn us that we were being followed, so let's not waste time playing games, Ms. Price. You had to know she'd tell us how she got that information anyhow. And I'm not really concerned about how you knew where to find us, either. I just want to know why you bothered to warn us and what you can tell me about that man."

"I don't know who he is," she blurted, her face growing pale. "I just know he's never been here before. I didn't say a word to him!"

"The receptionist said you gasped when he asked about us," J.D. said, allowing a sliver of ice in his voice. "I'm sure that's all he needed to hear to find out he'd guessed right about our being here." He paused. "Did he mention Miss Shaffer's name?"

"No," Eleanor Price said, shaking her head for emphasis. "He just asked about you and the sheriff. He asked if you had been here and who you had come to see. No one else's name was mentioned." She clasped her hands in front of her and words came spilling out. "He was fairly well-dressed, his coat and slacks were neat and clean, his shoes and his sunglasses were expensive brands. He wasn't some seedy derelict. I think he wore that cap just to hide his hair color, or whether or not he had hair... it was pulled down well over his ears. He had a goatee and a mustache but they were short. He didn't wear any jewelry. I mean, he didn't have any piercings that I could see. He might have had a watch or ring, but he kept his hands in his pockets except when he came in and left and he had to open the door. Overall, he was very well-groomed." She was breathing hard, her eyes swimming with tears. "I swear, Detective, I never said a word to him and he never gave any hint that he heard me gasp! I didn't do anything wrong!"

J.D. held up a hand. "Nurse, I appreciate all the information you've given me and I have to say it's more than I expected," he said. "But why would you think the sheriff and I would think you've done something wrong? We were told you were up front when he arrived and your sister told us you'd called...." He stopped when she let out a short, despairing laugh.

"I'm not stupid, Detective Wilder," she said, wiping at her eyes. "I saw the way the sheriff looked at me when he took Rosa aside to talk to her. I'm surprised he didn't want to talk to me himself. He'll probably never forgive or forget...." She stopped and pressed her lips together. "I'm sure you know what I'm talking about. So I don't know how to convince you I had nothing to do with that man following you. I tried to help you. That's all I'm going to say." She folded her arms across her chest and glared at J.D. defiantly.

He met her gaze steadily, though he was baffled. And growing irritated. He couldn't wait to get his hands on the sheriff and find out what it was that everyone else but he seemed to know. Eleanor Price had answers that he needed and he wasn't about to let her stonewall him any longer. "Look, Nurse, this isn't personal, no matter what you think. This is more than a possible breach of a patient's privacy; it's a matter of the facility's security. Someone buzzed in an unauthorized person and that person was looking for the sheriff and me. We don't know who that person was nor why he was looking for us, but he had no business being here. He didn't have an appointment, he didn't have authorization from the doctor, and he shouldn't have made it through the gate, much less all the way to the reception desk. Dr. Pruett said he didn't let him in, but someone might have used his office to allow this person into the facility. Are you sure you don't know who that might be? Did you see anyone near the doctor's office? You were on your way to the front desk when that person arrived. Is it possible that you saw someone, whether they had a reason to be around the doctor's office or not? Anyone at all?"

"I told you...."

"Absolutely nothing!" J.D. snapped, his patience at an end. He had been leaning across the table, but now he straightened up. "You've told me absolutely nothing and that's what's making me suspicious. You were out there," he said, jerking his head in the direction of the reception area, "when this man showed up. Supposedly you went to find out if there were more visitors scheduled. You couldn't pick up the phone and call the receptionist to ask her? You don't have a list of scheduled visitors at the nurse's station? You couldn't ask Dr. Pruett himself?" He had raised his voice and the nurse was wilting under his withering tirade, biting her lip and blinking back tears. He told himself to calm down before he crossed a line that might cost him his job and possibly RaeLynn her safety. He stepped back and took a deep breath. He saw the security guard peering through the window and raising a curious eyebrow at the commotion. He nodded at the man, who glanced at the nurse. She looked toward the door as well and gave him the tiniest nod. The security guard turned back around and J.D. addressed Nurse Price. "What are you so afraid of telling me?" he asked in a low voice.

Her head jerked up and she swiped a hand across her cheeks. Her eyes narrowed with anger and helplessness. "I need my job, Detective," she hissed. "You have no idea...."

"You're right, so clue me in," he said with a sigh. He folded his arms across his chest and leaned against the wall. He managed a nonchalant shrug. "You're under the impression that I know something about you that is apparently very incriminating and it's distressing you. Well, for what it's worth, I don't. I know nothing about you. I only know that, right at this minute, the way you've been acting would certainly put you at the top of a suspects' list if an actual crime had been committed. Technically, this man was trespassing, which is a crime, but not one that would get you, as an accomplice, arrested. Maybe fired from your job, but not arrested. You've already said you need your job and I'm not here to try to make you lose it. I want information. And if the information you give me jeopardizes your job, then if it helps me in solving my case, I'll do my best to make sure you're not penalized for it. Can you work with me, please?"

Her breathing had slowed and her tears had dried up. She bit her lip. "It's not that easy."

"It never is," J.D. responded, managing to keep the sarcasm out of his tone.

She shook her head. "I'm a nobody around here, Detective. I keep my job by keeping my head down and just doing what I'm supposed to do. I stay out of everyone else's business. And I wish they'd stay out of mine."

"If somebody's 'business' allows an unauthorized person into the clinic, compromising the clinic's security and the safety of the patients, Miss Price, then their business has become yours." He kept his voice low but she flinched as if he were shouting. "What did you see?"

"No one will believe me."

"Try me."

She sighed. "I might as well. Then I'll start updating my resume. Not that fast food joints care about my years as a health care worker, but that's all I'll ever be able to find in this town."

"Miss Price?" His politely spoken words didn't mask his impatience. She straightened up.

"Okay, Detective, here's what happened," she said. "After you and Rick left, Rosa had a brief meeting with the nursing staff, telling us that, even though we were cooperating with you two, you had no jurisdiction here and we were merely extending a courtesy. She also told us that it wasn't necessary for us to volunteer any information, just answer questions you asked us, and keep our opinions to ourselves. And she told us to mind our own business about this whole thing and keep quiet about what we hear and see." She drew a deep breath. "I was going to Dr. Pruett's office to escort the next group of visitors that were here to see a patient, just like I did with you. But before I got to his door, I saw Rosa come out of his office."

"Rosa never goes to Dr. Pruett's office?" J.D. asked, raising a brow.

"Well, yes, but you've met her," Nurse Price said with a grimace. "She always acts like she owns the place, or at least runs it. She makes it seem like even the doctors do things HER way. So when I saw her coming out of the doctor's office, it seemed odd that she just didn't fling the door open and walk out." Her face paled and she swallowed hard. "I saw the door open just a crack and someone looked out, toward the door to the reception lobby. Then I saw Rosa slip out and shut the door quietly, look around again, then she headed back to the nurse's station."

"She didn't see you?" J.D. asked incredulously. Eleanor Price's face flushed red again.

"No. When I saw the doctor's office door open and Rosa acting so sneaky, I... I slipped into the restroom just down hall," she said, waving a hand in the general direction. "I kept the door cracked open and watched. I told myself I'd have to make sure it looked like I had just stopped in on my way to the front, to wash my hands, before I brought back the visitors, in case she saw me and asked what I was doing. But she just kept going back to the nurse's station. I assume she never saw me."

"So the visitors must not have been in Dr. Pruett's office then?" J.D. asked.

Nurse Price shook her head. "No, they weren't. Neither was Dr. Pruett. It turned out that he had escorted them to the patient they were visiting, himself."

"Is that unusual?" J.D. asked.

"Well, it's not unheard of," she admitted. "Sometimes, we get a visitor who can't handle the truth about their loved one's condition. In spite of the comfortable and non-clinical atmosphere of the clinic, it's still a place to treat people who have substance abuse issues. And because it's a very exclusive type of clinic, many of the patients and their families don't like to admit that a loved one has 'that' kind of problem," she said dryly, making air quotes. "In those cases, the doctor on duty will escort the family so as to answer questions and explain things. Because apparently a nurse's word is never as trustworthy as a doctor's," she added bitterly.

"So Dr. Pruett wasn't in his office when Rosa went in there," J.D. said, trying to keep the nurse focused on his investigation. It was obvious there were several underlying issues regarding her employment and her relationship with the clinic staff... among other things. But he didn't have time to delve into it at the moment and he didn't want to give the impression that he could be swayed by emotional appeals.

She shrugged. "No. I went back to the nurse's station and Rosa confirmed that Dr. Pruett had taken the visitors himself."

"How did she seem when you asked her?"

Nurse Price was quiet for a few seconds, frowning. "The usual. But at first, she seemed... I don't know. Startled, maybe? She asked me where I had been. I told her I had stopped at the restroom on my way to escort the visitors. She didn't ask me anything else, so I assume she thought I hadn't seen her."

J.D.'s mind was racing. Was Rosa hiding something? Or was Nurse Price? What about Dr. Pruett? "When did you go up front to check for new visitors?"

"Right after I got back to the nurse's station. Rosa sent me to go see. And before you ask," she said, holding up a hand, "yes, we have a list, and yes, Rosa could have called to ask if there were any more visitors scheduled. But it wasn't my place to tell her that, so I just did as she said. That's why I happened to be up front when that man was here." She dug her hands into the pockets of her scrubs and took a deep breath. "Look, Detective, I know you couldn't care less about the fact that my career is pretty much over as of the minute you started asking questions. So I have no reason to not tell you everything I know. And I have. So are we done here?"

She looked resigned, exhausted, her eyes haunted. She seemed to be staring at nothing and a trembling hand brushed a lock of her hair out of her face. And yet, J.D. couldn't help himself. "I have one more question."

"Go ahead," she sighed, slumping against the table.

"Why did you refer to the sheriff by his first name?"

She jumped and sucked in her breath sharply. She grabbed the back of the chair in front of her to steady herself. "What?"

"You heard me," J.D. said, disguising his astonishment at her reaction. "All of a sudden, in the middle of your story, you called him 'Rick'. I don't even call him by his first name and I work with him. Care to comment on that?"

"I... You... I thought you knew...," she stammered. J.D. kept quiet, just raised an eyebrow. She stared at him. "You don't know," she said, her voice hardly more than a whisper.

"Surprise," J.D. said dryly. She drew a deep breath.

"I thought everyone knew. I thought that was the reason you were questioning me."

"You thought wrong on the first count, but you're absolutely correct on the second one. Now, would you please tell me what it is everybody seems to think I know?"

She sighed. "All right, Detective," Eleanor Price said. "I'm just not sure where to begin."

"Let's start with how you happen to know Rick Sutton."

Nurse Price shook her head. "I should think that would be fairly obvious, Detective Wilder. He was a resident here for a while."

"By 'resident' you mean 'patient', am I correct?" J.D. said, heroically managing to hide his shock at his suspicions being confirmed. The nurse nodded. "How long ago was this?"

"About five years ago. I'm sure you know why. He'd had some emotional trauma in his life that led him to engage in behavior that ultimately required him to come here for treatment."

J.D. was well aware of the "emotional trauma" that Nurse Price was referring to, and it was clear she thought that he knew the sheriff much better than he was letting on. He saw no reason to correct her impression. "How long was he here?" he asked, half expecting the nurse to tell him that such information was off-limits for her to discuss.

To his surprise, she went on. "Six weeks. That's the minimum amount of time any of our residents spend here. He had checked himself in; a lot of our patients are brought here by family members. They usually take much more time for treatment. I would say the fact that he accepted that he had a problem and really wanted to recover was the main reason he wasn't here longer."

"And what exactly was that problem?" J.D. was sure he knew, but he wanted to hear it from her and Nurse Price didn't mince words.

"Alcoholism. As you know, he'd had a few shocks in his life… losing a child and having his wife walk out on him. If I recall correctly, he started drinking to cope with the losses. It hadn't been a life-long thing with him. When he realized he was losing control of his life and his law enforcement career was in jeopardy, he took steps to get things under control."

J.D. wondered if he was going to regret this foray into the sheriff's personal life, but it occurred to him that Sutton knew this would come up. What Nurse Price was telling him cleared up a lot of questions J.D. had... and created many more. He knew that there was more to the story than what he'd already heard. "So you were here at that time. He was under your care."

"Yes," she said. "Not that he needed much medical attention. Once he got over the first couple weeks of withdrawal, his overall health was excellent. His addiction hadn't started creating the physical problems many alcoholics are prone to. His stay here was a focused effort to stop his addiction before it got completely out of hand. He spent a lot of time in counseling."

"So what, exactly, did your care of him entail?" J.D. wasn't sure where that question had come from, but nothing Eleanor Price was telling him was adding up. The color rose in her face. "If he didn't need to have his health monitored so closely...."

"He did while he was drying out," she said brusquely. "It was a hard time for him. Quitting cold turkey can create a lot of medical problems. His weren't as severe as those of a person who had been drinking for years and years, but still, he did have to be monitored."

J.D. decided to take a chance. "And you became very close to him."

Her eyes hardened. "It's not what you're thinking."

"What am I thinking?"

"That Rick – I mean, Sheriff Sutton – and I had a relationship of some kind."

J.D. thought about what the sheriff had said before sending J.D. to interview Nurse Price. He watched the young woman's face closely. "And?"

She drew in a sharp breath. "Of course not! That would have been completely unprofessional and... and wrong... and...."

"And good cause for termination from your job," J.D. interjected. She started to protest and J.D. held up a hand. "But you still have your job, so apparently that wasn't the case. I'm sure the clinic would have thoroughly investigated any claims of impropriety between the staff and residents." He folded his arms across his chest. "But there WAS an investigation."

She blew out her breath. "After a certain point, some residents are allowed to check themselves out for a few hours. It usually comes toward the end of their treatment. They can leave the clinic to go out to eat or to a movie or anything they want, as long as they're not exposing themselves to any temptation to fall off the wagon. So, no bars or clubs, or any place that might entice them to drink."

"The Pantry serves alcohol."

It was incredible to think that her face could have gotten any redder. "The state of New Mexico prohibits alcohol sales before noon on Sundays. We went for breakfast," she choked out.

"So you DID fraternize with a resident."

"It was completely harmless!" she snapped. "I felt sorry for him! He was getting antsy, wanting to get back home and go back to work and worrying if his career was going to be ruined by his time here! And what was he going back to? His wife was gone, his child was gone. I was just trying to cheer him up!"

"But your supervisors here at the clinic didn't think so?"

Her eyes grew frostier. "I think we're done talking here, Detective. I've told you what you needed to know in relation to your current investigation. Everything else I've told you is already over and done with."

J.D. inclined his head. "Thank you for your time, Nurse Price. If I have any further questions, I'm sure you won't mind answering them."

Her eyes narrowed but she didn't answer beyond giving him a tight-lipped nod. He gestured for her to leave the room before him.

She brushed past him and yanked the door open. Rick Sutton stood outside the door with a grim look on his face.

Chapter 15

Rick managed to mask his surprise when Ellie Price nearly walked right into him. One look at her shocked face, streaked with the snail-tracks of her tears, made him glad that Rosa had been called to check on a patient. The older nurse had made it clear that she didn't appreciate the disruption in the clinic's routine and she wasn't shy about voicing her opinion about who to blame for it. "It's not the first time there's been a breach in protocol here, Sheriff, and you, of all people, should know who is responsible for it!" she had snapped.

Ellie's eyes had widened at the sight of him and it was an obvious struggle for her to keep her composure. She mumbled an apology and swiftly went down the hall to the restroom to pull herself together. Rick glanced at Wilder as he exited the room, dismissing the security guard at the door with a nod. "I guess you didn't have much luck?" he asked. Wilder raised a brow.

"What makes you say that? Did you have any luck?"

Rick sighed. "Lately, most of my luck seems to be bad. I'm going to venture a wild guess. Nurse Price saw Rosa come out of Dr. Pruett's office, correct?"

If Wilder was surprised at Rick's guess, he hid it well. "In a rather suspicious fashion," Wilder said. He filled Rick in on his interview with Ellie although Rick was certain he wasn't hearing everything that was said in the conference room. "All right, your turn. I'm guessing Rosa is claiming she saw Nurse Price coming out of Dr. Pruett's office?" Wilder said.

Rick realized he was chewing his lower lip and stopped. He shook his head. "No, but she made it a point to state repeatedly that Nurse Price shouldn't be considered a reliable witness and that she has a history of skirting clinic policies which should have resulted in her termination a long time ago. It took me a while to get her to back to what I wanted to talk to her about. She says she hasn't seen anyone near Dr. Pruett's office who shouldn't have been there and that she hadn't gone down there herself."

"Interesting," Wilder said, raising a brow. "Do you believe Nurse Price saw her come out of Pruett's office?"

Rick didn't hesitate, even though he knew it was going to create even more questions in Wilder's mind... and more problems for himself. "Yes, I do. Why would she make up a story like that? With her history, it would only create more problems for herself, invite scrutiny of her past, and arouse suspicion. All she had to say was that she hadn't seen anything and that would have been the end of it. She knows she'll be in trouble if Rosa finds out what she told you."

Wilder nodded. "She's a lousy liar. I could tell she was hiding something. Unlike other people," he deadpanned, looking Rick dead in the eye. Rick tried not to flinch, but Wilder's eyes were like a hailstorm of bullets, drilling into him. "So now what?"

Rick was relieved to change the subject. He jerked his head in the direction of RaeLynn's room. "Rosa told me that RaeLynn is ready to receive visitors. Maybe if we back off the nurses a little, they might be ready to give us some more information the next time we talk to them. And maybe RaeLynn might have an idea who's been following us." Wilder said nothing, just nodded, but his piercing gray eyes seemed to pin Rick in place. Rick glanced at his watch and grimaced. "We're going to be getting home pretty late tonight. Sorry about that, Detective. I was hoping we'd have gotten a little more information by now."

"Funny you should say that," Wilder said dryly. "Maybe sharing some information on the way home will help pass the time and keep us awake."

Rick said nothing, but he met Wilder's gaze directly. Then he gave a brief nod before turning toward RaeLynn's room, Wilder right behind him.

Officer Debbie Yellowcloud still stood outside RaeLynn's room as they approached. A quick glance up and down the corridor didn't reveal any chairs or other seating and J.D. wondered if she ever took a break. As if in response, the young woman shook her head.

"I go off duty in about thirty minutes," she said. She indicated the two security guards on either side of the door. "They rotate out every four hours with two other guys. You'll be able to meet my relief before you go."

"Is Miss Shaffer awake, Officer?" the sheriff asked, getting right to the point. She gave him a quick, appraising look.

"She is. She's bathed and dressed and a good deal calmer than she was earlier. Rosa said you were back to see her." She must have decided that reminding them that they could call her by her first name was an exercise in futility. Her no-nonsense tone matched the sheriff's. "You can go in now," she added, reaching for the doorknob.

To J.D.'s surprise, Sutton shook his head. "Officer Yellowcloud, before we go in to see Miss Shaffer, there are a few questions I'd like to ask you. All of you," he added, glancing at the two security guards. They exchanged looks then turned to Officer Yellowcloud, as if asking her if she had objections. She frowned.

"This have to do with a supposed security breach earlier?" she asked.

"Were you questioned about it?" J.D. asked before the sheriff could respond.

"I wouldn't say 'questioned', Officer Yellowcloud said, forming air quotes. "At least I wasn't." The two guards shook their heads. She went on, "But I heard there was some concern about an unauthorized person entering the building. There was some snapping among the nurses and the doctor, about how it could have happened or whose responsibility it was. The poor maintenance people got some flak, but it was obvious they had no idea what was going on."

"But none of you were questioned at all?" J.D. asked, perplexed. The security guard who had stood outside the conference room while J.D. talked to Nurse Price spoke up.

"Detective, we were just told to make sure we stayed vigilant, that we didn't leave our posts for any reason. No one really explained why and it's really not our place to ask. The only thing we were asked," he went on, indicating the other guard and himself, "was if we had talked about our assignment to anyone. Which, of course, we hadn't," he said, shaking his head for emphasis. "That is strictly against our company policy. We don't discuss our assignments or even who we're partnered with. Not with our families or even our own coworkers," he said. He nodded to the other man. "We didn't know we'd be working this together, we don't know who our relief is going to be until they show up."

"Doesn't that open up the possibility of a security breach within your company?" Sutton asked. The man shook his head.

"Not really, Sheriff. Assignments of this level," he said, indicating the door to RaeLynn's room, "are never given to newer hires. We've both been with the company for over ten years. I have to assume that the guys who are relieving us have also been with the company for a long time as well. I guarantee they won't be strangers to us."

Officer Yellowcloud had been following the conversation closely. She tugged at her ponytail and cleared her throat. "For what it's worth, Sheriff, Detective," she said, nodding at them, "We were familiarized with the security measures already in place here in the clinic. Cameras and such. But we don't really know who has access to them."

"So you know the location of security cameras on the grounds?" J.D. asked.

"On the grounds and in the clinic itself," she said, jerking her head toward the ceiling above RaeLynn's door. J.D. could barely see a slit in the ceiling tiles that resembled a vent. "They're all over the place," Debbie Yellowcloud said. J.D. exchanged a glance with the sheriff.

"So there are cameras all over the inside of the clinic?" Sutton said.

"Yeah. You didn't know that?" the young officer said, her eyes widening.

"No," J.D. answered. He shook his head. "Do you know where they monitor the camera feed from inside the clinic?"

"No. We only know that the feed from the outside camera that monitors the front gate goes directly into the doctor's office. I'm not sure where the security room is."

"Thanks, Debbie," Sutton said. "We'll go in to see RaeLynn now."

"Sure," she said, eyeing the sheriff curiously. She rapped on the door and poked her head in. "Ready for some guests?" she asked. She stepped back and held the door open for J.D. and the sheriff. "I'll shut the door. If anyone else needs to go in, they'll knock before they enter."

Sutton nodded and led the way into RaeLynn's room. This time, the curtain was open and RaeLynn was sitting up. Her bruises were still stark against her pale skin, but her eyes were clearer than they were and her hair, though damp, curled softly around her face and shoulders. She managed a trembling smile. "Hi," she said in a raspy whisper.

"Hi, again," Sutton said, removing his Stetson and sitting in one of the two chairs beside the bed. J.D. nodded to her, but opted to remain standing at the foot of the bed. "I hope we didn't stress you out too much earlier when we stopped by."

She shook her head. "No, I was just surprised to see you."

"Do you know where you are?" he asked.

She nodded slowly. "Yes, Rosa – the nurse – told me. I don't know why I'm here, in Santa Fe, instead of Bonney."

"Don't you?" J.D. said. She looked at him, but her usual wariness was absent.

"Yes, I guess I do know," she said. She folded her hands in her lap, careful of the IV and the other tubes and wires attached to her. "You're trying to make sure no one finds me and... hurts me. Again." She drew a deep shaky breath. "Thank you."

"You don't have to thank us, RaeLynn," the sheriff said gruffly. He cleared his throat. "I'm sorry to have to do this, but we have some questions to ask you."

"I know," she said, a hitch in her voice. "I wish I had answers for you."

"We haven't asked the questions yet," J.D. said. She gave a shrug.

"It's not difficult to figure out. You want to know where I've been, who took me, who hurt me, and why. And the truth is, I don't know. Everyone probably thinks I do, because of my brother, Cliff, and him wanting me to get the money to bail my dad out of jail. But it wasn't Cliff. It wasn't anyone I know."

"Tell us what happened, RaeLynn," Sutton said. "Tell us everything you remember."

Her brow furrowed and her gaze grew distant. "It's hazy and all jumbled and confused. I mean, I remember leaving the campground store the night of the fiesta. Father Eloy asked me to help count the fiesta receipts. I didn't want to. I was afraid... afraid if the count was wrong, people would think that I took the money, especially if... if they found out about Cliff's threats."

"What happened when you left the store? Where did you go?" Sutton asked.

"I walked out of the laundry room door to the patio. I went to look around and see if anyone was out there. And Cliff was there," she said, her voice fading to a whisper. J.D. started to say something, but the sheriff held up a warning hand and RaeLynn went on. "He grabbed my arm and said I had to get him the money. Right away. He said if I didn't, then I'd pay for sure... and he said Mama would, too. That scared me so much. I begged him not to let anything happen to her and said he couldn't guarantee her safety if I didn't get him the money. So I said I would get the money... but he had to wait for me up by the gate. He didn't want to. He didn't trust me. He thought I was going to run or tell the police. He said he'd go with me but I told him we'd be sure to get caught if he was seen inside the store. So he told me I could go in to get the money, but if I tried anything, he'd make sure I'd be sorry. All I could think about was Mama getting hurt... but I also knew that I couldn't take the money, either. So I thought, if I take the money bags and make it look like they were full of money, he'd just take them and I'd have a chance to get Mama and leave...."

Her voice cracked and she covered her face with her hands, trying to control her sobs. Sutton handed her his handkerchief. "Then what happened?" he asked.

She took a deep breath. "Fr. Eloy was in the campground store when I went in. I was so scared that he'd seen Cliff, but he just asked me to count the money and that Maggie would count it after me to be sure the amount was right... I was terrified that he was going to stand there while I counted it and I'd never be able to get the money bags out to Cliff. But he said he'd be right back and left. So I hid the money under the signs Corrie keeps under the counter. You know, the ones that say 'Help Wanted'."

"And you left your guardian angel pin there, too."

She nodded, her face growing paler. "I didn't know what was going to happen. I wanted to try to let Corrie or somebody know where the money was. I didn't want Cliff to come back in and find it. But I was also afraid he'd try to get it from Corrie. I was so scared and I wasn't sure what to do! I grabbed the receipt books and stuffed them into the money bags and then I hurried out the laundry room door, hoping nobody would see me." Her lips trembled. "I saw Cliff standing by the gates, so I started to run over there, but when I went around the corner of the building, someone grabbed me. I tried to scream, but they covered my mouth. I tried to fight them off," she whispered as her tears began to flow.

"Them?" J.D. asked, breaking his silence. RaeLynn nodded, burying her face in Sutton's handkerchief. "There was more than one person? Was Cliff one of them?" he snapped, ignoring the sheriff's warning look.

She shook her head. "No. Cliff... he saw them grab me and he... he turned and ran. He left me," she said, her voice breaking. "Just... just ran off and left me with two guys. I'm pretty sure they were men," she added. "They were big and strong and their voices were deep. I tried to fight," she said again. Her body shook even harder. "I really tried to get away, but they were too strong. Then I felt a needle in my arm and then I... I don't remember what happened after that."

Sutton cleared his throat sharply and J.D. realized he was gripping the footboard of the bed so tightly it looked like he was going to break it. He let go and stepped back, sucking air into his lungs and willing his heart to stop pounding. One look at Sutton's face told him that the sheriff was also fighting the same rage deep inside, but doing a much better job of hiding it. Tight-lipped, the sheriff asked, "What's the next thing you remember? Do you remember anything that happened before you woke up in the hospital?"

She took several deep breaths, trying to calm herself before she spoke. "Nothing clearly," she said. "Everything seems so hazy, like I never really woke up before now. I kind of remember everything being dark and not being able to move much. I don't know where I was or who I was with. I don't even know how long this all went on." She frowned, her eyes narrowing as if she were trying to see into the distance. "I heard voices. Not always clear. I mean, I couldn't always make out what they were saying. I remember hearing voices and they were angry. Whoever was talking was angry and yelling and other voices were quieter. Like whoever was yelling was angry at them."

"Do you remember anything they said?" Sutton asked.

Tears welled up in RaeLynn's eyes. She looked away. "Yes." The word was barely audible. J.D. and the sheriff exchanged a glance when she didn't go on.

"You can tell us, RaeLynn. I know it's hard to talk about but we need to know," the sheriff said quietly. She shook her head and a slight moan slipped from her lips. "You're safe, RaeLynn. No one's going to hurt you. I promise we'll see to it you stay safe."

"You don't have to be embarrassed," J.D. suddenly said. "Look, if it makes it any easier, Miss Shaffer, I'll step out and you can tell the sheriff privately. You've known him all your life, and I know I'm still pretty much a stranger to you, so if you'll feel more comfortable talking to him alone, I understand."

He waited a few seconds until she turned to face him. When she spoke, her voice, though raspy, was firm. "Please call me, RaeLynn, Detective. And I trust you as much as I trust Rick so you don't have to leave. I'll tell you both what I remember hearing."

J.D. hid his surprise then he took the other chair beside her bed. She was still tense, but it seemed his action made her relax just a little bit. Sutton nodded. "Go ahead, RaeLynn."

She licked her lips. "My mind was still hazy, so I don't know if what I heard is actually what they said," she reminded them. "I don't know how many of them there were. They were angry, I could tell that from the tone of the voices. One man said he didn't have time for all the drama, he had a life to live. And one of them said, 'I'm going to get paid, one way or another' and another voice said something like, 'We don't have that much money, she lied about getting it to us'. I knew he meant me," she added, her face growing pale.

"You didn't recognize the voices? Any of them?" Sutton asked.

She nodded. "I know one of them was Cliff. He was the one who said I lied to him. He was throwing me under the bus to whoever he owed money to," she said, a sliver of anger in her voice. She straightened her shoulders. "I don't know who he was talking to. I thought the other voices sounded familiar, but I couldn't tell you who they were. One of them just said...." She faltered for a second, but then steeled herself to continue, "He said he was going to get what was owed to him. No matter," she swallowed, "no matter what it took." She closed her eyes for a second as her face went white. "The door opened. It was still dark in the room where I was. I couldn't move, I couldn't see anything clearly. Then the door shut and I felt... I felt...." A cry tore from her throat and she dropped her face into her hands as her shoulders heaved.

"Easy, RaeLynn, easy. It's okay, you're safe," Sutton said, getting up from his chair and sitting on the edge of her bed. His arms went around her shoulders and she turned into him, clutching at his jacket and crying hysterically. J.D. stood up as well, his hands clenched into fists and feeling more helpless than he ever had in his life. She didn't have to go on; it was evident what had happened to her, how her captors had decided to take their payment. And her brother had allowed it to happen to her? How long had it gone on?

J.D. recalled the injuries that had been inflicted on her, the report the doctors had given them about the drugs in her system. It was clear that whoever used her to get paid back what was owed to him had kept her drugged and then.... J.D. felt sick to his stomach at the thought of what she had gone through. And her brother had allowed it.

She had fought back; the injuries she had, the bruises and fractures, indicated that at times she had tried to fight off her assailants before they had resorted to drugging her. He raked his fingers through his hair, wishing he were somewhere else. Preferably in front of whoever had done this to her. Alone. With nothing to hold him back. Red-hot rage flooded his vision for a few seconds. He blinked and his gaze met Sutton's. It was evident the sheriff felt the same.

Sutton cleared his throat as RaeLynn's sobs began to subside and she struggled to pull herself together. She sat up and wiped her eyes. "I'm sorry, Rick. I'm sorry...."

"RaeLynn, you don't have anything to be sorry about," the sheriff said, giving her a little shake as he released her. She took several deep breaths and shook her head. "RaeLynn, you didn't do anything wrong," he insisted.

"I should have told you and Detective Wilder what was going on, before all that happened," she said, looking up to meet J.D.'s gaze. "And then I should have paid closer attention while they had me. I should have been able to...."

"Under the circumstances, Miss Shaffer – RaeLynn – I'd say you did a hell of a good job just staying alive," J.D. said. She looked startled and she glanced at the sheriff. He was nodding silently. "The thing is, your brother knows where you were and who kidnapped and assaulted you. And as you know by now, he hasn't helped us at all. That's why we're questioning you."

"He's afraid," RaeLynn said so softly that they almost didn't hear her.

J.D. and the sheriff exchanged a glance. "Afraid? Who's he afraid of?" J.D. asked.

"I don't know," RaeLynn repeated helplessly. "I don't know if it's only one person or a whole gang. I don't even know how many were there or how many of them...." She stopped abruptly, her face twisting in revulsion. "Cliff's voice was the only one I'm positive I recognized," she said. "And I'm not positive I recognized another man's voice. I just know it sounded familiar, but I don't know where I've heard it before." She leaned back against her pillows, looking drained and pale. "I'm sorry," she whispered. "I want to help you. But I can't anymore. I feel so tired and everything is growing hazy again. And I'm starting to hurt all over...." Her voice trembled and she closed her eyes.

The sheriff stood up, alarmed. "I'll get the nurse," he said. He looked at J.D. "Stay with her," he muttered, then he rushed out of the room.

J.D. moved to RaeLynn's side, not sure what to do. He lowered himself onto the bed and brushed the hair off her forehead. RaeLynn's eyes opened a slit. "J.D.... Detective Wilder...."

"You're going to be fine, RaeLynn," he said. He couldn't muster a smile, no matter how hard he tried. He only hoped his fear wasn't showing.

She groped for his hand and squeezed it with a strength he hadn't known she was capable of. Her lips moved and he leaned closer to hear what she had to say. "Take care of Corrie. She might be in danger," she said in a faint voice before she slipped into unconsciousness.

Chapter 16

J.D. leaned his head back against the headrest in the truck, wondering if two aspirin was going to be enough to stop the pounding in his head. Sleep was going to be out of the question for the next few hours, maybe even the rest of the night.

It was well after six in the evening before he and Sutton had finally left Santa Fe. The sheriff had insisted on remaining in the room while Dr. Pruett and Rosa had checked over RaeLynn. Once he'd been satisfied that her condition hadn't worsened and she was merely due more pain medication for her existing injuries, he and J.D. had excused themselves from RaeLynn's bedside. While Rosa, with the help of another nurse – not Eleanor Price – had finished assisting RaeLynn with getting ready for bed, the sheriff had taken the opportunity to question Dr. Pruett and the clinic's head of security about the cameras inside the clinic.

"Do you really believe Pruett didn't know about the cameras in the clinic?" J.D. asked as the lights of Santa Fe began to fade behind them in the gathering dusk.

Sutton let out a sound between a laugh and a snort as he kept his eyes on the highway. "About as much as I believe that those cameras aren't working and haven't been for years."

J.D. digested this, recalling the doctor's reaction when asked about the cameras. His eyes had grown wide. What cameras? Where? In the hallways? Outside the patients' rooms? They had taken him into the hallway to point out the cameras, which apparently had been so unobtrusive that the doctor had never been aware of them. They had not mentioned that Officer Yellowcloud had alerted them to their presence, preferring to let the doctor, along with the head of security, think that they had been the ones to see them. J.D. had been even more surprised at what the head of security had told them. "They disconnected those cameras about five years ago. There was some concern that there could be a breach in the patients' privacy, even though the recorded feed from the cameras was erased regularly." Was it a coincidence that the security cameras had been disabled around the time Sutton had been a resident at the clinic? J.D. was beginning to adopt the sheriff's attitude about coincidences. He cleared his throat. "Pruett's only been there for four years. I was under the impression he'd been there for a lot longer."

Sutton was quiet for a few seconds. "There are actually four doctors on staff, most are experts in treating addiction. The head doctor, like Pruett, is a general practitioner, with a background in addiction treatment. The previous head of the clinic retired five years ago. He was a good man."

"I guess you'd know," J.D. said. The sheriff nodded silently. He kept checking the mirrors, avoiding glancing at J.D. "Come on, Sutton, anyone who follows us is going to be easy to spot, now that it's dark and they'd have to have their headlights on. We got a little time to kill so why don't you finish filling in the blank spaces for me?"

"What do you want to know?"

"Are you kidding me?"

Sutton sighed. "Where do you want me to start?"

"I'd say the beginning, wherever that might be," J.D. said. The sheriff let out a laugh.

"That's a good way of putting it, Detective," he said. He said nothing for a few minutes and J.D. waited, knowing that Sutton would talk when he had his thoughts in order. There was no hurry; there were still over three hours to go on their trip home. "I guess the beginning was after I got married and began to realize that the woman I married wasn't the woman I thought she was. We met when we were both students at UNM. Her focus was business, but I wasn't interested in that. Sure, I planned on going to law school, but I wasn't going to be a corporate lawyer. Then I met a guy who talked me into joining the police academy. I figured it would come in handy to have some law enforcement background if I was going to become a criminal lawyer. And that was when I realized what my true calling was.

"Meghan and I weren't even engaged yet, and I thought this might be the end of our relationship when I decided to forget about going on to law school. She told me that all she cared about was that I was happy and was pursuing a career that I loved and that she didn't care where we lived as long as we were together. What she really meant was, as long as she had access to my bank account. Problem was, Bonney didn't offer a lot of opportunities for her to enjoy the 'good life'. After a year of pretending she was content to live in Bonney, she started pressuring me to move back to her hometown, Dallas, or someplace other than rural New Mexico."

"Maybe she just didn't want to live in such close proximity to your former girlfriend?" J.D. said, bracing himself for the sheriff's explosive response. Sutton merely shrugged.

"It was never an issue. On rare occasions, we ran into Corrie, but if truth be told, I think Meghan would have liked to have had more opportunities to flaunt her 'conquest' in Corrie's face. For instance, I knew what time Corrie went to Mass on Sundays, so I purposely started going at a different time. Meghan insisted on going to the same one Corrie went to... and before too long, she couldn't keep up that act and she started balking about going to church at all. Before our first anniversary, I was going by myself."

"She's not Catholic?"

Sutton shook his head. "She said if it mattered so much to me, she'd do whatever she needed to do to make sure we married in the church. It convinced me I was doing the right thing," the sheriff said. "It also convinced me that she really wanted the same things I wanted: a simple life, a home, a family." There was a hitch in his voice and J.D. knew things were about to get very personal. "I was hired by the Bonney County Sheriff's Department right out of the academy, started the day after Meghan and I got back from a month-long honeymoon in Europe. Maybe that was when she realized just what she had gotten herself into. She tried to pretend she was satisfied with our life, but she really wanted a lot more glamour and prestige than she had being the wife of a small town rookie deputy, no matter how wealthy he might be. Yeah, you know good and well that my family has money, but I never lived like it. It drove my mother crazy. The main reason she liked Meghan initially was that she thought Meghan would persuade me to live like my station in life warranted, instead of working for a living... and at a very poorly paid job, at that. I had both my mother and wife against me and you have no idea what that made my life like. It got harder and harder to look forward to coming home, with Meghan harping about what a dull, boring life we had and Mother basically encouraging her. Before too long, it got easier to offer to pick up extra shifts. Since the department was short-handed, no one questioned it. They just figured it was an example of my dedication and work ethic. And that I probably needed the overtime." He paused for a moment and rubbed the back of his neck.

J.D. cleared his throat. "You never considered maybe moving someplace else and being a LEO wherever she wanted to live?"

"We tried that," the sheriff said. "We compromised, moved back to Albuquerque. I started with the Albuquerque P.D. and she talked about going back to finish school. But she was enjoying the perks of having a husband with a lousy paycheck but a hefty trust income. When we divorced, she got half of our assets, which was what I managed to save of the trust income I received while we were married. If I'd let her spend the way she wanted to while we were married, she wouldn't have gotten a tenth of what she did end up getting after the settlement."

"Whoa," J.D. said with a whistle. "So she was all set?"

"She was disappointed – furious, actually – when she found out all she was getting was the interest from my trust fund. My parents actually set it up that I wouldn't get the bulk of my trust until I was forty years old, but I would receive quarterly payments on the interest earned. A lot of money, but nothing like what Meghan was expecting. She tried to sue me for more, claiming I misrepresented my assets, but the truth was there weren't any more assets. And there's no way she would have stuck out staying married to me any longer. Looking back, I'm impressed she made it to five years." Sutton shook his head. "Anyway, I tried every which way to make it work, but she was fighting just as hard to make it fail. I couldn't take living in the big city; after six months, we were back in Bonney. In all honesty, she wasn't any happier in Albuquerque. She still kept pressuring me to move to Dallas, to give up law enforcement, to go to law school and get a 'respectable' career in corporate law. Everything she had once told me I didn't need to do because she wanted me to be happy was suddenly the very thing I needed to sacrifice to make her happy. She started going off on weekend trips with her girlfriends from college or by herself. Eventually, they ended up being weeklong trips. At least, I assumed that she was by herself," he added dryly. He was quiet for a long time, but J.D. knew he was steeling himself for what he was going to say. "I started having a couple of stiff drinks after my shifts. Whenever I got home and found she was gone, when she wouldn't answer or return my calls, when I'd call her family and friends and they'd claim they hadn't seen or heard from her. And then, when she was home and the only conversations we had were just arguments, I'd end up staying up late just to avoid her, not able to sleep unless I'd had a few drinks. You think I drink a lot of coffee now, I swear if you'd cut me back then, I would have bled Crown Royal and Coke. Heavy on the Crown." He rubbed his face and sighed.

J.D. shook his head. He was seeing a side to the sheriff he couldn't have imagined had existed. The man who seemed to have everything under control…. "How long did that go on?"

"A couple of years. I hid it well. I'm not even sure if Meghan was aware of how much I was drinking… or if she even cared. At one point, I told myself that I was going to have to pull myself together and make things work. I told myself I owed it to her. Never mind that she wasn't in any mood to compromise at that point. Nothing short of me doing exactly what she wanted was going to satisfy her. So, I made her a promise that we would move; that I would try it for a while, doing things her way, and I promised I'd make a real effort to do what she wanted. I don't know if she believed me, but I told myself I had to do it. Why I cared so much, I'll never know."

"Because you're a man of your word," J.D. said, surprising them both. "You made a vow and you're a man of honor. You'd never walk away from that."

They were silent for several seconds and the sheriff finally nodded. "You're right," he said quietly. He let out his breath and his next words came out so softly that J.D. had to strain to hear them. "You have no idea how much heartache that's brought into my life."

J.D. waited a few seconds while it seemed that Sutton was lost in the past. Darkness had fallen over the highway. They hadn't passed another vehicle in several miles and a quick glance in the mirrors proved that still no one was following them. Finally, J.D. cleared his throat. "So what happened then? How long did you live in Dallas?"

The sheriff shook his head. "We never moved."

"Why not?"

Sutton turned to J.D. and, in the dim light from the dashboard, raw, searing pain flashed in his dark blue eyes. "Meghan got pregnant."

J.D. blinked. "And that changed your plans?"

"It ruined hers," Sutton said in a strangled voice. "I never questioned why she hadn't gotten pregnant during the previous years of our marriage. With all that was happening… it seemed like a blessing in disguise that it hadn't happened. But then… when it did happen, it seemed like a miracle to me. But to her, it was a disaster. There I was, thinking that everything was going to be all right, that things were going to work out, and no matter where we went, we'd have each other and our child. And she told me I had destroyed her life."

"What? Why? Didn't she want to have kids?"

157

"I thought she did. She let me think she did. If I'd known she was so opposed… it would have been a deal-breaker. I'd have never asked her to marry me." The sheriff cleared his throat. "Apparently she'd been on birth control the whole time. I never knew. She hid that from me. And it failed right when I had agreed to try life in Dallas, on her terms. Needless to say, it wasn't the happy time I had expected it to be. And then when Ava was born, premature, struggling for life, Meghan walked out and left me to deal with what happened afterward. I didn't see her for months. I only got communications from her lawyers. Everything was a blur. I wish I could say the booze dulled the pain, but it didn't touch it. It was like a slow, painful death." He sat up straighter. "Sorry if I kind of rushed over that last part, Wilder."

"Understandable." J.D. shook his head. "I have to say I'm surprised no one ever told me about all this. I thought there were no secrets in small towns."

"There aren't," Sutton said bluntly. "Trust me, everyone in Bonney knows just about everything that went on during that time. But in small towns, we look after our own, for the most part. You're still a newcomer, so it would have been a long time before you heard all the gossip. The locals will say it was for me to tell about, not them."

"Meaning, don't ask why Corrie never said a word to me about it?"

A ghost of a smile flitted across the sheriff's face. "Corrie… I tried to keep a lot of this from her. But she knew. I should have known better." J.D. frowned.

"So after your wife left you… you never considered…." He let the thought trail away.

"I'm Catholic, Wilder. I'm still married," Sutton said brusquely. "And I will be until and unless the marriage tribunal decrees otherwise. Problem is, I went to a lot of trouble to make sure that my marriage to Meghan was valid. Nothing that happened afterward matters. As you said, I'm a man of my word." He stopped and blinked rapidly for several seconds. "Anyway," he went on, "the only thing that seemed to be going right in my life was my career. I loved my job and, if I say so myself, I was damn good at it."

"Still are," J.D. interjected.

Sutton inclined his head in thanks. "I was working like a mad man, putting in crazy hours, trying to think about anything and everything but what my personal life was like. I hated going home to an empty apartment at the end of my shifts and, no matter how tired I was or how many hours I'd worked, I couldn't sleep. The alcohol knocked me out – after too many drinks – but it didn't touch the pain. I started...." He faltered for a second. "I started drinking on duty. It helped me push everything else back so I could focus on the job." He gave a hollow laugh. "At least, that's what I thought. I truly believed I was still in control and no one knew what was going on. The sheriff at the time was a man named John Garza. He was one of the finest law enforcement officers I've ever had the privilege to know and work with. And he knew. He made it clear that either I sobered up or I'd never work in law enforcement again. I'd already lost everything else; I couldn't stand the thought of losing my career as well."

J.D. stayed silent, digesting what he'd learned. "So you found that clinic in Santa Fe," he said. To his surprise, the sheriff shook his head.

"No. The credit for that goes to my mother." He raised his eyes heavenward and shrugged. "When she found out what was going on – I had hidden it really well from her – she was horrified. Bad enough I was an alcoholic, but now she had to find a way to help me without the whole world finding out." J.D. stared at him. Sutton lifted his hands from the steering wheel in a helpless gesture. "I told you Mother hated how I never seemed to take my station in life seriously. Well, this was the icing on the cake. She made sure I was going to get help and that no one would find out about it. Don't judge her too harshly, Wilder," the sheriff said mildly. "Her family name was important to her, especially since my father had done plenty to tarnish his own. But we'll save that story for another time," he added as J.D. sat up, startled. "After all I put Mother through, I figured the least I could do was keep my treatment under wraps." He paused and when he continued, there was a steel thread of anger in his voice. "So, yeah, there WAS a security breach in the clinic five years ago, but the cameras had nothing to do with it. At least, not initially."

"Nurse Price?"

"What did she tell you?"

He thought for a few seconds, recalling that he had told Eleanor Price that he would do his best to keep her from losing her job. However, it seemed that this wouldn't be the first time someone had helped her save it. "She thought I assumed she'd had a relationship with you, which jeopardized her job at the clinic," he said. Sutton let out a snort and shook his head. "She denied it, said she was just being nice to you because you were getting a little stir-crazy toward the end of your treatment. So you went to breakfast at The Pantry a couple of times. Because they couldn't serve alcohol till after noon on Sundays."

"She was just being nice," Sutton repeated. "That was the only part of the story that wasn't true."

"So, uh, you guys did go out...."

"Yes, but it wasn't a date, in any way, shape, or form," the sheriff cut in. "It's true that, by the time the fifth week of my stay in the clinic rolled around, I was getting restless. I knew that the clinic required me to stay for a full six weeks minimum before I was discharged. I had already dried out; that is, I had no desire for alcohol of any kind. I only wanted to go back to work. I wanted to go home, pick up the pieces of my life, and try to build a new one. And I knew that booze wouldn't have any place in it. The doctors agreed I was probably ready to be released, but, in order to maintain protocol, I had to stay for the full term. I'm sure I was getting on the staff's nerves at that point. I even offered to help the maintenance crew clean floors and bathrooms, help the kitchen staff prepare meals, help the grounds keeper cut grass, pull weeds, you name it. They didn't know what to do with me."

J.D. snickered. He couldn't help himself. He had a sudden image of the sheriff, a resident in an otherwise ritzy clinic that catered to well-off addicts, doing the work of the cleaning crew... and what that would have done to his mother if she'd known. Sutton cracked a smile.

"Go ahead and laugh. I don't blame you." His smile faded. "However, that's probably just another reason why Nurse Price – Ellie – did what she did."

That wiped the grin off J.D.'s face. "What was that?" he asked.

Sutton grimaced. "I told you that my mother was struggling with everything that was going on in my life and how it affected her. Mother had always been very proud of her family name and standing, and she knew lots of influential people and not just in New Mexico. She'd managed to come out of my father's scandal relatively unscathed – like I said, another time," he warned. J.D. shook his head and held up his hands. No matter how bad he wanted to know, he wasn't going to push. Not right now. The sheriff went on, "Anyway, my story had all the makings of a sensational tell-all book. At least, that was what Eleanor Price was told. She'd been caring for another resident, a former journalist-turned-author who specialized in digging up dirt on celebrities and other influential people, putting it between the covers of a book, and calling it a 'biography'. Apparently he'd been very successful but his last book had bombed, he'd been sued for slander, and took to drugs and drinking to deal with it all, so his agent sent him to the clinic, hoping he'd straighten out. Once he cleaned up enough to think clearly, he realized he was in a prime location to find his next book."

"You?"

"Me," Sutton said and rolled his eyes. "Ellie was a fairly new hire, just out of nursing school, and thrilled about working at a prestigious clinic. And maybe she was just a little star-struck. She was well aware of who this guy was. He apparently impressed her enough to get her talking about her work at the clinic and the other residents."

"The residents don't interact with each other?"

"Not until they reach a certain point and only if they want to. Remember, the clinic serves members of the community who, for various reasons, wish to remain anonymous. Privacy is a huge thing. So when Ellie happened to mention my name to this guy, he started to pressure her for more information."

J.D. whistled. "No wonder she was worried about losing her job. I'm surprised she still has it. But surely she knew what she was doing would get her fired?"

"Her weak spot was her nursing school debt. Santa Fe's not a cheap town to live in and she was saddled with bills relating to her care of a younger sister, Mandie, who was still in school, and a disabled mother, in addition to her living expenses and student loans. She was offered a lot of money to get my story and, if possible, allow the author to get a few pictures for the book. He got his agent to follow us and now he had photos implying that I was involved with one of my nurses." The sheriff sighed. "I found out about it, then the clinic found out about it, and that's when it all hit the fan. The author and his agent were sued, a gag order was issued, and they were about to fire Ellie." He chewed his lip. "I talked them out of it."

J.D. stared at Sutton. "Why?" he finally managed to ask. "She violated your privacy, not to mention compromised the clinic's security, almost got your name smeared in the tabloids...."

"She was a scared kid who was stressed out about finances. She made a stupid mistake. She wouldn't be the first or the last person who did something out of desperation. Getting her fired

161

wouldn't have helped anyone, least of all her. She'd have had a hard time finding another job in her field, especially as good as the one she has at the clinic. She was a good nurse. She still is," Sutton said with a shrug. "She might be removed from RaeLynn's care, now that they know there's a connection between RaeLynn and me."

"Was Rosa at the clinic at the time all that happened?" J.D. asked.

"I think she's been there forever," the sheriff said wryly. "Everyone seems to act like she runs the place. Anyway, I didn't see how getting Ellie fired would have... what's going on?"

A state police cruiser passed them, going in the opposite direction, then suddenly its brake lights and light bar came on. J.D. looked over his shoulder and saw the vehicle swing around and come after them, lights flashing but no siren. He glanced at the speedometer. "What does he want with us? You're not speeding."

"Let's find out," Sutton said as the sign for the exit to Clines Corners loomed ahead. He pulled off the highway and into the parking lot of the travel center. J.D. couldn't remember the last time he got pulled over for a traffic violation. He opened the glove box to retrieve the vehicle registration and insurance papers. He and Sutton had their identification and badges ready when the officer stepped up to the driver's side window, flashlight in hand.

"Evening, gentlemen," he said with a pleasant drawl. He seemed to be a few years older than they were, with a smooth bronzed face and piercing dark eyes. "Lieutenant Gary Lopez of the New Mexico State Police."

"Lieutenant," Sutton said, inclining his head. "What seems to be the problem?"

"Well, if you fellas happen to be Sheriff Rick Sutton and Detective J.D. Wilder of the Bonney sheriff's and police department, then I might be asking you that same question."

Sutton handed him their IDs and badges and the lieutenant checked them, considerately keeping the flashlight beam from hitting them directly in their eyes. "What can we do for you?"

"Well, maybe check your cell phones, for a start. I understand that y'all might be pursuing leads on a case you're working on, but your respective departments have been trying to get hold of you all day." J.D. and the sheriff exchanged a glance.

"Our departments asked the state police to help track us down?" J.D. said incredulously and the sheriff sighed and rubbed his forehead, shaking his head. The state cop shook his head, noting Sutton's reaction.

"Nope. It was a private citizen. And an awful persistent one, too."

"Cute, Corrie. Real cute," Sutton groused. "I can't tell you how much I enjoyed getting pulled over in the middle of nowhere at night. Why didn't you just mobilize the National Guard while you were at it?"

"Gee, I seem to recall, not one, but TWO, law enforcement officers who hounded me about getting a cell phone in order to always be available in the event of an emergency," she responded. J.D. could hear her exasperation clearly from the sheriff's cell phone. They had already sent a bemused Lieutenant Lopez on his way and checked their phones. J.D. had no fewer than fifteen missed calls, mostly from Corrie in the last hour. He could only imagine that the sheriff had about the same.

Now they stood outside the pickup truck in the parking lot of the travel center, drinking coffee and waiting for the firestorm to subside before they drove on. The sheriff was doing his best to keep calm but the events of the day were wearing on him and he couldn't keep the edge out of his voice. "We were a little busy, Corrie. We had our phones silenced. And cell service isn't the greatest where we are."

She wasn't in the mood to hear excuses. "Well, maybe if you guys checked your phones from time to time, or maybe – get this – let people know what you guys are up to and where you are, I wouldn't have to resort to having the state police track you down to get in touch with your departments!"

"You mean you have the state police looking for us all over New Mexico?" J.D. flinched as the sheriff's voice rose in disbelief. Corrie was silent for a few seconds.

"No, Rick," she said quietly. "Just the highways between Bonney and Santa Fe."

J.D.'s head jerked up. It was the sheriff's turn to be silent. He avoided looking at J.D. then he took a deep breath. "Okay, you found us. I'm sorry we made you worry. Now what's going on?"

Her annoyance had turned to concern. "Cliff Shaffer has been making a nuisance of himself with both the sheriff's department and the police department. My cousin even came by the campground to ask how to get a hold of you and J.D. Apparently, they're concerned that Cliff might be a little too close to the edge.

He's making threats about suing for false arrest and who knows what all. Charlie didn't get too specific. I talked to Dudley and he's gotten some calls from both Cliff and Teddy Shaffer. He didn't tell me what they were about, but it sounds like the Shaffers are scared. Of what, no one has a clue. Have you guys stirred up something in your investigation? And how's RaeLynn? Don't try to deny you've seen her."

"She's fine. I'll fill you in tomorrow," Sutton said bluntly. "I need to call Dudley."

"You mean you haven't talked to him yet? Then why did he send Deputy Mirabal to come stay at the campground store tonight?"

"Dudley sent Angie to stand guard?"

"Jimmy Watkins from the police department is outside in the campground, keeping watch. Angie said that she's supposed to stay here in the store, as an additional precaution. That wasn't your idea?"

"It probably should have been," Sutton said, glancing at J.D. They both got into the truck and the sheriff gunned the engine. "We'll be home in about three hours. Let me talk to Angie and then make sure you, and everyone else at the campground, do what she says. Got that?"

"Got it," she said dryly. "Anything else, Sheriff?"

"Yeah," he said, as he pulled the truck out onto the highway. "Remind me to treat all these state cops patrolling US 54 and 285 to donuts or pizza for their trouble."

Chapter 17

The next few weeks passed with a continual feeling of uneasy expectation. Corrie woke up every morning with her stomach in knots, dreading what the day might bring, and went to sleep every night breathing a prayer of thankfulness that nothing had happened.

Rick and J.D. had surprised her that first night by showing up at the campground instead of making her wait until the following day to hear what they had discovered in Santa Fe. With Deputy Mirabal and Officer Watkins keeping watch, she had invited both Rick and J.D. up to her apartment and made them sandwiches from the leftover meatloaf Jackie had made for their dinner, guessing that they hadn't had regular meals all day. They had filled her in on what they had learned, from RaeLynn's condition to the news that there was a mysterious stranger who had been following them. Corrie had listened without interruption, her brow furrowing with concern as J.D. told her that the last thing RaeLynn had warned him about was that Corrie could be in danger. "And that's it? She didn't say what kind of danger?"

"The only person she could identify with any certainty from the time she was taken was her brother, Cliff," Rick said. One look at his face told her that the day had taken more out of him emotionally than it had physically. J.D. kept glancing at him, worry etching more lines in his face than exhaustion. "Which means only Cliff can tell us who else was involved."

The following days brought no answers to any of their concerns. Cliff Shaffer voluntarily turned up at the police department the following day, but flatly denied any involvement in RaeLynn's disappearance and reappearance. It was his word against hers, and she was under the influence of painkillers and the residue of illegal substances. "Who's a jury gonna believe?" he had sneered. "Now leave me and my family alone!"

Oddly, the Shaffers, who had seemed so ready to leave town before, now seemed to be keeping very close to their trailer. Only Teddy was seen out and about and he kept away from everyone, speaking only when necessary. Rick had one deputy following him at all times, but he never went anyplace except to run errands for his family. "Are you waiting for him to lead you to someone in particular?" Corrie asked late one morning when Rick stopped by to see how things were at the campground.

"I'd like to know where Johnny Shaffer is… and has been," Rick admitted. "He hasn't been seen anywhere around, not even the casinos in Mescalero or at the racetrack, since before RaeLynn disappeared. His cars haven't been moved from where they're stored. Mike Ramirez chatted up a few of Johnny's girlfriends and they were wondering if he'd been arrested or something because they hadn't seen him around either."

"Johnny has never cared for life in Bonney. He only comes back on odd occasions. He might not even know what's going on with RaeLynn," Corrie pointed out. She refilled Rick's cup of coffee, taking advantage of the slow time at the campground that usually occurred during the weeks between Thanksgiving and Christmas. Renfro and Oliver had taken up their usual stations behind the counter and were enjoying the peace and quiet. It was early December and the weather had turned colder, but the area still didn't get the much-needed snow that would bring winter sports enthusiasts to the region to take advantage of the slopes at Ski Apache.

Thanksgiving had ended up being a very quiet affair. Unlike previous years when Corrie had hosted many of her employees and their families, this year it had only been her and the Pages, along with Rick and J.D., and she had been relieved that there had been none of the usual awkwardness that marked any occasion where the two men were together and not working as law enforcement officers. It had come as no surprise to Corrie that her cousin, Charlie, hadn't shown up for dinner, or even to have a piece of pie with her, but his absence still stung. Red and Dana Myers had extended their vacation until after Christmas and it amused Corrie how the lack of Dana's overly-chatty presence seemed to magnify how few friends gathered around the table. Shelli and her kids had always spent Thanksgiving with her, but now they were building a new family and new traditions elsewhere. Buster and Noreen had gone to spend it with her family in Arizona. Myra and Dudley, of course, had hosted their first Thanksgiving dinner as a married couple with the Kaydahzinne clan. Gabe Apachito and Dee Dee had stopped in for dessert after having had dinner with the young deputy's family and it appeared that his family was pleased about him and Dee Dee. And RaeLynn…. Corrie swallowed hard.

"Have you been to see RaeLynn lately?" she asked Rick.

He shook his head. "I get daily updates from her doctors but I haven't wanted to take a chance to go up there. We still don't know who was following us in Santa Fe last month. We don't have a single lead. None of the Shaffers are talking. In fact, it's amazing how they haven't popped on our radar for any reason; no complaints, no vandalism, no thefts or drug deals...."

"I thought no one reported anything the Shaffers did for fear of retaliation?" Corrie said.

Rick gave her a grim smile. "There's still the village gossip mill and no one seems to have any to share. At least, we haven't heard any." For once, he didn't seem to be in a hurry to leave. Perhaps the fact that it was evident that J.D. wasn't at the campground encouraged Rick to linger over a second cup of coffee. J.D. had been reporting in to work early every morning after grabbing a quick cup of coffee from the campground store and only returning when the deputy or officer on guard duty was ready to end his or her shift to take over for them. Rick must have noticed that J.D.'s Harley was gone and he thanked Corrie with his usual half-smile as she handed him the steaming cup. "Dr. Pruett says that RaeLynn is doing very well, physically and emotionally. She's still got a ways to go with her recovery, but it doesn't look like she's sustained any long-term damage from what happened to her. Of course, her therapists are being especially cautious; they don't want to rush her treatment just because she's doing well. So don't expect her to be home any sooner than the minimum of six weeks," he warned Corrie.

"I know that," she said. "But surely she's allowed visitors, isn't she?"

"Under normal circumstances, yes," Rick said, setting his cup down and leaning forward, resting his forearms on the counter. "By this time, she would have been allowed visitors, maybe even encouraged to go out to lunch or for coffee on occasion. The thing is, the clinic usually only allows immediate family members to visit and that's with the express permission of the resident. In RaeLynn's case, I made it clear when she was checked in that she was not to have any visitors, family or otherwise, except for certain law enforcement officers, until she was sufficiently recovered to make that decision for herself. The only time the clinic allows visitors who are not family is if the resident specifically requests them. And as of now, Corrie, RaeLynn has not requested any visitors, family or friends. Not even her mother."

"No one?" Corrie blurted, forgetting her resolve and knowing that Rick was far from done speaking. "Not even...?"

"No one," Rick said with emphasis. "And don't take that personally. Let me finish." He waited until Corrie nodded. "It's not that she doesn't want visitors, or rather, she doesn't want YOU to come see her. She's worried, Corrie. And scared. She knows someone tried to kill her. She doesn't know who it was or even why they wanted her dead. And she also believes you're in danger as well, although she's not sure what that danger is. She's also aware that her brother knows who's behind all this, and that he's refusing to cooperate with the police. As much as she wants to come back home, she knows she's safe where she is, for as long as she can be there, and she's hoping that, in the meantime, we can find out who hurt her and what it is they want." He paused and Corrie decided to take a chance and ask what had been bothering her.

"Everything is at a standstill in this investigation. That's what you're saying," she said and received a wary nod in response. "RaeLynn's under heavy guard and you might say I am, too," she added, jerking her head in the direction of the front window where Deputy Mike Ramirez could be seen, sitting in an unmarked car in front of the unoccupied cabin next to J.D.'s which had the clearest view of the campground store and most of the area leading from the highway. "And this has been going on almost since the moment RaeLynn was found on the highway almost a month ago. And nothing has happened."

"So far."

"Exactly."

"What are you getting at, Corrie?" Rick asked. He straightened up and his blue eyes darkened. She took a deep breath.

"Just that whoever was following you and J.D. in Santa Fe apparently knows you're on to them. He knows he was spotted. So he's aware that you know that he's looking for RaeLynn and maybe he already knew that she was at that clinic and just wanted to see how tight security was around there. And now that he knows he doesn't have much of a chance to get in, he's just laying low, waiting for some other opportunity."

"Someone at the clinic had to help him get in," Rick reminded her.

She nodded. "Which means he already knew, or at least had a reasonable suspicion, that RaeLynn was at that particular clinic. The fact that you and J.D. went there just confirmed it."

Rick had stiffened. "The person who let him in could have confirmed it, as well as what security measures are in place. They didn't have to see Wilder and me there to know."

"But maybe they wanted to see what you would find out from RaeLynn. They know she survived and is being treated. And they know that she's the only one who can identify them. They probably know there isn't a chance of anyone, except you and J.D., finding out anything from her. Maybe they're trying to find out what you and J.D. found out from RaeLynn."

"But she didn't tell us anything. She said she couldn't identify anyone except Cliff."

"The guy following you probably doesn't know that. He's laying low, waiting to see what you guys come up with. And if he's the one the Shaffers are taking orders from, it could explain why they haven't been up to their usual shenanigans." Rick stared at her.

"How long have you been thinking about all this? I don't believe this came to you in a sudden flash."

"You're right, Sheriff, because I do believe we've had this conversation before," she said dryly, and the look of growing enlightenment on his face told her he'd already figured out what she was getting at.

"If you think I'm going to drop the security measures around the campground because you think you can lure RaeLynn's attacker into the open...."

She raised a hand and motioned him to keep his voice down. He stopped and glared at her. She gave him a lop-sided grin. "You know as well as I do that, given it's been a month since RaeLynn was left out on the highway, whoever it is that tried to kill her isn't going to make another move. Not while he knows that I – and RaeLynn – are surrounded by cops and security guards. He's not that stupid."

"Neither am I," Rick growled. "There's no way I'm relaxing security, Corrie. It's too dangerous."

"So is letting this guy, whoever he is, go on keeping out of sight indefinitely. RaeLynn can't be guarded forever, Rick. You know that there's no way you or anyone else can protect her for the rest of her life and I'm willing to bet she won't put up with it that long. And neither will I," she said, drawing a deep breath. "I refuse to live my life in fear and I believe RaeLynn feels the same way. Right now, she's as safe as she can be but she'll be leaving that clinic soon and we need to find who attacked her and what it is that THEY are so afraid of."

She paused, expecting a barrage of arguments from Rick. He remained silent, chewing on his lower lip. She hardly dared believe that he was actually going to agree with her... or at least hear her out. "What, exactly, are you thinking?" he asked.

She was so stunned at his reaction that her mind went blank. He waited until she gathered her scattered thoughts. "He wants to know what RaeLynn knows and he can't get to her while she's in the clinic," she said. "Also, whoever is in cahoots with him at the clinic – you know, whoever buzzed him in – is probably not finding anything out, either. That means one of two things...."

"One is that RaeLynn really doesn't know anything more than what she's told us," Rick said, and raised a brow.

"And, two is that she doesn't trust anyone around her to talk about what she knows." She tapped on the counter. "Rick, she knows that someone who works at the clinic buzzed in that guy. Someone there knows what happened to her. But she doesn't know who it is. She only knows that person was in on her kidnapping and they might try to kill her again. They think she knows more than she does and they want to know who she's told." Rick's eyes widened.

"If there's a connection between the clinic and whoever attacked her, then this is bigger than we thought!" he said sharply. Corrie shrugged helplessly.

"You don't believe in coincidences, Rick. How else to explain that guy that followed you to the clinic? He probably made a connection there once he discovered that was where RaeLynn was. Which means...."

"There's money in this. Big money. Enough to buy information from a highly regarded medical clinic with tight security." He blew out his breath. "It's a wonder RaeLynn's safety hasn't been compromised."

"The security you're providing at the clinic is the only reason RaeLynn's safe for now. But once she's discharged, she's going to be a walking target. And that means that we – and that includes you and J.D. as well – are targets as well. Whatever it is that she knows, it's important enough that whoever attacked her wants to make sure that there are no loose ends." She drew a deep breath. "Look, Rick, I know you don't want to get me involved and I understand, truly, I do. Not just because you don't want me sticking my nose into a police investigation, but because it's your job to protect me as well as RaeLynn and Heaven knows you don't need someone else to look after." She paused when it seemed like Rick was going to say something but he shook his head, his gaze fixed on her face. She wondered if she had crossed some invisible line that kept him from responding like he normally would. "I just think that we need to stop waiting for him to make a move. I think we need to force his hand. Otherwise, RaeLynn will never be safe again." She stopped talking because the way Rick was staring at her was making her squirm.

After several long moments, when she was beginning to wish someone would come into the store or the phone would ring, he finally spoke. "What do you suggest?" he asked. He gave her his half-smile. "Don't pretend you don't already have a plan. You've thought this out very thoroughly so go ahead and tell me. Not that I'm promising to go along with it, but let's hear it."

She let her breath out slowly. She couldn't believe he was willing to listen, even if it was just to humor her. "I think I should go visit RaeLynn. You said she can have visitors...."

"If she requests them," he reminded her.

"Well, can't you suggest to her that I might want to come see her? I mean, I get it that she's worried about putting me in danger...."

"However, the fact that you're going to see her just might be what draws our mysterious shadow out, especially if he finds out that RaeLynn asked to see you. He'll think that she wants to tell you something. That's what you're getting at," Rick said. His expression and tone of voice had changed from concern, to faint amusement, to resignation. He let out a long sigh. "Right."

"You don't seem to be particularly upset by my suggestion," she said, eyeing him narrowly. "What are you thinking?"

"That you're right, as much as I hate to admit it."

She blinked. "Really?"

He chuckled. "That I hate to admit it? You should know me well enough by now to know how much I hate to admit when you're right about something I'm totally dead-set against."

She ignored his banter. "You mean you're going to let me go see RaeLynn and maybe get this guy to show his face so you can find out what it is he wants?"

"I don't see how I have any choice to do otherwise," he said. "What you've said is absolutely true. If RaeLynn's attacker, assuming he's the same guy who was following us, hasn't made a move by now, it's probably safe to assume he'll wait however long it takes to make his next move. And you're right, we can't keep up this level of security forever. So what's the plan, once I get RaeLynn to request a visit from you?"

"Well, obviously, I have to go to Santa Fe."

"Obviously. But you're not going alone," Rick countered.

"I wasn't planning on it," Corrie retorted, her customary irritation at Rick flooding back. "I'm well aware that it's too dangerous for only one person to go."

"I'm glad you're aware of that, but who are you planning to have go with you?" There was a curious tone in his voice and a glimmer of expectancy in his eyes. Corrie felt a rush of heat to her face. She hadn't really thought that far ahead; she hadn't expected to have gotten far enough along to even explain her idea to Rick.

"Well, I'm, uh, not sure. I mean, it seems the most natural choice would be to have Jerry and Jackie go with me...."

"Which means closing down the campground? The Myers aren't here to keep things running and you actually have a few guests staying right now. I doubt you want to go that route. And the Pages aren't of an age where they should be putting themselves in any kind of danger." Rick shook his head as Corrie shivered.

"Exactly," she said. "So I wondered if you'd allow Deputy Mirabal to go with me." Rick blinked. Was he surprised that Corrie had requested Angie Mirabal? He actually looked more disappointed than surprised. She shrugged. "I mean, wouldn't it make sense that I'd be safer with a law enforcement officer than with anyone else?"

"Yeah," Rick said, his voice flat. Corrie stared at him.

"Is there a problem, Rick?" she asked. He cleared his throat.

"No, not really. I just thought maybe, uh, you'd want me to go with you."

If that wasn't enough to make Corrie's jaw drop, the next thing that happened did: for the first time in her life, she saw Rick's face turn brick red. "You want to go to Santa Fe with me?"

He drew himself up stiffly. "Well, you just said you'd be safer with a law enforcement officer, right?" he snapped. "And how well do you know Santa Fe? Would you know how to find the clinic? Besides, I've got security clearance to get in. And...."

"Okay, okay, you've got a point. Several points, in fact. More points than a porcupine," she said, holding up her hands to slow down his torrent of words. He stopped and drew a deep breath and his color returned to almost normal. Corrie had to bite back a smile, but she didn't want him to think she was laughing at him. "I just didn't think you'd be able to get away to go with me. You're usually so busy and I wouldn't want to impose on your time. I mean, just because we're old friends...." He removed his Stetson and set it on the counter. His hands were shaking slightly and she wondered what was bothering him. She moved closer to him and gently touched his forearm. "Rick, I'm sorry, I didn't mean to hurt your feelings. I don't want you to feel like you owe me anything. And I can never repay you for everything you've done for RaeLynn... and for me."

He turned to her. "You owe me nothing, Corrie." And before she could respond, he reached for her and she found herself in his arms, his lips on hers, and for the first time since she was seventeen, she was kissing him as if the last fifteen years hadn't happened. Her heart raced like a runaway horse and she was sure she could hear Rick's heart pounding through the blood rushing through her head. She tried to shut down the part of her brain that was telling her she was making a mistake and that they had to stop, but her thoughts were scrambling in a million different directions. It took every ounce of will power for her to pull out of their embrace just as Rick did the same. They moved an arm's length away, their breathing ragged, and she wondered if she had the same wild, disoriented look in her eyes as he had in his. Her hands went up to her cheeks and she licked her lips as if to quench the burning she still felt. He ran a hand over his face and cleared his throat. "I... I don't...."

She swallowed hard. "I, uh, don't think we should have done that."

"Are you sorry?" he asked, his voice hoarse. A fire burned in his blue eyes. She gulped.

"Uh, not really," she stammered.

He drew back, as if snapping out of a trance. "Well, we should be. Both of us. I'm not... I can't... I should have never done that, Corrie. I'm... I'm sorry."

"Wait a minute," she said as he grabbed his Stetson. He turned quickly but she caught his arm before he reached the door. She was torn between fury and concern and she wasn't sure which emotion would win out. "Rick, don't. You can't just leave like this! Talk to me! What's going on?" He stopped and sighed, but didn't look at her.

"Nothing. I mean, nothing I can talk about. Yet. Look," he said, finally turning to face her, "don't take this the wrong way, but I really didn't mean for that to happen. I never wanted to put you in that position. And if you don't want me to go with you to Santa Fe now... well, I'll understand. But I'd really like to be able to forget this happened."

She shook her head and let go of his arm. She took a step back. "Maybe it's easy for you to forget—it wouldn't be the first time you did—but how do you expect me to forget?" He winced. She wrapped her arms around herself and tried to calm her racing heart. "I wish, just once, you'd tell me what you're thinking. If you still want to go to Santa Fe with me, that's fine. If you don't want me to talk about what just happened... that's not fair but, okay, I won't. But forget it happened? I can't promise that." She moved back behind her counter, giving them both some space. "I just hope that someday you'll explain all this. I think you owe me that much."

"I owe you more," he said quietly. He took a deep breath and tried to make his voice sound casual. "How about we go to Santa Fe the day after tomorrow to see RaeLynn? I need a day to make arrangements. Is that all right?"

"Fine," she said. It was all she could do to keep her voice from shaking. She heard him say something under his breath as he slipped out the door, the bell eliciting a "woof" from Renfro, and her tears began to flow.

Rick pulled over to the side of the road a half mile from the campground, threw the Tahoe into park, and shut off the engine. He snatched off his Stetson, flung it onto the passenger seat, and dropped his head into his hands, wishing it was a massive migraine that was making his temples throb. At least the pain would make him forget what an ass he'd made of himself.

What on earth possessed him to do something so stupid? His phone call to the diocesan marriage tribunal earlier that morning had been a mistake. He hated to make a nuisance of himself, but it had been months since he'd filed his appeal and he hadn't heard a word back yet. Yes, his advocate had warned him that it would take time and not to hold out hope for a quick answer, let alone the answer he wanted to hear. But the strain of the investigation of RaeLynn's attack, the feeling of needing answers to at least one case in his life, prompted him to break protocol and contact the tribunal office directly. The woman who answered the phone was sympathetic but all she could tell him was that, even though there was a backlog of cases and they were doing their best to expedite responses, it took time and the most she could promise is that he would hopefully receive an answer before the end of the year. Three more weeks.

But she didn't promise it would be the answer I wanted, he reminded himself as he let his head fall back against the seat. He closed his eyes and wished he could stop seeing the look on Corrie's face. If she had looked properly offended, affronted, horrified... he could have dealt with that. It's what he would have deserved for jumping the gun and taking liberties and he wouldn't have blamed her one bit.

But beside the stunned look he had expected, there was something else. What was it? A look of surprised delight? Subdued joy? Or worse... hope? Had he given her hope that maybe, somehow, by some miracle, he HADN'T succeeded in contracting a valid marriage with Meghan ten years ago? That maybe, somehow, by some miracle, he and Corrie might have a chance at what they had started when they were still in high school?

Had he kindled a hope that he might have to cruelly extinguish?

He shook his head and started the Tahoe's engine. He had to put this out of his mind, the whole thing. He had work to do that would keep his mind off what had just happened. When the letter arrived, then he would know. And he'd go from there. He took a deep breath.

And said a fervent prayer.

Chapter 18

"You sure you want me to take your truck?"

"Were you planning to take her on your Harley?"

"The thought had crossed my mind...."

"Well, you can forget about it," the sheriff snapped. "It's likely to be freezing cold up north and I doubt you have cold weather gear for her. And I'm not sure she'd feel safe riding on that thing." He practically shoved the truck keys at J.D. and once again, J.D. wondered what exactly was going on.

A terse phone call from Sutton as J.D. got off duty a few hours earlier still had him scratching his head. Corrie had told J.D. the day before that she and the sheriff were going to Santa Fe to visit RaeLynn and hopefully draw whoever had been following them out into the open. Besides J.D.'s surprise that the sheriff had agreed to Corrie's plan, he was even more surprised that the sheriff was asking him, J.D., to take Corrie to Santa Fe.

He bit back his initial retort. "Tell me again what the plan is. I thought you were taking Corrie to see RaeLynn."

Sutton threw a cold glare in J.D.'s direction but spoke in a carefully controlled voice. "I was, but I got a call from the Otero County courthouse earlier. I have to be in Alamogordo tomorrow and the day after to testify in a court case that's been tied up for the last sixteen months. I can't get out of it and I already made the arrangements for Corrie to go see RaeLynn tomorrow. I can't reschedule it with the holidays coming up. The most I could do was change it to have you going with her instead of me." He drew a deep breath. "I also don't want to put off this plan any longer than I have to. We need to try to find out who's threatening RaeLynn before she comes home. And time's running out."

J.D. nodded, refraining from asking anymore questions. He knew Sutton well enough to know that he wasn't in the mood to talk about whatever was bothering him. Whatever it was, it was affecting Corrie as well. She'd looked confused when J.D. had informed her that he was taking her to Santa Fe, and not exactly thrilled about it. He was stung by her subdued reaction; he had hoped she would have been a little more enthused that he, J.D., would be taking her.

What had surprised him even more was that the sheriff had made plans for an overnight stay in Santa Fe. "It's two rooms," he'd informed J.D. pointedly, handing him an envelope with a reservation email, confirming two rooms at one of the nicer hotels near the Plaza. Even Corrie had seemed surprised, but she didn't comment other than Jackie was going to have something to say about it. Sutton had, so far, avoided entering the campground store, but now he did to brief Corrie and J.D. about what to look out for, to be cautious about who was present when they talked to RaeLynn, to...."

"I think I got it, Sheriff," J.D. interrupted, trying not to sound insulted, even though he didn't appreciate Sutton telling him how to do his job. The sheriff stopped and inclined his head, muttering an apology to J.D. Another shock. Almost as shocking as how quickly the sheriff said good night and left, barely looking at Corrie.

It was eight in the morning when J.D. pulled the sheriff's Silverado up to the door of the campground store. The morning was chilly and he was glad to see that, while he stowed their overnight bags behind the seat, Corrie went in and filled travel cups with piñon coffee. She also held up a thermal lunch bag. "Breakfast burritos. I figured you wanted to get going right away so we don't have to stop to eat. No green chile on yours."

He grinned. "I ever tell you that you're a sweetheart? And this gets us on the road, but we're not going to rush this. You're scheduled to see RaeLynn at around three o'clock this afternoon, and also at ten o'clock tomorrow morning. When was the last time you visited Santa Fe or Albuquerque?"

She laughed and it was good to see a smile on her face. "I couldn't tell you. But when have *you* been there?"

"I don't count my brief sojourn when I landed in Albuquerque and drove home from the airport when I came back from Houston a few months ago. Or my trip with the sheriff a few weeks ago. So I'm going to see both places with fresh eyes, with someone who, I hope, is just as eager to see them."

"Sounds like you have a plan," she said, eyeing him suspiciously. He held the truck door open for her and gallantly ushered her in. He gave a cheerful wave to Jerry and Jackie, who stood at the door of the campground store, their concern and misgivings plain to see, though tempered with the knowledge that Corrie would be as safe with J.D. as she would be with the sheriff. He climbed into the driver's side and reached for her hand, giving it a reassuring squeeze.

"What better way to make our mysterious shadow not suspect our motives for going to visit RaeLynn than making this look like a pleasure trip? And what better way to make this LOOK like a pleasure trip than actually MAKING it a pleasure trip? So we just loosen up, have fun, and make sure we keep our eyes open for trouble. Piece of cake."

"If you say so, Detective," Corrie said with a grin. "So now what?"

He started the engine. "We eat our breakfast, enjoy the trip, and see what we can flush out from our unknown friend. And with any luck, RaeLynn will be safely home for Christmas."

"That's the best news I've heard all day."

By 11:30 in the morning, they had arrived in Albuquerque. J.D. had decided to take a slightly longer route than he and Rick had taken previously, with the idea that it might make a nice getaway for them both along with possibly throwing off anyone who might decide to follow them. Corrie had managed to evade J.D.'s subtle probing about what was bothering Rick – and her – for most of the trip. The fact that they were both discovering parts of New Mexico that neither of them were familiar with helped. She admitted that she hadn't been to Albuquerque since her father's initial illness when she was seventeen… and she stopped before she went on. The look J.D. gave her, full of compassion and understanding, told her that he made the connection between Billy's recovery and end of her relationship with Rick. He changed the subject and instead asked her to use his phone to find a place to stop for lunch.

Old Town Albuquerque wasn't too busy on a weekday between holidays. J.D. was able to find a parking spot on the street in front of the shops that were directly across the plaza from San Felipe de Neri church. Though there were several public parking lots within easy walking distance, Corrie was glad that Rick's truck would be in sight of the restaurant that she had found. Dos Hermanas was relatively busy for the lunch hour and they were seated near a large party that included an elderly priest in a threadbare cassock; an older couple – the man very British and correct, the woman looking like the neighbor who always shows up with a casserole; a young Native American man and an older one who seemed related to him; a young, college-age man with curly locks of hair and a dreamy expression; and a vivacious dark-haired woman who was engaged in banter with a nondescript middle-aged man who had his arm around the shoulders of an exotic-looking woman of exquisite beauty. They were seated near the window, ostensibly to keep an eye on the two animals waiting

179

outside the restaurant in an old Bronco: a regal-looking Savannah cat and a dog that looked to be part anteater. They were joined by an older man in a rumpled jacket with a gravelly voice, whom J.D. identified as a cop under his breath. "How do you know that?" Corrie hissed at him. J.D. merely grinned.

"We know our own, Corrie, no matter where we go." He squinted one eye at the man who seemed to sense J.D.'s gaze. He turned, gave J.D. a once-over glance and nodded. "He's a homicide detective," J.D. added, raising his iced tea glass in greeting.

Corrie felt a pang as the waitress darted around their large table delivering drinks and food with the ease of familiarity. Despite the festive holiday decorations in the restaurant and around the plaza, she couldn't work up any joyous expectancy about their trip. She hadn't felt so out of place in her entire life; she knew no one and no one knew her. J.D. seemed to feel a sense of camaraderie, just because he recognized a fellow cop in a city that was as strange to him as it was to her. But she suddenly felt homesick for Bonney, even though they'd only been gone a few hours, and lost and alone, even with J.D. by her side. She could only imagine how RaeLynn must have been feeling these last few weeks.

After lunch, they continued on to Santa Fe. Corrie began to feel anxious. She and J.D. had been conversing about inconsequential things – anything to keep him from asking about what had happened between her and Rick – but she realized that neither of them had been on the lookout for anyone who might have been following them. As they reached the outskirts of Santa Fe on Interstate 25, she began to pay closer attention to cars that passed them and the ones they passed, particularly any white car, Honda or otherwise, even craning her neck to look back over her shoulder. J.D. threw her a quizzical glance. "What are you doing?"

"I know you said we had to act like this was just a pleasure trip, but we have to remember that we really do have an important job to do. And we've been failing miserably."

"Oh, have we?" He cocked an eyebrow at her.

"Yes, we have," she snapped. "We're supposed to be on the lookout for that guy that was following you and Rick. The whole purpose of this trip was to draw him out into the open. We've been so busy chit-chatting that we've forgotten all about that!"

He laughed and shook his head. "Corrie, I haven't forgotten. I've been looking for him just as intently as you have... only not as obviously." He gave her a pointed look. "We don't want him to know the real reason why we're going to see RaeLynn, so we can't let him know we're looking for him. You're going to have to be a bit more discreet."

She felt a rush of heat to her face. "Was I that obvious?" She could kick herself. Had she already blown their cover? He reached over and squeezed her hand.

"Don't worry about it. Chances are he's not even following us yet."

"Yet?"

"He has an accomplice at the clinic. If that person found out about our visit, then he doesn't need to go all the way to Bonney to tail us. He can just wait for us in Santa Fe and follow us from there. That's when we need to be on our guard."

"Oh," Corrie said, relieved. She shrugged. "That's why I told Rick it would be best for a cop to come with me."

J.D. nodded. "But I'm going to need your eyes, too. Remember, I'm still a relative newcomer to Bonney. I only have this guy's description and not a very clear one, either. He was pretty well disguised. If he turns out to be someone from Bonney, I might not know who he is. And I'm willing to bet he's not driving that white Honda anymore."

"If he's in a different vehicle, how will we know we're being followed?" Corrie asked.

J.D. gave her a lop-sided grin. "We're trained to notice things that most people don't. And like I said, he won't bother to follow us here. It's once we leave the clinic that we'll have to keep a sharp eye out."

"We're going to be surrounded by strangers in Santa Fe," she said. She shivered and tugged her jacket closer around her even though the heater was on in the truck.

"Don't worry, Corrie," J.D. said softly. "I'll make sure to protect you and RaeLynn. We have to find out who wants her dead and why."

"I know; and I know it was all my idea to come talk to her. But I have this feeling I can't shake. A bad feeling. Don't take it personally," she added quickly, turning to J.D. "It's not that I don't trust you. You know I do. And I know Rick trusts you, too. It's just..." She stopped when J.D. continued to look at her curiously and she felt foolish. She forced a smile. "Sorry. I've got a lot of stuff on my mind and it's making me sound crazy."

"Not at all. You have every right to feel a bit unsettled."

You have no idea, she thought, fighting back another shiver.

They arrived at the clinic. J.D. had been scanning the area for anything that seemed out of place, but the whole area appeared to be deserted. He used the code the sheriff had given him to allow them access to the clinic and he noticed Corrie's interest sharpened as they pulled into the clinic parking lot. "You've never been here before, have you?" he asked.

She shook her head, looking around at the high wall around the clinic, the tall building, and the immaculately groomed grounds. Despite the cold, only a few patches of snow were on the ground. "No. I've only heard about it." That was all she said and J.D. decided not to press.

They entered the lobby and the same receptionist that had greeted him and the sheriff on their previous visit was already waiting to escort them to the door leading into the clinic. She gave Corrie a quick nod and then looked at J.D. expectantly. "There was no one on the street when we came in," he assured her.

"Thank you, Detective," she said, relief plainly on her face and in her voice. "Come this way, please."

"She didn't ask for my I.D.," Corrie whispered to J.D. as the security guard opened the door for them.

He shrugged. "You can thank the sheriff for that," he murmured, as they followed the receptionist down the hall past Dr. Pruett's office. The door was tightly shut and it wasn't clear if the doctor was in or not. The receptionist waved them on, saying she needed to get back to the front. They went straight to the nurse's station where Rosa was ensconced behind the desk, as usual. Her brows rose when she saw J.D. with Corrie.

"I thought Sheriff Sutton was coming back to see Miss Shaffer," she said tartly, her eyes boring into J.D.'s. She gave Corrie a suspicious glare, as if wondering if Corrie had been the one to make the change. Corrie just gazed back at her calmly and let J.D. do the talking.

"Sheriff Sutton had something important come up and couldn't make it. He didn't want to change the appointment so he asked me to accompany Miss Black. And he did clear this with the clinic," he added. Rosa's face reddened slightly.

"Miss Shaffer is in the day room. I believe she's the only one there."

"And her security?" It was J.D.'s turn to be sharp.

"They're with her, of course," Rosa snapped as she rose from behind her desk. "Sheriff Sutton said they were to be with her constantly, unless he specifically says it's all right for them to leave." She threw a challenging glance at J.D.

He drew an envelope from an inner pocket of his jacket and handed it to the nurse without saying a word. She practically snatched it from him and read the email that was enclosed. J.D. cleared his throat. "Dr. Pruett specifically forwarded that to you, as you can see," he said. "I have the same privileges and authority as Sheriff Sutton does, so if there is a problem, we can discuss it with Dr. Pruett...."

"I haven't seen him today," Rosa muttered, setting the envelope and email down on her desk. "He's been in his office all morning and said he's not to be disturbed." She pressed her lips together and avoided both his and Corrie's eyes. "I'll take you to the day room."

Behind her back, J.D. looked at Corrie. He shook his head at her and she gave a single nod. She understood not to say anything or ask any questions. They reached the end of the corridor where there was a set of double doors with narrow windows. The same two security guards who had been outside RaeLynn's room stood on either side and they recognized J.D. immediately. They checked Corrie's identification, and J.D.'s as well, as Rosa stood by, tapping her foot impatiently. "Is Officer Yellowcloud still providing security as well?" J.D. asked.

"Yes," answered one of the men. "She's with her right now. There's a nurse there, too, just doing routine checks. Debbie said you could go right in when you got here."

J.D. thanked him, aware that the security guards seemed to be more well-informed about their visit than Rosa was. The sheriff had advised him of their suspicions regarding the connection between RaeLynn's abduction and someone at the clinic. He reached for the door just as it swung open and Nurse Price started when she saw them. "Oh! Detective Wilder?" She stared at him, then stammered, "I thought Rick... uh, Sheriff Sutton was coming?"

"You must be Ellie," Corrie said, making Nurse Price jump. She stared at Corrie in confusion then her eyes widened in dawning realization as Corrie went on, "Rick told me about you. I'm Corrie Black and I'm here to see RaeLynn." Her manner was polite, but she didn't smile and Eleanor Price's face paled slightly.

"Oh, you're... you're...." She cleared her throat. "Yes, Miss Shaffer is expecting you. I'll leave you alone now." She moved past them, her eyes fixed on the floor, and she hurried down the hall, Rosa behind her.

J.D. shook his head and held the door for Corrie. She stepped into the room and he heard RaeLynn gasp.

"Corrie!"

"RaeLynn!"

He halted just inside the door and watched as the two women rushed to each other and embraced. He smiled and caught the eye of Officer Yellowcloud who was also smiling at the reunion. She moved over to J.D. and extended her hand. "I can wait to be formally introduced. How are you doing, Detective?"

"Doing well, Officer." He shook her hand. She looked the same as she had the last time he saw her nearly a month earlier. He nodded toward Corrie and RaeLynn. "Miss Shaffer looks like she's doing a lot better."

"She's gained some weight, gotten some strength back, some color in her face," Debbie said, nodding. "She couldn't wait to see her friend. She's been on pins and needles all day."

By this time Corrie and RaeLynn had moved to a loveseat on the other side of the room, still chatting excitedly and totally ignoring J.D. and Officer Yellowcloud. J.D. smiled to himself. He'd told Corrie to get RaeLynn aside to talk to her privately while he kept security and the nurses away. He cleared his throat to get Debbie's attention. "What do the doctors and nurses say about her condition?"

She cast another glance toward the two women then, seemingly satisfied that everything was fine, she turned her full attention to J.D. "She's been examined by Dr. Pruett three times a week and the counselors have had regular visits with her every other day. I've been with her every time, even during her counseling sessions, with her express permission, of course. Not sure what the counselors think of that, but it seems to me that she doesn't need the therapy. It's more just to follow the clinic's treatment protocols. I'm not a healthcare professional but I think she's doing really well."

"Has she expressed any concerns to you about... anything?" J.D. asked.

Debbie Yellowcloud shook her head, sending her long braid swinging. "She hasn't gotten really chummy with me or anyone else," she said. "In fact, the best way to describe her is 'painfully polite'. This is the most emotion she's shown since you and the sheriff came to see her last month. Wait, that's not true," she corrected herself. "Yesterday, when the sheriff called to make arrangements, she became particularly animated when she got off the phone with him."

"Miss Shaffer talked to the sheriff directly?" J.D. asked.

Debbie nodded. "Yes. Dr. Pruett took her to his office to tell her that she had a call from the sheriff. He handed her the phone and she talked to the sheriff for a few minutes. She didn't say much. But her eyes lit up and then she looked panicked for a few seconds, but then she calmed down and said 'yes' a few times. She looked nervous and excited when she handed the phone back to the doctor and she told him that she did want to have her friend come visit, if that was all right. Pruett agreed and said he'd make the arrangements. So I walked her back to her room and she was pretty restless the rest of the day. Probably the excitement of having a visitor."

J.D. nodded. Out of the corner of his eye, he saw RaeLynn take her hand out of the pocket of the cardigan she was wearing and lay it flat on the loveseat cushion and push it toward Corrie. As Corrie's fingers moved toward RaeLynn's hand, J.D. hurried to say something else to keep Officer Yellowcloud's focus on him. "No other visitors have come to see her?"

"Nope, and she hasn't requested any, except for you guys." She glanced toward RaeLynn and Corrie and J.D. held his breath as he looked that way. The two women were holding each other's hands and he was sure he saw tears on both their faces. As much as he was itching to go see what they were talking about, he knew he had to keep Officer Yellowcloud away from them. "Man, she's really happy to see her friend. Who is she, anyway? She wouldn't tell me anything about who was coming to see her."

"They've been friends since they were kids," J.D. said, wishing he could find a way to get the security officer out of the day room, but he doubted she would blatantly ignore the sheriff's strict orders. "Corrie's been very worried about RaeLynn and RaeLynn probably feels bad that she made Corrie worry." Debbie continued to eye them and she pursed her lips.

"I hope Miss Shaffer isn't getting too worked up. The nurses won't like that." She made a move as if to go check on RaeLynn, but J.D. touched her arm, shaking his head.

"She's fine, trust me. She needs this more than anything the doctors or counselors can do for her." His words seem to stop the security officer, though she continued to watch the two women. "Believe me, Officer Yellowcloud, I've worked narcotics for many years and I've seen just about everything that you can imagine. She'll show more improvement after this visit than you've seen in the last few weeks."

Debbie looked at him and a corner of her mouth lifted. "I think you're right, Detective Wilder. I'm just making sure I don't relax my guard. Sheriff Sutton made it seem like she was in imminent danger. Hardly anything has happened except for that one incident when you and he came last time and someone got into the building without authorization."

"Nothing else has happened?" J.D. asked.

The young officer shook her head. "Not that I'm aware of. But if you don't mind me saying so – and I realize it's probably nothing or not my business – I've noticed there's been a bit of tension among the nursing staff."

J.D.'s brows rose. "Really? Anyone in particular?"

Debbie jerked her head toward the door while keeping her eyes on Corrie and RaeLynn who were now laughing with each other. "Mainly between the two nurses, Rosa and the other one, Ellie. Rosa tries to keep Ellie away from Miss Shaffer, even if there aren't any other nurses on duty. The clinic doesn't have a large amount of residents right now, so Ellie naturally has time to do extra checks on them. Anytime she goes near Miss Shaffer's room, Rosa suddenly shows up and asks her if she has anything else she needs to be doing. Rosa's probably not happy that she was in doing a routine check on her when you guys showed up."

"Is it a common practice to check on patients when they're in the day room?" J.D. asked.

Debbie frowned. "I don't know. I mean, I suppose they check their vitals and all on a regular schedule. I haven't noticed if they do this with all patients."

"Something to inquire about," J.D. said under his breath. Debbie looked alarmed and J.D. quickly told her, "Don't worry about it, Officer. It's just something that occurred to me."

"It should have occurred to me," she muttered. "Maybe I should ask the other guards if they've noticed."

"Not a bad idea," he said. Officer Yellowcloud looked uncertainly back at RaeLynn and Corrie then at J.D and bit her lip, torn between what she considered her duties. "Would you rather I talk to the security guys about it?" he asked. She looked slightly alarmed.

"No, no, I'll ask them. I wouldn't want Sheriff Sutton to think I'm not doing my job."

"I won't say a word," J.D. said. "I'll go say hello to Miss Shaffer while you go talk to them. I'll make sure she's safe," he assured her. Debbie nodded and slipped out the door and J.D. made a beeline for the two women. They looked up as he approached them and perched on the edge of a chair near them. "Sorry to interrupt, ladies, good to see you, Miss Shaffer, I've only got a second, how's it going?" he said all in one breath, careful to keep his voice low.

Corrie rolled her eyes and shook her head. "Hi, J.D., everything's fine," she said dryly.

RaeLynn smiled, her eyes brighter than they were the last time J.D. had seen her. "Hi, Detective Wilder. Thanks so much for bringing Corrie to see me. You have no idea how much I appreciate it."

J.D. nodded. "We don't have much time...," he began but RaeLynn cut him off grasping his hand. He nearly drew back in shock but she gripped it tighter.

"I know," she breathed, pressing something into his palm, then pulled her own hand back. Her voice was slightly louder and brighter as she went on, "I'm so glad you were able to come, even if it was just a short visit. But you'll be back tomorrow morning, right?"

"At ten o'clock," J.D. said automatically. RaeLynn folded her hands into her lap as Officer Yellowcloud came back into the room. "If that's all right with you and your doctors, of course," he added, glancing up at the young officer. "Officer Yellowcloud, you haven't had a chance to meet Corrie Black. She's an old friend of Miss Shaffer's."

"Hello," Corrie said, standing up and offering a hand to Debbie Yellowcloud. Whatever RaeLynn had passed to Corrie was neatly concealed. She went on, "Sorry my manners went out the window when I came in, Officer."

"Call me Debbie. And no apology needed," Debbie said, her braid, which was almost as long as Corrie's, swinging as she shook her head. "Detective Wilder explained the situation."

RaeLynn stood up as well as Rosa reappeared in the doorway. "I guess my visiting time is up. We only get a half hour a day, unless Dr. Pruett allows a longer one." Her excitement and animation faded as they moved toward the door. Rosa was already looking at her watch and J.D. wondered if she would dock them time tomorrow if they went over their allotted time today. "Thanks so much again for coming, Corrie. I know it's a long trip...."

"That's why we asked to see you tomorrow as well. I wish we could stay longer, but I do have to get back to work," Corrie said with a grimace.

RaeLynn nodded then hugged Corrie fiercely. "I can't wait to go back to work. I'll be home as soon as I can," she whispered, blinking back tears. J.D. had to glance away and his eyes caught the gaze of Rosa, focused on the two women. Her face was a mask of suspicion and impatience which she tempered when she caught J.D. watching her. She cleared her throat.

"I expect you're tired after your visit, Miss Shaffer," Rosa said. "Would you like something to help you rest?"

"No, thank you," RaeLynn said. "I'm fine. I'll go to my room and read for a while."

Rosa nodded and said nothing else as Corrie and J.D. stepped into the hallway. As she escorted RaeLynn back to her room, Nurse Price approached them, blatantly ignoring Rosa as she passed her. "I'll show you both out," she said. She didn't make eye contact with either of them. Officer Yellowcloud and the two security guards had followed Rosa and RaeLynn. As Nurse Price started to follow them down the hallway, J.D. caught Corrie's arm and slowed his steps to let them get out of earshot. He cleared his throat and Nurse Price glanced at him. A look of alarm crossed her face and she looked toward the other group but they had already rounded the corner, heading to the patients' rooms.

"Mind if I ask you something, Nurse Price?" J.D. asked. He kept his voice low and she had no choice but to move closer.

"I can't give you any information about any of the patients," she said firmly.

"I'm aware of that," J.D. said. "I'm just curious about how often the patients have to undergo routine care checks. You know, temperature, blood pressure, all that."

There was a wariness in Nurse Price's eyes. She shrugged. "It depends."

"On what?"

"Lots of things," she said tersely. "The patient's condition, doctor's orders...."

"Do you do checks wherever the patient happens to be or do you normally do them in the patients' room?"

Before Nurse Price could answer, Rosa came back around the corner. Her eyes narrowed as she glared at the younger nurse. "Don't you have other duties to tend to?" she asked sharply.

Eleanor Price straightened up, her cheeks flaming red. "Detective Wilder had a question for me. About Miss Shaffer's condition."

"Miss Shaffer is perfectly capable of answering questions about her own condition and care, Detective," Rosa snapped. She whipped an envelope out of her pocket and handed it to J.D. "I almost forgot to give you this. Don't keep Nurse Price, I'm sure she has a lot of work to catch up on," she huffed as she turned and stalked off down the hall. Ellie stared after her and J.D. noticed she was trembling. He exchanged a glance with Corrie. She had noticed it, too.

"Are you all right, Miss Price?" he asked.

She spun on him. "Why are you asking these questions, Detective Wilder?" she hissed. She shook her head. "Your visiting time is up and I have to get back to my duties. Now please, let me escort you out before I get into any more trouble."

He held a small white card out to her. "We're not here to make trouble. If you can't talk to me here, call me. We'll be in town till tomorrow afternoon. We can meet wherever you want at whatever time."

The look on the young woman's face was a mixture of fear and frustration. She snatched the card and stuffed it into a pocket. "You need to go," she said firmly.

Chapter 19

As they drove to the hotel from the clinic, Corrie was relieved that J.D. was too focused on watching for anyone following them to talk much. Random flecks of snow were beginning to fall from the gray sky and she pulled her coat tighter around herself despite the warmth from the truck's heater, though it wasn't the weather that made her feel chilled.

She was glad Rick had told her that Ellie was still at the clinic. He hadn't wanted her to be caught unprepared, as he had been. She could almost feel sorry for the young nurse, but she wasn't as forgiving as Rick was... at least, not when it came to anyone who tried to hurt the people she cared about. After five years, she was surprised that her anger had flared up for a moment, only to be replaced by curiosity as to why Eleanor Price was still working there after everything that had happened.

The hotel wasn't far from the Santa Fe Plaza and the Cathedral Basilica of St. Francis of Assisi. Corrie hoped she might be able to attend a Mass there the next morning, and she hoped J.D. didn't mind a quick walking tour of the area. Under normal circumstances, she wouldn't have worried about going by herself, but she was sure that wandering alone in a strange city with the possibility of being followed by a dangerous individual was out of the question.

"Do you really think Nurse Price is going to call you?" Corrie asked, breaking the silence. They were circling the area around the hotel, trying to find which one-way street allowed them access to the hotel's parking garage.

J.D. shrugged. "Hard to say. If she's scared enough, she might. I just wish I knew who or what everyone is so afraid of. Of course, then the case would be solved," he added dryly.

"No one's been following us?" she asked, barely refraining from looking over her shoulder. She hoped if someone was watching them, they would think she was just another rubbernecking tourist.

"If they are, they're being way more careful than the last time," he said, finally getting a break in the line of cars to turn into the parking garage. The attendant asked for their reservation number and parking voucher, since they hadn't checked in yet, and it made Corrie feel better to see a sign that said only hotel guests were allowed to park in the garage and it had 24-hour security. As if reading her mind, J.D. shook his head. "That doesn't mean we can let our guard down. Not for a second. We don't know who this guy is or what he wants."

"I'm assuming it's whatever is in these notes RaeLynn slipped us. She said she had one for you, too," Corrie said, slipping a tightly folded piece of paper out of her jeans pocket. It was barely the size of a quarter and about three times as thick, and it was neatly wrapped in a piece of chewing gum foil.

"Keep it stashed for now," J.D. warned, as he found a vacant parking space between two smaller and far more expensive vehicles. He wasn't surprised that the parking attendant had given Sutton's truck a rather dubious look, as if J.D. might be in the wrong place. "At least until we can get someplace where no one will see us. Just don't throw it away by mistake," he added. Corrie poked him in the arm.

"Where's yours?" she asked.

"In my jeans pocket." He pulled an envelope out of his jacket, checked the contents, then handed it to her. "That's our reservation confirmation," he said. He looked around and then reached over the back seat and grabbed their bags. He slung his over his shoulder and picked hers up by the handle. "Let's go," he said.

"I can carry mine," she protested. He shook his head and smiled.

"I know you can, but I was raised better," he said.

She rolled her eyes and laughed, but she noticed he was still scanning the area without seeming to as they made their way to the elevator that took them up to the hotel lobby.

There weren't many people at the registration desk and J.D. made sure to be able to keep a full view of the doors that opened to the street as well as the elevators, stairs, and the lounge that opened off of the lobby. They waited until the other guests had left before Corrie approached the desk clerk and handed him the envelope with their reservation information.

"Oh...." The clerk grimaced and Corrie felt a twinge of alarm.

"Is there a problem?" she asked. J.D. turned toward her and raised a brow. He drew closer as the clerk tapped on the desk.

"Well, yes. Um, there's been a water leak in one of the two rooms you have reserved, ma'am. A pipe burst in the wall and took out the power in the room as well, so that room is closed until we can get a contractor in there to fix it. I'm afraid there's only one room available."

"What?" Both Corrie and J.D. yelped, causing a few heads in the lobby to turn their way. The clerk jumped, and Corrie waved at J.D. to back off and let her handle it. She cleared her throat. "Are you sure there isn't another room available?" she asked, keeping her voice low.

The clerk shook his head. "I'm afraid we're fully booked, ma'am. The holidays, you know, the city gets a lot of tourists. I'm sure a lot of the other hotels are booked solid as well. Of course, we'll give you a full refund on the other room, and a voucher for dinner at a local restaurant. And two free drinks in our lounge," he added hurriedly, as if afraid Corrie might ask to speak to his manager and get him fired. J.D. had edged closer and Corrie avoided his eyes as she felt the color in her face rise.

"Well, I guess we'll have to take the room," J.D. said. "I mean, it's got two beds in it, right?" The clerk blushed.

"Um, no, sir. I'm afraid all the rooms only have a double bed."

Corrie wondered if this could be any more awkward if it were Rick who had accompanied her on this trip. "It'll be fine," she said, firmly. The clerk didn't bother to hide his relief. He quickly gave them their key card and paperwork for the room and told them to take the stairs to the second floor.

They didn't say a word as they reached their room, easily identified by the workmen standing in the doorway next to it. The men apologized for the noise and assured them that they would stop work at 5 p.m. and put a "Do Not Disturb" sign on the door to prevent anyone from trying to get into the room. J.D. set their bags down, took the key card from Corrie, then motioned for her to stand aside. She nodded and waited while he opened the door and quickly checked their accommodations, wondering what the workmen would think if they saw him draw his gun to sweep the room. "Okay," he said and she grabbed the bags and slipped inside. She was stunned at how small the room was, despite its obvious luxury. A queen-size bed, overflowing with pillows and cushions dominated the floor space, leaving a narrow path to the bathroom. The only other furniture in the room were an antique armoire, a writing desk with a phone and lamp, and two wing chairs situated on either side of a door that led into the adjoining room. A single window looked out onto the busy downtown street; there was no balcony. J.D. edged his way around the bed and tested the window and then checked the door to the adjoining room to make sure both were secure. Corrie leaned against the wall and cleared her throat. "Aren't we being a little paranoid?" she asked. "I mean, no one, except for you and Rick, knew we were going to be staying here. Even I didn't know."

"You know what Sutton says about coincidences," J.D. said grimly. "I don't particularly care for the timing of one of our rooms being suddenly unavailable. You're probably right," he added, holding up his hands, "but get used to me being overly cautious until this case is solved."

Corrie rolled her eyes. "If you say so, Detective." She straightened up and slipped her jacket off and draped it over one of the wing chairs. "Do you think it's safe to look at those notes RaeLynn passed us?"

He nodded. "Let's do it." They took the foil-wrapped notes from their pockets, unable to resist a quick look around the room as they did so, and then unfolded them. There was silence for a few seconds as they read the words on the scraps of notepaper. Corrie looked up with a frown.

"Not much information here," she said. "It just says, 'I was locked in a small room with just a bed and they kept me handcuffed to it most of the time. It was dark and there were no windows. I could hear them talking through the door. There were three men besides Cliff. I also heard Teddy's voice once or twice. But I never saw their faces, not even the one who,'" Corrie paused, swallowed hard and blinked tears out of her eyes before she went on, "'who assaulted me. He wore a ski mask every time, but he had dark brown eyes. He was tall and husky, and he usually wore dark blue sweat pants and a black sweatshirt. He wore some kind of strong aftershave. Maybe I can recognize it, if I ever smell it again. I don't remember if he ever said anything. I blocked out a lot of what happened, but I'll try to remember anything else I can. I know I recognized the voice of the one who seemed to be in charge, but I can't remember where I've heard it. There's another voice that sounds familiar, but I don't know who it is, it sounded like he had a sore throat or maybe he was trying to disguise it. They talked about money that was owed to them. I don't remember what they said it was for, but I think it might be guns or drugs. The leader of the group was angry, said it was time to make people pay up, that he was getting ready to make a move to bigger things and he wasn't going to let those people stand in his way. I don't know what people he was talking about. He told Cliff he better not make the same mistake again because he didn't have another sister. I think Cliff owed him money and when he didn't get it, Cliff told him to take me instead. If I tried to fight back, they would beat me and shoot me up with drugs. After a while, they started whispering instead of talking in normal voices so I couldn't hear them. That's when I knew they were going to get rid of me, because they thought I knew too much. But I don't know anything else.' And that's all that my note says," Corrie finished bleakly. J.D. had been reading his note silently as she read hers, nodding along the way. He looked up at her, his gray eyes stormy.

"No descriptions that'll help us. She doesn't even indicate that she knows where she was. It could have been Bonney or some other place. If she ever heard those men's voices again, she might recognize them, but she couldn't prove it was who she heard, no matter how positive she might be. Same goes for that aftershave. I mean, thousands of guys in the area probably wear it." He sighed, then gestured for Corrie to hand him her note. She did and he laid them side by side on the writing desk and took out his cell phone.

"What are you doing?" Corrie asked.

He took several pictures of the two notes with his phone, then of each note individually, making sure the text was clear in each photo. "I'm texting photos of these notes to the sheriff and to Officer Camacho. That's the fastest way to make sure they don't get lost even if...." He stopped and glanced at Corrie.

She nodded. "In case anything happens to the originals," she finished for him.

He gave her a wry smile. "Yeah, that's one way of putting it. And maybe they can start looking for any signs of these men." He took a minute to add an explanation to the photos before sending the texts. Corrie glanced around the room while he was focused on sending his messages. The bed was certainly big enough for two people but THAT was definitely not going to happen. She had no idea what J.D. was thinking about the whole situation. She had a fleeting thought of asking the desk clerk if the hotel had a rollaway bed or cot they could use, but there was hardly enough floor space to walk in the room, let alone get another bed in. He spoke up, breaking into her thoughts. "I know it's barely four-thirty, but maybe we should go get an early dinner. It gets dark early and there's snow in the forecast for tonight."

"Sounds good," she said quickly, turning away before he saw the flush of heat on her face and grabbing her jacket. "Any ideas where...?"

She stopped as J.D.'s cell phone buzzed. He sighed. "Probably Sutton wanting to ask questions," he muttered as he unclipped his phone and swiped it open. He frowned, then his forehead cleared. "I'll bet I know who this is," he said. "Detective Wilder. Yes, Miss Price, we're still in town." He glanced at Corrie and gave her a thumbs up sign. "Sure, we can meet. Wherever you like." He paused and listened intently, raising a brow. "Okay, what time is good for you? Okay, we'll be right there. Thanks for calling." He hung up and returned his phone to its clip. "You're not going to believe this," he said.

"Wait, wait, let me guess!" Corrie said dramatically, closing her eyes and pressing her fingers to her forehead, as if reading J.D.'s mind. "Um, Nurse Price has decided to talk to us! Am I right?" she said, opening her eyes and grinning at J.D.

"Funny," he said. "And you're right, but you won't believe where we're meeting her. Get your coat on and let's go!"

The streets were getting busier as the end of the work day drew closer and the downtown area was crowded with pedestrians. Bits of snow swirled in the cold air and bright lights from the Christmas decorations adorning the majority of businesses created a near-kaleidoscope effect as J.D. and Corrie made their way toward their meeting place with Eleanor Price. It wasn't far from the hotel, so J.D. suggested walking instead of having to deal with finding a parking spot for the truck. He kept a sharp eye out, even though he knew that the dozens, if not hundreds, of people shopping and making their way to restaurants, stores, and bars presented an almost impossible obstacle to recognizing anyone following them. Especially since the majority of people were wearing heavy coats and hats and scarves.

They reached San Francisco Street, which ran past the Plaza. Turning right would take them into the teeming crowds enjoying an outdoor Christmas concert; the sounds of a mariachi band floated through the chilly air. J.D. could tell that Corrie was enthralled by the music, but also apprehensive about the crush of people. Her relief was palpable as he took her arm and steered her to the left.

"Do you have any idea where we're going?" she finally asked, keeping as close to him as possible even as they weaved around people who seemed to be striding far more purposefully than they were. He surprised her by taking hold of her hand and nudging her away from the street so that he was between her and the curb. Even through their gloves, she could feel the warmth and strength of his grip and it made her feel immediately safer.

"We're almost there," he said as they crossed Burro Alley and walked past the Lensic Performing Arts Center. He glanced around quickly as the number of pedestrians thinned out and then he stopped. "What do you think?" he asked her with a sly grin.

At first, she had no idea what he was talking about then her eyes widened as he pointed ahead of them. She looked up and saw the barrel-shaped sign hanging over the sidewalk. "Noisy Water Winery?" she gasped. J.D.'s smile widened.

"I found out they have a tasting room here before we left Bonney and I was going to surprise you, but then Nurse Price suggested it. We're a little early to meet up with her. Care for a glass of Jo Mamma's White while we wait?"

"Are you sure that's a good idea?" she asked as they entered the tasting room. A few people perched on stools at the bar, enjoying glasses of wine and platters of cheese and crackers, and the cheerful young woman serving them offered a warm greeting and told them to sit where they liked. J.D. guided her to a table near the front window. They could only see one end of the street, but they couldn't be seen unless anyone looking for them came into the tasting room.

"It'll be fine. We don't want to look like we're suspicious or threatening. We're just out for a relaxing evening," he said with a wink. A blush rose up to Corrie's cheeks and she hoped J.D. would attribute it to the cold air outside and the warmth inside the tasting room. She busied herself removing her coat and hanging it on the back of her chair. J.D. did the same and then went over to the bar to place their order.

Corrie looked out the window and tried to relax. She felt wound up, tense, and it wasn't just from RaeLynn's cryptic notes. She tried to stay focused on the purpose of their visit to the winery and not what might come up later. Rick's kiss, despite his subsequent apology, was something she relived several times a day, though she felt guilty every time she did. She was so confused; mixed signals from Rick and obscure signals from J.D. If he was signaling at all. Maybe it was all in her imagination.

He came back to their table with their wine glasses, hers filled with her favorite Jo Mamma's sweet white wine, his with a dark red one. "Thank you," she said, picking up her glass. "What are you having?"

"Reserve Cabernet Sauvignon." He held up his glass and she touched the rim of her glass to his. "I've got a cheese platter coming, too. Something to hold us over until dinner."

Corrie nodded, taking a sip of her wine. She told herself not to look out the window too often, following J.D.'s lead, although she was certain he was scrutinizing every person that passed by the winery. The cheese platter arrived and Corrie wasn't sure she would be able to eat much; her stomach was tied in knots. "What time is Nurse Price supposed to get here?" she asked, setting her wine glass down before her shaking hands dropped it.

J.D. glanced at his watch. "Still another half hour or so. She had to wait till she was relieved at the clinic before she could meet us." He leaned across the table and touched her wrist. "Hey, it's going to be okay. Just relax."

She forced a smile. "I just wish I knew what RaeLynn's note meant. And that this was all behind us and she was home safe."

He waited, a look of expectation on his face. She wondered if he was hoping she would go on to say that she wished they were on an actual weekend getaway. Again, the memory of Rick's kiss flashed into her mind and she felt her face flame. One glance at J.D.'s eyes and she had to look away. She toyed with a cracker on the plate and picked up her wine glass. The buzz of J.D.'s cell phone gave her a welcome distraction. He repressed a sigh as he glanced at the screen and swiped the phone open. "Howdy, Sheriff," he said dryly. "What took you so long?"

Corrie could hear Rick's voice though it was slightly muffled and she looked nervously toward the other patrons at the bar. She was relieved when J.D. turned slightly so his back was to them, but she could still hear Rick. "Just got out of court. I'm still in Alamogordo and I have to come back tomorrow. I might just stay here tonight."

"You got my texts?"

"Yes. You got any ideas?"

"I was hoping you might," J.D. admitted. He looked at Corrie and she shook her head. "There wasn't much to go on. She didn't know where she was being held, how far away."

Rick grunted. "Still nothing going on with the Shaffers. Dudley says Cliff is really laying low. He hasn't left the trailer at all today." He was silent and both Corrie and J.D. waited, knowing he wouldn't speak until he had his thoughts in order. "But now we know Cliff and Teddy were involved, which means that, wherever RaeLynn was all that time, it was probably close to Bonney. Which means it's possible those other three men have connections to Bonney as well." His voice became brisk. "You're still going to see her tomorrow?"

"We've got another visit at ten in the morning," J.D. affirmed. "Maybe she'll have more to tell us. The fact that she slipped us these notes the way she did tells me she knows there's a breach in security at the clinic, but she doesn't know who it is, either."

Corrie glanced out the window, letting Rick and J.D. continue their discussion. Foot traffic on the sidewalk had increased, many people making their way to the parking garage directly across the street from the winery. The wind had picked up and the snow was beginning to fall heavier than earlier. She was glad she had brought a heavy coat and boots and she wondered what the weather back in Bonney was like.

As the stream of people thinned slightly, she noticed a person – she couldn't tell if it was a man or a woman – walking slowly in the opposite direction of the majority of the pedestrians across the street. He, or she, was staring in the direction of the winery, seemingly unaware of the teeming crowds, and wearing a dark gray trench coat that completely covered his or her outfit, a knitted hat and scarf obscuring his or her face, hands deep in pockets. Could it be Ellie Price? Was she checking to see if Corrie and J.D. were in the winery before coming in? Or was she checking to see if anyone else was around? Afraid to take her eyes off the figure in case it should suddenly take off running, she slid her hand around their wine glasses and poked J.D.'s arm.

Out of the corner of her eye, she saw him look up from his call and she made a slight motion for him to look out the window. He stiffened and she looked at him.

"I'll call you back," he told Rick as he stood up. Corrie stood as well. The person glanced up and down the street and started to jaywalk in their direction. J.D. gestured for Corrie to sit down. "I think that's her. She's a little early, but...."

Suddenly, Ellie – if it was Ellie – stopped dead in the middle of the street, oblivious to the vehicle traffic, and stared toward J.D.'s and Corrie's right, in the direction of Sandoval Street. Neither Corrie nor J.D. could see what had attracted her attention because a group of customers entering the winery blocked their view through the window, but Ellie spun around, narrowly missing being hit by a car, and sprinted back across the street.

"Stay here!" J.D. hissed at Corrie as he made for the door, shouldering his way past the people entering, and made a dash after the fleeing figure.

"J.D.!" Corrie cried as she jumped up. The young woman behind the bar looked up, concerned. She took one look at Corrie's face and waved at her to follow him.

"His tab's paid up. Go ahead!" she said. Forgetting about their coats, Corrie also ran for the door.

Once on the sidewalk, she took a second to look around to see where they might have gone. Neither J.D. nor Ellie Price were in sight, but a small group of people who had stopped and were looking down a side street gave her a clue. Fortunately a break in traffic allowed her to cross the street without incident. Snow was falling harder, making the street and sidewalks slippery but she ran as fast as she could, hoping she was doing the right thing. The side street wasn't as busy as the main road but still she had to weave around several people, glancing into shops along the way, in the event that they had ducked inside one of them.

Suddenly Corrie came to a dead stop and her heart began to pound with the realization that Nurse Price had run scared. But from whom? She hadn't seen J.D. yet and she was planning to meet him; she wouldn't have run from him, would she? There had to have been someone else.... She spun around, dread closing up her throat, scanning the people around her, expecting to see someone running in her direction, also intent on catching J.D. and Nurse Price. But no one seemed to be taking any note of her. She shivered. She had left her coat behind, as J.D. had, and the wind was slicing through her like a knife. She started running again, not quite sure where she was, but sensing she was heading back in the direction of their hotel. Snowflakes stung her cheeks and she prayed she wouldn't get lost. Part of her wanted to yell out J.D.'s name but she didn't want to draw unnecessary attention to herself. She had no idea if he was anywhere nearby, anyway. She gritted her teeth, bent her head against the driving snow, and, without breaking her stride, turned left at the next corner, running smack into....

" J.D.!"

"Corrie!" he cried, catching her as she slipped on the icy sidewalk and nearly took them both to the ground. She gasped, clutching at his shoulders as his arms slid around her waist. "Are you all right?" he said.

"I'm fine," she stammered, as he drew her out of the way of the crowds. She looked around. "Was that Nurse Price? Where did she go?"

"Good question," J.D. said grimly. It was then that Corrie noticed that he was clutching a knitted hat and scarf in his hands along with a familiar-looking gray trench coat. "I found her disguise, but she's disappeared."

"You're sure it was her?" Corrie asked, as her teeth began to chatter.

J.D. took her arm firmly and they began to make their way back to the winery, stepping carefully around patches of ice that had collected on the sidewalk. "Let's get out of the cold. To answer your question," he said, his dark gray eyes looking like storm clouds, "I didn't see her face so I wouldn't be able to swear to it in a court of law. On the other hand, who else knew we were meeting at Noisy Water? She set up the appointment...." His voice trailed off and he stopped and turned to Corrie, concern creasing his forehead. "Did you happen to see what spooked her?" he asked.

"I didn't even think about it until a half block ago," she admitted ruefully. "I just ran after you and didn't look anywhere except the direction you went."

He shook his head, clearly annoyed with himself. "I should have thought of that," he muttered, as they resumed walking. They arrived at the winery and brushed off the snowflakes that had accumulated on them before walking into the cozy warmth. The young woman at the bar looked up in relief.

"I'm so glad you're back," she said, making her way from the back of the room. The patrons at the bar had thinned out and she hurried toward J.D. and Corrie with a look of apprehension on her face. "I hope everything's okay. After you left, I kept an eye on your table, but then I got busy and when I was ringing up a sale, a man went over and picked up your jacket," she said addressing J.D. He stared at her.

"Picked it up? You mean he took it?" he asked in disbelief.

The bartender shook her head. "No, no, when I saw him, he was holding it in his hands, looking it over. I told him that table was occupied and that you would be right back. He didn't seem startled, just put your jacket back on the chair and said something like, 'Okay', and then he left." J.D. and Corrie exchanged a glance.

"You're sure it was a man?" he asked. The young woman nodded. "Did you happen to get a good look at him?" he asked. She bit her lip and grimaced.

"I saw what he was wearing," she admitted. "Dark shades, which he kept on the whole time he was here. He had a dark mustache and goatee. And a long gray trench coat, knitted hat...." Her voice trailed away as she saw what J.D. had in his hands. "And a scarf," she finished. "Just like those," she added, gesturing at the items. "After he left, I took both your jackets into the back to make sure it didn't happen again, and I'll get you a fresh cheese platter and wine, but I don't know if you had anything in your pockets that he might have taken. I didn't notice him until he was holding it in his hands."

"It's all right," J.D. said. "There wasn't anything in my pockets except my gloves and...." He stopped and frowned. "Listen, don't worry about the wine and cheese. We're going to have to be going anyhow."

"Oh, but you didn't finish. Let me get you a refund or at least a voucher...."

"No, that's fine," he said, squeezing Corrie's arm in case she should argue. Which she had no intention of doing. "If we can just get our coats...."

"Yes, of course, right away," she said, scurrying to the back room. Corrie nudged J.D.

"What did you have in your pocket besides your gloves?" she hissed.

"Tell you once I check," he murmured as the bartender came back. He thanked her and, once again refusing a voucher or refund, they left the winery.

They didn't speak as they made their way through the crowded streets, until they reached the corner where Corrie had run into J.D. He pulled out his wallet and fished out two slips of paper. "Dinner vouchers," he said. "Pretty nice place, too. The hotel wanted to make sure we didn't give them a lousy review."

"I'd have almost settled for a fast food joint," Corrie said. J.D. chuckled as they went in. The place wasn't too crowded for a weeknight this early in the evening. After being seated and ordering iced tea and a plantain and salsa appetizer, Corrie's patience ran out. "Well?" she demanded.

J.D. fished in his jacket pockets and shook his head with a grim smile. "Yes, something's missing. It was the letter that Sutton gave me to give to the clinic. Well, it was an email, actually," he said. "You saw that envelope I gave Rosa. She gave it back to me just before we left the clinic, while Nurse Price was escorting us out."

Corrie blinked. "Why would someone want to steal that?"

"I don't think they did," he said. "I think they believed it was something else, information that RaeLynn wanted us to have." Corrie's mouth dropped open.

"You mean... they think they got the information that RaeLynn wrote in those little notes to us? They think that's what was in the envelope?"

"Why else would they steal it? What use would it be to them?" He stopped as the server approached their table to take their order. After he left, J.D. frowned.

"What is it?" Corrie asked. He looked at her, his brow furrowing.

"Who knew that I had that envelope?" he asked quietly. "Besides Rosa? And she knew what was in it, so she would have no reason to want it back."

Corrie's eyes widened and she sucked in a deep breath. "Ellie Price?" she whispered. She looked around the room and J.D. touched her hand and shook his head, warning her not to be too obvious. "She might have known that RaeLynn would try to tell us what she knew without anyone else finding out about it. Do you think she's the one that RaeLynn doesn't trust at the clinic?" she asked, trying to look nonchalant.

"Possibly, or it might be someone that Nurse Price is passing information to. Our mysterious tail," J.D. said, keeping his voice low as well. "She distracts us and he makes a move to try to get that envelope from us. That was her reason for meeting us at the winery. She knew he could slip in and probably get it but, as luck would have it, the bartender was too sharp."

"He took a big chance that you'd still have it with you," Corrie responded. "How did he know you wouldn't leave it in the truck or our hotel room?"

J.D. shrugged. "Probably figured I wouldn't want to let it out of my sight or that I would expect him or them or whoever to search our room...." He stopped abruptly and a look of alarm suddenly came into his eyes. He quickly searched through his jacket pockets once again, and once again, came up empty. He stopped and let out a sigh of exasperation. "Great," he mumbled, shaking his head.

Corrie felt her heart nearly stop. "What? What is it?"

J.D. looked at her grimly. "That wasn't the only envelope in my jacket. I also had the one with our hotel reservation in it. Which has our room number on it."

Chapter 20

Corrie's concerns about the sleeping arrangements in their hotel room were put to rest with the discovery that whoever had been following them knew where to find them. J.D. positioned one of the wing chairs in front of the door leading to the adjoining room and, due to the limited floor space, was easily within a few feet of the door leading to the corridor.

"You can't sleep in a chair all night," Corrie had protested.

"Who said anything about sleeping?"

"Well, you can't stay up all night, either!"

"Watch me."

Which she did, for the most part. Deciding that it would be more prudent to sleep fully clothed instead of changing into her usual nightwear – for more reasons than one – Corrie lay in the darkness on the edge of the bed, too nervous to close her eyes. The only light came from the moonlight shining in the window and the sliver of light coming from the partially opened bathroom door. Despite J.D.'s numerous admonitions to go to sleep, she merely dozed off from time to time, waking with a start, only to find him wide awake and alert. He was a mere shadow in the dim light, sitting upright in the wing chair with his gun resting against his thigh. Every time she opened her eyes, it seemed he was watching her and he'd give her a slight grin. "You're supposed to be watching the door," she sighed, sitting up.

"And you're supposed to be sleeping."

"As if I could," she mumbled. The bedside clock gave off a soft glow and showed the time to be two-fifteen in the morning. She groaned. "Maybe we're overreacting."

"Maybe," he responded, keeping his voice to a whisper.

"Maybe we should have alerted the front desk that there was a possibility someone might break into our room."

"And they would have stationed a security guard or another employee to stand outside the room and scared off our mystery guy." J.D. stood up, holstered his gun, and stretched. He went to the door and tested it to make sure it remained locked. "I want to catch him. I want to know what it is he wants."

Corrie nodded. The silence seemed to press in on them. She lay back down, wishing she could drift off to sleep. She'd never had an opportunity to enjoy such luxury – the comfortable pillows and mattress and the ridiculously soft sheets – and she doubted she'd ever have another chance again. Somehow, jeans and a flannel shirt didn't enhance the experience. J.D. went back to his chair in front of the door leading to the other room, moving silently as a shadow. She watched him settle in the chair and she closed her eyes.

Then she heard a noise from the room next door.

Her eyes popped open.

She sat bolt upright in bed, stifling a gasp. J.D. sprang up then moved closer to the door and listened carefully, slipping his weapon out of its holster. He motioned to her to duck down on the far side of the bed, but she was already slithering over the edge of the mattress, dragging the comforter and blankets with her. He carefully unlocked the adjoining door and began to turn the handle, but it wouldn't move.

It was locked from the other side.

He spun around and rushed toward the door leading to the corridor, unlocked the deadbolt, and dashed into the hallway. Corrie leaped to her feet and fought her way out of the tangle of bedding. She had just succeeded when she heard J.D. say, "Police! Freeze! Put your hands where I can see them!"

He was standing in the doorway of the room, his gun aimed at someone inside. She heard a shaking voice saying, "Hey, man, I'm sorry, don't shoot! I'm not doing anything wrong!"

"Who are you and what are you doing in this room?"

Knowing J.D. was too preoccupied to take notice of her, Corrie edged up behind him and stared at the intruder next door. A young man, short and pudgy, with a dark buzz cut and wearing black pants and a dark blue shirt with the hotel's logo on the front pocket, stood looking dumbfounded and trembling, unable to take his eyes off the gun. "I, I, I'm Josh," he stuttered, his eyes as round as saucers. "I, I, I work here. Don't shoot m-m-me!"

"Okay, Josh, what are you doing in this room?" J.D. said, keeping his voice low and stepping into the room, as he lowered his weapon. Corrie was right behind him, glancing over her shoulder down the hallway. She was surprised that no one had heard the commotion; she half expected all the guests to be congregating outside their rooms to see what was going on.

"I, I, I was looking for something," the young man stammered. "The guest that stayed here before, he said he left something in the room. In one of them. He told me the room numbers. He asked if I could come in and look for it for him. Said it was an important document. He said it couldn't wait till morning. I knew this room wasn't occupied so I checked it first, and then I was gonna have to knock on your door next," he went on, nodding toward their room, "I hated to bother you, but this guy said it was urgent and he gave me twenty bucks, said he'd give me another twenty when I got him the envelope...."

"He's downstairs now?" J.D. asked sharply. At Josh's faint nod, both Corrie and J.D. turned and sprinted for the stairs.

"And he was gone when you got there." The sheriff finished J.D.'s narrative for him.

"Yep," J.D. said with a sigh. "Apparently he paid the night clerk fifty bucks to have someone check the rooms. Of course, when they checked the hotel records, they discovered he wasn't the guest who checked into those rooms. But at least we got a description of him."

"Let me guess. Dark trench coat, knitted hat...."

"You got it." J.D. couldn't stop pacing back and forth in their hotel room, which meant he could go two steps in either direction before turning around. He knew he was getting on Corrie's nerves, but she said nothing, just brewed them both a cup of coffee with the in-room coffee maker. He thanked her with a nod and went back to his conversation with the sheriff, who seemed to have been awake when J.D. had called him, despite the early hour. "He must be pretty desperate to find out what information we were given to try to have someone get it from us in the middle of the night."

"That's what worries me," Sutton said. "He apparently thinks RaeLynn knows more than she does." He was silent for a few seconds and J.D. waited, picturing him chewing on his lip as he did when he was thinking. "Who saw Rosa give you that envelope?" he asked at last.

"The only person around was Ellie Price. The security detail was around the corner and out of sight, escorting Miss Shaffer to her room. Rosa just handed me the envelope and said she'd almost forgotten to give it to me. Nothing she said indicated that it might be from Miss Shaffer, or gave a clue as to what was in it."

"So Ellie just guessed that what was in the envelope was information RaeLynn was passing to you about the people who kidnapped her? That's kind of a stretch," the sheriff said.

"I agree, but why else would someone be so intent on getting it? And for what it's worth, we think Nurse Price might be trying to get the information for someone else... our mysterious friend in the trench coat. Who might be one of the men who was holding Miss Shaffer hostage," J.D. added.

"So there *is* a breach at the clinic," Sutton said. He said nothing else, but J.D. knew what he was thinking: that Eleanor Price had once again sold out a patient's privacy, but this time, more than just a reputation was at stake. "You need to get hold of Miss Price. Someone's using her to try to get that information. It's got to be someone who knows her prior history at the clinic and they're using that as leverage to get her to cooperate."

"I tried calling the number she used to contact me. She didn't call from her personal cell phone or from home. It's the clinic's number and the night staff said they couldn't release her personal information. I tried looking her up, but she's not listed, and neither is her sister that works at The Pantry." He rubbed the back of his neck and took a sip of his coffee. "Since we don't have jurisdiction, I'd have to get the local LEOs involved if we try to get her number from her workplace tonight... or today," he amended, glancing at the clock. "Wasn't sure if you wanted me to go that route...."

"I'd rather not," Sutton said when J.D. paused. "Clinic opens at eight for visitors," he went on. "The staff comes on duty at seven-thirty, if my memory is correct."

"We'll be waiting at the curb at seven," J.D. said, glancing at Corrie. She paused with her coffee cup halfway to her lips, then gave him a weary smile and a thumbs up.

They sat in the truck, parked a half block from the clinic entrance, at five minutes till seven in the morning. Neither of them had gotten much sleep in the few remaining hours and they had checked out of the hotel by six-thirty. Now they clutched steaming cups of coffee they had picked up at a local bakery along with bagels. Corrie shivered, despite being bundled up in her warmest sweater and her winter coat. "I wonder if Bonney got any snow," she murmured.

"Probably not this much," J.D. replied. The clinic's neighborhood easily had twice the amount of snow than the downtown area had received. He was eyeing the vehicles that passed by on the road carefully. It was dark still, and the streets were fairly empty except for those motorists heading to their jobs and an occasional die-hard jogger willing to brave the cold. "It would help if we knew what her car looked like," he added.

"She might carpool with someone else," Corrie pointed out. "Or maybe her sister drives her to work. The Pantry serves breakfast early. Maybe we already missed her."

"You're being awfully pessimistic," J.D. said, glancing at her. He raised a brow. "Something bothering you?"

"Yeah, all of this," she said, gesturing with her coffee cup. "The whole thing seems like we're missing something right in front of us. Whatever it is they think RaeLynn knows, it's bigger than we even imagine and it connects with the clinic and her kidnapping... and probably even bigger than that. It has to be or they wouldn't be trying so hard to find out what she told and who she told it to. And if that's the case, why can't we see it?"

He was silent for a few seconds, staring out the windshield, and she studied his profile. His face seemed carved from granite. She felt a twinge of guilt that she had ever considered he might have entertained less than professional thoughts about their lodging situation the night before. Even if he had, he would have never acted on them. And that, she realized, was what was really bothering her. She still had no idea what his feelings toward her were. Now her guilt was stabbing at her. She had no one to blame for that but herself. She'd been cool, downright frosty, to him since RaeLynn's disappearance. If she looked at the whole picture honestly, she could see that she hadn't been fair to him. She constantly took RaeLynn's past into consideration whenever she felt the need to defend her actions, but she never bothered to consider J.D.'s past and where he was coming from. She just expected him to see things the way she did simply because she told him that's how they were. She had dismissed his concerns and feelings because they didn't align with hers. She was grateful for the darkness in the truck cab that hid the rush of heat to her face. She stared into her coffee cup, wondering how, and if, she could ever apologize to him. And she wondered what, if anything, that would accomplish.

She felt his gaze on her and she managed to meet his eyes. He shrugged. "You make a good point," he said and she kept quiet because she was scrambling to remember what she'd said before she started woolgathering. "Maybe it's so big we can't see it from up close or from the inside. But whatever it is, Miss Shaffer is probably the only person who can stop it. Because she knows something, whether she realizes it or not, that can blow this whole thing up."

"You think so?" Corrie said, her eyes widening. J.D. nodded.

"Oh, yeah. That's why they're so intent on silencing her. And anyone else she might have talked to about what she knows."

Corrie swallowed hard and huddled in her coat. She was finally beginning to see just why Rick and J.D. were so overprotective of her... and everyone around her. She couldn't think of anything else to say and the morning was growing brighter. Traffic picked up on the street and more vehicles began arriving at the clinic. J.D.'s attention was focused on the arrivals and before long, it was after eight a.m. "You didn't see her, did you?" Corrie said, breaking the silence.

J.D. shook his head and started the engine. "Let's see what's going on."

"Nurse Price has never called in sick, never even been late in the last five years, Detective. I can't understand why she hasn't shown up today. It's simply not like her to not show up for work."

The receptionist wrung her hands in agitation. J.D. wondered if Dr. Pruett and Rosa had been hounding her to see if Eleanor Price had showed up. "Did you call her to see if everything was all right?" he asked, masking his own concern.

"Twice," she confirmed. "The only number I have on file for her is for her cell phone and it's gone to voice mail both times, which isn't set up. Her only other contact person is her sister, but her cell phone is off, as well. I understand she works in a restaurant and Nurse Price told me that she isn't always able to answer her phone when she's busy. The roads are so icy this morning. I'm afraid something awful has happened to her."

Me, too, J.D. thought, though the driving conditions had nothing to do with his fears. Forcing a calm tone, he asked, "Would you be able to give me her home address? Unless you already have someone checking on her...."

"Well, I'd have to clear it with Dr. Pruett," the receptionist said. "We're not supposed to give out personal information. And it's not standard procedure to go check on someone who has called in sick."

J.D. cleared his throat. "I'd like to speak to Dr. Pruett, then. And we'd like to see Miss Shaffer, even if we're a little early for our scheduled visit."

"I'd have to check with Rosa about that," the receptionist said, her concern over Nurse Price turning into nervousness at the thought of having to disrupt Rosa's routine. "But let me call Dr. Pruett's office to see about getting you Nurse Price's address. To be honest, I haven't even seen the doctor today. Either I missed

210

him or he came in earlier to catch up on paperwork and hasn't left his office," she added as she reached for the phone on her desk.

J.D. exchanged a glance with Corrie. He could see the same thought had occurred to her. Both Dr. Pruett and Nurse Price were not at work? The receptionist had punched in his number and was now frowning as her call went unanswered. She glanced at the security guard. "Jimmy, have you seen Dr. Pruett this morning?" He shook his head and she turned back to J.D. and Corrie, her face turning white. "I don't understand what's going on...."

"Ma'am, we'd appreciate it if we could speak to Rosa or whoever else might be in charge. And we need to see Miss Shaffer immediately." It was clear from J.D.'s tone that it wasn't a request.

She didn't argue. She motioned to Jimmy to escort them to the back. Just outside of Dr. Pruett's office they met Rosa who didn't seem particularly surprised to see them. "We'd like to see Dr. Pruett," J.D. said without preamble. Rosa's mouth tightened into a grim line.

"So would I," she said. "I don't know why he's deliberately avoiding me...."

"What makes you think he's here and avoiding you?" Corrie interrupted her.

The nurse turned frosty eyes on Corrie. "Because his car is in the parking lot and he's not answering his phone. He's nowhere else in the building and his office door is locked...."

J.D. let an oath slip. "Call security and the local police! Now!" he barked as he took a step back and kicked Dr. Pruett's door open.

Corrie sat in the day room along with RaeLynn, Officer Yellowcloud, and one of the security guards. The other guard stood outside the door, talking to the local law enforcement. A glance at RaeLynn showed that she was as shocked and dazed as Corrie felt. Even Debbie Yellowcloud looked shaken. She had already been questioned by the Santa Fe police and by J.D., who was assisting them. It had been an hour since Dr. Pruett's body had been removed from the office by the medical examiner. He refused to comment on the cause of death until he'd had a chance to take a closer look at the doctor. From where Corrie stood, it could have easily been a stroke or heart attack that killed him, but the fact that Nurse Price was still missing made it a very convenient coincidence.

She was beginning to share J.D.'s and Rick's opinion on coincidences.

She wasn't sure if she should ask questions, but she did, hoping Debbie would have some answers. "So you never saw Dr. Pruett leave the clinic last night?" She kept her voice low.

Debbie shook her head, then frowned. "I saw him leave his office, a little after four o'clock that was," she said. "But I never actually saw him leave the building. I was on duty until almost six and I never saw him come back either."

"And he looked like he was leaving for the day?" Corrie pressed. Debbie shrugged.

"He had on a coat, you know, like a parka. It was dark blue. He was pulling it on when he came out of his office and then he locked the door. I thought he was heading home. I didn't speak to him or anything," she added quickly. "I was at the end of the hall by Miss Shaffer's room, like always. He never looked my way."

Corrie was silent, thinking hard. She knew J.D. would reach the same conclusion she had: Dr. Pruett's death wasn't natural. "What time does the receptionist leave? I assume she would have seen him when he left the clinic."

"The front office closes at five, but he didn't go that way," Debbie said. She pointed with her chin in the direction of the corridor that led straight out from the doctor's door. "That's the hallway that leads to the staff entrance. All staff members come in through the back, never through the front door through the lobby. It's a privacy thing."

So Pruett could have left and come back later, Corrie thought. Could he have been the man who was looking through J.D.'s jacket in the winery? But Debbie just told her he'd been wearing a dark blue parka, not a dark gray trench coat. Of course, he could have changed, that would be simple enough. Did he follow Nurse Price to find out if she was responsible for the security breach, or did he send her as a diversion so someone else could search J.D.'s pockets?

Had he been working with whoever attacked RaeLynn?

She looked at RaeLynn and her heart twisted. Tightly controlled fear was all Corrie could see in her face. She was no longer safe here and she knew it. Dr. Pruett was dead and Nurse Price just might be, as well. And they still didn't know who was responsible and what they wanted.

They all looked up as J.D. strode back into the room. As if on cue, Debbie and the other security guard both got up and left. J.D.

waited until the door shut behind them. His face was grim, his eyes burning with anger and frustration. "Miss Shaffer, get your things together. We're taking you home right now."

"Right now?" she gasped as she stood up, clasping her hands. Hope sparked in her eyes. "The clinic is going to release me?" J.D. gave her a crooked smile.

"What the clinic wants to do is irrelevant. I caught the sheriff before he went in to court. He's already raised Cain with every doctor and nurse on staff he could get hold of, being as how Dr. Pruett is no longer able to give his approval. Rosa is getting some papers for you to sign yourself out of the clinic, basically absolving them of any responsibility. The local LEOs are done with us; they'll call if they need anything else, but they agree it's in your best interest to get you out of here as soon as possible."

"I'm ready," she said, giving a little bounce on her toes. "Let's go!"

"Hold on, RaeLynn," Corrie said, standing up and putting an arm around her. "Don't you need to pack your stuff?" RaeLynn shook her head vehemently.

"It doesn't matter, Corrie. What I'm wearing now is more than what I came with a few weeks ago. I don't even know where I got the clothes I have...."

J.D. had a very good idea where they came from but he was sure Sutton wouldn't care if they got left behind and donated to charity. "Well, I hope you have a coat, because you'll need it, Miss Shaffer. But let's go get those papers signed and get out of Dodge."

They stopped by her room long enough to grab her jacket. Debbie Yellowcloud had taken the liberty of packing up RaeLynn's clothes and personal items in a plastic bag. The young officer looked concerned. J.D. assured her that he would inform the sheriff that she and the security guards had done their jobs admirably. She nodded, tight-lipped, her troubled eyes on RaeLynn. "Watch yourselves, Detective," she said, shaking their hands.

Rosa looked pale and shaken, her hands trembling as she pushed the papers across the desktop for RaeLynn to sign. Corrie noticed that J.D. was studying her intently. Once RaeLynn finished signing and collected her copies, he cleared his throat. "Mind if I ask you a couple of questions, Rosa?"

Her gaze darted toward the doctor's office where the local police were finishing up. "I don't know what else I can tell you,

Detective," she said quietly, none of her usual frosty demeanor in evidence. In fact, she looked as if she'd aged a lifetime in the last hour. "I left at my usual time, four p.m. I never saw Dr. Pruett after that."

"You went to his office?"

She nodded. "I stopped in to let him know I was leaving and that the evening shift nurse had arrived. I didn't really talk to him. He was on the phone and it seemed like an important call... at least he looked extremely serious. He wasn't saying much, just 'yes' and 'I understand' and, at one point, he said, 'I'll take care of it'. He barely acknowledged me, so I just left."

"Did Nurse Price leave at the same time you did?" J.D. asked. Rosa blinked.

"No, she actually left earlier... she said she had an errand to run. Of course, I told her that she needed to do her errands after her work hours were up, but she said it couldn't wait till after five, which was the end of her shift. We have staggered shifts," she explained. "I wasn't happy about it, but I really couldn't stop her. She did seem rather agitated."

"And she didn't show up this morning. She didn't call in, either?" J.D. asked.

"Highly unusual, I have to admit," the nurse said grudgingly.

"Can you tell us how to get a hold of her?" Corrie asked.

At first, Rosa hesitated, but then she glanced down the hall toward the doctor's office and she shivered slightly. She sat at the computer and tapped a few keys, then scribbled some information on a yellow slip of paper. "Here's her home address and her cell phone number, as well as her sister's, and the number for her sister's place of employment."

They thanked her and made their way out of the clinic. They paused for a moment as RaeLynn took a deep breath of cold, clear air and tears glazed her eyes. She turned to Corrie and J.D. "Thank you," she breathed.

Corrie gave her a squeeze and J.D. let out a grunt. "Don't thank us yet. We still have a ways to go before everything is okay."

Chapter 21

Calls to both Nurse Price's cell phone, as well as to her sister's, went unanswered. J.D. called The Pantry and was informed that it was Mandie's day off. The GPS led them to a house on the seedier side of Santa Fe, but there was no sign of anyone being home and no vehicles sat in the driveway. "Now what?" Corrie asked.

"We head home," J.D. said with a shrug, although he looked frustrated. "I could go around and ask the neighbors if they've seen the Price sisters, but I doubt we'll get any useful information and I don't want to attract too much attention. We've done everything we can here, I've informed the local cops about what's been going on and they're the ones who are going to have to look for Nurse Price. I've told them all we know about what she and Dr. Pruett might have been involved in, which isn't telling them much at all, and their problem pretty much goes away when we do."

"Meaning I'm the reason they're both dead," RaeLynn said softly, tears welling in her eyes. Corrie squeezed her arm.

"It's not your fault, RaeLynn. They got involved in something, and they probably knew it was dangerous. And besides, we don't know that Nurse Price is dead also." She looked at J.D. with a question in her eyes. He shrugged and shook his head as he started the truck.

"We don't know a lot of things," he admitted. "But for sure, we know you're not to blame for any of this, Miss Shaffer. You're lucky you're alive."

"They probably still think I know something," RaeLynn said, her voice a raspy whisper. "Or else they think I told you all and they want to know what it is. So now you're in danger, too." She drew a shaky breath. "Maybe it's best if you don't take me back to Bonney. I couldn't live with myself if something happened to you because of me."

"Don't say that," Corrie said, giving her arm a shake. "We'll find out what it is they're after and then J.D. and Rick will be able to catch these guys and you'll be safe. We'll all be safe," she added, throwing J.D. a hopeful look. To her chagrin, he glanced pityingly at RaeLynn and gave a slight shake of his head. "It's going to be okay, RaeLynn," she said firmly.

RaeLynn forced a tiny smile, then her gaze turned inward. She was trembling and wrapping her arms around herself. Despite her coat and the truck's heater blasting away, she looked cold, but

Corrie was positive it had little to do with the snowy winter weather. Before she could ask, J.D.'s cell phone buzzed. He unclipped it from his belt and handed it to Corrie. "See who it is. This is a hands-free call only city and I don't need a ticket," he said dryly.

Corrie looked at the screen. "Doesn't say who it is, but it's a 505 number...."

"Give me that," J.D. reached for the phone. They were on the outskirts of Santa Fe, heading toward US 285, and the traffic was light. Corrie swallowed a gasp as she relinquished the phone and J.D. swerved onto the snow-covered shoulder and threw the truck into park, answering the phone as he did. "Detective Wilder," he said, punching the speaker button.

"It's Ellie. I swear I didn't know! I didn't know they were following me! Please, Detective, you have to believe me...." The voice was a frantic whisper. RaeLynn gasped and Corrie sat up straighter, looking around the truck and chiding herself for thinking the nurse would be anywhere nearby.

"Where are you? You have a lot of questions to answer," J.D. snapped as he glanced around as well, making Corrie feel less foolish. RaeLynn shrank down in the seat between them, as if to hide from anyone who might be looking at them.

A smothered whimper came from the phone speaker. "I know. I'm sorry. I have to talk to you, tell you everything."

"That'd be fabulous, Miss Price," J.D. said sourly. "Start talking."

"Not on the phone. I'll meet you."

"How do I know you're not planning to ambush us?" J.D. snapped. "You set us up once before. Whatever you have to say, tell me now."

Corrie heard Ellie Price make a sound between a sob and a laugh. "I know, I know, I shouldn't expect you to believe me or trust me. But please, Detective, this is not a trick. I have something to give you. You need it for your case. I have to get it to you before something happens to it... or to me."

Corrie's eyes met J.D.'s and RaeLynn's head jerked up. J.D. put the truck in gear. "Where are you?" he asked as he pulled back onto the highway.

"I'm at a gas station on 285, off Colina Drive. If you're heading to Clines Corners, it'll be on the left."

J.D. flirted with the wrong side of the speed limit as he drove to the gas station. It didn't look like they were being followed, but he wasn't sure if Eleanor Price had been followed. He knew they could very well be driving into an ambush, despite Ellie's assurances... one that even Ellie might not be aware of. "Do you think she's setting us up again?" Corrie asked.

"No idea," J.D. said. "She sounds terrified, but she just might be a great actress." He looked at Corrie and RaeLynn and his gut twisted. Whatever they were driving into could be dangerous – not just for themselves, but for Ellie as well. RaeLynn's face was white and her lips were trembling, but her eyes once again looked faraway. He wondered what she was thinking.

He turned into the parking lot of the gas station. At the far end, a single car was parked by itself. He had no idea what Nurse Price drove, but he was willing to bet it was a battered white Ford Focus. He pulled up cautiously, the truck's tires crunching on the partially frozen snow patches. The white car had the engine running and the window rolled down. He could see Eleanor Price sitting in the car, her face drawn and pale. He lowered the truck window. "This better not be a trick, Miss Price," J.D. said grimly.

"Dr. Pruett's dead," she blurted out, looking at them with haunted eyes. She stared when she saw RaeLynn was in the truck as well.

"We know," J.D. shot back. "He put you up to all this? What was he after?"

"Someone made him do it," Ellie wailed. "He was following someone's orders. They wanted to know what she knew. Miss Shaffer, I mean," she said with a sob. "She's got information that they wanted...."

"Who are 'they', Ellie?" Corrie snapped, scooting forward in her seat. RaeLynn shrank down further and Corrie jerked a thumb at her. "Who thinks she knows something? The people who put her in the clinic? The people who tried to kill her?" She pointed at Ellie. "You have to tell us who 'they' are! No one is safe until they're in custody!"

"That's enough, Corrie," J.D. said quietly. He stared hard at Nurse Price. "Right now, Miss Price, you are the only lead we have on whoever tried to kill Miss Shaffer. Whoever sent you and Dr. Pruett to get the information from her is linked to the person who shot her full of drugs and left her on the highway in Bonney. Might even be that same person. So tell us what you know."

Tears spilled down her cheeks. She swallowed hard. "I don't know a lot. Honest, Detective Wilder. I... I lied to you about Rosa being in Dr. Pruett's office. I was the one in his office. He had already taken me aside and told me about the case you and Rick – the sheriff," she amended hastily, the color rising in her face. He didn't have to turn his head to know that Corrie's stare had turned a little colder. "He told me about Miss Shaffer's case. He also said that I was to get close to Miss Shaffer, find out what she knew. He said that I had already proved I was good at that," she said in a choked voice. She shook her head. "He didn't realize how seriously that security detail the sheriff had hired took their jobs. That Debbie Yellowcloud, she never left Miss Shaffer's side. I couldn't take her temperature or assist her with dressing or anything without her being right there. The doctor was getting angry and impatient. He said he needed to know what she remembered about her accident. He called it an accident, but even before you and the sheriff showed up, I knew it wasn't that. In spite of everything, I am a competent health care professional."

"He had no idea what the nature of that knowledge was?" J.D. asked. Ellie shook her head. "He didn't ask Rosa or anyone else to try to get information from Miss Shaffer? Just you?"

She let out a helpless laugh. "Rosa would never agree to anything like that. He knew that. She has too much pride and integrity. She would have reported him without any hesitation. And he knew I wouldn't do anything to jeopardize my job. I told you why. He said my job depended on my cooperation." She drew a deep breath and gripped the steering wheel. "I went in his office that day, to see if I could find out what it was he was looking for. He was out of his office and I took a chance. I couldn't find anything. But I didn't know what I was looking for, either. I knew that it had to do with that man that sneaked into the clinic, the man that was following you."

"Dr. Pruett let him in," J.D. said, shaking his head. "He was the only one who could."

Ellie nodded. "He started to get antsy about finding out what Miss Shaffer knew. It was getting close to time to release her and... he must have been getting pressured to find out. I don't know, I swear to you, Detective, that I don't know who was pressuring him. He'd get phone calls that would leave him agitated. I got scared," she said, her voice barely above a whisper. "I saw what had happened to her. I didn't want those people to get to me or my sister. But I didn't have a choice. Dr. Pruett... he was so afraid of whoever was pressuring him that I was afraid he would throw me under the bus to save himself." She swiped a hand under her eyes.

"What happened last night?" J.D. asked. He'd been scanning the area around them, alert for anyone who might be watching them or any suspicious vehicles that might approach them. "Was it Pruett you saw at the winery last night? Is that why you ran?"

"No," she said, her voice shaking. "I mean, I saw Dr. Pruett. He was standing on the curb near the winery and he was watching me. He's the one who sent me to get the information he thought you had…."

"That envelope Rosa give me," J.D. said. "I guess you know now that it wasn't what you thought." She flinched and looked down at her hands. "What happened that made you run?"

"Another man came up to him. The man that had followed you to the clinic. He stepped up behind Dr. Pruett and… and I could see that Dr. Pruett was startled. No, he was terrified when he saw the man." She looked up at J.D., her lips trembling. "The man tugged on his arm and, even though I could tell he didn't want to, he went around the corner with him. As soon as they disappeared, I ran. I knew… I just knew…."

"You were right," J.D. muttered. "That guy decided to get the information himself. And when he found out it wasn't what he expected…."

"I took Mandie and we hid. I'm not telling you where. Once I give you this, we're leaving. No one will find us." She picked up a sheaf of papers from the seat beside her. "I got into his office yesterday. He'd gone to lunch and told us he didn't know when he'd be back, but he made it a point to tell me he wanted to see me as soon as he got back. As soon as he left, I went to his office. I wasn't sure what I would do, but I was shocked that he hadn't locked it. He always locks it. That scared me even more; apparently he was so keyed up he forgot to lock his office. I went in and his computer was on. I worked fast. I printed out Miss Shaffer's case history, and I found emails that had been deleted, but they were still stored in a separate file. I printed them out. I didn't take the time to read them all, but I read enough. They were from whoever had him trying to find out what information Miss Shaffer might have." She stopped and took a deep breath. "I had just gotten back to the nurse's station when he came back. He took me into his office and told me to call Detective Wilder and tell him to meet me at the winery. I was so nervous, afraid he'd somehow know that I had been in his office and messing with his computer that I never even asked why."

"What name was on those emails?" J.D. barked.

She shook her head as she handed him the papers. "It's not a real name. Just a string of letters and numbers. But maybe you have someone who can trace them from the information about the server and all that stuff." She took a deep breath and put her car in gear. "I'm sorry about everything, Detective Wilder. You, too, Miss Shaffer. And you, also, Corrie," she added, looking past J.D. and RaeLynn at Corrie. "Rick – Sheriff Sutton – gave me another chance and I blew it. I have no one to blame but myself." She shook her head. "I'm so sorry... I can't say it enough and it will never be enough. I just hope I've given you something that will help you. I have to go now."

"Miss Price," J.D. said, raising his voice. She was staring straight ahead, but he waited until she turned her head and looked directly at him. "You have my number. Call me if you think of anything else. Or if you need anything."

She blinked rapidly, nodding her head, then she spun her tires as she sped out of the parking lot and drove off.

The trip home to Bonney was uneventful. Although Corrie and RaeLynn scrutinized the emails Nurse Price had given them for the slightest clue, they had been kept deliberately vague. The person who sent them took no chances and hadn't seemed to have trusted Dr. Pruett to be as discreet as he should be. Even Eleanor Price's name was kept out of the messages, the only references to her being "the nurse" and "your employee", along with veiled warnings of dire consequences if orders weren't followed. The only real chance they had at discovering anything would be if Aaron Camacho or Gabe Apachito could somehow trace who had sent the emails.

At Corrie's insistence, J.D. took a detour from their planned route at the intersection of US 54 and 380. He drove down and picked up US 70 in Tularosa, making their trip home about an hour longer. "You'll thank me later," Corrie said cryptically, as J.D. grumbled about the delay. "I know RaeLynn will be happy."

It was almost two in the afternoon when they arrived on the outskirts of Mescalero and Corrie directed J.D. to take a left onto a road that seemed to lead into a residential area of the reservation. They came upon a low-slung, flat-roofed adobe building with a parking lot in front of it with a few vehicles, but no sign indicating what it housed. RaeLynn stifled a squeal of delight and clapped her hands.

J.D. stared at Corrie, perplexed. "Here?" he said.

"Yep, here," Corrie affirmed. "And you know we haven't been followed and I know we're all hungry, so let's get inside."

"Corrie, I haven't been to the Old Road in ages!" RaeLynn cried happily as she followed Corrie out the passenger door. Though the weather in Mescalero was almost as cold as Santa Fe, there wasn't any snow, but RaeLynn's cheeks were pink with excitement. "Oh, I hope the menu hasn't changed much!"

"I don't think it's changed at all," Corrie remarked as they went in. The warmth from a woodstove just inside the entrance had them shrugging their jackets off almost immediately. J.D. wasn't surprised when the young woman behind the counter greeted Corrie with the familiarity of someone who had known her for years, then instructed them to sit where they liked.

J.D.'s stomach growled as the delicious aromas of Mexican food wafted from the kitchen. They walked across the Saltillo-tiled floor to a corner table near a window that looked out into the parking area and afforded a clear view of the sheriff's truck. Red chile ristras and original Apache artwork adorned the rough adobe walls, and a giant Christmas tree dominated the space between their table and the woodstove, almost blocking the door from their view. With a start, J.D. realized that Christmas was only two weeks away and that it was nearly three months since RaeLynn had been kidnapped. RaeLynn smiled with a radiance J.D. had never seen before as she looked around the room. She waited until the waitress delivered menus, chips and salsa, and three glasses of water before she spoke. "Oh, Corrie, this is such a treat! Thank you so much!" She lowered her voice, realizing she'd attracted the attention of other tables in the room and a few people at the counter picking up to-go meals. "I never thought I'd ever leave that clinic or even see home again, much less eat another Old Road Special. I can never thank you enough."

Corrie squeezed her hand and it seemed she couldn't find any words to say. She swallowed hard and looked at J.D., her lips trembling. "The food here is great, but sometimes the chile has a real bite to it, no matter if it's red or green," she offered as a friendly warning as she blinked the moisture out of her eyes. "Try the salsa and if you're okay with it, you might be fine with the chile. They have burgers, if you'd rather not take a chance," she added.

"I'm not that big of a wimp," he teased, realizing that this was an emotional moment for the two women and he sensed Corrie didn't want it to get too intense. "Just tell me what's good on the menu and what you recommend."

"Everything," Corrie and RaeLynn answered together and then laughed. J.D. felt his anxiety loosen a bit. For now, they were safe; for now, there was nothing he could do. He'd instructed Corrie to take pictures of the emails with his phone, making sure that the information in the headers was especially clear, and text them all to Deputy Apachito and Officer Camacho. The two LEOs both assured J.D. they would work on them immediately, even though it was Aaron Camacho's day off. Knowing that worrying or wondering about their progress wouldn't make them find answers any faster, he decided to focus on lunch. His growling stomach helped with the task.

They had no sooner placed their orders when the door opened again and, to J.D.'s surprise, Sutton walked in. The waitress stopped and greeted him on the way back to the kitchen. "Well, hello, Sheriff, long time no see! The usual?"

"Yes, please," he said, removing his Stetson and glancing toward their table. For a brief second, J.D. felt a stab of hurt and he shot a look at Corrie. The expression of astonishment on her face turned the hurt into guilt; it was clear she hadn't known the sheriff was going to stop in. It was just the man's incredibly lousy timing, not that lunch with Corrie was going to be a very romantic event with RaeLynn along. Sutton walked over to their table. "This a private party or may I crash?"

"We saved you a seat," J.D. said smoothly, recovering from his surprise and indicating the chair across from him. Sutton took a second to see how good a view he had of the room and the door, which was what J.D. had done also, before he sat down. Sutton's view wasn't as great as J.D.'s, not that there were any clear views due to the Christmas tree being in the way, but he seemed to feel comfortable enough not to suggest another table. "I thought you were in court today," J.D. remarked.

The sheriff was dressed in a charcoal gray suit with a pale silver-gray shirt and matching tie. He removed his badge from his lapel and slipped it into his pocket as he set his Stetson down on a nearby chair. He sighed and shook his head. "Guy lost his nerve and changed his plea, after wasting the court's time for a week. Wish he'd lost it sooner, I had more important things to do." He gave RaeLynn a half smile and patted her hand. "How are you doing?"

She bit her lip and nodded, then surprised them all by jumping up and giving Rick a fierce hug that barely lasted two seconds before she let go and plopped back into her seat, her face flaming red. "I don't know how to thank you, Rick. I mean, Sheriff. I mean....."

Sutton's own face had a hint of color. "RaeLynn, you can call me 'Rick' and you don't have to thank me. At least, not yet. We're not done with this case yet." He turned his attention to J.D. and Corrie. "I heard the news about Pruett on the radio. Fill in the blanks for me."

J.D. repeated the information that Eleanor Price had given them and that he had already sent photos of the emails to both the sheriff's department as well as the police department. Sutton nodded and J.D. went on, "I told the Santa Fe cops to keep me posted if there were any developments. They're positive it wasn't suicide or a heart attack that killed Pruett, even though someone took pains to make it look like that but, since they don't have any proof, it might be a while before they find a suspect. And the only description we have of the only suspect...." He let his words trail away as the sheriff shook his head and their plates were delivered.

For the next few minutes, there was silence around the table as they all enjoyed their meals. J.D. had opted for the same meal RaeLynn had mentioned which was basically a sampler of the menu. Despite the heat from the red and green chile sauces – and no way of telling which was hotter to him – he decided it was some of the best Mexican food he'd ever eaten in his life... besides Corrie's, of course.

The sheriff frowned, although he seemed to be enjoying his beef burrito plate smothered in green chile. He looked up at J.D. across the table. "Do you have those emails on you?"

"Sure," J.D. said, delving into his jacket pocket. He handed the folded pages to Sutton. The sheriff took them and shuffled through them quickly.

"Is this all the correspondence between Pruett and our mystery guy?" he asked.

"I'm not one-hundred percent sure," J.D. admitted with a shrug. "Nurse Price said she found a file in Pruett's email account that had all this correspondence regarding RaeLynn. It was deleted, but obviously not completely erased. She said she printed it out and I'm assuming she meant the entire file. Of course, there may be another file she doesn't know about. It seems hard to believe that in the last five weeks or so, they only exchanged, what? About two dozen emails? I'd think they'd be keeping in touch every single day, even more than once a day."

Sutton nodded. "He might have called on occasion. If we need to subpoena Pruett's phone records and get access to his computer, we will, but it will take time and maybe Gabe and Officer Camacho can get us the information quicker." He turned to RaeLynn who was trying not to wipe her plate completely clean. J.D. concealed a smile; while she had been well-fed at the clinic, she had obviously missed good home cooking, and this was pretty close. The sheriff pretended not to notice as he asked, "RaeLynn, did Officer Yellowcloud or any of the security guards ever say anything about Dr. Pruett or Nurse Price and their behavior? That they noticed anything unusual?"

She swallowed and wiped her lips. "No," she said, shaking her head. "They hardly ever talked to each other in front of me. When they did talk, it was directly to me and it was never about the doctor or nurses."

The sheriff shrugged. "I take my hat off to them. They did their jobs exceptionally well."

Corrie had been listening and watching them intently. She cleared her throat. "Did Officer Yellowcloud or either of the security guards see Dr. Pruett return to his office after he was supposed to meet us at the winery? He was found in his office, so he must have come back on his own. It would have been too noticeable if someone had carried him in or even helped him come back. He had to have been killed in his office."

J.D. shook his head. "Officer Yellowcloud said she never saw him come back to his office after he left at four o'clock. She went off duty at six when her relief arrived and I presume the security detail switched out at that time, too."

RaeLynn's head jerked up. "Five-thirty was when the evening shift nurse came in and checked my vitals and everything. You know, the routine check. Officer Debbie was with me when she did, like she always was. The two guards were directly in front of my door. I don't think they can see the doctor's office from there."

Sutton nodded. "It would mean split second timing, but that's probably when Pruett came back to his office. Whether he was alone or not...." He stopped as J.D.'s cell phone buzzed.

J.D. raised a brow when he saw who the caller was. "Detective Wilder speaking. Yes, Lieutenant." He glanced at the sheriff and mouthed "Santa Fe". Sutton nodded and they all leaned forward to listen. "Okay. Yes. You're sure? Yeah, you have my information. If you wouldn't mind forwarding that to my email, I'd appreciate it. Definitely. Thanks for everything, we really appreciate all your help." He ended the call and gave them all a wry smile. "Well, no surprise, it wasn't natural causes and it wasn't suicide, unless Dr. Pruett was flexible enough to get his arm around to inject himself in the base of the neck with a combination of heroin, cocaine, and who knows what else...." He stopped when RaeLynn sat up straight with a gasp, her tawny eyes wide, her hands flying to cover her mouth. J.D. glanced at the sheriff and Corrie. They were both staring at RaeLynn in surprise and he leaned toward her. "Uh, is there something wrong, Miss Shaffer?"

"The syringe!" RaeLynn whispered, her face growing pale. "The evening nurse... I can't remember her name. Serena, or something like that. I heard her out in the hall after she checked on me. She sounded like she was further away than the nurses' station and she was yelling at the rest of the staff, asking who left a syringe on the floor! She was threatening whoever did it with getting fired, saying it was a biological hazard and dangerous and that Dr. Pruett and Rosa would have a fit when they found out...."

The sheriff was already punching in the clinic's number on his phone while J.D. called the Santa Fe police department back. Corrie looked around the room nervously. "Shouldn't you guys wait until we have a little more privacy?" she asked in a low voice.

J.D. gave a quick shake of his head as Sutton reached his party. "We can't take a chance that that syringe got disposed of. It might have fingerprints on it." He broke off as his call was answered. After a few seconds of whispered conversation, he and the sheriff ended their calls and drew deep breaths. "RaeLynn, this might be the break we've been waiting for," he said, giving her a smile.

RaeLynn took a deep breath, the color returning to her face. "I can't believe I didn't remember that," she murmured. "So much was going on...."

"Well, Officer Yellowcloud and the other security officers didn't mention it, either," J.D. said. He glanced at Sutton. "You might want to look into that."

"I intend to," the sheriff said grimly, but RaeLynn spoke up quickly.

"Oh, Rick, please don't get Debbie into trouble!" she said. "She was so nice to me and she and those security people kept me safe. They were the only reason I was able to sleep at all the whole time I was there! I'm sure there's a reason they didn't mention it." She stopped, blushing a deep red. She stood up. "Excuse me, I... I need to go to the ladies' room," she stammered. She turned and headed toward the stairs that led to the downstairs restrooms, until the waitress intercepted her and directed her to the handicapped restroom on the dining room level, explaining that the downstairs ones were out of service. RaeLynn nodded and hurried away. J.D. and the sheriff looked after her.

"You guys have to realize she probably became close with Debbie after all those weeks of not having visitors," Corrie said quietly. The sheriff shrugged.

"I'm still going to look into it," he said, keeping his voice low as a couple of tables cleared out toward the register near the door. "Once RaeLynn is back in Bonney, we're going to need to keep a close eye on her. She's not going to go back to her parents' home...."

"Of course not! She'll stay with me," Corrie said, folding her arms on the table. She looked from the sheriff to J.D. and back. "No objections, I take it?"

"With round-the-clock security. No objections, I take it?" Sutton shot back. She rolled her eyes and started to say something, when her eyes widened and she gasped.

Both J.D. and the sheriff spun around, rising from their seats. A tall, powerfully built man, clean-shaven with dark hair and eyes, stood near their table with an amused expression on his face. He was wearing an expensive wool trench coat, but no hat, despite the cold weather. Well-polished boots, not made for wet winter conditions, peeped out from under his sharply creased designer slacks. He bowed slightly to them all and winked at Corrie. "Well, well, look at this gleesome threesome," he drawled. He nodded to Corrie and the sheriff, greeting them by name and then nodded to J.D. "And you're Detective J.D. Wilder. Heard of you – who hasn't? – but haven't had the pleasure yet." He didn't extend a hand, not that J.D. would have taken it based on the sheriff's and Corrie's expressions. His unspoken question was answered by the man himself. "Johnny Shaffer. Not to sound conceited, but I'm sure you've heard my name. Looks like you've made yourself some friends in Bonney, Detective. Hope I'm not interrupting anything important." His eyes flicked to the fourth empty plate on

226

the table at RaeLynn's place and J.D. sent up a quick and fervent prayer that Johnny Shaffer wasn't staying for lunch and that RaeLynn would take her time in the ladies' room until her brother left.

"It's been a while, Johnny," Sutton said. He remained standing, his voice and stance casual, but J.D. knew better. "Haven't seen you around. Visiting family for the holidays?"

Johnny smirked. "Yeah, sure, gonna help Ma put up the Christmas tree and dear ol' dad carve the Christmas goose. Then maybe me and Teddy and Cliff will build a snowman and go sledding before we hang up our stockings." They all waited a few beats while Johnny glared at them with a challenging gleam in his eyes.

"What about your sister? Aren't you looking forward to spending some time with RaeLynn during the holidays?" Corrie snapped. She didn't stand up but sparks flew from her dark eyes and J.D. was positive she was doing everything she could to keep from blurting out anything else. Especially when Johnny Shaffer threw his head back and laughed.

"Oh, yeah, sure. Of course. I'll help her bake cookies for Santa or somethin'." He threw a challenging stare at Corrie. "What's it to you, anyway? Since when do you care what me and my family do? Oh, that's right, since you turned RaeLynn against us, made her think she was too good for us because she worked for you."

"When did you talk to RaeLynn?" the sheriff said quietly. Johnny jerked his head around to glare defiantly at Sutton. Out of the corner of his eye, J.D. saw RaeLynn stop in the doorway of the dining room, her mouth open in shock. He didn't make a move but he stiffened, hoping Johnny wouldn't see her. To his relief, she slipped back through the door before Johnny turned to look at J.D. as well.

"I haven't 'talked' to RaeLynn in years," he snapped, addressing both J.D. and Sutton. "Not even when I come around Bonney. I hear things about what happens around the old home town, what my brothers and dad supposedly do, so, yeah, I heard that RaeLynn took off a couple months ago. I said 'good riddance' when I heard. Figured she was probably getting ready to do her usual disappearing act whenever the need for drugs would get too strong. Surprised she stayed clean this long, but it never lasts. Yeah, don't look so shocked, Corrie," he sneered, his eyes cutting toward her. "You're not so special. She played on your sympathy, took advantage of you, then went back to her old habits. That's the way she's always been. She's no better than the rest of my family but she tries to pretend she is. Why do you think I stay away? I got no time for their drama. I have a life to live."

"You know someone kidnapped her, assaulted her, and tried to have her killed?" Sutton said, his voice low and cold.

"And?" Johnny shot back.

"Got anything to tell us that might help us find out who did it?" J.D. asked. Johnny's head swung in his direction.

"No. Haven't been around in months, don't know what's going on, haven't talked to her. And since I feel I'm being harassed, I guess I'll go elsewhere for lunch. Have a nice day," he said. He started to turn and the sheriff cleared his throat sharply.

"I might be in touch, Johnny. Hope you're planning to hang around for a few days."

Johnny Shaffer swung around and glared at them through narrowed eyes. He shook his head in disgust and stalked out of the restaurant. The sheriff moved closer to the window and peered around the Christmas tree. J.D. joined him in time to see an expensive sports car pull out of the parking lot and speed away, tires squealing. Snow was starting to fall and J.D. shook his head. "He'd better be careful driving like that in this weather. Those don't look like snow tires on that Beemer. He'll end up with more than a scratch on the paint if the roads get slick."

Sutton shook his head. "He's always been rough on his toys. He always seems to be able to get a new one. Still has dealer plates on it." He and J.D. turned back to the table as RaeLynn came up. Her face was stark white and she was trembling.

Corrie jumped up and went to her. "It's okay," she said soothingly.

RaeLynn shook her head. "I heard what he said." Her voice shook and tears spilled down her cheeks. Corrie put her hands on RaeLynn's shoulders.

"Don't listen to him," Corrie said. She sounded like she was trying to soothe a frightened kitten. "You know I don't believe a word he said. I know you didn't relapse. You didn't leave of your own free will."

RaeLynn shook her head and drew a quavering breath. "No, no, not that," she breathed. "What he said... about not having time for drama and having a life to live. I heard that before." She stared at Corrie, then looked at J.D. and the sheriff. "Remember? I told you I heard that when I was... when I was being held." Her breath came faster, in shallow gulps, and her eyes grew wild. "It was Johnny's voice I heard. One of the voices I heard that I thought I recognized. I'm positive it was Johnny!"

"You're sure?" the sheriff said, his voice as sharp as a razor. J.D. glanced at Corrie; she looked as stunned as he felt. "You're positive it was Johnny's voice?"

"Yes, Rick! I know it was him!" RaeLynn cried, then flinched as other people in the restaurant looked their way. She lowered her voice. "I haven't seen him in so long... almost a year since I heard his voice. That's why it didn't sound familiar when I was... when they...."

"Okay," J.D. said, taking her arm and easing her into her seat. Corrie sat beside her but both he and the sheriff remained standing. He scanned the room, which had emptied out, and saw no one was near them nor paying any attention to them. "So we know that all three of your brothers were with two other men who held you captive," he said, keeping his voice down. "But you still don't know who the other two men are."

She shook her head. "One man's voice sounded familiar, too. But I don't know who it could be."

"Everything points to this all happening in Bonney," the sheriff said quietly. J.D. looked up into the sheriff's grim eyes and nodded.

"That's where we'll find who's behind all this," he said.

Chapter 22

The drive to Bonney took longer than expected. The snow storm had followed them down from Santa Fe and had swept down over Lincoln and Bonney counties. By the time they reached Ruidoso, five inches of snow covered the road and visibility was so poor that J.D. kept the truck's speed down to only fifteen miles an hour. Corrie tried not to let her nervousness show. They could barely see the taillights of Rick's Tahoe just a few feet ahead of them. Though it was only a little after four in the afternoon, the winter storm had made it dark early. She hoped that Rick and J.D. would be able to get them safely to Bonney.

If Bonney would actually be safe for them now.

She looked at RaeLynn, sitting between her and J.D. She was trembling and it had nothing to do with the driving conditions. The danger they thought they had left behind was already waiting for them in Bonney. At home.

J.D. broke the silence with a low whistle as the truck slid on the icy road as they rounded a curve just outside of the village of Ruidoso limits. "At any rate, it's going to be a white Christmas," he remarked.

Corrie nodded, not sure if she should voice the concerns she had in mind, but RaeLynn did it for her. "Do you think Johnny knows I'm back in Bonney?" she whispered.

Corrie grimaced, remembering how Johnny's gaze had fallen on the fourth plate at their table at The Old Road. She was positive he knew and she was equally positive that RaeLynn already knew it as well. J.D. cleared his throat. "It's possible he knew before we left Santa Fe," he said. "He might have been the mysterious guy showing up at the clinic and following us."

"That doesn't make sense," Corrie said, stifling a gasp as another icy patch on the highway caused the truck to drift slightly. "Why follow us around suspiciously? He's RaeLynn's brother. He's her family. He had a legitimate reason to be at the clinic, even to get in to see her!"

"Except the sheriff had made sure that the clinic wouldn't allow her to have any visitors that she didn't personally request or that he approved," J.D. reminded her.

RaeLynn shook her head. "I'd have never asked for any of my brothers or father to come see me. Maybe just my mother, but I didn't want to make things hard on her... and I didn't want everyone else to know where I was."

"They found out somehow," Corrie said dryly. They passed a sign that indicated it was still ten miles to Bonney. At the rate they were going, it would take them almost forty-five minutes to get there and who knew what the road conditions were like as they went on. Rick's tire tracks were quickly being covered up by blowing snow and neither the lines nor the shoulder of the road were visible. Corrie prayed Rick could see well enough to lead them into town without mishap. She looked at J.D. and noticed he was frowning. "What is it?" she asked.

"I'm just wondering who could have found out that RaeLynn was in Santa Fe. I'm positive that the sheriff and I weren't followed. And no one went back up there before yesterday when we went up." He shook his head. Corrie could see his knuckles, as he gripped the steering wheel, were white and his arms were rigid with tension. It was clear that in all his years in Houston, he'd rarely dealt with near-blizzard conditions, and that was only adding to the stress of the investigation. She shrugged off a chill that had nothing to do with the weather.

"Corrie, I can't stay with you," RaeLynn spoke up suddenly. Her tawny eyes glazed with tears. "It's too dangerous. We know my family knows I'm back. There's no way they can't know. And if my brothers are in this, none of us are safe as long as I'm around. It's me they're after. I won't put you or Rick or Detective Wilder in anymore danger."

"Don't be ridiculous, RaeLynn!" Corrie snapped. "Rick and J.D. are going to keep you safe! They'll keep us all safe! You can't go back to your family."

"I wasn't planning on it," RaeLynn said quietly. "I'll just leave. I won't even tell you where I'm going, for your own safety. Once I'm gone, you'll all be safe."

"You're not going anywhere in this weather," J.D. said dryly. RaeLynn blinked back tears and bit her lip. "Corrie's right," J.D. went on. "If you stay at the campground with her, you'll be safer than anywhere else in town. We can keep an eye on both you and Corrie."

"For how long?" RaeLynn said, a sob in her voice. "You can't protect me forever. That's not fair to any of you!"

"It won't be forever," Corrie said firmly, giving RaeLynn's hand a squeeze. "They'll find out who's behind all this and then everything will be fine. Right, J.D.?"

He slid her a sideways glance that warned her not to be too optimistic, but she glared back at him and he gave a quick nod.

"Right."

Driving into Bonney gave J.D. a shock; the heavy snow blanketed the village and most of the businesses along the main road were closed and dark. Very few residences along the way showed any lights but they were dim and wavering. Only the police department, sheriff's department, and medical center were well-lit and even then, not as brightly as usual. "Power must be out," he muttered. "I doubt they'll get it restored anytime soon if the snow keeps up."

"Wonderful," Corrie groused. "The campground has a generator, but we never use it unless it's an absolute emergency. I hope my guests are doing all right."

"I'm sure Jerry and Jackie have it under control," J.D. reassured her. "You don't have any tent campers and the cabins are empty except mine. And you only had about three RV guests besides your year-rounders." She nodded, but her forehead remained puckered with concern. "Worst case scenario is you could have them all camp out in the main store, if the weather doesn't clear out soon and the power restored."

They made the turn into the campground, J.D. slowing down to allow the sheriff's Tahoe to descend the ramp and get out of the way before he guided the pickup down the icy incline. He only fishtailed slightly at the bottom and then pulled up to the door of the office. Sutton was already waiting at the curb and a feeble light shone in the window. He motioned for J.D. to wait before they got out of the truck. The door opened and Jerry ushered him in. J.D. tapped his fingers on the steering wheel, even though it only took the sheriff a few minutes to make sure the store and apartment were clear and secure. Quickly, J.D., Corrie, and RaeLynn scooted into the building, grateful to be out of the storm. Jackie brought a pot of coffee which she had brewed on the gas stove in the kitchen, with apologies to everyone for not having made piñon coffee. The cold had seeped into their bones and no one complained.

"Phones have been out for a couple hours," Jerry informed them, his walrus mustache bristling. "Same with the power. Good thing we're on propane out here so we can stay warm, and we're not on a well, so we have water. The storm's supposed to sock in till morning then move on, but they're expecting up to a foot and a half of snow in some places before it's over."

"We'll have a lot of cleanup to do tomorrow," Sutton said. He was chewing his lip and shook his head. "All our communication is cut off. Radio and cell towers must be affected. I can't get hold of anyone at the sheriff's office or the police department."

"Great," J.D. muttered. He knew what the sheriff was thinking; they had to get to their respective departments and take care of business. He looked at Corrie and RaeLynn and his gut twisted. He turned to Sutton. "What do you think?" he asked, knowing what he was going to say.

"I don't like this," Sutton said. "We have to get back to the village, but leaving RaeLynn and Corrie here, along with Jerry and Jackie, knowing that Johnny's back in town and still not knowing who's behind RaeLynn's kidnapping or Pruett's murder...." He let his voice trail off.

"We're not the only people in Bonney you two are responsible for," Corrie said. Her voice was firm and her chin was set, but J.D. could see a flicker of controlled fear in her eyes. She went on, "I know we have to be on our guard, but the chances of anything happening in this storm is slim. We'll be fine. You guys have to do what you have to do." She looked at RaeLynn and the Pages and they all nodded.

RaeLynn spoke up, the bravery in her tone masking her anxiety. "Thank you for all you've done for me, Rick, Detective Wilder," she said. "I wouldn't be alive right now if it weren't for you. We'll be fine and I'm going to do my best to remember exactly what happened and who was involved and I'll do everything I can to make sure my family never hurts anyone else again, no matter what happens to me. I promise," she added, setting her lips in a firm line.

J.D. didn't know how to respond to that. He glanced at the sheriff; his eyes were fixed on Corrie, as if he were sending her a private message. She moved next to RaeLynn and put an arm around her. Jerry and Jackie stepped in closer and it was clear that they were all going to rally to her defense if need be. Sutton nodded, then he looked at J.D.

"Let's go."

Corrie took a deep breath and tried to calm her racing heart. Jerry had trekked back to his and Jackie's RV to retrieve his police scanner, in the event that communications were restored. He also brought his shotgun. They were all in Corrie's apartment where they only had one door to watch and the windows were all on the second floor. Her concerns about her guests had been alleviated by Jerry's assurance that he and Buster had gone around before the storm got bad and suggested that they find alternate accommodations in the village of Bonney or Ruidoso. Almost all of them had taken the advice and Buster was able to leave before the snowfall had gotten too heavy. The generator was keeping the heat on, but they chose to leave the lights off in order to make it look like no one was in the building.

Though Corrie had been able to provide accommodations for everyone, no one was sleeping. Raelynn stood by the window that looked out over the front of the building, staring into the blank view of the world outside. Corrie moved close to her and gently touched her arm. "You should try to rest," she said softly, though she was in no danger of waking anyone.

RaeLynn's lips twisted into a smile, but her eyes never left the swirling white vista outside the window. "As if I could," she murmured. Her smile faded and she shook her head. "I keep trying to remember more of what happened while I was... gone," she said, her voice trembling slightly. "Nothing makes sense," she went on. "I mean, why are they still after me? I can't prove anything. I can't positively identify them, not even my own brothers, because I only heard their voices. And even though I know I recognized that other voice, I still don't know who it was. They never talked about anything that sounded like it was something they wouldn't want the police to know about."

"That you know of," Corrie said.

RaeLynn shrugged. "Money was all that was mentioned. But nothing was ever said about where the money was coming from. It could be drugs, it could be gambling, it could be robbery... but I don't know. I never heard...." Her voice trailed away as she started to tremble and she blinked back tears. "But they must think I did hear something, that I do know something. Why else would they still be after me?"

"Maybe one of them let something slip that might not mean anything to you, but it might mean something to someone else. And they're afraid you might repeat it to the wrong person...."

RaeLynn let out a groan and dropped her face into her hands. "How will I ever figure it out, Corrie? How do I know what they meant?"

"You don't have to know," Corrie said, pulling her hands down from her face. Even in the dim light, she could see the fear and despair in RaeLynn's tawny eyes. "You have to try to remember everything you heard. EVERYTHING, RaeLynn! Every tiny little thing they talked about, no matter how inconsequential or unimportant you think it is. Even if it's just deciding what kind of pizza they want to order or saying 'excuse me' as they pass each other in the hallway!" She took a deep breath as RaeLynn's eyes widened. "Just write down everything you can think of," Corrie insisted, guiding RaeLynn to the desk in the small bedroom that she had converted into an office. She pulled a notepad and a pen from the drawer, then switched on a small, battery-powered lantern she kept on the desk. "I'll be right outside the door," she assured RaeLynn who sank into the chair reluctantly, shaking her head. She thought of saying something encouraging but she'd already said all she could think of. Now it was up to RaeLynn. She moved out of the room, shutting the door softly behind her.

Both the sheriff's department and village police department were scenes of controlled chaos. Despite the lack of radio chatter and ringing phones, there was plenty of noise to indicate that every one of the officers or deputies on duty were busy... and many who weren't scheduled had made it a point to report for duty. Those that had personal vehicles capable of making their way through the snow drifts and had winches were already out patrolling the roads, ready to help motorists who were stranded in the ever-increasing storm. Others were preparing emergency kits of food, water, and medical supplies to deliver to the residents in the outlying areas of Bonney who were otherwise safe, but might not be able to leave their homes for a while once the storm subsided. "I take it this isn't the first time you all have experienced this kind of weather," J.D. remarked as he and the sheriff made their way through the blowing snow to the Tahoe after making sure things were under control at the police department. No way was J.D.'s Harley going to be of much use in this weather, or even the sheriff's pickup truck, for that matter.

Sutton shook his head as they got into the Tahoe and he tried the radio. It was still out. "This is the worst storm we've had in years," he said as they pulled out of the parking lot. "Are all your officers accounted for?"

"All but Ray Herman," J.D. said. He shrugged as the sheriff shot him a look. "I asked Charlie White about him, since they used to pal around together a lot, but Charlie seemed to be a bit annoyed that I asked. Said he didn't know, it wasn't his day to watch him, and then said that Ray had told him he might be going out of town on his day off—which was today—but didn't say where he was going or when he'd be back. He's supposed to report for duty tomorrow morning, but if he left town and didn't get back before the storm...."

"And no way to get hold of you till the phone lines are restored," the sheriff finished for him. "He's the only one out?"

"Just as well," J.D. admitted. "I'm on the verge of taking disciplinary action. He's late for duty way too many times, violates the dress code for patrol officers, doesn't do so great on firearms proficiency, and still hasn't tried to start, let alone finish, his training. I don't know what LaRue was thinking when he hired a lot of these guys, but so far, Ray Herman is the only one who's been a real liability. Even his buddy, Charlie White, hasn't been hanging around him as often and started taking the job more seriously."

"Corrie's cousin," Sutton said. "He's not a bad guy but he's always been a follower, and usually of the worst kind of leader. Maybe he's seen Ray's true colors and is breaking away from him. Smart move."

J.D. nodded, a feeling of uneasiness creeping up on him. It had been nearly two hours since they had left Corrie and RaeLynn at the campground. The snow had started falling harder. Most residents were prudent enough to stay home and not risk getting stranded or having an accident on the icy roads. Even fewer would attempt to go anywhere on foot. It was ridiculous for J.D. to be worrying about the possibility of anyone attempting to go to the campground if they discovered Corrie and RaeLynn were back.

And still he couldn't shake the feeling that something might happen.

The sudden lurch of the sheriff's Tahoe as it slid across the snow-covered road and bumped into the two foot high berm left by the snowplows earlier in the day got his attention. Sutton muttered under his breath as he wrestled to get the Tahoe back under control, and J.D. felt his stomach drop as the tires spun on the slippery pavement. Sutton let out his breath as the tires managed to grip the icy road and J.D. realized he'd been holding his breath, too. Sutton shook his head. "We're not going far like this. Should have put the chains on."

"Are we headed to the Black Horse?" J.D. asked, looking out into the swirling snow. The headlights barely pierced ten feet ahead; beyond was complete darkness.

"Not till I get chains on this vehicle," the sheriff muttered. He managed to turn around at an excruciatingly slow rate of speed. He shook his head. "It hasn't been this bad in years. The police station is closer...."

"I'm sure there's a spare set of chains," J.D. said. A reasonable person would ask if it was really necessary to put themselves – and possibly others – at risk by making the trip out to the Black Horse. Surely there was no way that Corrie and RaeLynn were in any danger from RaeLynn's attacker or his cronies. Surely the blizzard would prevent anyone from making a move to finish what had been started. Surely....

His thoughts ground to a halt as the sheriff stopped the Tahoe at the curb outside the police station. They got out and the sharp wind cut through J.D. like a sword, and he ducked his head against the onslaught of snowflakes stinging his face as they hurried inside and headed to the storeroom where the snow chains were kept. To J.D.'s surprise, Officer Charlie White was standing outside the storeroom, wearing a heavy winter parka, gloves, and a hat pulled well down over his ears. He was just putting on a pair of snow boots when he looked up and saw them. "Good, you came back," Charlie breathed straightening up. "I was thinking I was gonna have to go after you."

"What's up?" J.D. asked, narrowing his gaze. Usually Charlie had a cocky attitude that bordered on contemptuous and flirted with insubordinate. He looked agitated, but it appeared to be from distress and uncertainty. "Something wrong?"

"Yeah. Maybe," Charlie said, jamming his hands into his pockets. He glanced around as if looking for a definite answer somewhere in the room. No one else was there and he shrugged, shaking his head. "Or maybe it's nothing. I don't know."

J.D. glanced at the sheriff, who only raised his brows, but managed to keep his impatience under wraps. "Well, just tell us and we'll figure it out. What's going on?"

"Remember I told you Ray went outta town yesterday?" J.D. nodded and Charlie went on, "Well, seemed strange to me, that he didn't tell me where he was going or what he was doing. And he usually does. He likes to brag about stuff. If he was going hunting, he'd be telling me he was gonna bag the biggest elk I ever seen or if he was going fishing, then he'd be rubbing it in about how he knows the best places to catch rainbow trout. He never kept anything a secret, you know what I mean?"

"Yeah," J.D. said, still not sure what Charlie was getting at and he was getting antsy. He wanted to get the chains on the sheriff's Tahoe and get to the Black Horse as soon as possible. Charlie pushed his cap back on his head and J.D. noticed his hand was shaking slightly. "So you think there's something suspicious about him not telling you where he was going?"

"He's been kinda flush with money the last few months," Charlie said, the words tumbling out of his mouth. He hesitated, as if wishing he could call them back but it was too late. "I know it ain't my business, but it seems weird. He likes to show off how he can afford stuff, but he doesn't talk about where the money is coming from. Can't be gambling, 'cause God knows he'd be bragging about his luck for sure. And I can't see him getting a second job. At least...." He hesitated a second then looked directly at J.D. and Sutton. "At least not a legit one."

"Okay," J.D. said, his patience wearing thin. "What, exactly, do you think he's gotten himself involved in?"

Charlie rubbed his face. "Look, Wilder, I know I shouldn't have looked in his locker, but it was unlocked...."

"But you did, apparently," J.D. snapped, and now both he and the sheriff were giving Charlie their full attention. "What did you find?"

Charlie let out his breath and fumbled in his pocket. He fished out a crumpled envelope and thrust it at J.D. "That," he said. "There's another one in there, but it's stuffed full of money. Fifties and hundreds. I didn't count it. I put it back. I thought... if you have this one and you find out something, before he gets back in town, you can do what you have to do with the other one."

Sutton had his gloves on before J.D. could say a word. He took the envelope and carefully fished out the folded paper inside. J.D. said to Charlie, "You don't have any idea where he might have gone yesterday? Even a slight clue?"

"It's not far, I know that," Charlie said. "He said he'd be back to work tomorrow, even if he was a little late. I told him he couldn't keep coming in late, that he was gonna get himself into serious trouble, maybe even lose his job. He didn't like that I said that, and he didn't talk to me anymore after that. Just muttered something about me watching myself and minding my own business... or else I'm gonna have to learn a lesson, too, he said."

"He said 'too'?" J.D. asked sharply. Charlie nodded, a wary look in his eyes. Sutton stepped to J.D.'s side.

"Did he say who else is learning a lesson?" the sheriff snapped. He held the letter that was in the envelope. Charlie shook his head. Sutton held the letter out to J.D. "See this address?"

J.D. didn't touch the paper, but the two addresses listed below the words, "Take care of this", written in bold block letters, seemed familiar. When he saw the initials "J. S." at the bottom, it suddenly clicked. "Is that the Black Horse Campground's address?"

"And the Shaffers' trailer park address," Sutton confirmed. "And that has to be Johnny Shaffer's initials." The sheriff grabbed the snow chains from a shelf in the storeroom and he and J.D. broke into a run back to the Tahoe.

Chapter 23

Corrie tried to stop pacing, but the nervous energy in her wouldn't allow her to sit still, much less try to sleep. Jerry and Jackie managed to doze from time to time, but every time she scuffed her foot along the floor or made some other small noise, Renfro would wake up with a whimper which would rouse the Pages. She checked the battery-powered clock on the wall; it was nearly midnight. The wind seemed to be dying down, though the snow was still falling as thickly as before. Corrie shivered, despite the warmth in her apartment. She'd checked in on RaeLynn twice. Half of the sheet of paper Corrie had given her was filled with scribbled lines, but nothing seemed like it was important enough to warrant the danger

"So much of what I remember sounds pointless," RaeLynn had said miserably the last time Corrie checked... when was it? An hour ago? "None of it seems important. How am I ever going to be able to help find out who else was there besides my brothers?"

"Something will come to you," Corrie had assured her, perhaps too optimistically. She was beginning to wonder if they were hoping for too much. RaeLynn had been through so much trauma, it was a wonder she hadn't blocked that entire time from her mind. But time was running out for RaeLynn to try to remember more. As much as Corrie hated to, she decided to check in and see if anything else had popped up in her memories.

She went to the door of the small office and tapped on it before pushing it open. "It's me again," she called out softly. "Did you miss me?"

A hoarse cry that turned into a shriek burst out of RaeLynn's throat as she jumped up from the desk and backed into a corner. Corrie froze in mid-step, dumbfounded. In the dim light of the lantern, RaeLynn looked like a ghost, her face stark white and her mouth open in a scream. Her arms were up over her face and she huddled down, shaking, crying, her screams dissolving in sobbing words. "No, no, no, please, no...."

"RaeLynn!" Corrie gasped as Jerry and Jackie materialized behind her in the doorway.

"What happened?" Jackie asked. Corrie shook her head then stepped into the room, motioning for the Pages to stay back.

"RaeLynn," Corrie said softly. RaeLynn's cries faded into a whimper but she continued to tremble as she curled herself into a ball. "RaeLynn, it's just Corrie. It's okay, no one's going to hurt you." She made her voice low and soothing, as if she were calming a terrified kitten. She wanted to reach out and touch RaeLynn but decided it would only frighten her more. "Everything's okay. You're safe."

"Corrie?" A raspy, haunted whisper. Corrie took the lantern from the desk and turned down the intensity so that a warm glow illuminated her and the Pages. "Corrie...." RaeLynn sat up, her arms still wrapped around herself. Her eyes were still wide and her lips trembled but a hint of color came back into her cheeks. She took a deep, shuddering breath. "Oh, my God...." Her eyes widened.

"RaeLynn, what is it?" Corrie asked urgently, as she squatted beside her friend. "You just remembered something, didn't you?"

RaeLynn nodded. "That's what he would say. The man who...." Her voice faltered for a second then she cleared her throat. "He said it every time he came in. Just what you said. 'It's me again. Did you miss me?' Every time." Tears started rolling down her face. She shook her head. "I forgot all about it. No. No, I didn't forget," she corrected herself, drawing a deep breath. "I just didn't want to remember. But now I do. I remember that."

"We don't blame you, honey," Jackie said soothingly as she and Corrie helped RaeLynn to her feet. Jerry wisely stayed back as the three women made their way to the sitting room and RaeLynn sank into the recliner. She rubbed a hand wearily across her forehead. Corrie pulled a chair over from the dinette table and sat beside her friend.

"What is it? You remembered something else," she said. RaeLynn nodded.

"Give me a minute," she said. Corrie and the Pages waited silently. In the shadowy light, Corrie could see RaeLynn's tawny eyes looking at something half-hidden in her memory. She blinked rapidly, her lips moving, then she nodded. "He came in one time, and I knew what he was going to say and I... I tried to block him out. I knew what was going to happen and I tried to... to go away in my mind. So I focused on everything but him." Her breath came in gulps and she shook her head. "I heard them talking in the other room when he came in. He always shut the door behind him, but this time, it didn't close all the way. So I could hear some of what they were saying. I could hear my brother, Teddy, saying, 'Why do you let him do that to her?' and then I heard Clifford telling him to mind his business, that all he had to do was follow orders.

Teddy started to argue with him, then I heard the other man – the man whose voice I kind of recognize – come in and say they didn't have time to waste, they needed to move some...." She stopped abruptly and shook her head.

"What?" Corrie asked, fearing that RaeLynn would forget what she was going to say.

"This is going to sound silly," RaeLynn said with a nervous laugh. "But I swear I heard him say they needed to move some more wheelbarrows."

Corrie blinked. Jerry and Jackie exchanged a glance. "Wheelbarrows?" Corrie repeated.

"I told you it would sound silly," RaeLynn said, tears pooling in her eyes. "I mean, that doesn't even make sense. Why would they – especially my brothers – have anything to do with wheelbarrows? What's the big deal?"

Corrie shook her head. What RaeLynn told them made no sense and yet... why would her captors have been talking about wheelbarrows? "Is there something your family has been involved in that would require the use of wheelbarrows?" Corrie asked.

"Gardening," Jackie murmured and Jerry scoffed.

"That's too much work for the likes of Jake Shaffer and his boys. Sorry, RaeLynn, but that's the truth," he said gruffly, patting the younger woman on the shoulder. "You and your ma are the hardest working members of the family."

"I know," RaeLynn said, shaking her head. "Mama would have liked a garden, but there wasn't enough room in our yard. Not with all the cars my brothers kept bringing home and working on."

"There's only one kind of crop Jake would've planted," Jerry added sourly. "But that would've been too much work for him. He'd rather just sell it than grow it."

"Well, what else would you use a wheelbarrow for?" Jackie said. "Moving dirt...."

"Cement," Jerry added.

"You can move a lot of things with a wheelbarrow," Corrie said with a sigh.

A tear trickled down RaeLynn's cheek. "I told you it didn't make sense."

"It's okay, RaeLynn," Corrie said. "It has to mean something. It must have meant something in particular to your brothers and the other men who were holding you, or else they wouldn't have been talking about it." Before anyone else could respond, they heard a faint tapping and what sounded like a voice shouting over the wind. Renfro sat up and growled. Jerry hefted his shotgun and went to the door, Corrie right behind him.

"Oh, no," Jerry said, stopping her as she reached for the doorknob. "You're staying right here, Corrie." He didn't have to say anything to Jackie and RaeLynn as they huddled together in the dark apartment. But Corrie shook her head.

"You're not going down alone," she argued. She snatched up the heavy flashlight from the small table by the door. "You've got your hands full with your gun. I'll take the light. You're going to need it down there."

"It's too dangerous," Jerry insisted. Corrie sighed.

"Jerry, think about it," she said. "Who on earth could be out there? If it were someone bent on hurting us, why would they knock? It might be someone stuck out in the storm, someone whose car went off the road and they need help. Even if it were someone who was looking for RaeLynn and me," she added and RaeLynn shrank closer to Jackie, "how do they expect to get away in this blizzard? I don't think they'd be that stupid."

"Now, see here, young lady," Jerry began, his mustache bristling. Jackie cut him off.

"Honey, Corrie's got a point. You need back up, even if it's not someone who's a threat. And she's the only one who's probably going to be of any use to you," she added.

Jerry sighed, knowing he was beat. "You let me go first," he instructed Corrie. She nodded as she opened the door and they crept down the stairs.

It was pitch dark in the campground store, but Corrie didn't turn on the flashlight. She and Jerry knew their way around. The tapping came again, from the direction of the side door, almost lost in the howl of the wind. Corrie felt a chill when she heard her name again, barely rising above the storm. She clutched the back of Jerry's shirt as he made his way toward the side door. He put his face to the glass, but all he could see was the blackness outside. Corrie pressed the flashlight into his hand. He raised it to the glass pane in the door and flicked it on.

For a split second, nothing could be seen but swirling snowflakes. Suddenly a face appeared in the light, shadows making the eye sockets look hollow and snow and ice crusting on the thin mustache and beard. Corrie gasped as the spectre flattened a mittened hand against the glass and the mouth opened again in a cry: "Corrie!"

"Who…?" she stammered and Jerry let out an exclamation.

"It's Benny Gonzalez!" He handed Corrie the shotgun and swiftly unlocked the door and the half-frozen man stumbled across the threshold, nearly knocking Jerry over. "Benny, what are you doing here?"

"Oh, thank God," Benny croaked, leaning heavily on Jerry. "I was so afraid no one was here and I didn't know what I'd do…."

Corrie rushed to find something for Benny to sit on, not bothering to shut the door. Jerry kept the beam of the flashlight aimed at the floor so as not to blind any of them as they made their way across the room to the front desk. Corrie pulled the stool out from behind the counter and she and Jerry eased Benny onto the seat.

"Benny, what on earth are you doing out in this blizzard?" Corrie demanded. "How did you even get here?" she went on before he could answer. She leaned the shotgun against the wall and fumbled her way to the coat closet. She pulled out one of the heavy winter jackets she kept in there for emergencies, and draped it around the old man's shoulders. Benny nodded his thanks weakly and she went on, "What happened?"

"I didn't think this storm would come so quick," he said in a raspy whisper. "I got a… a friend to take me to town, I needed to get some stuff and pay a bill. Didn't wanna keep 'em waiting so I told 'em I had a ride back home. But that wasn't true. I planned on walking 'cause I didn't wanna take advantage…."

"Good God, man," Jerry thundered. "You mean to say you walked from the village in this storm? Why didn't you stay somewhere in Bonney?"

"Because I was already a mile or so from here when the storm hit," Benny said, shaking his head. "I don't walk too fast to begin with, but this blizzard slowed me down a lot more. I don't even know where I was. Think I was just wandering lost out there…."

Corrie looked out the windows and frowned. She sensed, rather than saw, the skeptical look on Jerry's face. It wasn't completely impossible for someone to wander blindly through a raging snowstorm and somehow find themselves outside the door of the campground store, but…. "It's a miracle you found the building," she said, hiding her alarm. Benny nodded.

"You're right about that," he said and cleared his throat. "Are you both here alone?"

"Nope, the missus is here, too," Jerry said quickly. Again, Corrie sensed the look Jerry was giving her and she simply nodded, although no one could see it in the dark.

"Oh, that's good," Benny said. "Guess everyone else in the campground got evacuated before the storm got too bad, huh?" Corrie didn't answer and neither did Jerry. The uneasy feeling she'd had since Benny had arrived grew stronger, but she had no idea what to do. The phones weren't working, the power was still out, and the storm, though it seemed to be lessening, was still howling outside. She jumped when Benny spoke again. "I heard a rumor that that nice young lady that worked here—Jake Shaffer's girl—that she came back home."

"Who told you that?" Corrie asked sharply. Benny flinched and turned toward her, raising a hand to block the flashlight's beam.

"Oh... just something I heard in town. Some folks were talking about it...."

Corrie stopped herself from asking which folks. She heard footfalls and a dragging sound, like a chair being pushed across the floor, from upstairs and wished that Jackie and RaeLynn would stop moving around. She noticed Benny's gaze turn toward the stairs leading to the apartment and tried to think of something to say to distract him.

Suddenly, she heard glass breaking, followed by an unintelligible shout; then a scream then the sound of a gunshot, then two more. Another scream, muffled shouts, then footsteps pounding down the stairs. Corrie swung around, her heart in her throat, realizing too late that the shotgun was still leaning against the wall by the door. To her shock, Benny jumped up, showing more energy and strength than she had ever seen, and he gave Jerry a vicious shove, wrenching the flashlight from his grip and knocking him to the floor.

"Benny, no!" Corrie screamed as Benny raised the heavy flashlight and brought it down on the older man's head. Jerry let out a moan and slumped to the floor. Corrie lunged for Benny, barely making out his upraised arm in the darkness. "What are you doing!"

All at once, the light beam was directed into her eyes, blinding her, and the next instant, she was off her feet, a strong arm catching her around the waist and lifting her, as a wave of strong cologne filled her nose. She shrieked and kicked, but the arm tightened around her midsection, and her scream turned into a yelp of pain. She pounded her fists against the forearm crushing her abdomen, kicking though her feet didn't make contact with anything, and she couldn't draw a deep enough breath to do more than groan and whimper. She heard Benny yelling, "You idiot! Where's the girl?"

"Out the window," a frighteningly familiar voice said behind Corrie's head. She stopped fighting in shock and the arm tightened even more. "She threw something through the window when I got the old broad and climbed out. By the time I got to the window, she was gone...."

"What did you do to Jackie?" Corrie managed to croak, but both men ignored her.

"You let her get away?" Benny roared, starting toward the other man. She heard a sharp click and remembered the gunshot she'd heard earlier. Corrie wondered if Benny had a weapon as well, not even trying to figure out what was going on, and she squeezed her eyes shut and struggled harder to break the grip around her waist. An ugly chuckle sounded in her ear.

"Where's she gonna go, Benny?" he sneered. "She probably fell off the roof and broke a leg. We'll find her and if we don't, she won't get far in this cold with no coat on. Besides," he went on, jerking Corrie around to face Benny, "we got this one. She's all we need."

"The other girl knows what we're doing! If she gets to the police...."

"Big 'if'," the other man retorted. "We'll pick her up outside, no problem. And this one," he added, giving Corrie a shake, "will be our guarantee we get away."

Silence filled the room for several seconds before Benny spoke. "Let's go get her and get out of here. And you better be right about this, Ray."

Ray Herman didn't respond. He merely chuckled.

RayLynn flattened herself into the valley on the roof, shivering as the blowing snow stung her face and the cold bored through her sweater. She could only hope that Ray Herman believed she fell off the roof and escaped. She thought about Jackie and prayed that she was going to be all right after Ray hit her in the head with the butt of the gun. She just had to get away, find a way to get to Rick and Detective Wilder and tell them what she knew.

She trembled but it wasn't from the cold as she recalled the strong, musky aroma that permeated the small apartment as the door swung open, and the words that alerted her that they weren't alone. *"It's me again. Did you miss me?"* She had frozen in place, then, in the dim glow of the table lantern, she saw him raise the gun, and she acted quickly.

It helped that he hadn't expected her to fight back. His eyes were trained on hers, and he grinned as he saw the horror of recognition in them. He didn't see the wooden chair she gripped swing toward him and crack him in the shins. He stumbled over it, muttering and cursing, as she grabbed the lantern and heaved it at the window. His roar of pain and fury propelled her up onto the windowsill and she dove through the screen. Her shriek of panic was muffled as she landed face down in the fluffy snow on the roof, her breath catching as the freezing cold cut through her clothes and enveloped her body. She scrambled away from the window opening, sliding and rolling and terrified she would suddenly reach the edge of the roof and fall twenty feet to the ground. Dimly, over the wind's whistle she heard Ray yell her name and two shots from the gun in his hand made her bury her face in the snow, even though he was shooting blindly into the darkness and the storm. She shook uncontrollably from fear and cold and then she realized he'd turned from the window and gone downstairs to where Corrie and Jerry were.

Stay put. The order came from somewhere deep inside and, though she wanted desperately to go help Corrie, she knew that doing so would only get them all killed and let Ray Herman get away.

"And Benny Gonzalez," she whispered to herself. The shock of realizing who the other semi-familiar voice belonged to gave way to agonizing self-reproach. How could she not have recognized Benny's voice? After all the years of living down the street from him, after the many times he'd spoken to her kindly after one of her father's rampages? During those weeks of imprisonment, she'd never once connected her captor to the poor neighbor she pitied for being lonely, disabled, and the object of Jake Shaffer's wrath. She had sometimes baked him cookies and he'd acted grandfatherly to her, even shown her once how his scanner worked to pick up emergency frequencies... and with a jolt, she realized that was how he found out she was in Santa Fe. She never would have suspected Benny or Ray....

If she didn't get away, no one else would, either.

She cautiously raised her head. The wind was dying down though the snow continued to fall. The power was still out, and it was pitch black, and she had no idea where exactly she was or how close to the roof's edge. She crept forward, plowing her bare hands through the snow, hoping the rough surface under her numb fingers was the roof shingles, until she felt the sharp edge of the gutter. She slowly looked over the edge, not sure which side of the building she was on. In the darkness, she saw a dim light moving away from the building and she heard voices. One of them was Corrie's.

"You're not going to get away with this!"

"Keep quiet and keep moving!"

"Ray, we have to find that girl!"

"Forget her! She'll be dead before anyone finds her and this is our chance to get away!"

RaeLynn crouched back although it was unlikely that any of them would look up and, even if they did, it would be almost impossible to see her. She heard the muffled sounds of a vehicle's doors slamming... when had they driven up to the building without any of them hearing it? She heard an engine roar into life and saw two headlight beams cut through the night. She sank lower into the snow until the truck lurched out of its parking spot and began to turn toward the road. She held her breath as the tires spun and then the chains gripped the icy, snow-packed pavement, moving quickly toward the ramp leading to the highway. The driver gunned the engine and, with the blurry taillights swaying from side to side in the darkness, the vehicle made it to the top of the ramp and disappeared into the storm.

RaeLynn realized she'd been holding her breath. She let it out and became conscious of how cold she was. Shivering, she made her way back up the roof, feeling for the window. She had to get back inside before she froze, had to see if Jerry and Jackie were all right. And then she had to find a way to get hold of Rick and Detective Wilder. She had to warn them about Benny and Ray. And find Corrie before it was too late.

Chapter 24

J.D. was torn between caution and impatience as the Sheriff pushed the Tahoe as fast as he could through the snowy night. The fact that the headlights pierced the darkness ahead by only about twenty feet and the vehicle kept drifting on the icy pavement made his gut twist with anxiety as he fought back the fear that they might be too late.

The wind had died down, but snow continued to fall and the view through the windshield looked like a tunnel of shooting stars. J.D. knew the edge of the road was protected by a wall of snow, left by a snowplow hours earlier, but running into that wall would probably disable their vehicle. Sutton said nothing as they partly slid down the curving highway, unmindful of where the dividing line might be. His focus was on getting to the Black Horse as quickly as possible. Besides their side arms, the sheriff had also grabbed a powerful rifle and there was a shotgun in the vehicle as well. There was no telling who or what they might encounter.

Into the silence came the crackle of radio static. "… anyone hear me? Please respond…."

J.D. grabbed the mike. "Bonney County sheriff and village P.D. here. Who is this?"

More static, then, "… Watkins here. Communication coming back up. Power company trying to restore… hospital and public safety…."

"Have everyone check in, county and village. Anyone near the Black Horse Campground or Riverside Trailer Park, please respond. Repeat…." J.D. waited, shaking his head in exasperation as broken transmissions came in. "I can't tell if anyone got that."

"What about cell phones?" Sutton asked. J.D. shook his head as his phone screen glowed with bold black letters: No Service. The sheriff muttered something under his breath, then said, "There's still a chance that Jerry has his police scanner on and that he might be able to get a signal. If so, then he's heard us by now…."

"And should be responding," J.D. said. The fact that he wasn't meant one of two things: either Jerry didn't have his scanner on… or something had happened to keep him from answering. J.D. knew it was taking everything in the sheriff's power not to stomp on the gas and try to get to the campground faster. Getting them stuck in a snowbank or killed in a crash wasn't going to help, no matter how frantic they both felt at how slow fifteen miles an hour felt. Before J.D. could key the mike and try again, a faint, static-blurred voice came through:

"Hello? Can anyone hear me... Rick... Detective... anybody... please, help...."

"RaeLynn?" Sutton said in astonishment. J.D. grabbed the mike, his heart in his throat.

"Miss Shaffer? RaeLynn? It's Detective Wilder. What's going on?"

"... took Corrie!" A half-sob, half-wail, cut through the static. "Ray Herman...."

"What?" J.D. blurted. He felt the Tahoe lurch ahead as the sheriff instinctively hit the gas and he grabbed the dashboard as the vehicle fishtailed. "When?"

"... half hour ago... Jerry is okay... Jackie... ambulance... have a gun...." J.D. felt his blood run cold.

"Do you know what he's driving?" he barked. Silence, broken by spurts of static, greeted him and his heart began to pound harder. He keyed the mike again. "Dispatch, do you copy?"

A garbled mix of static and words came over radio, then Charlie White's voice. "Wilder... Ray's truck... gray dually...." The rest was lost in a snowstorm of static. J.D. switched to the county frequency with the same result. He flung the mike down, muttering under his breath.

"If they're heading toward the village, we should be seeing them soon," Sutton said. He didn't have to say that if they were heading in the opposite direction, they might never catch up to them in the storm, not with a thirty minute head start. He tapped the brakes to take a sharp curve ahead in the road that was bordered by a stand of pine trees.

The Tahoe kept going forward.

The sheriff let out an expletive as he tried to keep the vehicle on the road. The Tahoe fishtailed wildly as the sheriff fought to get it under control but a sheet of black ice, hidden under the snow, made it impossible. "Hang on!" Sutton yelled as the Tahoe slid across the shoulder sideways, and the rear end dropped over the edge of the roadway, coming to rest with a hard thud against a large tree. Heavy clumps of snow showered down on the Tahoe from the branches above, nearly burying the vehicle. Both J.D. and the sheriff had the presence of mind to fling the doors open before the snow barricaded them inside. The blast of frigid air nearly took J.D.'s breath away. He fumbled for the shotgun that was racked in the Tahoe while the sheriff retrieved his rifle and a high-powered flashlight.

They floundered up the incline through the knee-deep snow until they reached the road. The wind had died down but the snow continued to fall and J.D. felt the slick ice under his boots once they reached the pavement. The sheriff's flashlight beam barely cut through the darkness and J.D. shivered. Nothing looked familiar; everything was blanketed in white, looking ghostly and menacing. For a few seconds they stood, getting their bearings, and the silence was broken by the hum of an engine and the sound of tire chains on the icy road... from the direction of the Black Horse Campground.

Sutton swung his light toward the sound as a pair of powerful headlights pierced the snowy night. As the vehicle drew closer, J.D. felt his heart leap. It was a dually pickup truck, its gray paint partially obscured by snow and ice sticking to it. The sheriff shoved the flashlight into his hands and moved out into the middle of the road, leveling the rifle at the driver's side of the windshield, blinking as the driver hit the high beams, blinding him. At that instant the interior light burst on and J.D.'s blood ran cold.

"Don't shoot, Sutton!" he yelled. "Corrie's in there!"

The dome light went off, hiding the view of Ray Herman's sneering laugh and his right arm locked around Corrie's neck, pulling her in front of him like a shield as he aimed the half-ton truck directly at the sheriff.

Sutton hesitated; at first, J.D. thought he was debating about his ability to take out Ray Herman without hitting Corrie, but then he realized that the sheriff was trying to get his footing on the slippery road surface. The truck's grill work was barely a couple feet from the sheriff before he was able to lunge for the side of the road.

His right foot slipped on the ice. The truck's engine roared as it lurched forward. Sutton scrambled to get his footing and managed to launch himself at the snowbank on the shoulder of the road, but not before the front of the truck caught him in the side. J.D. yelled his name again and watched in horror as the blow spun Sutton several feet in front of the truck. Somehow the sheriff managed to slide away from the front tires. J.D. tried to run toward him but lost his footing on the slick surface of the road. He managed to get to his knees as the truck lumbered past, flinging bits of packed snow and ice from the tire chains. J.D. raised the shotgun in his hands and dropped it again helplessly, knowing he couldn't take a chance on hitting Corrie.

He could almost hear Ray Herman laughing as the truck roared into the night.

Corrie stared out the windshield in horror. Off to the side of the road, she could make out the front of the Tahoe protruding from a drift. Through the swirling snow, illuminated by the headlights of the big truck, she saw Rick standing in the middle of the road. He held a rifle in his hands, aimed straight at Ray's head. Ray's arm tightened around her and yanked her in front of him as he laughed and shouted, "Go ahead and shoot, Rick! I dare you!"

She gasped as Ray stomped on the gas. Benny let out a scream as the dually fishtailed then surged forward toward Rick. Ray's arm tightened around Corrie, making it impossible for her to make a sound. She saw Rick turn to get out of the truck's way and then... her stomach did a flip when she felt the impact. "No," she whimpered, as Ray let out a roaring laugh. Tears threatened to escape her eyes and she squirmed to free herself from Ray's grasp, while Benny shouted, "Have you lost your mind? You ran over the sheriff! We'll never get out of this mess!"

"They have to catch us first, and they won't!" Ray shouted back. "This will all come down on the Shaffers, like always. Only Corrie knows we're the ones involved and once I make sure she's never found...," he growled, giving her a shake, "... the Shaffers will take the fall, like always. We're home free!"

Corrie's blood ran cold for a second, then Ray bent his face toward hers. "Too bad Rick won't be around to find out that I got to have a little fun with you before...."

Corrie saw red. She drove her feet down hard against the floorboard, ducked her chin down, and propelled her body upward. She felt the top of her head connect hard with Ray's jaw, the click of his teeth slamming together, his arm around her growing slack. For a second, she felt dizzy and feared she had hit him hard enough to knock herself out, then she heard Benny's scream and she realized the dizziness was from the truck spinning out of control on the slick road. Ray slumped toward the driver's side window, his left hand dropping from the steering wheel. She grabbed the wheel with both hands and braced herself. She sensed rather than saw Benny fighting to get out of his seatbelt, a string of curse words erupting from his lips. He managed to free himself and fling the passenger door open. A blast of icy air froze Corrie to her bones and seemed to rouse Ray. He half sat up in the driver's seat, shaking his head, then he let out a scream as he stared through the windshield, throwing his hands up in front of his face. Corrie buried her face in Ray's jacket as glass exploded from the windshield and the deafening screech of metal crumpling made her want to cover her ears. The truck stopped suddenly, throwing her forward under the dashboard.

"Sutton!" J.D. got to his feet and slipped and skidded his way to the sheriff's side. Sutton had rolled on his back, groaning, his breathing labored. J.D. dropped to his knees in the snow, shining the flashlight on the sheriff's pale face. "You hurt bad?" he asked.

The sheriff started to shake his head and sit up, but he sucked in a sharp breath and fell back, his face contorting with pain. "Think I cracked a rib," he finally managed.

"Great," J.D. muttered. He threw a glance down the road where Ray Herman's truck had disappeared. "Hold still," he told the sheriff. He picked his way back to the Tahoe, struggling to keep his footing. He keyed the mike, praying the radio worked and he could get a signal. Dead silence greeted his efforts. He muttered under his breath and made his way back to the sheriff. "Hate to tell you this, Sheriff, but we're on our own. Can't get a signal and no way I can get the Tahoe out. You'd best wait in the vehicle while I go for help...."

"No," Sutton grunted. He tried to stand up, but the pain was too much. J.D. grabbed his arm as he slipped back onto the snow with a grimace. "We have to help Corrie."

J.D. shook his head in frustration. Ray Herman's truck was gone into the frozen night. Short of a miracle that someone would stop him—without getting Corrie hurt in the process—they'd never catch up to him. And the sheriff....

J.D. glanced at Sutton and shone the light on him. His breathing was labored, with a rattling, gurgling sound, his eyes closed and his face chalky. "You have to stay in the Tahoe, Sutton. You don't look so good. I'll have to get back to the station...."

"Medical center is closer," Sutton whispered. He reached up toward J.D. "Just help me up. I'll manage. Let's get going."

Arguing was going to be a waste of time and it was getting colder every second. He helped Sutton to his feet though it was obvious that the man was in agony at the slightest movement. Walking was going to be hard and painful for the sheriff; the fact that nearly every step had them floundering through snowdrifts and slipping on the ice underneath made it worse. The wind gusted from time to time, blowing snow across the road and obscuring their view. J.D. worried that they weren't heading in the right direction, but it was hard to see, even with the flashlight. But they had no choice.

They kept walking.

Dead silence.

Corrie opened her eyes in the eerie, cold darkness. She became aware of tiny sounds of the engine ticking, doors creaking on hinges, broken glass tinkling down like raindrops. She thought her heart had stopped, then she heard the blood roaring in her ears and she began to move tentatively. She waited for a rush of pain, but there was nothing except for the sting of tiny cuts on her arms. She unfolded herself from under the dashboard, holding her breath, and looked around. The dome light sputtered dimly, allowing her to see inside the cab. Her heart leaped up into her throat as she saw Ray, slumped over the steering wheel, his face bloodied. Part of her wanted her to get away as quickly as possible, but she forced herself to check if he was alive. Her trembling fingers found a pulse and she didn't know whether to be relieved or not.

Shivering, she edged her way to the passenger side door, only dimly surprised to see that Benny wasn't in the passenger seat. The door hung open and Corrie grabbed the handle, squinting to see in the darkness. Snow blew outside the door and she frowned. The ground seemed awfully dark; she expected to see a carpet of thick snow. She eased herself onto the floor of the truck and stuck her foot out feeling for the ground....

She drew back with a gasp. There was no ground under the truck.

She scooted backward and looked wildly around for a flashlight. She felt for the glove compartment and yanked at the door until it fell open. She scrabbled among the items until her fingers closed around a thin metal cylinder. Praying it wasn't a tire pressure gauge, she fumbled with it until she found a switch and clicked it on. The beam was barely the strength of a birthday candle, but it was enough for her to see that the truck was hanging over... a ditch? A cliff? She had no idea where they were. She looked around but everything was covered in snow and ice and all she knew for sure is that a large tree stump and a broken, twisted guardrail were all that kept the truck from plummeting who knew how far into the darkness. Swallowing hard, she strained to make out the sounds she heard. Was it the river far below her or was that the sound of the wind in the trees? She brushed strands of hair out of her face, feeling the sting of snowflakes biting into her cheeks. She had to get out of the truck before Ray woke up or before it fell into whatever abyss it was hanging over.

She scrambled over the back of the front seat of the crew cab. She had no idea if she could get out through the back doors, but she had to try. She found the passenger side door jammed shut, but the driver's side door had popped open slightly from the impact. Holding on to her tiny penlight, she shouldered the door open and aimed the beam downward. She saw snow below the door but how solid was it? She gingerly put one foot out the door and into the snow drift. She held on as tightly as she could as her foot went deep into snow, almost up to her knee, when she felt something solid under her foot.

She hoped it was the ground.

Still holding on to the door, she gritted her teeth and put her full weight on first one foot, then she slid the other out. The rapidly dimming light in her hands showed a vast field of white all around her. Her heart began to pound. Nothing looked familiar; she knew Ray had been driving toward Bonney, but she couldn't make out any landmarks in the dark, snowy landscape. Her teeth began to chatter. She had to find someplace, a house, a business, before long or she would freeze to death. And though she had forced herself not to think about Rick, the image of him, knee deep in the snow in Ray's headlights rushed back into her mind. Was he all right?

She blinked back the tears and concentrated on putting distance between herself and the wrecked truck. Pushing through the snow, with her jeans and sneakers becoming freezing cold and wet, she struggled to where Ray's tire tracks still showed and started following them back in the direction from which they had come.

At first, she was able to move easier by half walking and half jogging in the tire tracks, despite her numb feet, though she kept stumbling. But as the snow continued to fall, she found it harder and harder to see the tire tracks. Panic gripped her; if she didn't find help soon, some kind of shelter....

She bent her head and kept walking.

Chapter 25

J.D. shivered. He tried to estimate how far he and the sheriff had walked—make that shuffled—and how long it had taken them to go that far but decided it wouldn't help.

Sutton's breathing was labored and J.D. knew that they didn't have much time to find help. At this point, leaving Sutton behind was out of the question, although he was slowing J.D. down. Every step elicited a hiss of pain from the sheriff and J.D. wondered if they were both going to end up lost and frozen in the darkness.

He stopped when he heard a low, buzzing noise over the sound of the wind in the trees. Sutton nearly fell to his knees and it was all J.D. could do to keep him upright. "You hear that?"

Sutton nodded. "Snowmobile," he managed to say, then two sets of headlights pierced the thick snowfall ahead. J.D. stiffened, wondering if it was Ray Herman or if it was really help arriving. The riders blinked their lights and then pulled up to the two men.

"Wilder? Sheriff? What happened? You guys okay?" Officer Charlie White asked, pushing his snow goggles up on his head

"We've been better," J.D. said. He nodded toward the sheriff and addressed Deputy Mike Ramirez, whose signature handlebar mustache was apparent under the goggles. Mike immediately moved forward to assist him. "He needs to get to the medical center. Cracked rib," J.D. said. Mike nodded and Sutton didn't argue as the deputy helped him aboard the snowmobile. J.D. turned back to Charlie. "Ray Herman has Corrie. We tried to stop his truck and he tried to run over the sheriff. We need to go after him, but we also need to check on the Pages and RaeLynn Shaffer at the Black Horse...."

Charlie was nodding. "We picked up RaeLynn's radio call and we got chains on some of the emergency vehicles. Watkins is right behind us, along with Deputy Klinekole. They're driving the ambulance. Not sure what we're gonna find out there...." He stopped and glanced at Deputy Ramirez and the sheriff. Sutton was beckoning to J.D.

J.D. moved toward him as Mike started the snowmobile. Sutton grabbed hold of J.D.'s jacket front and tugged him closer. J.D. bent down and heard the sheriff's rattle voice. "Find Corrie," he grunted.

"That was the plan," J.D. said dryly. Sutton tried to say more, but J.D. shook his head and motioned for Mike to get going. The sheriff grabbed on to the back of the deputy's jacket as the snowmobile lurched forward. J.D. hoped that the sheriff would be able to hold on till they arrived at the medical center. As the snowmobile roared off into the darkness, J.D. turned back to Charlie White. "We need to find Ray Herman. He was heading toward the village."

Charlie nodded, then grimaced. "Probably going to have a hard time catching him. And his tire tracks are probably already covered up by the snow."

"We don't have a choice," J.D. said. Charlie gave a brief nod then jerked his head toward the seat behind him. J.D. swung his leg over and quickly checked to make sure he had his weapon secure. He grabbed hold of Charlie's jacket and was about to tell him to go when he realized that the man was shaking like a leaf and, as bundled up as he was, it couldn't be from the cold. J.D. leaned forward. "Hey," he said, raising his voice over the wind and the idling motor. "Charlie? You okay?"

"That's my cousin, Wilder," Charlie said hoarsely. He turned in the seat and his eyes locked with J.D.'s, even though J.D. couldn't actually make out any of his features in the darkness. "She's my blood. In the Native culture, she's my sister. No matter what's come between us... and it's not her fault, she always tried to be family to me... I mean...."

"It's okay," J.D. interrupted, giving him a shake as he started to ramble and his voice scaled higher. "She's gonna be fine, man. We're gonna find her. Let's go." He slapped Charlie on the back and it seemed to help him gather himself. He gave a nod, adjusted his goggles, and they roared into the night.

Corrie felt light-headed. She plowed through the deepening snow, stiff-legged, feeling as if she were wearing casts made of ice from her feet to her hips. Adrenaline had kept her warm in her sweatshirt and hoodie, but now the cold was beginning to penetrate her consciousness... which seemed to be fading fast.

She bent her head against the wind and kept going.

The tire tracks she had been following had long since been covered by blowing snow. She had no idea where she was, nor how far she had walked. She thought she was walking in a straight line, but she couldn't be sure and she fought the urge to look behind her because she was afraid of becoming even more disoriented than she already was. And as tired as she was, she didn't dare stop for even a second, terrified that if she stopped moving, she'd never move again.

Ten more steps, she told herself. Then, *ten more*. She had lost count of how many times she had told herself that, urging herself to keep going. She raised her head, expecting to see nothing but bleak, never-ending blackness and was shocked to see a patch of... well, maybe not light, but less darkness. She almost stopped in surprise and stared, holding up a hand to ward off the snowflakes striking her face. Could she really be seeing a dim glow ahead? For a brief moment, she wondered if perhaps she was freezing to death, slipping away, and the glow was her way out of this nightmare.

No! She shook her head. She wasn't going to give up, not until she knew Rick and J.D., Jackie and Jerry, RaeLynn, the people she loved, were safe. She wouldn't drop dead in the snow. She HAD to get to that light....

A rumbling sound suddenly cut through the cold haze in her mind, and she instantly snapped to full alertness. The sound grew louder and she realized it was the sound of an engine or motor. And it was coming closer.

Frantically, she looked around, hoping to find a place where she could hide. While it was possible that the sound meant she could be rescued from the cold, it was also possible that Ray or Benny had managed to find a way to come after her. She couldn't take that chance, but she also couldn't see where she could get away either. She decided her best bet was to run.

Floundering through the knee high snow was hardly going to win her any medals in a fifty-yard dash, but fear sent a surge of adrenaline that helped her pick up her previous pace considerably. Now she could see the outline of the building that was casting the dim glow through the flurry of snowflakes. It was the medical center.

Her heart leaped in her chest and began pounding, making her feel almost giddy. She was halfway across the parking lot of the hospital when another light cut through the darkness and the sound of the engine grew louder. She realized that it was coming, not from behind her, but from off to her right. She almost stopped but fear spurred her to move faster toward the blurry square of light that indicated where the doors to the emergency room were. The cold was forgotten as she half-skidded, half-ran across the section of the parking area that had been partially cleared and she wildly scrabbled to get the doors open.

"Corrie? Miss Black?"

She spun around, holding a hand up to shield her face from the headlights of the vehicle that slid to a stop a few feet away. At first she couldn't make out the faces of the shadowy, snow-covered figures that dismounted the snowmobile, but she could see that one of them was having a hard time walking. The other helped him toward the doors and Corrie instinctively moved toward them, her previous feeling of terror forgotten.

"Corrie…." Her heart nearly stopped as she recognized the ashen face and the faint voice.

"Rick? Oh, thank God! I thought you… what happened?" she stammered. She looked at Deputy Mike Ramirez and his usually jovial face looked grim.

"You got no idea how glad we are to see you," he said. "He said Ray Herman had you in his truck."

"Ray hit him with the truck. I was afraid…." She swallowed hard and slipped an arm around Rick's waist, helping him make his way into the medical center. "What happened?"

"Think I broke a rib," Rick muttered. He stared hard into her face, his jaw working. Corrie blinked back tears, not sure if it was from the snow or the lights from the medical center or from the overwhelming relief of seeing Rick alive. He blinked as well. "Thank God you're safe," he whispered.

By this time they were inside the emergency room lobby and two men in scrubs moved toward them. Deputy Ramirez answered their questions as they produced a wheelchair and helped Rick into it. Corrie fell in step as they made their way down the corridor to the emergency ward. They stopped outside the door. "Ma'am, I'm afraid you can't come back here," one of the men said apologetically.

"I'm not leaving him," Corrie said stubbornly. "Not till I know he's all right."

"Corrie, it's okay," Rick rasped out. He was breathing heavily, despite the fact he wasn't walking. In the dim light of the corridor, she could see he was chalky white. "Soon as they check me out, I'm sure they'll let you in to see me." He turned to his deputy. "Keep an eye on her. See if you can get hold of Wilder and let him know she's safe. And try to find Ray Herman." The orderly manning his wheelchair started to push him forward.

"The truck crashed into a tree." Corrie said. "Ray was unconscious when I left him. I don't know how long ago that was or if he's okay." She took a deep breath and fought off a shudder. "Benny Gonzalez was with him," she added.

Rick stopped the orderly and wheeled the chair around. "Benny Gonzalez?" he asked sharply. "Where is he now?"

"I don't know," Corrie admitted. "After the truck crashed and I got out, I didn't see him. The truck was hanging over a ledge. I don't know if he fell or ran away. I never saw him after the crash. I don't even know if he was hurt or not."

"Put out an APB on Benny Gonzalez," Rick snapped at Mike. "Get hold of Wilder, somehow, and let him know. I don't know what Benny's got to do with all this...."

"He's the man who took RaeLynn," Corrie broke in. Mike and Rick both stared at her. "Benny's behind all this. Ray was the one who... assaulted her, but Benny was the one giving the orders. No one would ever suspect him, but it wasn't the Shaffers behind it all."

Rick tried to stand up but pain flashed across his face and both orderlies grabbed him and eased him back into the wheelchair. "Sheriff, you need to have a doctor look at you. You don't look good at all. Something's seriously wrong."

"I'll take care of things, Sheriff," Mike said firmly. "Don't you worry."

"Don't let her out of your sight," Rick grunted, gesturing toward Corrie. A faint smile lifted the corner of Mike's handlebar mustache as Corrie rolled her eyes.

"I'll do my best," Mike promised. He nodded at the orderlies and they wheeled Rick away. Corrie took a deep breath as the doors shut behind them, her mind flashing back to the day when RaeLynn was discovered on the highway and was brought to the emergency room. She shook her head and turned to Mike. "Where's J.D.?"

"Me and Charlie found the sheriff and Wilder on the road. He and Charlie went to go look for you while I brought the sheriff here. We'd heard from Mr. and Mrs. Page and RaeLynn. They musta gotten Mr. Page's police scanner working. They're all right, but an ambulance was on its way out there to get them." Corrie shook her head.

"They're NOT all right," she stammered. "Benny knocked Jerry out. I don't know what Ray did to Jackie... I heard gun shots...." She sucked in a breath and smothered a whimper. Mike took her arm and squeezed it gently.

"They're getting help," he said softly. "We just gotta pray they're okay."

Corrie nodded and swallowed her tears. Mike released her arm and motioned for her to follow him away from the doors to where he could attempt to make his radio calls and keep an eye on her.

The hospital corridors were dim and it soon became apparent that they were operating on emergency generators. Only lights that were absolutely necessary were on and the entire building was cloaked in gloom. Corrie shivered and pulled her sodden jacket tighter around herself. She was thankful she was out of the storm but it was still cold inside the building. Mike came back, shaking his head, his mustache drooping and not just from being out in the storm.

"Can't get hold of nobody," he said. "Only dispatch and they're only getting spotty reception. Can't even tell who's callin' in or where they're at." He glanced at her and his look of concern deepened. "You're gonna freeze to death, Corrie. The sheriff's gonna have my head. Let me find you a blanket or something."

"I'm fine," Corrie managed to stammer. She tried to make it look like she was smiling while she tried to keep her teeth from chattering. "There probably isn't anyone around who could help you find one anyhow," she went on. "The hospital is probably on a very skinny skeleton crew and they've got their hands full right now with Rick."

Before Mike could respond, there was a blast of cold air from the double doors. Mike instinctively reached for his weapon as a tall figure, dressed in ski clothes and a heavy parka stepped into the waiting room and leaned a pair of skis and poles against the wall. A cascade of blonde hair tumbled out of the ski cap and Corrie was surprised to see Noreen Adler. The nurse seemed just as surprised to see them. "What are you doing here, Corrie?"

"Long story," Corrie said dryly, then gestured to the emergency ward. "Rick's in there. Possibly a broken rib. I didn't think anyone was able to get calls."

"I didn't get called," Noreen said grimly. "I figured it would be best for me to be here in case I'm needed. Oscar wanted to drive me, but I told him it would be impossible for either of our cars to get through this, even if we put chains on them, so I told him I'd come in on my skis."

It took Corrie a second to process that Buster's given name was Oscar since Noreen was the only one who ever called him that. She started to say something else when Noreen's brow furrowed. "Corrie, you're going to catch pneumonia. I've got a spare set of scrubs in my locker and you need to dry off and get warm. Come on," she said, jerking her head toward a door that led to the staff room. "You can fill me in on what happened while we change."

J.D.'s stomach rose and fell like he was on a rollercoaster as the snowmobile swooped over the snow drifts but part of the sensation was from anxiety. Did Charlie know where he was going? Everything looked the same to him; even the powerful headlights and the searchlight he was using showed only icy white everywhere. Trees drooped from the weight of the snow and the wind swirled falling flakes and kicked up pockets of powdery snow. It was like being in a violently shaken snow globe. Charlie slowed down and pointed to the left, indicating that J.D. should aim the light in that direction. He shouted over his shoulder, "The river bank is that way. No guardrail in some places." J.D. slapped Charlie on the back to let him know he understood. It would be very easy for a driver to miss the curves in the road and go over the edge, although the tire tracks would have been covered up a long time ago from the blowing snow.

Charlie slowed down further as J.D. swept the searchlight and strained to see any sign of a vehicle. The snowmobile's engine blocked out every other sound and J.D. wondered if they'd miss the sound of someone calling for help. Suddenly, the searchlight beam caught a snow-crusted, rectangular outline, too straight and geometric to be caused by the snow and trees. He slapped Charlie on the back again and yelled for him to stop. Charlie glanced in the direction that the light was aimed and steered toward it. J.D.'s heart leaped and his throat closed up with dread.

Practically hidden in the stand of pine trees lining the edge of the drop-off into the river was a large pickup truck. Even before he and Charlie dismounted and slogged toward it he could see it was Ray Herman's dually. The rear tires were nearly buried in a snowbank and the front end of the truck was tipped downward. The front passenger side door was hanging open, and J.D. immediately moved toward it. Charlie's grabbed his sleeve. "Hold on, Wilder. No telling how far over the edge the truck is hanging. You gotta go slow."

If anything, that news only increased J.D.'s dread. By now, they had approached the truck and he could see the front end practically wrapped around a thick tree trunk, with mounds of snow covering up the cab. Any evidence of anyone having left the truck had long since been covered up by drifts. Charlie found a long tree branch sticking up out of the snow and he pulled it out and handed it to J.D.

Using the branch as a probe and training the light alongside the truck, J.D. tested the snow, poking hard until, just beside the passenger door, it gave way to a dark, empty space and he could clearly make out the sound of the river below over the wind in the trees. He heard Charlie mutter an oath behind him and his heart crashed against his ribs. He turned the light beam to illuminate the interior of the truck cab.

It was empty.

He hadn't realized he'd been holding his breath until he felt light-headed, partly from the lack of oxygen, but mostly from relief which lasted only a second or two. He turned and shone the light all around but the darkness of the night seemed to press down on him.

"What? What is it? Is Corrie in there?" Charlie shouted, trying to move past him to look for himself. J.D. grabbed his sleeve and shook his head.

"No one's in there," he said. He tried not to think of the drop off into the river but it occurred to him that if the back door of the truck was hanging open, then it was probably likely that was how the occupants got out.

But how long ago? And where did they go?

They made their way around the back of the truck and checked the driver's side. Both doors were shut but that didn't mean someone hadn't gotten out that way, although there was no sign of any tracks. "Now what?" Charlie asked, hopelessness in his voice.

The question chilled J.D. to the bone because he only had one answer. "We need to find them, but we're going to need help. We have to head back to the station."

Charlie didn't answer. Silently, they both mounted the snowmobile and made their way back toward the village.

Chapter 26

Corrie paced the waiting room, shuffling in the borrowed pair of sneakers that Noreen kept in her locker. She was able to adjust the scrubs to keep them from falling off, but Noreen was much taller than she and Corrie could only lace the sneakers on so tight to keep them on her feet. However, she was barely aware of her too-big apparel. She was fighting back her fears over Rick's condition, not sure how much the doctors could do with their limited resources. X-rays? Scans? What if Rick was badly hurt enough to need surgery? She shook her head, pushing the thought out of her mind. *He'll be fine*, she told herself. If only she could make herself believe it.

She jumped when the doors to the emergency ward opened up and Noreen came toward here. A glance at the clock told her it had been almost forty-five minutes since they had arrived. Noreen was shaking her head and Corrie's heart plummeted. "No, it's not that bad," Noreen said with a grim smile as she noted Corrie's reaction. "But that man is as stubborn as a mule."

Corrie felt her knees go weak. "Tell me something I don't know."

"Fractured ribs," Noreen said in a brisk tone. "Yes, plural," she added at the look of shock on Corrie's face. "Three, as a matter of fact, and one is the same one he cracked earlier this year when he was shot. My guess is that it never healed properly because he never followed the doctor's orders and took it easy. If he ever even saw a doctor for it."

Corrie smiled wearily. "Just the EMTs. They taped it up for him."

"Well, he's taped up pretty good now," Noreen said. "We gave him painkillers but he refused anything strong. Says it just needs to take the edge off and he has work to do. He's arguing with Dr. White as we speak. He'll probably change his mind once he tries to walk."

Corrie doubted it, but she nodded. "Can I see him?"

"Yes," came a stony voice from the direction of the doors. Rick, walking carefully and buttoning up his shirt over a thick layer of bandages, made his way across the waiting room. He tried to tuck his shirt in, but stopped with a grimace and shook his head impatiently. Corrie's concern almost wiped out the wisp of a smile she felt; it was evident that looking sloppy and unprofessional pained Rick more than his fractured rib did. Noreen rolled her eyes.

"Sheriff...," she began but Rick held up a hand.

"Noreen, I already talked to Dr. White and signed a waiver. I'm not holding either of you or the medical center liable for anything. Whatever you're going to say, I've already heard from him, so don't waste your time." He gave her a half-smile to take the sting from his words, but Noreen already looked resigned.

"I'll let your own body and pain get the point across," she said. She glanced at Corrie. "Good luck with him. I'd better go see Dr. White." She turned and went back into the emergency ward.

Corrie looked at Rick closely. His color was a little better than earlier; apparently the pain had abated, but not by much. He still looked shaky and his steps were halting. He searched her face, his blue eyes reflecting his relief at her safety. "You sure you're okay?" he asked.

"I'm fine, Rick, but what do you think you're doing?" she asked, taking his jacket that he was holding over one arm. If he was expecting her to help him put it on, he was disappointed. She stood back, clutching his jacket to her chest. "There's no way you're going back out there, not injured the way you are."

"Corrie, I'm fine," he said, firmly. "Just a little sore." He almost succeeded in hiding the flash of pain in his eyes. "I don't have a choice. Wilder and Charlie are out there looking for you. We can't get hold of them on their radios. They think you're out there with Ray and they don't know about Benny. They could be ambushed. I can't stay here and do nothing."

"I can go, Sheriff," Mike Ramirez said, coming up behind them. He gestured toward Rick's midsection. "You ain't gonna feel so good on that snowmobile, even if you are taped up. And I don't wanna take a chance on you getting hurt any worse. I can go look for Wilder and White." Rick was already shaking his head.

"Mike, I don't want you going alone, either. It's too risky." Corrie held up a hand.

"Look!" She pointed toward the glass doors that led to the parking lot. Flashing lights cut through the blowing snow as an emergency vehicle crawled into the bay. Noreen and the two orderlies suddenly appeared and rushed out to meet the ambulance. Officer Watkins and Deputy Klinekole exited the cab and went to open the rear doors. Corrie found herself pushing past Rick and Deputy Ramirez to meet RaeLynn as she emerged.

"We're okay," RaeLynn managed to say as Corrie enveloped her in a hug. She was wearing Corrie's heavy winter coat and had a knit hat pulled down over her ears. "We're okay," she repeated, as the two LEOs pulled out a gurney holding a heavily wrapped Jackie, followed by a bundled up Jerry, sporting a bandage wrapped around his head. Corrie's heart plunged and then she heard the familiar back-and-forth bickering between the Pages.

"Jerry! Jackie!" she cried and rushed over to the gurney. Jackie half sat up and Jerry immediately barked at her not to move. "What happened?"

Jackie, her head and face wrapped in a scarf, ignored Jerry and reached for Corrie and drew her into a fierce embrace, the tears on her cheeks freezing cold against Corrie's skin. "Oh, thank God, you're safe! I was so afraid...."

"Well, that makes two... or three... or however many of us!" Corrie's words and laugh were choked with relief. She looked up as Deputy Klinekole and Officer Watkins cleared their throats. "Oh, yeah, I'm sure you all want to go inside where it's warm," she stammered.

They made their way in, with Corrie peppering the Pages and RaeLynn with questions which stopped when Rick stepped forward. "Jackie, what happened?" he asked, his voice wavering between relief and stern authority. He looked at Jerry and RaeLynn, including them in the question as well. He managed to hide his own pain, masking it with concern, and Corrie decided to keep it under wraps as well.

"A lot of things," Jerry said gruffly, taking Jackie's hand and squeezing it as if letting go of it would never be an option. "Benny Gonzalez came to the door of the campground, claiming he'd gotten caught in the storm." He related what happened up until Benny knocked him unconscious. Jackie sat up, brushing away the hands that tried to get her to lie back down.

"I don't know how he got in or how long he'd been there," she said. "But Ray Herman suddenly appeared after Corrie and Jerry went downstairs. He had a gun." She cleared her throat. "I don't think he even noticed me at first; he had his attention focused on RaeLynn." She and RaeLynn told Rick what happened when he lunged at RaeLynn. "She managed to get out the window," Jackie said. "He shot at her and, thank God, he missed. I came up behind him and hit him with Corrie's baseball bat. I guess I didn't hit him hard enough," she said almost apologetically. "He turned around and it was dark in the room and he just fired the gun blindly. I didn't even think about it, I just... cried out and fell to the floor. I don't know if he even saw me, but he must have thought he shot me and he ran for the stairs. I was terrified. I didn't know if Jerry and Corrie had heard what was going on. Then I heard the commotion downstairs. I was so torn... RaeLynn, Jerry, Corrie. I didn't know what to do...." Her voice started to tremble and Jerry patted her hand.

"The good thing is, he didn't hit Jackie," he said, his own voice becoming gruffer as he tried to hide the tremor in it. "And once I was able to sit up and focus, we got the scanner working. That was when RaeLynn stumbled down the stairs. You don't know how glad we were to see she was safe," he said.

"She was a trooper," Jackie said, taking RaeLynn's hand. "Jerry told her how to work the scanner so I could try to patch up his head. We didn't know if anyone heard us...."

"It was patchy," Rick said. For once he wasn't jotting down notes and Corrie suspected it was partly from the pain in his ribs and partly because he was overcome with relief that they were all safe. He looked at RaeLynn. "I know this probably isn't the best time to ask you this, but can you positively identify Ray Herman and Benny Gonzalez as your kidnappers?"

RaeLynn started to nod then frowned. "Do you mean, did I see their faces? No, Rick, I never did. But I know their voices. Isn't that enough?"

"Ray practically admitted what he'd done to RaeLynn," Jackie began as she sat up and motioned to Noreen, who was approaching them, to turn her attention to Jerry, but Rick shook his head.

"I don't mean just about kidnapping RaeLynn. After all, we'd have enough to charge him and Benny both with assault, kidnapping, and attempted murder after all that's happened tonight. I want to know if, now that you know both Ray and Benny were involved with your abduction, you have any idea WHY they did it." RaeLynn was shaking her head hopelessly, tears pooling in her eyes, when Corrie straightened up and grabbed her arm.

"RaeLynn, wheelbarrows. Remember? You said you heard them talking about moving wheelbarrows." RaeLynn's eyes widened.

"That's right," she breathed. She turned to Rick and her face flushed. "I know it sounds ridiculous, but they did talk about wheelbarrows. That they needed to move more. But I don't understand... I mean, I don't know anything about wheelbarrows that my family would have been involved in or that Benny and Ray would...."

"It's got to mean something," Corrie put in. "Maybe it's a code word for something else."

Rick frowned and chewed on his lower lip, then winced. Corrie fought the urge to tell him to sit down, knowing if he was deep in thought, he wouldn't listen anyway. He let a breath out slowly. "Wheelbarrows...," he muttered, the frown lines deepening. "Where have I heard that recently?" he said almost under his breath.

A blast of cold air startled them all and they turned toward the entrance where two snow-covered figures were stumbling through the door. RaeLynn gasped and gave a little shriek as she backed away and both Rick and Deputy Ramirez reached for their weapons. Then Corrie caught a glimpse of silver-gray eyes.

"J.D.!" she cried and the other figure moved forward.

"Cousin! You're safe!" Charlie White hollered and threw his arms around Corrie in a freezing cold embrace. Startled, she almost pulled back but her cousin's bear hug, despite the icy snow clinging to his parka, had a warmth she hadn't felt from anyone in her own family in a long time. She locked gazes with J.D. and he grinned at her.

"My sentiments exactly," J.D. said. He looked at Rick. "What are you doing up and around?"

"I was going to go look for you. Ray Herman isn't the only danger we got out there." Quickly, he filled J.D. and Charlie in with the news that Benny Gonzalez was also involved in RaeLynn's kidnapping and was probably the mastermind behind the Shaffer's illegal activities. "The only thing we don't know is what exactly those activities are," Rick finished, his hand slipping inside his shirt to clutch at the bandages covering his injured ribs.

J.D. shook his head and looked at RaeLynn who was staring at the floor, lost in thought. "Glad you and the Pages were able to get away, Miss Shaffer," he said. Her head jerked up as if surprised that he was addressing her. Corrie managed to disengage herself from her cousin's embrace and stepped to RaeLynn's side.

"Wheelbarrows," Corrie said, looking at J.D. "That's what she remembers them talking about. We don't think it means actual wheelbarrows... it might be a code for something else. Does it mean anything to you? We've all been drawing a blank," she said, hoping against hope that J.D. might have an answer.

He shook his head and shrugged. "No idea. I mean, that isn't something you'd associate with either Benny, Ray, or the Shaffers." He looked at Officer White. "Doesn't mean anything to you, does it, Charlie? Has Ray said anything to you about a wheelbarrow?"

Charlie shook his head and then let out a laugh. "Nah, just that stupid joke Jessup likes to tell all the time. Ray overheard him telling it to one of the county guys and he got all upset and told him to shut up, that everyone was tired of that joke and it wasn't even funny anyway. Duane got testy, told him he wasn't talking to him, blah, blah, blah. Ray ended up just storming out, but it seemed kinda weird that Ray would get all irritated over something like that. Duane makes dumb jokes all the time and we mostly just kinda tune him out."

Rick had straightened up and exchanged a glance with J.D. Corrie noticed the look. "What?" she asked, feeling tension knot in her stomach.

"What's the joke?" Rick asked. Charlie seemed surprised.

"The joke? Oh, geez, I'm not sure how it goes. It's one of those long drawn out story ones, about some guy who used to work in a factory and everyone thought he was stealing stuff from the factory… something like that, but I don't remember the whole joke, just that the punch line was wheelbarrows."

"Oh, I know that story," Jerry spoke up, despite Noreen's ministrations to the bump on his head. "Guy working in a factory for twenty years, every day he leaves, pushing his tools in a wheelbarrow. The security guards are convinced he's stealing something from the factory and selling it, 'cause they find out he's getting extra money from somewhere, so they search the wheelbarrow every day, but they can't find anything. This goes on, every day, for twenty years until the guy is about to retire. On his last day, the security guards stop him and say, 'Look, we know you've been stealing stuff all these years but you've been too clever for us to catch you. You're retired, we can't do anything to you anymore, so tell us what it is you've been stealing and selling.' And the guy says, 'Wheelbarrows'." There was dead silence in the room.

"That's a joke?" J.D. said.

Jerry shrugged. "Aw, Duane Jessup is a talker, you know. He'd tell it way better. But it'd probably only be funny the first time you heard it."

"Um...." RaeLynn raised a hand, as if she were sitting in a classroom. "I don't get it."

Corrie bit back a smile, but then shot a look at J.D. as if warning him not to laugh at RaeLynn's question. He raised an eyebrow at Corrie then gave RaeLynn a gentle chuckle. "The guy left every day with a wheelbarrow and the security guys were so focused on what he might have IN the wheelbarrow that he was stealing that it never occurred to them that it was the actual wheelbarrows he was stealing." RaeLynn nodded, grateful for the explanation but Rick straightened up, letting out a grunt of pain.

"That's it," he said, his eyes widening. "That's got to be it. My God, it's been right in front of us all these years!"

Everyone stared at Rick. Corrie glanced at J.D., to see if he knew what he was talking about but he looked just as perplexed as she felt. "What are you talking about? What's been in front of us, Rick?" she asked

Instead of answering her, he turned to RaeLynn. "RaeLynn, listen to me. Have you ever, in all the years you've lived in your family's home, seen them deal drugs? Or any other illegal substances?"

RaeLynn stared at him, her mouth open. She blinked, her face turning red. "Uh, well, it always seemed like my brothers had... lots of it on hand...." She shook her head and gave an uncertain laugh. "I mean, gosh, Rick... you and just about every cop in the county know that...."

"That's not what I'm asking," he interrupted with an impatient wave of his hand. "What I'm asking is, have you ever actually seen them sell or distribute drugs? Not just use them, even on a weekly basis. I mean, actually make money from selling or distributing them?"

She was shaking her head before he finished speaking but it was from confusion. "No, I mean... I don't think so. I don't remember ever seeing anyone come to get drugs from them...."

"And yet," Rick went on, "there have been different vehicles—cars, trucks, whatever—at your family's home almost on a daily basis, at all hours of the day or night, for years. Do you remember seeing different people coming to the house?"

"N-no," RaeLynn stammered, her eyes growing wider. "Rick, what are you getting at?"

"Wheelbarrows," J.D. spoke up, a glimmer of comprehension in his face. "It wasn't what was IN them that was important, it was the wheelbarrows—in this case, the vehicles—that was

273

important!" He turned to RaeLynn. "Your brothers are pretty good mechanics, aren't they? And they always seem to have a new vehicle around?"

"It's the vehicles," Corrie breathed as all the pieces fell into place. She looked around and saw understanding dawn on everyone's faces. "The vehicles weren't transporting drugs or stolen goods to sell. The Shaffers were stealing the vehicles and selling them or the parts. Is that what you mean?"

"That, or something like it," J.D. agreed. RaeLynn still looked dazed. "They were making a lot of money and they had high-end vehicles coming through, nothing second hand. But why no one ever mentioned stolen vehicles...."

"That's something we'll have to look into once this storm clears," Rick said. "In the meantime, we've got Ray and Benny at large, armed and dangerous. We need to...."

"You're not going anywhere, Sheriff," J.D. said. He pointed at Rick's side. "I don't care how much padding the doctor put on your ribs, you're in no condition to track down two fugitives in this storm. Since everyone's safe, I think it's best we don't take chances with anyone's safety and wait out the storm. I doubt Ray and Benny will get very far."

"J.D.'s got a point, Rick," Corrie said.

"And if they take shelter in some innocent person's home? No one would turn them away in this weather and there's no way to warn anyone with communications down. Other people could be in danger," Rick argued.

"Rick's got a point, too," Corrie said, as J.D.'s forehead puckered in concern. He glanced around the room.

"Well, we've got enough manpower here to start a search. We'll concentrate in the area where Ray's truck crashed." He glanced at Charlie. "Any idea how many homes are in the area?"

Charlie shook his head. "That area is part residential, part business. Lots of places they could take shelter, even if they didn't find someplace where someone would let them in."

"We need to check back in at our respective stations," Rick said. In spite of himself, he rested his hip against the receptionist's desk, wincing as he did so. Corrie knew that he realized, though he'd hate to admit it, he would only hold up any officers or deputies who would be out searching for Ray and Benny. He avoided her eyes. "We need to notify everyone we can about Ray and Benny. I guess I can stay here and man the radios and phones...."

"Great idea," J.D. said. The other LEOs in the room snapped to attention, realizing that J.D. was taking charge. Quickly he made assignments, sending all four of them back to the sheriff's department to man two more snowmobiles and pair up with four more officers and deputies to start the search. Once they were out the door, he turned to Rick.

"Level with me, Sheriff," he said. "How are you, really? We all know you're in pain and probably a lot worse off than you care to admit, but we have a right to know. Especially me. I don't want to take a chance on you being seriously injured and going on as if nothing's wrong."

Rick was silent for a few seconds, his eyes locked with J.D.'s, as if engaged in a silent battle of wills. Finally he let out a sigh. "Dr. White hopes it's not more than fractured ribs. At the moment, he can only do x-rays... no CT scans or MRIs are possible until full power is restored to the hospital." He tried to draw a deep breath, but it ended up as a painful grunt. He shook his head. "He's worried I'll develop pneumonia if I can't draw deep breaths, especially after being out in the storm. And he can't tell if there are internal injuries to my lungs or other organs. I shouldn't be up and moving around, I know," he said, holding up a warning hand, although no one seemed ready to say anything. "I know I'm hurt bad. But we're all in danger here, and so are the people of Bonney, and it's my sworn duty to serve and protect."

"Not at the expense of your own health," Corrie protested.

Rick didn't answer. He glanced at J.D. instead, who cleared his throat, "Corrie, I'd be doing the same thing," he said quietly.

She looked at RaeLynn, at Jerry and Jackie, at Noreen and the other nurses, and understood. She glanced away to hide the tears stinging her eyes and took a deep breath. "After all these years, I guess I should know you well enough by now." She turned to face Rick and J.D. and gave them a shaky smile. "Both of you are cut from the same cloth. I don't know why I waste my time and energy arguing with either of you." They both gave her grim smiles, well aware that she was trying to lighten the mood. "What do you need the rest of us to do?" she asked, nodding toward her friends. Rick raised a brow and J.D. let out a short laugh.

"Oh, something you're really going to hate," he said, gesturing toward the conference rooms. "Unless the doctor says you need to be in a hospital bed, you're all going where we can keep an eye on you until we find Benny and Ray. Because we can't do our jobs if we're worrying about your safety."

Chapter 27

Deputy Bobby Fletcher shook his head as the snow continued to fall, not as hard as it had earlier, but without any sign of stopping. All deputies had reported in for duty and several were still around the department, waiting for a call and ready for anything. He himself had taken on the duties of dispatcher and wasn't having much luck with getting a clear signal on either his or the department's phone or any radio. Spotty calls had come through, one which had sent Deputies Mike Ramirez and Daniel Klinekole out to the Black Horse Campground. They had taken two of the department's fleet of four snowmobiles to the police department to pick up reinforcements and then to the medical center to get the ambulance. So far, he hadn't heard much back from them, except spotty transmissions that were garbled or full of static.

Dudley Evans, the unofficial undersheriff, kept coming to him, asking for any updates and growing visibly worried that neither Sheriff Sutton nor Detective Wilder had checked in. Bobby wished he could do something to make the radios and phones miraculously start working, or do something to improve his standing in the department. He could hear Deputy Evans making assignments to the other deputies, sending them on patrol or having them prepare emergency vehicles for calls. Bobby knew that he was assigned to dispatch because of his latest performance evaluation and also because he'd twisted an ankle two days before doing a traffic stop—just by tripping over his own feet. He'd been thankful that Sheriff Sutton hadn't been around when that happened, but Deputy Evans' silent response and curt assignment to desk duty were enough to make Bobby wish for an opportunity to save the day.

He looked up as a blast of cold air from the front doors signaled to him that someone was coming in from the storm. Instead of one of his fellow deputies, a dark, hunched over figure, covered in snow and ice, stumbled across the room toward him. "Help me," came a faint, wheezing plea as the figure collapsed on the floor.

Deputy Fletcher froze in place for nearly a half minute, his mouth hanging open in shock. It was only when the figure on the floor moaned that he snapped into action. Quickly he hobbled over to the figure as fast as his sore ankle would allow, grimacing from the pain and trying to decide if he should call for help or take care of the person himself. Without thinking, he reached down and brushed the snow on the person's face and hair. "Benny? Benny Gonzalez?"

"Help me, please." Benny's voice was a muted croak and Deputy Fletcher drew back, confused. How did Benny Gonzalez get all the way to the sheriff's department? Where had he come from? What was he doing out in the storm? Benny raised his head and one hand, reaching toward Deputy Fletcher. "You have to help me. I'm in danger."

"Danger?" The deputy straightened up, his hand going to his weapon as he frantically looked around. He couldn't see much outside because of the swirling snow. His wounded pride was the only thing that kept him from calling for another deputy to come assist him. "What happened?" he asked as Benny managed to get to his feet.

"I'll explain later," Benny wheezed, clutching his side. "I need to...."

"What's going on here?"

Deputy Fletcher jumped and quickly spun around, the pain in his ankle shooting straight up his leg, but he managed to squelch the screech of surprise and pain that threatened to erupt from his throat. Dudley Evans stood behind him with his hands on his hips, his expression stern. He looked at Benny then back at Deputy Fletcher and raised a brow. Deputy Fletcher swallowed hard and tried to hide his grimace.

"Uh, Mr. Gonzalez here," he said, gesturing to the shivering figure, "He, uh, he just came in." He winced at the stupidity of the statement. "I was just asking him if he was all right."

Deputy Evans narrowed his eyes and looked Benny over closely. "Does he need medical attention?" he asked.

"I... I don't know," Fletcher stammered, shooting a glance at Benny. He hadn't thought to ask and the older man didn't seem to be in any hurry to answer. "He was out in the storm...."

"Look, take him to the medical center," Deputy Evans interrupted with an impatient shake of his head. "It won't hurt to have him checked out and he'll be able to stay warm there until he can get home. I need you to get over there right away. The sheriff's been injured. Ray Herman practically ran over him with his truck. There's a BOLO for Ray and his pickup truck. He's considered armed and dangerous."

Fletcher stood with his mouth hanging open again and it wasn't until Benny Gonzalez spoke up that he remembered to shut it. "Oh, that's terrible, Deputy Evans. Will the sheriff be all right?" Benny inquired meekly.

Deputy Evans turned to Benny. "He'll be fine, Mr. Gonzalez. Thanks for asking." He turned and shot a withering glare at Fletcher who finally managed to snap his lips shut.

"Why would anyone, especially Officer Herman, do such a thing?" Benny asked plaintively. Deputy Evans ignored his query as he drew Fletcher aside.

"Listen, Fletcher," Deputy Evans said urgently, "we don't know the whole story so you need to get over there and find out what's going on. Communications are still spotty, so you might have to come back with anything you learn. I didn't get a lot of information but I'm under the impression that the sheriff's condition is serious. Deputy Klinekole and Officer Watkins also brought in the folks from the Black Horse to get them all checked out, and I'm not sure who all that means. I've got to stay here or I'd go...."

"You can count on me!" Fletcher said, snapping to attention. His attempt to click his heels together ended with a grimace and a barely suppressed grunt of pain and a weary sigh from Deputy Evans.

J.D. kept one eye on the security monitor and the other alternately on Corrie and the sheriff. He had suggested Sutton work on trying to establish communications using the medical center's phones and radios. Corrie, RaeLynn and the Pages were camped out in the tiny lounge area near the dispatcher's station where both J.D. and the sheriff felt comfortable enough to be able to work without worrying about them. Occasionally J.D. would check his cell phone only to see "No Service" flash on the screen. He was getting impatient; the storm was dying down but it would be a long time before full service to all phones and radios would be restored. And Ray and Benny were out there somewhere.

J.D. glanced at the sheriff. Sutton was propped up painfully in a chair, leaning on the desk to take the pressure off his broken ribs. Despite his assertion that he was fine, it was obvious to everyone that he was NOT fine; the ghostly whiteness of his face, his labored breathing, and the coughs he kept trying to suppress indicated that he was seriously injured and doing his best to hide it. J.D. knew that calling attention to his condition would only make the sheriff even more stubborn so he kept a close watch on him and was thankful that at least they were at the hospital. Just in case.

The lights in the corridor, already dimmed to conserve energy, flickered and J.D. shook his head. The security monitor screen blinked several times, then blurred and froze before clearing up. It had happened several times already. The camera was trained on the emergency room entrance, and showed the doors, the sidewalk outside the doors, and the curb where the ambulance would pull up. The picture was in grainy shades of black, white, and gray, motionless except for puffs of snow that would swirl past the entrance. He was glad that the main entrance and employee and maintenance doors were securely locked; they only had one way in and out of the medical center to worry about. "I don't suppose a coffee maker would be considered essential equipment?" he said as he stood up and stretched.

"It should be," Sutton muttered. The silence in the room was punctuated by bursts of crackling static over the radio and the sheriff's repeated efforts to get an answer to his radio calls. J.D. glanced over at Corrie. She was awake, her face drawn with exhaustion and worry, her eyes darting back and forth between him and Sutton. RaeLynn and the Pages had drifted off to fitful sleep in the uncomfortable plastic chairs with blankets wrapped around them. He caught Corrie's gaze and gave her a grim smile.

"Go to sleep," he said. "Everything's under control."

"Which is why we're all in the medical center instead of at home," she said dryly. Before either of them could say anything else, the security monitor flickered again and J.D. sighed irritably. Then Corrie jumped to her feet, pointing to the screen. "Look!"

J.D. and the sheriff both spun toward the monitor but the screen was frozen, and the image was of the wide open double doors. The bottom half of two tires and the lower part of a vehicle were visible at the curb, the bottom part of a door partially open, but it was impossible to see what the vehicle looked like or the passenger, for that matter. They moved closer to the screen, but the images didn't move. "C'mon," J.D. muttered, slapping the side of the monitor. After a second or two, the screen blurred and there was movement. A well-bundled figure with a pronounced limp was already halfway across the pavement outside the emergency room doors and in a few steps had moved beyond the frame.

"That looks like it might be Deputy Fletcher," Sutton said with a grunt. "He hurt his ankle the other day. Must've gotten pretty bad for him to come to the ER in this weather."

Corrie leaned between them, squinting at the screen. J.D. glanced at her. "What is it?"

"Thought I saw a shadow," she said. She pointed at the sidewalk area just outside the doors. "Just before Deputy Fletcher walked in. Like someone had come in ahead of him."

The sheriff shook his head. "Any way we can back up the camera feed?" he asked J.D.

J.D. shook his head. "No idea, and it'll be faster if we—that is, if I—go check it out," he said pointedly. He nodded toward Corrie, RaeLynn, and the Pages. "You don't need to be aggravating that rib and someone needs to stay with them." He turned to Corrie. "You're sure you saw a shadow?"

"Not a hundred percent, no," she admitted. "Maybe it's just my nerves, but it almost looked like someone walked in ahead of Deputy Fletcher."

"You're right," the sheriff said suddenly, as he straightened up and his hand went to his side and unstrapped his weapon. "Someone had to come in with Fletcher. That's the passenger side door on the screen; Fletcher was driving. Someone else got out of the patrol vehicle and went in before him. Let's go find out who it was."

"Sheriff…," J.D. began, but Sutton cut him off.

"You might need backup. Could be nothing, but we're not taking chances. Corrie," he said, turning to her and jerking his head toward the conference room next to the lounge, "get Jerry, Jackie, and RaeLynn and go in there and lock the door. Don't open it unless Wilder or I come get you. Understood?"

For once, Corrie didn't argue. She nodded mutely and turned back toward her friends who had already roused themselves and were heading toward the conference room. She glanced back at them over her shoulder, not masking her concern, and then went in. As the lock clicked, Sutton looked at J.D. and nodded.

"Let's go."

Benny Gonzalez didn't linger over the unconscious form of Bobby Fletcher, sprawled face down on the polished tile floor. It had been a big risk to pretend to help the limping deputy by offering him a supporting arm, but it had been surprisingly easy to grab the service pistol out of his holster and bash him on the head with it. Deputy Fletcher had never seen it coming.

But now Benny had to find a place to hide before someone showed up.

Tucking the weapon into his waistband, he took off down a dark corridor. He knew it would be a matter of minutes before someone came across the deputy. He'd have preferred to shoot him and make sure he wouldn't be able to talk about what happened, but he couldn't risk the sound of the shot alerting anyone till he got away. He had to find Corrie and RaeLynn and the Pages and eliminate them as witnesses, even if it meant taking out the sheriff and Wilder as well. It was a slim chance for him to escape, but he had no choice. It was pure luck that Deputy Evans hadn't already heard that he was involved. He'd already taken care of the Shaffers, at least the ones most likely to turn on him. Ray Herman was now a loose cannon and, if Benny got the chance, he'd make sure Ray wouldn't throw him under the bus.

Assuming Ray had survived the crash.

Sticking to the shadows in the dim corridors, he silently made his way through the darkened medical center.

"Fletcher!"

Sutton made his way painfully toward the huddled form of his deputy as J.D. immediately unholstered his weapon and swept the area. He caught sight of the emergency call button next to the registration desk. He backed toward it, covering the sheriff, and pressed the button with his elbow. He heard a buzz and before a voice could answer, he barked, "We need medical assistance in the registration area! Officer down! And we need security if there's any available!" He released the button and stepped toward Sutton. "How bad is he?" He grimaced as he noted a trickle of blood seeping from the wound behind the deputy's ear.

"He wasn't shot, thank God," Sutton muttered as a medical team burst through the doors with a stretcher. "Looks like he was hit in the head, probably with his gun," Sutton told them and J.D. saw the deputy's empty holster confirming the sheriff's suspicions. Sutton got to his feet and moved away to let the medical team work on Fletcher. He had his own weapon in his hand as he stepped next to J.D. "There isn't any armed security on the premises, except for us. Someone else DID come in with him," he said under his breath.

J.D. merely nodded; none of them had seen who it was and now that person was armed with Fletcher's gun. Suddenly his attention was riveted on a spot on the floor where the reduced lighting reflected off a small puddle of melted snow. There was another one just beyond it. He nudged Sutton. "I'm gonna take a guess he went that way," he said.

"Let's hope he's got plenty of snow on his shoes," Sutton grunted as they headed down the corridor.

For several minutes, they went silently down the hallways, searching rooms, utility closets, and offices. The puddles had shrunk to nothing and now it wasn't clear which direction they should go. The medical center was practically empty; no surgical or maternity patients, and only one patient in the hospice ward who was in a coma. Staff was severely reduced and most of the nurses and aides who remained were close to the emergency department, in the event of new patients coming in because of the weather. The few staff members they encountered hadn't seen anyone, much less an older man, who shouldn't be in the building. They checked stairwells that led to locked doors; everything had been locked down once the emergency generators had kicked in. J.D. wondered if perhaps Fletcher's assailant was leading them in circles. It would make more sense for him and the sheriff to split up, but one look at Sutton's face and the sound of his labored breathing told J.D. that he would need help if they ever caught up with the fugitive.

"Let's go back," J.D. said, when the sheriff stopped and leaned against the wall to catch his breath. "You look like you're about to drop."

Sutton didn't argue. He nodded toward the hallway ahead. "That will take us back to the waiting room by the dispatcher's station. We should check on Corrie and everyone else, too."

J.D. felt a chill run down his back. If their quarry was ahead of them, then it was possible that he had already reached the location where Corrie and her friends were. He was about to tell Sutton he needed to pick up his pace when he heard a door slam and several screams.

It was all he could do to keep up with the sheriff as they raced toward the conference room.

Chapter 28

Corrie made no secret of her nervousness. Sitting in a chair was out of the question so she leaned against the wall near the door. It was frustrating that the door didn't have a window, but she knew the last thing Rick and J.D. would want her to do is to be seen by anyone, so she hoped she would at least be able to hear something. Anything.

Jackie and Jerry sat bolt upright in two chairs at the far end of the room, holding hands tightly, as still as statues. RaeLynn paced back and forth, her steps no louder than falling snowflakes. The silence was suffocating; Corrie wished her heart wouldn't beat so loudly. She pressed her ear closer to the door.

Then she heard it, and she knew it wasn't her imagination because Jackie, Jerry, and RaeLynn all looked toward the door.

Footsteps outside the door. Slow. Stealthy.

She drew back from the door as the handle shifted slightly, but didn't move more than a fraction of an inch. She held her breath. It was locked, there was no way the person outside could get in, they were safe....

"Corrie...."

She stifled a gasp. The voice was low, rasping, labored. She looked wildly across the room. Both Jerry and Jackie were shaking their heads. RaeLynn's hands were up over her mouth, her eyes as wide as saucers. Corrie took a deep, silent breath, trying to calm her racing heart, then she heard the voice again, growing fainter, and then....

"Corrie... it's Rick... open up...."

"No!" Corrie barely heard her friends' frantic whispers or her own good sense warning her. The image of Rick clutching at his injured ribs and his white face twisted in pain blotted out everything but the overwhelming panic that drove her to open the door to help him.

She turned the handle but before she could say a word, the door flew open with a vicious shove, banging against the wall, and Benny Gonzalez burst through with a laugh. RaeLynn and Jackie screamed as Benny grabbed Corrie's arm and jerked her in front of him. Jerry made a move toward them but Benny jabbed the gun into Corrie's side and shook his head. "Don't think I won't shoot her, old man!" Benny snapped. He glared at RaeLynn and jerked his head toward the door. "You, girl!" he snarled. "Get over here! You and your friend have cost me everything!"

"Let Corrie go," RaeLynn said, tears spilling down her cheeks, her voice trembling. "You know it's me that you're mad at. I'm the one you want to kill. Please, Mr. Gonzalez, just take me and let everyone else go. I promise I won't make trouble."

"Too late!" Benny snapped. "You've made more trouble than you're worth! You and your friend and your family, too! And now thanks to you, I've got to take care of the sheriff and that detective, too! So forget offering yourself to fix everything, missy, you're going to have plenty of company when I...."

"Drop your weapon, Benny."

Corrie swallowed a scream as Benny spun around, pressing the gun harder against her ribs. Rick and J.D. both stood with their guns aimed at Benny. Benny uttered a curse and stepped into the conference room, ducking behind the wall and yanking Corrie in front of him as a shield. RaeLynn stood paralyzed until Benny snarled at her, "Don't even think about running, girl, or your friend will pay the price." He jerked his head, motioning her to sit in a chair. She did and Corrie was certain RaeLynn's shaking legs wouldn't have held her up much longer.

Corrie shuddered. "Benny, you can't win," she said. "Let us go. No one has to get hurt."

"Shut up!" Benny squeezed her arm and twisted it. She bit back a yelp of pain. He raised his voice, "Sheriff, you and that detective better drop YOUR weapons and forget about playing super heroes! I've got all the cards and I'm calling all the plays. You wanna stop me, go for it, but you can't do it unless these people in here die. If that's how you want it, then hang onto your guns. Otherwise, drop 'em and step in here. The best I can do for you is to let you be with your friends when you all die!" There was silence and then Benny raised his voice once again, "I'm not playing, Sheriff! The next sound you guys hear is gonna be gunshots!"

Corrie bit her lip and watched as RaeLynn's face paled and then she gasped as the sound of Rick's and J.D.'s guns hitting the floor reached her. Without prompting, the guns were kicked into the room. Benny grunted approval then raised his voice again.

"That better be the only weapons on you. Now put your hands on your heads and come in here, and walk slowly. No tricks."

Corrie felt her heart sink as J.D. and Rick stepped slowly into the room. They had their hands on their heads, and it was apparent that Rick was in a great deal of pain. He could barely stand upright, but the agony in his eyes was more from seeing her in Benny's grasp with a gun pointed at her… and knowing there was nothing either he or J.D. could do. She glanced at J.D. and saw the darkness in his eyes, fury and frustration mingling in his gaze. She could sense his feeling of helplessness and it was almost more than she could bear. She swallowed hard and prayed even harder, but Benny tugged at her arm, pulling her toward the door.

"Years of hard work," Benny rasped, his voice thick with anger. "Years of planning and making connections and running my business like a well-oiled machine. And now it's all gone."

"You can't save your business anymore, Gonzalez," J.D. said. "It's over. All you can do is let us bring you in. You kill us all and you'll never be able to get away." Benny let out a laugh.

"No one's gonna stop me in this storm, Detective. Once you're all dead and I make my getaway, no one will find me again. Hadn't planned on retiring this soon, but I got enough to live out the rest of my life as I like." He edged toward the door, backing out into the hallway. He pulled Corrie along, the gun pressed hard against her back. All she could see were the faces of the people she loved—Jackie and Jerry, RaeLynn….

Rick.

J.D.

"Say good-bye," Benny hissed in her ear.

She smothered a sob as gunfire roared in her ear. Shrieks exploded around her and she slumped to the floor, feeling as if she were being dragged down, blood puddling on the floor beneath her. She heard her name, over and over again, but she couldn't tell who was saying it. Dimly, she could see both J.D. and Rick lunging toward her and, fearing for their safety, she impulsively tried to turn toward Benny to intercept his next shot, but she couldn't move.

Benny's body lay across hers, pinning her down. Then she realized that it was Benny's blood on the floor, not hers. It was Benny who had been shot….

"Back up! Rick, you and Wilder back away from those guns and put your hands up! Do it NOW or I guarantee I won't miss when I pull the trigger!"

Corrie stared in disbelief. Standing over her and Benny's lifeless body was Johnny Shaffer. His face was twisted in fury and his black trench coat dripped icy, melting snow on her and Benny, but what chilled her even more was the sight of the gun in his hands. She wanted desperately to crawl out from under Benny, but

Johnny's unwavering aim, coupled with his palpable anger, encouraged her to remain completely still.

He seemed to be unaware of Corrie as he stepped over her and Benny. She turned her head just enough to be able to see out of the corner of her eye and her blood ran cold. Johnny was an arm's length from RaeLynn, his arm extended and the gun pointing directly at his sister's head. He seemed oblivious to anyone else in the room but Corrie knew—and she was certain everyone else did, as well—that any move would be sure to end with RaeLynn dead. She held her breath as she widened her gaze. She couldn't see Jerry or Jackie, but she could see J.D. He'd frozen in mid-lunge toward the weapons on the floor, his face twisted in a grimace of anger and frustration and he had one arm flung out as if to shield RaeLynn. A low groan almost directly behind her head sent her heart plummeting. Even without looking, she knew Rick was on the floor, probably reaching for the weapons and probably having injured his ribs even more. She could tell by the smirk on Johnny's face that he knew he had them all at his mercy and none of them were getting out of the hospital alive.

She inched her way out from under Benny, careful not to move her head or arms, hoping Johnny wouldn't look her way. J.D.'s eyes were directly on Johnny but she knew he could see what she was doing. She just prayed Johnny would keep his focus on everyone but her.

"You happy now, RaeLynn?" Johnny hissed. "You proud of yourself for being so honest and law-abiding? Is that gonna make up for what you did to your family?"

"What did you do to Mama?" she cried, rising from her chair. Johnny took a step toward her, but she looked past the gun; neither she nor Johnny wavered. Tears stood in her eyes, but her hands clenched into fists. Johnny frowned.

"What do you think? You think I'd hurt her?" He almost sounded insulted. "I talked Benny out of it. He gave Teddy and her an hour to get their stuff together and get out. Even let him take one of the better vehicles. Didn't take them five minutes to get going… didn't bother to take anything. They split before the storm got worse. Who knows where they are by now, but what's it matter to you? You're never going to see either of them again." As he spoke, he closed the distance between them and Corrie held her breath, hoping she would get a chance to do… something. He had ignored Rick and J.D.'s weapons; if she could reach one of the guns....

She had stretched her hand out unconsciously and the movement caught Johnny's attention. He swung around, aiming his gun toward her, and she gasped. Instantly, Rick dove for the weapons and Johnny spun back around, unleashing a roar and a vicious kick that connected directly on Rick's injured ribs. Dimly she heard J.D. yelling "No!" but she didn't take the time to plan her next move.

She sprang to her feet and threw herself at Johnny Shaffer, hoping she could grab the gun or knock it away before he could pull the trigger. Her foot slipped on the blood and melted snow on the floor and she only managed to connect with the back of Johnny's knees before she fell flat on her face. With a yelp of surprise, Johnny's knees buckled and he fell backwards, his arms flailing as he tried to keep his balance. A shot rang out, shattering the overhead light fixture and plunging the room into darkness before he landed heavily on top of Corrie, knocking the breath out of her. Screams and shouts echoed in Corrie's ears and Johnny's already considerable weight suddenly became crushing and she struggled with all her might to get out from under him. The weight lifted off her and she managed to roll over. In the dim light from the doorway, she could make out the shadowy figure of J.D. hauling Johnny to his feet as a few of the hospital orderlies and nurses arrived and a couple of the brawnier men helped J.D. subdue him. Corrie crabbed backward across the floor, trying not to get stepped on or get in the way, when she collided with Rick, who was sprawled facedown behind her.

"Rick!" she gasped and, as she reached for him, she was aware of a wet, stickiness on her fingers and the coppery smell of blood filled her nose. In horror, she rolled him over and saw the dark stain on the front of his shirt.

"Rick! Oh, my God! *Rick!*"

Chapter 29

Corrie sat motionless in the waiting room of the emergency department, surrounded by the Pages and RaeLynn. Her eyes were fixed on the doors to the emergency ward and it was all she could do to keep herself from jumping up and bursting through them. Her mind kept replaying the last hour....

She squeezed her eyes shut and drew a deep breath. *Rick is alive*, she kept repeating to herself. In the pandemonium after Johnny Shaffer's gun had gone off, she had thought the blood down the front of Rick's shirt had come from a bullet wound. Her relief that he hadn't been shot had been short-lived. Once the nurses had been able to tend to him, while J.D. and two of the orderlies kept Johnny under tight restraint, it was soon evident that he was badly hurt, his face a ghastly shade of white as he coughed up blood and struggled to breathe. Ignoring Corrie's repeated pleas for information, they managed to get him onto a nearby gurney and rushed him off to the emergency room. One of the nurses insisted on having Corrie checked out as well, since the scrubs she had borrowed from Noreen were stained with blood, though none of it was hers. As soon as they were satisfied she wasn't hurt, she was shooed out into the waiting room and they turned their attention to Rick. She could still hear their shouts for oxygen, IVs, medical terms, and codes she couldn't comprehend. She only understood the urgency.

The doors opened and J.D. stepped into the waiting room, looking drained. Corrie sprang up but the questions in her mind wouldn't come out. He ran a hand over his head and moved toward her. The Pages and RaeLynn remained seated. J.D. motioned her to sit down, but she couldn't. He took a deep breath.

"Benny is dead. But you already knew that. Deputy Fletcher has a concussion, but he'll be fine. Johnny is under arrest and being held in a private office under guard until we can get him back to the lockup. Luckily, Benny hadn't taken Fletcher's handcuffs." Before he could go on, Corrie broke in impatiently.

"What about Rick? How bad is he hurt?"

"It's serious," J.D. said, taking her by the arm and easing her into a chair. "When Johnny kicked him, he snapped two of the sheriff's broken ribs and they punctured his lung. He's losing a lot of blood. They need to operate."

Corrie sucked in a silent breath and covered her mouth with her hand. The dim lighting in the corridors told the story. Could the doctor operate with the facility on standby electricity? J.D. seemed to hear the question.

"Fortunately, he's the only critical patient they have. They're prepping him now...."

The double doors flew open again and Noreen came through, her face grim. Corrie leaped to her feet, her heart pounding with dread.

Noreen went straight to the point. "We have a big problem. Rick is going to need a lot of blood in order to make it through this surgery. However, he has an unusual blood type—B negative. As of right now, we only have one pint of B negative blood on hand and that's the one Rick donated a week ago, plus another pint from a universal donor...."

"That would be me," J.D. interjected. "I'm O negative." He stepped forward, pushing his sleeve up. "I know it's only been two weeks since I donated, but I'm willing to donate again. How much do you need?"

Noreen's face convulsed for a brief second, then her eyes went to everyone else in the room. Corrie's heart sank; she knew that neither she nor any of her friends had a compatible blood type. And she also knew the answer to J.D.'s question from the look on Noreen's face.

"Detective Wilder," she said softly, "it's... it's not just a pint we need...."

"Then take what you need," J.D. snapped. "Come on, there's no time to waste. I can assure you my blood is healthy. Let's go!" He strode into the emergency ward without a backward glance and Noreen hurried after him.

J.D.'s concerns about keeping Johnny in custody, dealing with the fact of Benny's death, and not knowing what had happened to Ray Herman receded in the wake of the knowledge of Sutton's condition. He had no idea just how much blood he needed, but he didn't want to consider the possibility that, no matter how much he gave, it wouldn't be enough.

"Can I see him?" he asked Noreen as they made their way toward the triage unit. She stopped, her eyes troubled, and she nodded.

"Not sure if he's conscious. They're getting ready to take him back. We need to hurry."

"I just need a minute," J.D. said, his throat closing up. Noreen nodded and motioned him toward a curtained off room.

The minute he walked in, the medical team working on the sheriff stepped away to give them some privacy. J.D. nodded in thanks and moved to the side of the bed. He caught his breath as he saw the wires and tubes snaking from various locations under the white sheet that was only slightly paler than the sheriff's face.

Sutton's eyes opened a slit. "Wilder," he breathed.

"You're gonna be fine," J.D. hissed. His vision blurred but he blinked until it cleared. "I'm not donating blood for it to go to waste, you hear me? I hate needles."

A ghost of a smile flitted across Sutton's face. "Promise me, Wilder...."

"What?"

"...Corrie. You'll take care of Corrie. If I don't...."

"Oh, no, you don't!" J.D. growled, grabbing Sutton's shoulder, unmindful of the tubing and wires. The sheriff winced, but J.D. gave him a firm shake. "You're not doing me like that! I'll fight you, fair and square, for her, Sutton, man to man, on your feet at twenty paces if I have to, but you're not going to pull the unforgettable dead hero card! You understand me? I won't be first runner-up, taking over if you step down. So you better make up your mind right now that you're gonna pull through this even if it means I give you every last drop of blood in my body!"

"Detective Wilder?"

He turned. A young man in a lab coat stood in the doorway. "We need to go draw your blood, sir. And they have to take Sheriff Sutton in right away."

"Right," J.D. said. He stepped away from the bedside. The sheriff's eyes had closed and J.D. felt a cold hand clamp around his heart. He tore his eyes away and set his jaw. "Let's go."

Corrie stared out the double doors leading to the parking lot. The snow had finally stopped, with over a foot covering the parking lot. She shivered and rubbed her weary eyes. Under normal circumstances, she would have been relieved to have all the people she cared about under one roof. But right now, her stomach was in knots and it seemed like time was standing still.

It had been over two hours since J.D. had gone back to donate blood for Rick's surgery. She had no idea what was taking so long. She only knew that Noreen had warned her not to expect any word on Rick's condition for at least four hours. She bit her lip and tears stung her eyes. She hadn't even had a chance to see either of them before they went into the emergency ward. She hadn't had a chance to tell either of them....

They'll be fine, she told herself fiercely, stopping her thoughts from going to a dark place. The Pages and RaeLynn were sleeping on gurneys that the hospital staff had brought out to them. They had been invited to use a few empty hospital beds to get some rest, but they refused to leave Corrie alone—and she refused to leave the waiting room, although she had been assured she'd be notified immediately of any updates.

The double doors opened and Noreen poked her head around it, motioning to Corrie. She hurried over, her insides quaking at the thought of what news the nurse might have.

"J.D.'s asking to see you," she said quietly. Any hopes she might have had of not waking anyone were in vain as the Pages and RaeLynn quickly sat up, instantly alert. Noreen's face was haggard; Corrie wondered when she'd last slept. "I can't let anyone else in; to be honest, I shouldn't be letting anyone in, but he was pretty adamant and... well, all the rules are out the window at this point, so it won't hurt."

Corrie nodded and followed Noreen down the hall. "Any word on how Rick is doing?" she asked, praying for an answer but at the same time dreading what it might be.

Noreen shook her head. "Not yet. It's going to be a while. His lung collapsed when the broken ribs punctured it. I wish I could tell you not to worry, but his condition is very serious. They're doing everything they can in there, and I promise you, there's a lot of praying going on as well." She paused before letting Corrie in to J.D.'s room. "Try not to be alarmed when you see J.D.," she said, her eyes dark with concern. "He's drifting in and out of consciousness and he's very pale. We've got him hooked up to a monitor, just as a precaution...."

"A precaution?" Corrie stared at her. "For what? All he did was donate blood...."

"Three and a half units," Noreen said with a weary sigh. "Over thirty percent of his body's volume. He was insistent we take four or five units and wouldn't listen to reason. He blacked out and that's when we stopped. He'll be fine, but he's exhausted, he's very weak, he's got a lot of stress, and who knows when he last ate anything...."

Lunch at the Old Road. Corrie almost laughed. Was that just today? Yesterday? She shook her head as Noreen opened the door. Corrie stopped short and gasped. J.D. was propped up in a half-sitting position and his bronzed face was a sickly yellow color. An IV was in his left arm; his right arm was bandaged. He opened his eyes and managed a faint smile.

"Pardon me for not getting up," he murmured. He raised his hand toward her as she hurried to his bedside, but then he frowned at the IV needle in his arm, then looked at his other arm and the bandages. He managed a shrug. "I guess they left me some," he said.

"No thanks to you," Corrie managed to say. She touched his hand, shocked at how cold it was. She wrapped both of her hands around it as he shivered. She pulled the blanket up around his shoulders. "Do you need another blanket?"

"Don't think it'll help," he whispered. He shook his head and blinked painfully. He managed to focus on her face. "The sheriff?"

"It's too soon to know," she answered. He frowned. "He's only been in surgery a couple of hours," she explained. "He's in serious condition."

"He'll be fine," J.D. muttered. "He'd better be." He took a deep breath and cleared his throat. "How's everything else?"

"Deputy Fletcher has been discharged, not that he can go anywhere. He's restricted from driving for two days and there's a foot of snow outside. The orderlies who are watching Johnny are enjoying the job way too much, so you have nothing to worry about there. You might have two new applications for jail guards." She stopped when she saw his eyelids drooping. "Am I boring you, Detective?" she said, hoping her light-hearted tone hid her alarm.

He opened his eyes and gave her hand a gentle squeeze. "I'm fine," he said huskily. He nodded toward the tray on the bedside table. "I'm supposed to be drinking some of that stuff to help build up my strength."

"You should get some sleep," she said, taking one of the cups and adjusting the straw so he could sip without sitting up straight. He let out a weak laugh.

"Shouldn't we all?" he said. He sipped at the juice and grimaced. "Any idea if communications are back up?"

"I haven't even thought about it," she admitted. "Should I go see?"

He shook his head, then shrugged. "Probably, but I'm feeling selfish and I don't want you to go." He squinted at her, focusing his eyes on hers. "How are you doing?"

"I'd be better if we were all out of here and back at the campground," she said. She shook her head. "I'm fine, J.D. I'm not hurt and neither is RaeLynn, and Jerry and Jackie are fine also."

He started to say something, when Noreen came into the room. "Sorry to interrupt, but Corrie, you're going to have to step out. Detective Wilder needs...."

"... to get out of here," he interjected, sitting up. Immediately, Corrie and Noreen grabbed his arms as he began to slump forward.

"Well, THAT'S not happening," Noreen said dryly. "You're being ordered to rest for the next few days, so as soon as you can get a hold of one of your officers, you are assigning one of them to be next in command and you're shutting your phone off. No arguments. We're going to have enough trouble making the sheriff take it easy for the next few weeks."

"Is he all right?" Corrie said, her head jerking up to stare at the nurse.

Noreen's lips twisted. "We're hoping. It will still be a while before he goes to recovery, but, off the record, he seems to be doing well, under the circumstances. You didn't hear that from me," she warned them. J.D. shook his head.

"I'm all right," he said stubbornly. "I have work to do."

"Right now, your work is to rest and recover," Noreen countered.

"I need to find out if the phones or radios are working. You all took my phone and weapon when you took my blood. I have to get hold of my officers or some deputies. I need to know what's going on," he said doggedly. Noreen sighed irritably.

"I'll go get your things. I guess you'd better stay," she added to Corrie, "and make sure he doesn't try to get up. And DON'T try to get up," she said, turning back to J.D. "I'm not kidding, I don't have enough help to get you back onto the bed if you pass out. Understand?"

He merely grunted and lay back against the pillow. Corrie gave Noreen a crooked smile. "I'll do my best," she said. Noreen nodded and slipped out of the room. Corrie shook her head. "You won't be able to get Johnny to the jail right now, you know. The snow...."

"It's not Johnny I'm worried about," J.D. interrupted. "He's not going anywhere. But the fact that Deputy Fletcher wasn't aware about Benny has me worried about whether or not anyone else knows about Ray Herman. We're only assuming that the rest of the departments got word about him. So far, we only know that the deputies and officers that we actually spoke to tonight are aware that he's dangerous." He stopped as Noreen came back.

"Here's your cell phone," she said, handing it to him. "And your gun," she added, setting it on the bedside table. "Your wallet, keys, badge, and any other less important items are in this bag." She set a clear plastic zip-top bag beside the weapon. "Just so you know, Detective, now that the wind and snow have died down, linemen have been able to start working on the power lines, so the medical center and law enforcement offices should be getting power on soon. Cell service is spotty, so your phone may or may not work."

"Thanks," he grunted, swiping his phone open. He frowned and quickly punched in a number. "Hello? Deputy Evans? Can you hear me? It's Wilder." He grimaced and sat up straighter, grabbing for the side rail of the bed to keep himself steady. "You're breaking up, Evans, just hold on a minute and listen carefully." He relayed all the information he could think of to Sutton's second-in-command, emphasizing the danger to the community at large and the sheriff's condition. "I think he'll be fine," he repeated over and over. "It's too soon to know what his condition is." He listened for a few seconds, shook his head, asked Deputy Evans to repeat himself, then, "Listen, Evans, I need you to send a couple of deputies or officers, if you can get hold of anyone in my department, and send them here to the medical center if you can spare them. I need some LEOs that aren't incapacitated." He listened for a few seconds, then, "Thanks," he said and ended the call. He sighed. "No sign of Ray anywhere. They knew about him, but they didn't know about Benny. That's how Fletcher ended up driving Benny here. He showed up at the police department and they thought he needed medical attention. I have to hand it to Benny; he was a heck of an actor. Made everyone feel sorry for him, thinking he was a disabled old man. I just realized, he must have been our mystery man in Santa Fe and I'm betting he's the one who killed Dr. Pruett. Fletcher got lucky he only got a concussion."

Corrie shivered, hugging herself. She tried not to think about how long it would be before an officer or deputy showed up and what might happen if Ray were to show up before they did.

J.D. noticed her concern. "I'm not completely helpless," he told her. She noticed he didn't make an attempt to sit up. "As soon as I can get up without Noreen having a meltdown, I'll come out to the waiting room with you." He flashed her a smile, then he sobered. "How is Miss Shaffer holding up?"

"As well as can be expected," Corrie said, feeling her heart grow heavy. "She's relieved that her mother is safe or, at least, that neither Johnny or Benny hurt her, but she still doesn't know where she and Teddy are or what happened to her father and her brother, Cliff. I can tell she's worried but she isn't saying anything."

J.D. grimaced and shifted his position in the bed. "Whatever the Shaffers had going with Benny must have been a pretty big operation. And they brought Ray into it. I wonder if he's the reason things went south for them. He wasn't too discreet about having extra money. Your cousin told us that Ray's been flush lately."

Corrie's breath caught in her throat. "Charlie isn't involved, is he?"

"No, he's not," J.D. said. "I think he finally saw Ray's true colors. And he's been really concerned about you. If nothing else, maybe you'll regain a family member when all this is over." He reached out and patted her hand with an understanding look. His eyelids drooped and he lay back against the pillow. In spite of himself, his own blood loss was making him weak and tired. She relaxed, hoping he'd sleep, and then J.D.'s cell phone rang.

He immediately came wide awake, glanced at the screen, and swiped it open. "Evans, what's going on?" He listened for a few seconds, then sat up, alert. "Deputy Ramirez and Officer Charlie White went with Officer Watkins and Deputy Klinekole from here at the medical center. What time? I don't know," he glanced at Corrie as if asking her. She shrugged helplessly. "It's been over three hours, at least." He listened again and shook his head. "No, I haven't heard from them. Let me know as soon as you do. Yeah, thanks." He blew out his breath as he shut his phone. "They found an abandoned snow mobile. No tracks or anything leading away from it, but the wind's been blowing the snow around so any tracks could have be obliterated. No telling how long it's been there."

"Where?"

"About two miles from where Ray wrecked his truck. Still has gas in the tank. No reason why it would be left somewhere… unless the riders went after someone on foot."

Corrie gasped. "And you don't know who the riders are?"

J.D. shook his head. He sat up and swung his legs over the side of the bed, barely managing to stay upright. "Get Noreen or one of the nurses to get this IV out of me."

Noreen appeared in the doorway. "Detective, you're in no condition to get up, much less go anywhere," she began.

"I'll pretend you're a mind reader and weren't eavesdropping," J.D. said dryly. "However, if you don't get this IV out of me, I will and then I'm gonna need a bandage because I'm getting up and checking on my officers and deputies!"

"J.D.," Corrie began, but Noreen had already taken him seriously enough to begin detaching him from the IV needle. She waited while Noreen slapped a cotton ball on the spot where the needle was removed and stuck it in place with a strip of adhesive tape. "J.D., what is it you're planning to do?" she asked.

He stood up, swaying slightly, and waved off their assistance. He took a deep breath. "I have to find those men. They might have found Ray, or he found them. Either way, they're in danger and it's my responsibility to find them."

"You're in no condition to help them!" Corrie cried. "J.D., you can barely stand up straight! What do you think you can do?"

"I have to try," he said doggedly, grabbing hold of the bed rail. He hadn't taken a step yet, but he shook his head to clear it. "Corrie, I can't just stay here...."

"You can't save everyone," she said softly. She clapped her hands over her mouth, shocked to find her cheeks wet with tears. He stared at her. She glanced at Noreen, but her expression didn't change and Corrie felt her heart sink. There was no guarantee that J.D. had even been able to save Rick... and now J.D.'s own life was in danger.

She couldn't bear the thought of losing both of them.

He sagged onto the bed, blinking; whether from dizziness or from something else, Corrie couldn't tell. He sighed. "All right," he said in a husky voice. "Just... get me to a radio. The ambulance outside," he added, nodding toward the emergency entrance, "has an emergency radio. I need to try to get hold of everyone I can, to try to find those men. It's the least I can do."

Corrie looked at Noreen. "Let's get a wheelchair," Corrie said but J.D. shook his head.

"Let me have a little dignity, huh? I'll lean on you," he said, giving her a lopsided smile.

Chapter 30

If J.D. had been feeling better—if the loss of blood hadn't made his brain so fuzzy, his eyes so blurry, his thinking and reflexes so slow—he would have sensed there was something wrong as soon as he walked into the waiting room. Corrie was focusing on him, watching him carefully to make sure he didn't start to black out, so he should have been the one to notice. But it took a second or two too long for him to register that the emergency room doors were wide open, making the waiting room freezing cold. Jerry, Jackie, and RaeLynn were sitting too stiffly in the hard plastic chairs, and they didn't turn to look when J.D. and Corrie came in.

Corrie's gasp came at the same time he saw Ray Herman—shivering, wet, disheveled—standing with a shotgun in one hand, aimed at the people in the waiting room and a pistol pointed at him and Corrie.

The fog cleared as J.D. realized that going for his own weapon would be a fatal mistake. Ray gave a low, guttural laugh and he used the pistol to wave J.D. and Corrie toward the rest of the group. "Believe it or not, I'm glad to see you, Wilder. I'm already disappointed that Rick is out of my reach... for now." His face twisted in rage. "Drop your weapon and step away from it, Detective. Do it slow, but no tricks."

J.D. drew a deep breath and straightened up. Moving deliberately, he took his gun and set it on the floor, with the fleeting thought that he'd already done this once earlier. He raised his hands and took a step back, nudging Corrie behind him. "Benny is dead," he said, hoping he wasn't slurring. His vision wasn't as sharp as he'd like. Ray's face went in and out of focus and he couldn't tell what his reaction was. J.D. tried to control his racing heart, not wanting to increase his chances of passing out. "Johnny is in custody," he went on. "It's over, Ray. Just give yourself up and no one has to get hurt. You have enough problems. Don't make it worse."

"It can't get worse!" Ray yelled. Even through blurry eyes, J.D. could tell Ray's hands were shaking. "It's all over! We've lost everything! The only thing I got left is to make you all pay! And then I'm out of here, with whatever I got left! But not till I make you all pay!"

"Police! Drop the weapon, Ray!" Charlie White had slipped through the open doors, aiming his service pistol at Ray. Behind him, Deputy Mike Ramirez had a shotgun aimed at him as well.

Both men were covered in snow, their faces grim. Shock registered on Ray's face for a split second, then a sneer twisted his features.

"You don't have the guts, Charlie. You're a follower, not a leader... and I've been your leader for months. So you drop your weapon or your cousin and her friends are gonna be dead and it'll be your fault."

Charlie didn't waver. "You got one more chance, Ray."

"Or what?" Ray threw his head back and laughed and J.D. took his chance. He launched himself at Ray's midsection. With a roar, Ray went down, squeezing off a shot from the pistol that miraculously hit no one. Corrie grabbed Jackie and Jerry and pushed them to the ground. J.D. felt the room spinning and things growing dangerously dark, but he was aware of Charlie and Mike wrestling with Ray to get his weapons away from him. He managed to roll out of the fray and lay face down on the tile floor, trying to catch his breath and praying he wouldn't pass out. Dimly, he could hear Corrie calling his name and the next thing he heard made him wonder if he was hallucinating.

"RaeLynn, no!"

"Miss Shaffer, put the gun down."

He instantly came alert, but his body wouldn't cooperate. He turned his head and forced his eyes open and stared in disbelief. RaeLynn had picked up the weapon he had dropped—his own gun—and was now standing over Ray Herman, who was being held down by Officer White and Deputy Ramirez. She had the gun aimed directly at Ray's head and it was the steadiest aim J.D. had ever seen in his life. The expression on her face chilled him to the bone... or rather, lack of expression. Both LEOs were holding on to Ray, but neither was in a position to do anything. Ray's face was exhibiting an array of emotions from disbelief to rage, but mostly terror.

"Miss Shaffer... RaeLynn...," J.D. said, not sure if anyone but himself heard the words. He summoned his strength and rose up on his elbows. "Don't...." He felt he was going to collapse back to the floor.

RaeLynn spoke, but she addressed Ray. "I'll make sure you don't get away. I'll make sure you pay... for what you did to my family. For what you did to me." Her breath hitched. Everyone else in the room seemed frozen in place. RaeLynn's hands didn't waver, even though her voice did. "You won't hurt anyone ever again," she whispered. J.D. managed to get to his feet, moving as slowly as he could.

"Miss Shaffer," he said, his voice low but authoritative. "It's all right. I know you're angry and you're hurt and you have every right to be." She didn't move; he wasn't sure if she was hearing him. He moved closer to her, praying he wouldn't make a wrong move. He lowered his voice even more, trying to sound soothing but also in control. "What he did was wrong and what he did to you was terrible. And he will pay for what he did. But not like this, Miss Shaffer. Don't let him make you do this. Give me the gun. He won't hurt anyone again."

She stood still, tears pooling in her eyes. J.D. could see that Mike and Charlie's eyes widened as the gun shook for the first time. RaeLynn bit her lip. "You promise?" she whispered. "You promise he won't ever...?"

"I promise," J.D. said firmly. He stepped to her side and took the gun from her hands. With a whimper, her legs crumpled under her and J.D. managed to catch her before she hit the floor. "Corrie," he said, and she was there before he said another word, helping RaeLynn to her feet and guiding her into a chair. J.D. shook the cobwebs from his brain before he turned his attention to Ray, but the deputy and the officer already had him restrained in handcuffs and were reading him his rights. He turned to Corrie who had her arms around a sobbing RaeLynn and she looked up at him.

"I think I need to sit down," he said, then everything went black.

Corrie sighed as she opened the blinds in the campground store and flipped the "Closed" sign around to "Open", not that she had to worry about a crowd of customers rushing the store first thing in the morning. A three-inch layer of fresh snow blanketed the campground and she shivered. The campground was nearly empty except for her year-rounders, as it usually was in late December. It was Christmas Eve, two weeks since the harrowing night of the blizzard that shut down the entire village of Bonney.

Two weeks since Rick and J.D. had ended up in the hospital, both fighting for their lives.

She closed her eyes and breathed a prayer of thanksgiving, something she had been doing a lot of lately. J.D. had reluctantly spent two days in the medical center, ordered to bed rest and then light duty for a week upon his release. Rick had stayed in the hospital for twelve days and had been released the day before, just in time to be home for Christmas, although his road to recovery was going to be a long one. He was on leave for the next two months, although he was on his laptop and phone from home every day and stopping in to the sheriff's department every other day, to the amused exasperation of Undersheriff Dudley Evans.

RaeLynn had moved in with Corrie… she had no intention of ever returning to the shabby trailer her family had vacated. Her brother Clifford had turned himself in when the storm abated, having escaped from Benny, Johnny, and Ray the day the snowstorm hit. Jake Shaffer hadn't been so lucky. And no one had heard from Teddy or Mrs. Shaffer since they were given a chance to leave. The shock of her family having been shattered, especially the fact that her mother had left without a word of good-bye or even concern, sent RaeLynn into deep despair and depression. Counseling and intensive therapy helped, along with Corrie's unwavering support, but she was going to need a lot of time to heal. She quietly took up her duties at the campground again, relieved that she had some semblance of normalcy in her life.

Corrie smiled as she watched J.D. leave his cabin, bundled up in a heavy jacket, and make his way through the snow to the side door of the store. She opened it as he stepped up on the porch and stamped the snow off his boots. "Coffee's ready," Corrie said as he came in.

He grinned. She was glad to see his color had returned to normal. She pushed away thoughts of how close he had come to losing his life. "And I'm ready for coffee," he said. She led the way to the courtesy table and poured two cups of piñon coffee. He looked around the campground store and shook his head. "You and RaeLynn and the Pages did a great job fixing up the place for Christmas. You can hardly tell it was a crime scene a few weeks ago."

"It's been a crime scene far too many times this past year," Corrie said dryly. Jerry had grumbled that it looked more like a Christmas store than a campground store, but Corrie, with RaeLynn's eager assistance, wanted to erase all signs of what had happened earlier that month. "What's the word on Johnny, Cliff, and Ray? RaeLynn still worries about them going free."

"They won't be," J.D. said as RaeLynn came down the stairs.

"Who won't be what?" she asked, eyeing J.D. warily. She still looked thin and frail from her ordeal, but there was a healthier color in her face and a more purposeful way of carrying herself.

She accepted a cup of coffee from Corrie as the front door opened and Rick walked in, shaking the snow off his sheepskin jacket and Stetson.

"Tell me you have regular coffee," he said in greeting. His voice was still hoarse, the result of his injuries and the lingering effects of the pneumonia he ended up battling while recovering from his surgery. He moved carefully, although most people wouldn't notice it, still nursing his healing ribs and patched up lung. Corrie shook her head.

"You shouldn't be out in this weather. It can't be good for you to be breathing in cold, damp air," she chided as she filled a cup for him. He didn't smile as she handed the cup to him, but his gaze fastened on her intently. She wondered if he was just masking his pain or if there was something else on his mind. She was aware that J.D. was watching them, so she cleared her throat. "RaeLynn was asking a question," she said to him hurriedly, glancing away from Rick as her face burned.

RaeLynn looked toward J.D. apprehensively. He gave her a smile. "It's good news," he said. "Both Ray and Johnny were in such a hurry to throw each other under the bus, they started confessing to everything before they thought to make a deal. Not that one was being offered," he added, "because once Clifford turned himself in and started blabbing, they had more than enough to charge them with theft, money laundering, fraud, kidnapping, you name it... and then they had to make it worse by assaulting police officers. They're going to prison for a long time, if not the rest of their lives. Clifford's the only one who's got a chance to get out early, but he's had enough of Bonney. I suspect if he manages to plea his way to a lighter sentence, he'll be gone for good." RaeLynn let out her breath, her relief palpable.

"So what was the business they were running?" Corrie asked. "I know you figured it had to do with stolen cars, but how did no one ever figure it out?"

"It wasn't cars they were stealing, exactly," Rick spoke up. He had sunk down onto a tall stool to rest. Corrie's heart twisted, but she was glad that everyone pretended not to notice. He went on, "They had a network of car repair and body shops all over the state of New Mexico, even in Arizona and Texas, that worked with high-end, newer vehicles. Whenever they did routine maintenance, they would switch out expensive parts for cheaper ones. Then, when the vehicles would have problems with the cheaper parts, they would charge the owners for repairs using the vehicle's original parts. They were careful to make sure they took advantage of owners that had a lot of money and very little knowledge about cars." He cleared his throat. "They also found a way to transport drugs and stolen goods in the vehicles they were working on. They'd tell the customer that it would take a few days before their car would be ready, then they'd use it to transport whatever contraband they were moving. That was why there were never drugs in the Shaffer home, but it kept our attention focused on that location instead of where the illegal activities were actually taking place." He took a deep breath. "And the reason the drug dealing was so hush-hush... that's where Pruett's clinic came in. Along with several other clinics that catered to well-to-do addicts. They paid off unscrupulous doctors and nurses who provided them with contacts—they literally sold them the names of potential customers. Several clinics were shut down and a lot of doctors lost their licenses when it was discovered they were taking advantage of the people they were supposed to help. Not all the healthcare workers were in on it, just the ones who were in desperate need of money and willing to sell out their patients' well-being for the sake of making a buck."

"That's why Nurse Price was an easy mark," J.D. put in. "Pruett had heard about what happened to her when the sheriff was there five years ago. He threatened her job if she didn't go along with it."

"How did they get Dr. Pruett to go along with it?" Corrie asked.

"He was a gambling addict who had a lot of debt," Rick said grimly. "He kept that hidden from the board when they hired him. It was just their lousy luck that I arranged to have RaeLynn taken there... and had additional security that wasn't on their payroll. Nurse Price warned Pruett about me but he was already in too deep. She was lucky she got away with her life."

"Almost thirty years' worth of illegal activities," J.D. intoned. "Jake and Benny started it then staged the falling out they had so no one would connect them. It worked. Then Jake brought his boys into it as they got old enough. Teddy was probably the only one who balked... probably because of RaeLynn," he said, nodding toward her. "His conscience was bothering him and that made Clifford nervous. Johnny realized that he had to bring in someone else to take the heat in case his brothers bailed. Ray Herman was greedy enough to accept the proposal. And that's why he applied to the police department," he said. "And he brought Charlie in with him, probably because he wanted to make it look legit. They were friends, so it wouldn't look suspicious if they both decided to become cops together. Charlie had no idea what was going on," J.D. said quickly, as Corrie's breath caught in her throat. "He's kicking himself for not seeing through Ray. He's applied to the police academy and he's become an exemplary officer. I think he's doing it for you and for his family. And he's hoping to mend some fences along the way."

Corrie let out a sigh. "We were close as kids. I'm glad he's straightening out."

J.D. chuckled. "He said to tell you he's sorry he hasn't come by lately. He's been busy, but he said he'd like to stop by tomorrow. Says it's been too long since you all have spent a Christmas together."

"Well, I hope you're all coming for Christmas dinner tomorrow," she said. She smiled at RaeLynn. "We've been planning it for days and RaeLynn's been baking up a storm, since Rick hasn't been in any condition to do his usual holiday magic, so we're going to need plenty of help to eat it all!" She had feared that there wouldn't even be a Christmas celebration this year at all, and she wanted as many of her friends around the table as possible.

"Of course," J.D. said. She looked over at Rick, who seemed to be wrestling with himself. Surely Rick wouldn't miss Christmas at the Black Horse? For years, she had hosted Christmas Day dinner for her friends and employees and Rick had always been there. This year, her guest list had dwindled; Shelli was gone. Myra and Buster had new families to spend the holiday with. The Myers wouldn't be back till after New Year's Day. A lump formed in her throat. Midnight Mass had been their tradition, then a cup of coffee and sweets at the campground afterward, then dinner at noon. Now RaeLynn would be joining them, and J.D., too, so surely Rick would....

She stopped, realizing she was mentally babbling. Rick studied her face, then nodded.

"Sure, I'll be here."

Chapter 31

Snow had begun falling as Corrie and her friends made their way back to the campground after Midnight Mass. Her heart felt like it would burst; sitting in the pew, surrounded by the people she cared about most, it had been all she could do to keep from sobbing throughout the entire service. She felt her heart lighten as they pulled up in front of the store with colored lights twinkling around the windows and lining the roof. She could see the Christmas tree they had set up near the counter shining through the window. Oliver sat on the window sill, watching for them, and she knew Renfro would sleep until the door opened, then meet them with his tail wagging, hoping for a bite of cookie or sweet bread before going back to sleep.

Rick parked the Tahoe in front of the building and Jerry pulled their Bronco in beside it. J.D. helped Corrie and RaeLynn step out of the Tahoe as they carefully kept their skirts out of the deepening snow and stepped with caution to keep from slipping on the icy pavement. Corrie watched Rick slowly step down from the vehicle, moving carefully to protect his damaged ribs. She fought the urge to hurry to his side to help him, knowing he didn't want to be treated like an invalid. He seemed to sense her scrutiny and his eyes met hers. He managed a smile that didn't look like a grimace and they made their way inside.

The sweet smell of sugar and cinnamon greeted them, along with the aroma of piñon and regular coffee. It drove away the chill of the early morning air and Corrie and RaeLynn bustled ahead to pull the coffee breads out of the warming oven. Jackie hurried after them to help pour the coffee. They gathered in the TV room where a table had been set with holiday linens.

Corrie smiled as she watched her friends help themselves to the sweets and settle into their chairs with their plates and coffee mugs. She felt a glow start in her heart. All but Rick, who had a look of patient resignation on his face, there was a feeling of camaraderie and peace. RaeLynn's eyes shone with wonder as she looked around the table, and Corrie realized this was her first true Christmas celebration and she felt her heart lift; RaeLynn would be all right. J.D. lounged in his chair, listening to Jerry and Jackie reminisce about past Christmases, looking comfortable and at home.

After an hour, they reluctantly stood up and prepared to depart for home. Rick was the one who had to travel the farthest;

for a moment, Corrie wondered if she should offer to let him stay the night. "I need to check in at the department before heading home," he said, heading off her offer before she could voice it. No one argued. They all knew it would be useless.

Jerry and Jackie left first, promising to be over "not too early" the next morning for breakfast and to help with the dinner preparations. RaeLynn excused herself to head upstairs, her tawny eyes glistening with tears. Corrie realized that she needed a few minutes to collect herself.

That left J.D. and Rick.

Rick shrugged into his coat and took his Stetson off the hook on the wall. He looked at Corrie, and then glanced at J.D. Corrie felt her heart skip a beat and her face burn with embarrassment. Usually Rick wished her a merry Christmas with a hug and kiss on the forehead. She had no idea what his plans were for tonight, but it was obvious that J.D.'s presence was complicating things.

"Take it easy in the morning," she said to Rick. "And let me know when you get home safe. You know I worry about you driving in these conditions."

"Sure," he said. He reached out a hand to J.D. "Merry Christmas, Wilder. I don't know how to thank you...."

"Then don't," J.D. said with a wry grin, clasping Rick's hand. "Because I don't know what to say, except that you don't have to thank me. Besides, I didn't know what to get you for Christmas."

Rick inclined his head and cleared his throat before he turned to Corrie. "Merry Christmas, Corrie." His voice was slightly unsteady and he reached out and gave her an awkward side hug. She was surprised; he'd never done that before.

"Merry Christmas, Rick," she whispered. "See you tomorrow?"

He hesitated. He glanced at her then at J.D. again. She wasn't sure what he was thinking but he straightened up, his face as stony and expressionless as always. "Sure. See you tomorrow." And he made his way out the door to his Tahoe.

Corrie stared after him, watching him back out and drive away in the snowy night. She was perplexed and alarmed. She wondered what could be bothering him....

Behind her, J.D. cleared his throat. "I think I know," he said quietly, as if reading her mind. She turned and he stood, holding his jacket and a white envelope that was addressed to Rick. He moved toward her. "It was in the pocket," he said and he held it out to her.

Her breath caught as she looked at the return address printed on the envelope: Office of the Marriage Tribunal, Diocese of Las Cruces. She stared at it, shaking her head. J.D. said, "I think he wants us to read it."

Corrie took the envelope with shaking hands and pulled out the letter. Her eyes blurred as she read, *"Dear Mr. Sutton... regarding your appeal in the matter of the petition for a decree of nullity of your marriage to Meghan Stratham... the tribunal finds that the marriage is indeed valid...."*

The letter dropped from her hands. She stared up at J.D. and she could tell that he already knew what it said. A look of pain flashed in his eyes, mirroring the razor-sharp sensation in her heart. He opened his arms and she stumbled into them. She clung to him tightly, her emotions whirling, as she heard him curse Rick under his breath.

"Merry Christmas, Corrie," he whispered, as her tears began to flow.

Acknowledgements

Note to Readers: There really was a Noisy Water Winery location in Santa Fe, New Mexico, just as mentioned in *On A Dark Deadly Highway*. But, as with many things in 2020, COVID messed that up. Look for a new location in Old Town Albuquerque near the plaza, and while you're there, stop by Treasure House Books and Gifts to pick up the rest of the Black Horse Campground mysteries!

It's hard to believe it's been almost nine years since *End of the Road*, the first Black Horse Campground mystery, was published and here we are with the seventh book.

Thanks to husband and best friend, Paul, for helping me write through the craziest year we've ever had, and this book is dedicated to everyone who struggled through 2020. May the coming years be better for all of us!

Of course, I have several people to thank, namely: Paul, for giving me the gift of being able to dedicate my time to what I love doing most, Cynthia, for her invaluable insights and spot-on editorial comments, Carla Morrow for understanding my book cover vision and bringing it to life, the Noisy Water Winery crew for keeping me on board when things got crazy, and Mike Orenduff for letting me borrow his characters for a fun crossover in this book!

Other books in the Black Horse Campground Series

End of the Road
Book 1

Corrie Black, owner of the Black Horse Campground, hopes for a successful summer season, but the discovery that long-time guest Marvin Landry has been shot dead in his own RV and $50,000 in cash is missing does not herald a good beginning, especially since the victim's handicapped wife and angry stepson show little interest in discovering who murdered him. Is the appearance of a mysterious biker with a shadowy past and a recently deceased wife merely a coincidence? Despite opposition from former flame, Sheriff Rick Sutton, Corrie is determined to find the murderer. But will she find out who is friend or foe before the murderer decides it's the end of the road for Corrie?

No Lifeguard on Duty
Book 2

At the Black Horse Campground in Bonney County, New Mexico summer means warm sunny days, a cool refreshing pool... and murder? Corrie Black welcomes the summer with a party to celebrate opening the pool. The shock of discovering Krista Otero's body in the pool the morning after the party is bad. What's worse is that the death wasn't an accident. And Krista's closest friends all have something to hide. Corrie is determined to find out who used her swimming pool as a murder weapon and her home as a base for illegal activities. But someone wants to keep Corrie out of their business... even if it means killing again!

No Vacancy
Book 3

"Close the campground Saturday. This is your only warning. Your life is in danger." So reads the note shoved under the door of the Black Horse Campground store as Corrie Black and her staff celebrate the first "no vacancy" day of the season. When a man suspected of writing the note is found dead in a cabin, it seems the threat is gone. Until the man's identity is revealed. Someone who knew a lot about the Black Horse family, a lot more than even Corrie knew. With the help of Bonney County Sheriff Rick Sutton and former Houston PD Lieutenant J.D. Wilder, Corrie digs into secrets her parents kept from her. But the deeper she digs, the more she finds out things that could change her life forever... if not end it!

At the Crossroad
Book 4

Trouble often comes in threes. It's no different at the Black Horse Campground. On his first day as detective with the Bonney Police Department, J.D. Wilder finds three cold case files on his desk – three women who disappeared over a fifteen year period. It seems no one has ever properly investigated them. Then a woman from his past arrives to ask for his help. Again. The timing couldn't be worse, since he's finally about to ask Corrie on a date. But Corrie also has a visitor from her past show up. And Sheriff Rick Sutton has his hands full dodging his ex-wife, Meghan, who insists on digging up a painful memory. When three bodies are discovered that prove the missing women were murdered, J.D.'s investigation reveals that all of their visitors have some connection to the victims. But which one of them killed three women? And will there be a fourth victim?

A Summer to Remember
Book 5

Police detective J.D. Wilder's attempt to focus on his budding romance with Corrie Black, owner of the Black Horse Campground, is thwarted when the cold cases he thought he had solves are reopened, and the killer is poised to strike again. But who held a grudge against the three cold-case victims? And who is the next target? With the help of Bonney County Sheriff Rick Sutton, J.D. probes the memories of Bonney residents who knew the victims and begins to make connections.
Then another death occurs, and Corrie is attacked. The attacker and the cold-case murderer could be the same person, but Corrie's condition is critical and she's lost memories of recent events, including the identity of her attacker and even having met J.D. Will she survive long enough to remember what happened? Or will she end up as a memory?

Fiesta of Fear
Book 6

Fun. Games. Food. Murder.... Corrie Black, owner of the Black Horse Campground in Bonney County, New Mexico, has her hands full. She has offered to host the annual San Ignacio church fiesta at the campground, she's helping her best friend Shelli deal with a missing ex-husband and troubled teenager, and she's trying to keep the peace between the parish's two most vocal members. When the high school principal is found dead in the church cemetery, Corrie needs answers: Who are the 'ghost girls'? What is causing Shelli's son to get into so much trouble? What is causing the tension between the church secretary and the church treasurer? Are these connected to the murder? And most importantly to Corrie, what is the secret her coworker and friend, RaeLynn Shaffer, is hiding? With the help of Bonney County sheriff, Rick Sutton, and Bonney Detective J.D. Wilder, Corrie tries to unravel the threads that connect all the mysteries to the fiesta and the Black Horse Campground. But the threads turn into a net that could snare Corrie and her friends in a deadly trap!

CPSIA information can be obtained
at www.ICGtesting.com
Printed in the USA
JSHW050902090322
23651JS00001B/31